THE FACE IN THE WATER

IRON ON IRON

BOOK ONE

GREGORY ASHE

H&B

The Face in the Water
Copyright © 2023 Gregory Ashe

Published by Hodgkin & Blount
https://www.hodgkinandblount.com/
contact@hodgkinandblount.com

Published 2023
Printed in the United States of America

Version 1.05

Trade Paperback ISBN: 978-1-63621-065-0
eBook ISBN: 978-1-63621-064-3

As in water face answereth to face, so the heart of man to man.
—Proverbs 27:19

1

"I'm not catastrophizing," Teancum Leon said as he wheeled his luggage into the lobby of the Santaland Resort and Convention Center, conveniently located in the middle-of-nowhere known as Auburn, Missouri. "I'm simply stating a fact: by coming to rural Missouri, we're statistically more likely to be murdered by hillbillies."

His husband, Jeremiah Berger, who went by Jem, smiled at an elderly couple passing them. But he said, "And."

"And if that murder were to be preceded by events like those in *Deliverance*, which, by the way, I still don't know why you made me watch—"

"Because it's amazing."

"—then we shouldn't be surprised."

When Tean paused to orient himself in the hotel lobby, Jem reached over to smooth down his collar. "And."

"And we would likely end up being made into masks of human skin."

"You didn't even watch *Texas Chainsaw Massacre*. You said it was too scary."

"So, you can see my point: this is objective reality. That's all."

Jem considered him. He seemed to be speaking to himself when he said, "We should have gotten you more tweed."

Tean blinked. "What?"

"More tweed. You're this bigwig—"

"I'm not and have never been a bigwig."

"—specially invited to attend a prestigious conference—"

"Missy invited me to be on her panel, Jem, at the annual conference for a third-tier association. Most of these people are hucksters. And I'm not even the keynote speaker."

"—and we should have gotten you those pants the horse guys have to wear, the really baggy ones. Only out of tweed."

"Jockeys?"

Jem smirked. "Boxers, but I wanted to surprise you." Before Tean could formulate a reply to that, Jem caught the eye of an older woman passing them. "This is my husband," Jem said. "Teancum Leon. He's a bigwig speaker who got invited to be on a panel."

The woman smiled at them and gave Tean a second look.

"I'm not—" Tean began.

"You can have his autograph for five dollars," Jem said over him.

And because he was Jem, the woman laughed. She even touched Jem's arm as she passed.

When Jem looked back at Tean, he said, "What?"

Tean refused to answer, but judging by the grin playing behind Jem's beard, Tean thought he already knew anyway. "And I don't know why I have to wear tweed—"

"You're not wearing tweed," Jem murmured. "A problem I intend to solve."

"—when you get to wear—well, that."

That was a neon pink and green *Beverly Hills 90210* t-shirt that fit Jem like a dream and vintage Adidas shorts (gray and purple because, well, Jem) and flip-flops.

"I seem to recall the last time I bought you a pair of shorts being told, 'I have chicken legs,' which, for the record, I disagree with, and I like how you look in shorts."

"That's not the point," Tean said. Although he felt like he might have lost track of what the point actually was.

Because the whole *Deliverance*-squeal-like-a-pig thing wasn't getting any traction, and the clothes thing had been a flop, Tean gestured at the lobby of the resort. True to its name, Santaland had gone all out with the Christmas decorations. Plastic Christmas trees, of course, filled every corner, shedding multicolored light from big, old-fashioned bulbs. Plastic reindeer perched in ornamental spaces overhead, looking down at conference-goers from where they bounded and leaped and frolicked in plastic snow. Plastic garlands draped the mantel of an enormous fieldstone fireplace, where orange plastic streamers shimmered. No actual fire in August, thank God— Tean was still soaked with sweat after the short walk from the car. Plastic elves wore jaunty plastic hats. And, of course, no fewer than eight plastic Santas were staged in various positions: one in a sleigh, of course, and another with a sack of toys over his shoulder. One appeared to be bending over and pulling down his red velour trousers. Background music played softly, and at least one of the hidden speakers had blown. It sounded like

Irving Berlin had suffered a stroke. The only concession to the conference were signs and banners for the International Habitat Conservation and Protection Association.

"Do you know—" Tean began.

"You get one, so make it good."

For a moment, Tean floundered. He went with "They have too many bucks. If these were real deer, when they went into rut, they'd trash this place."

Jem made a face. "Really? That's the one you picked?"

"No, hold on—"

Laughing, Jem put a hand on his nape and steered him toward the registration desk. "You're going to have fun. You're going to cut open snails and ride walruses and throw fish back into ponds, and one of you is going to have to wear the shame antlers, and there will be so much animal urine, you'll be like a kid in a candy store."

"One time," Tean said, "I had coyote urine in my pocket one time, and it should be a lesson to you not to snoop, much less open things that don't belong to you."

Jem smiled at an older man passing them, and because he was Jem, the older man smiled back.

"If I'd smiled at him," Tean said, "he would have burned me at the stake."

"Get it all out of your system, or your friends are going to make you wear the shame antlers when you do the annual penguin dive."

"What are the shame antlers? What is a penguin dive?"

"Like you don't know."

"It's going to be three unbearably boring days, Jem. In fact, it's going to be so boring that we should turn around right now, and we can fly back tonight, and—"

"This lady is coming to talk to you."

"—and I'm going to tell her I've got giardia, and don't you dare contradict me."

"Never," Jem said through a smile as the woman reached them.

It had been years since Tean had seen Missy Bennett—since grad school, actually—and she'd changed. They both had, of course. She'd gotten rid of most of her dark hair (thanks to Jem, Tean knew it was called a bald fade), and she'd opted for a baggy t-shirt and jeans that accentuated the androgynous look. The heart-shaped gauges were new, but the earbuds worn around her neck weren't—and neither were the dark, friendly eyes.

"Missy—" Tean began, lurching into a hug when Jem propelled him from behind.

At the same time, Missy said, "Teancum—"

She laughed. Tean tried to extricate himself. Jem, when Tean glimpsed him out of the corner of his eye, was beaming.

When they separated, Missy turned toward Jem, holding out a hand. They shook, and Missy said, "You must be—"

But Jem said over her, "He doesn't have giardia."

It was an interesting experience, Tean thought through the distant ringing in his ears. He'd never been swallowed by a black hole in slow motion before.

Then Jem grinned and said, "I'm Jem."

And somehow, because he was Jem—again, over and over again—Missy only laughed and said, "Missy. I've wanted so badly to meet you. Ever since you made Tean get Instagram."

"He didn't make me get it," Tean said. "He stole my identity and created the account himself."

Missy's smile got bigger. "I see rings."

"Yes," Tean said, touching his gold band absently, "and it's always getting caught on something. With my luck, I'll probably get my hand ripped off during the walrus ride."

Missy turned a look on Jem.

"He's been under a lot of pressure," Jem said, slinging an arm around Tean. "Walrus fever."

Missy laughed again, as though that made sense—as though any of it made sense—and Tean decided he was going to become a hermit. Nobody ever came and bothered hermits, and if they did, hermits were legally allowed to shoot at them with .22s until they left.

"Did you register already?" Missy asked. "The desk is over here."

She led them past a sign that said WELCOME DELEGATES AND OVERSEAS VISITORS, with the message repeated in Spanish, French, and what Tean guessed was Chinese. Jem studied the sign, a tiny furrow between his eyebrows until he realized Tean was watching him. Then he frowned as though he had caught something in Tean's expression.

"Nope," Jem said as he urged Tean forward. Then, in a whisper, he added, "I know that look, Teancum Leon. You are not allowed to become a hermit."

"I can do whatever I want."

Jem actually snorted at that.

"Heather," Missy said as they approached the registration desk at the far end of the lobby, "this is Dr. Leon, with the Utah Department of Wildlife Resources. And this is his…" She let the sentence trail.

"Troublemaker," Jem said. "Jem Berger."

Heather was an older woman, white, with a wattle of crepey skin. Her color was bad, and although it was hard to tell because she was sitting behind the table, she looked too thin, with only a hint of residual weight around her middle. She searched through the badges until she found Tean's, and then she started putting together a welcome kit—a tote bag with a conference program, flyers from industry and academic journals, some sort of little spongy thing that was probably meant to be for stress.

"Do you know the environmental toll of printing waste—" Tean began.

Jem cleared his throat. When Tean shot him a look, he was innocently studying one of the plastic reindeer overhead, whistling "White Christmas."

"I can connect you with your dog," Heather said as she passed the bag over. She had a gravelly voice, and she coughed before continuing. "If that would help."

Missy made no effort to hide rolling her eyes.

"Like, long distance?" Jem asked.

"No, thank you," Tean said.

"How did you know we had a dog?" Jem asked.

"We're fine, thanks."

Heather smiled at them: yellow, crooked teeth. "I can sense him with you. A black dog. I get the feeling of bigness. Is he big? Does he have a big personality? His aura has melded with yours." She frowned. "Did you lose him recently?"

Jem's mouth opened in shock. "I did. How did you know that?"

"We didn't lose him," Tean said, taking Jem's elbow and trying to pull him away. "You took him for a walk without a harness, and he got stuck in the McCoys' fence."

"He's speaking to me right now," Heather said, closing her eyes and touching her temples. "He misses you a great deal."

Jem nodded at Tean with a grin, and Tean spotted the dog hair on his sleeve that had, against all odds, survived a full day of travel.

Brushing away the fur, Tean said, "If anything, he's getting so many treats that he's going to have diarrhea or bloat or pancreatic failure or diabetes by the time we get home. Maybe all of them."

"Yes, well, if you're worried about him—" Heather opened her eyes and fumbled for a card. "—I also perform remote healings."

"No," Tean said.

"I'm interested." Jem snagged the card. "Very interested. Thank you so much."

"Heather," a woman snapped. "I told you: this is a professional organization, and there's no place for that kind of nonsense here. If you're going to bother the participants, I'll have someone else staff the registration table."

The speaker was a broad-shouldered, big-chested woman, her skin dark and lined from the sun, and she looked militant in a khaki shirt with epaulettes. The only thing missing, Tean decided, was a riding crop.

As she approached the table, Tean tugged Jem backward until they'd joined Missy. The woman planted herself in front of Heather. "What's the status of my room?"

Heather's shoulders curved in, and she sank down in the seat, not meeting the other woman's eyes. "The resort staff say it's all cleaned up, but they don't know how the cats got in—"

"Cats," the woman said and gave an unpleasant laugh.

"That's Yesenia," Missy whispered. "She's the president of the association."

It looked like Yesenia might have said more to Heather, but at that moment, screams erupted from the front of the lobby. They all turned to watch as two Santaland security guards—whose street cred, Tean considered, was probably undermined by the red jackets with white piping—dragged a struggling young woman toward the doors.

"No!" she was screaming as she kicked the air and writhed in their grip. "No! Let me go! It's not real!" Her labored breathing had the quality of real panic. "It's all a lie! I have to tell them!"

The automatic doors slid shut behind her, and the muffled screams slowly faded into the distance.

"Jesus," Jem said under his breath.

"I have to see to that," Yesenia said, striding toward the doors. "Don't let me catch you again, Heather."

Heather, still shrunken in her seat, sent a gray-faced scowl after the other woman.

"Uh." Missy gave an unsteady laugh. "Sorry about that, Jem. There are always people who show up at these kinds of events. The ones who think we're not doing enough. And the other side, who think we're doing too much already."

When Jem looked a question at Tean, he gave a tiny shake of his head: a silent answer of *Yes, but not like that*.

"I think we'll get our room," Tean said. "Grab our luggage, unpack."

"I'm so happy you're here," Missy said, wrapping him in another hug that, once again, Jem propelled Tean into. "Thank you for coming."

"It's really—"

"No, seriously, thank you."

Tean wondered if wriggling was ineffective; maybe he should duck and try to slip under her arms.

"It means so much to me," Missy said, and she sounded, all of a sudden, on the brink of tears. She released him then, stepping back, blinking rapidly. "Go on, get your room. But please, we have to grab dinner one of these nights. We have so much catching up to do. And I want to get to know Jem—I mean, I don't even know what you do."

"Real estate," Jem said. "I'm literally the most boring person you'll ever meet. Ask me about escrow accounts."

Tean couldn't help the laugh that erupted, and he changed it into a fit of coughing when Jem whapped him on the back.

They got the card keys to their hotel room and retrieved their luggage from the rental car. Even though it was evening, the air was so hot and humid that it felt like they were swimming in a broth of skin cells and off-gassing decomposition and redneck conservatism. Tean was explaining this to Jem in the elevator, at length, until he saw the smile on Jem's face and made himself stop.

Their room was clean, small, and cool, with the mini-split AC churring happily. It had a connecting door that, Jem checked, was securely bolted from their side. More importantly, they had a big bed, and even though they'd been together years, Tean blushed when Jem bounced on the bed, reclined on an elbow, and waggled his eyebrows.

"Come on," Jem laughed and flopped onto his stomach. "I want to call the girls."

Tean joined him on the bed as Jem placed the call. A moment later, the video started, and a giant, wet, black nose snuffled across the screen. Squeals of laughter filled the background.

"They thought that would be hilarious," Hannah said. Tean's friend—and co-worker at the DWR—appeared a moment later as Scipio, their black Lab, moved away from the camera. "Here they are. Scipio says hi, by the way."

"No, he doesn't," Tean said. "We could die in a fiery plane crash—"

He grunted when Jem elbowed him, and then the girls were there.

Sofia was ten, her hair still in the braids that Jem had done, and she was filled with a ten-year-old's outrage. "It's my turn on the Switch but Anahí won't let me have a turn even though she died and Hannah said when she died it was my turn!"

"Hi, sweetheart," Jem said and laughed.

The patter of feet announced Anahí, and Sofia sprinted away—doubtless, Tean decided, to reclaim the Switch. Anahí was only six, her dark hair short, a bow in it already falling halfway out. She was holding a slice of pizza—well, a fraction of a slice of pizza, since Hannah had clearly cut it in half for her.

"We're having pizza!" Anahí screamed and then ran away.

"Are you being good?" Jem called after her, but excited screams were the only answer.

Hannah appeared a moment later, tucking chestnut-colored hair behind her ear. "They're being wonderful. Although nobody mentioned the exploding toy boxes."

"Just leave it," Jem said. "We'll pick up when we get home."

"They're not supposed to be having pizza," Tean said.

Until then, Tean hadn't known people could share an eye roll over FaceTime.

"Vegetables—" he tried again.

"We did pizza salad," Hannah said. "And yes, they both ate their salads. And in case you're wondering—"

"I'm not," Tean said.

"—they're much, much easier, and more pleasant, to be around than their foster dads."

"Thank you for taking care of them," Jem said. "I'll Venmo you some money for the pizza."

"Oh my gosh," Hannah said. "Do you want to talk to Scipio again?"

They disconnected. Jem kicked off his flip-flops and went down a rabbit hole on TikTok. Tean had trained himself to tune it out, but he was fairly sure, from the bits and pieces that filtered through, it was about animal psychics. Tean checked his email, did a quick scan of his paper, and then, when he realized it was total crap, decided to rip it down to the studs and start from scratch. It would be considerate, he decided, if hotels provided metal trash cans so you could burn things more easily.

"Nope," Jem said, kissing him on the side of the head as he took the laptop away. "Either we're going to do something incredibly wicked in this giant bed, without children or dogs or neighbors to distract us—"

"If you'd closed the blinds last time like I asked—"

Laughing, Jem kissed him again, on the mouth this time, a little slower. He leaned back, smiled, and said, "Take a shower, and we'll go to sleep. I'll ravish you in the morning."

It turned out the shower part wasn't quite so straightforward—getting any hot water required a complicated series of movements, turning the faucets this way and that, that Jem described as "a *Nintendo Power* code." But eventually, they got it to work. They got ready for bed, and in the dark, smelling like Santaland soap (peppermint and rosemary, which was weirdly wonderful), with Jem warm around him, Tean should have fallen asleep immediately—they'd had an early flight, a layover, a long drive. But he twisted and squirmed and pushed the blankets down and pulled them back up again.

Finally, with a growl, Jem pulled Tean against him. He nuzzled into Tean's shoulder, and when he spoke, his voice was muzzy with sleep. "One."

Tean let out a tiny laugh in spite of himself.

"It'd better be a really good one," Jem mumbled.

"Do you know if people reused just two feet of holiday ribbon every year, we'd save 38,000 miles of ribbon? That's enough to tie a bow around the planet."

Jem's mouth was rough as he kissed Tean's shoulder and settled them together a little more comfortably. Tean was at the edge of sleep when, from a great distance, he heard Jem murmur, "With that much ribbon, imagine how many geese you could strangle."

2

Jem was bored.

It wasn't anybody's fault. It wasn't Tean's fault—he'd told Jem he didn't have to come on this trip, although he'd agreed, once Jem pointed it out, that they hadn't had much time alone lately. It wasn't Santaland's fault. God knew they'd tried hard enough to make things interesting. Even something as simple as navigating the resort became, at Santaland, a puzzle to be solved. The building was a maze of hallways that ended abruptly, of unexpected ramps and stairs and doorways where additions had been tacked on with total disregard for the height of the existing floors. It wasn't even the other conference-goers' fault; Jem had spent the morning perfecting his animal psychic bit, which was honestly a kick-ass game and one he wished he'd thought of himself. He'd only had one hit—a guy with long, chestnut-colored hair, carrying a Barbra Streisand wig under one arm, who kept asking Jem to contact his puppy but who wouldn't stay quiet long enough for Jem to actually do anything—he'd mostly talked about his boyfriend, often in explicit detail. Jem still took him for sixty bucks, but it was the principle of the thing.

But for the most part, he watched, and he hung back, and he felt keyed up and on edge. It was a new place, and Jem found that taking a toll on him that he hadn't expected. There were only so many hours he could spend shambling through the halls before he got bored, and, as the last panels of the day ended, and the halls of the Santaland Resort and Convention Center filled with conference-goers again, Jem realized he had hit his limit.

He had to be good. He was trying, desperately, to be good. For the doc, obviously.

Hearing himself think of his husband by that name made Jem pause for a moment. He hadn't thought of Tean that way—didn't think of him that way—for a while now. It was a nickname he used, occasionally. But it wasn't the way he thought about Tean, not anymore.

Ahead, in one of the lounge areas that broke up the maze of hallways, a man in a washed-out Sonic the Hedgehog tee was looking up and down the hallway. It would be an easy hook; the man was clearly waiting for someone, clearly nervous—the way he dried his hands on his jeans, the restless pacing. Jem even had a golden way in, what with his own Super Mario tee, the one with the original NES graphics. He wouldn't even have to disguise the first contact. No need to bump into the man. No fumbling for an apology. He could walk straight up to him, point to the Sonic shirt, and give him shit about Sega. Maybe it could be as simple as a free coffee— they'd start talking, end up at one of the resort's coffee shops, and Jem would realize he'd forgotten his wallet. Bingo, he just got a free coffee. And a cookie—are you sure you don't mind?

But no. Jem dragged himself away from the mark. No, this trip was about Tean, about how smart he was, about how respected he was, about all his smart, respected friends, and all the smart, respectable things they talked about. Jem had tried to listen to a panel and had (almost) literally been mummified by boredom. So smart he didn't understand any of it. Which was why it was a good thing—definitely a good thing, totally, unmistakably, clearly a good thing—that Tean had politely, and kindly, and considerately suggested Jem not come to dinner with all his smart friends.

When he glanced back, the guy in the Sonic shirt was bending over to tie his shoes, and his wallet fell out of his pocket.

Jem suppressed a groan. That wasn't fair. That was—that was like the universe testing him.

His feet carried him in a loop back to the lounge. The guy in the Sonic tee, oblivious to the loss of his wallet, was already scuttling away. Apparently, his nerve had broken, and whatever he was waiting for—sex, drugs, rock and roll—he'd scared himself out of it. Jem would do the responsible thing. He'd pick up the wallet before some random stranger found it, and he'd take it to the front desk, and he wouldn't even tell Tean he'd done a good deed.

He most certainly wouldn't copy down any of the credit card numbers. Even though it pained him. A little. Even after years of being exposed to Tean's unwavering goodness and Tean relentlessly being an upstanding citizen and Tean sometimes even feeding quarters into other people's parking meters (while telling Jem he shouldn't be doing it, he was furthering antisocial behaviors like poor planning and carelessness and disrespect for law and order, all of which would bring an end to civilization as we know it). Even though Jem still remembered what it was like to be hungry, and how to get an easy meal, and to watch his back because, aside from Tean, nobody was going to watch it for him.

So, he didn't copy down the credit card numbers. And he didn't take the Missouri driver's license. But he did take the eight hundred and thirty-six dollars in cash.

"Jem!"

Jem jerked upright, automatically discarding the wallet by tossing it into a potted plant. He scanned the hallway, looking for the source of his name while shoving the cash into a pocket of his shorts (today's were green nylon with an eye-watering graphic print).

Missy came down the hall toward him, waving both hands like he might miss her. Or like she was directing an airplane. Jem tried again to read her tattoos—on her wrists and on one biceps—but the font was that tiny, curling one girls loved to get, and it was still hard for him to read stuff like that. Especially when it was moving towards him at thirty miles an hour.

"Oh my God, I'm so glad I bumped into you!" She went for a hug, and then she released him almost as quickly and took a nervous step back. "I'm so sorry. I didn't even ask, and I know I don't really know you."

"No worries," Jem said. "But you're lucky you give good hugs."

Missy laughed. "The first time I hugged Tean, he literally snaked his way free and walked into a door jamb."

With a smile, Jem glanced around. "Is he with you? I thought you were going to dinner."

"Oh, we are." She gave a little furrow of her forehead. "He said you were going to do your own thing. I promise we're not that boring." She laughed again. "Ok, we are, but I still want you to come. I never get to see Tean, and I want to get to know you."

Which wasn't what Tean had said to Jem at all.

"Thanks, really. But I want Tean to have a night when he doesn't have to worry about including me—you know what I mean? If I go, he'll try to make sure I'm involved, and since I can't tell, uh, a hawk from…an owl, I guess, I wouldn't be very good company."

"We mostly get drunk and bitch about everybody else here. Trust me, after the third round, nobody's going to be able to tell a hawk from an owl." Her eyes widened, and in a rush, she said, "Oh, not Tean, though. He'll probably slide out from under the table and escape—"

Shouts down the hall broke through the stream of words, and when Jem glanced over, a ragged crowd of observers was watching as a woman straightened herself. The cause of her near fall was obviously the man who was striding away, back stiff. Jem only got a glimpse of him: acid-washed denim, one of the heavy belts country boys liked to wear, a stringy mullet flopping over the collar of his western shirt.

Missy made a vexed noise and headed toward the onlookers. Jem thought that might be his chance to get away, but Missy glanced back and waved for him to come. So, he strolled after her.

The woman who had nearly fallen was petite, her blond hair in a pixie cut, and red eyed behind a pair of glasses. She was fighting to plaster on a smile as Missy reached her, and when Missy asked something in a low voice, she shook her head. A few of the looky-loos lingered, hoping something else might happen, but the crowd broke up and drifted away.

"—because he's an asshole, that's why," Missy was saying. Over her shoulder, to Jem, she added, "Rod ran into her on purpose. Jem, this is Kristin. Kristin, Jem. Kristin's a veterinary anesthesiologist."

Kristin shook her head, blinking back tears, a wavy smile still fixed in place. "It could have been an accident."

"It wasn't," Missy said. "I repeat: he's an asshole. He did the same thing to Yesenia the day before, about knocked her over."

"The guy with the mullet?" Jem said.

"Rod Horton. He's a redneck son of a bitch, and he thinks he's God's gift to the universe."

"He's got a bit of an ego," Kristin said.

Jem glanced down the hall, but Rod was gone. "Why would he run into you like that?"

"Because he hates Kristin," Missy said.

"He doesn't like me." Kristin's grin sharpened and looked, for the first time since Jem had seen her, genuine. "He hates you."

"If it were me, he probably would have used a knife."

"Let me guess," Jem said. "He's an ex. Or it's money. Or both."

Missy and Kristin shared a look, and then both women burst out laughing.

"No," Missy said, through laughs.

"Nothing like that," Kristin said as they both settled down.

But Missy was still grinning. "God, even the thought—puking isn't enough. No, he's a joke, that's what he is. And he shouldn't be here, not that anyone can keep him out."

"What?" Jem asked. "Is he doing animal experiments? Is he a mad scientist?"

"He runs a big cat sanctuary," Kristin said. "Right here in Wilder County, actually."

"Like, what? Tigers?"

"Tigers, bobcats, I think he even had a lion for a while." Missy shook her head. "It's disgusting."

"Well, it's not ideal," Kristin said, "and I'm not saying Rod is the example we should follow, but someone has to do something. People buy these animals when they're small—you wouldn't believe how easy it is to get a tiger cub, actually—and then they have no idea what to do when it grows up into a three-hundred-pound adult. So, they let it go. Literally. Some people just leave the gate open and hope the poor thing will go away. With a big cat sanctuary, at least you know they're being taken care of."

"They're being monetized. He makes a fortune off admission fees, and he's got that crazy army of volunteers. And he's not a vet, but do you think he'll let anyone who's actually trained go in and check on those cats?"

"It's a legitimate operation," Kristin said to Jem. "He's certified, has the necessary inspections, everything. We don't like it, but as you can tell, we disagree on how much we don't like it."

"So, what's the problem?" Jem asked.

"He did a one-man panel this morning." Kristin and Missy paused to share an eye roll. "He was talking about sustainability—"

"Talking out his ass," Missy put in.

"—and I asked if part of his sustainability was to support efforts to end wildlife trafficking since, you know, that's where most of his animals come from."

Jem grinned in spite of himself. "He didn't take it well?"

"He lost his shit," Missy said.

"Not as bad as Yes," Kristin said.

Missy flushed and put a hand to her face.

"In public," Kristin said. "In the lobby, Missy."

"I know," Missy groaned.

"Really?"

"I said I know!"

"Yes?" Jem asked. Then he realized it wasn't *yes*, but a nickname. "Yesenia? We saw her yesterday at check-in. She's the president or something?"

"Or something," Kristin said drily. "She's the reason we've got people like Rod in IHCPA." She said the acronym like *hiccup*. "She's also the reason Missy is going to be drinking a lot of tequila tonight. Oh, Jem, you're coming, right? Everyone wants to meet you. I heard Kevin asking Tean if you'd be at dinner."

No, Jem thought. No, I won't be. Because—how had Tean put it? *You don't have to come. It'll be boring. I don't want you to be bored.*

But before he had to respond, Missy said, "I know I should have kept my mouth shut, but in my defense, I was a little drunk."

Kristin patted her shoulder. To Jem's questioning look, she said, "Missy and Yes had it out in the lobby last night."

"She seemed...intense."

"That's one word for it. She's rigid, I guess. And yeah, she's tough. She runs an exotic animal safari in the Boot Heel—that's what we call that weird little corner of Missouri."

Jem made an understanding noise. "So, she gets elected president—"

"Which is a good thing," Kristin rushed to add, "because you wouldn't believe how bad things had gotten—'me too' kind of stuff, the old boys, it was horrible."

"—but once you've got your president running a safari, it's hard to keep the big cat sanctuary guy out."

"Or the animal psychics," Kristin said with a roll of her eyes.

Jem couldn't help his own grin.

"And it doesn't hurt that Rod has gobs of money, while the rest of us are scrabbling for grants," Missy said. "Yes is the same way; she has oodles of it. She's opening another park, you know. In Osage Beach."

"Which means safe living space for animals who don't have a natural habitat here," Kristin said.

"Yes, thank you," Missy said, "I remember that talking point from when Yes screamed it in my ear. It's gross, that's all. Turning them into a spectacle."

Kristin opened her mouth to say something, and something flashed across her face. What she said instead was, "Oh my God, we're going to be late. You're sure you're not coming?"

Jem waved for them to go. "I don't want to crash the party."

"Come!" Missy said. "I'll have too much to drink, and I'll ask wildly inappropriate questions. We'll have fun."

"Tean will be so embarrassed he might catch on fire," Kristin said with a smirk.

With a laugh-track laugh, Jem shook his head, and a moment later, the two women were gone.

He turned the other direction, just in case. He wouldn't want to bump into Tean and his friends by accident. He wouldn't want to embarrass the doc. Which was silly, he told himself as he shuffled down the hall. The last panels of the day were letting out, the doors of multipurpose rooms swinging open, bodies pouring into the hall. It was silly because Tean loved him, and had never once been embarrassed by Jem, wouldn't ever be embarrassed by him. Jem knew that. It was a fact. It was …this place. And these people. And a nagging part of him that wondered, had there been a tone? Had something slipped into Tean's voice, something he hadn't meant Jem to hear, when he said, *It'll be boring. I don't want you to be bored*.

He was still trying to pry apart that particular pretzel of craziness when a man emerged from the throng of bodies and grabbed Jem's arm. Jem twisted free automatically. He bumped into a woman behind him, who let out a startled squawk. Jem mumbled an apology, but his gaze was fixed on the man who had grabbed him. He was short, with sandy-brown skin and a potbelly, and an ostrich feather earring dangled from one lobe. When he caught Jem's eye, he said, "Zach?"

The part of Jem's brain that was always alert, always processing, always ready to riff, launched into action. His subconscious had already put it together, and he was nodding before the connections made their way to his conscious mind: the two white guys, both of them wearing '90s-era gaming t-shirts, in this particular hallway of the Santaland Resort and Convention Center. You should say no, a part of his brain said, even as Jem nodded. The doc would say no.

But this seemed a hell of a lot more interesting than moping while Tean went to dinner—*I don't want you to be bored*—with his friends.

The man jerked his head, and Jem plunged through the river of bodies to follow him. They ended up in a vestibule, where a couple of vending machines made the air uncomfortably warm and full of the smell of corn chips. Bodies streamed past them in the hallway, but nobody seemed to be paying particular attention to them.

The man with the ostrich feather earring studied Jem. Then he said, "You're shit at describing yourself, you know that?"

"Who are you?" Jem asked.

"Who the hell do you think I am?" A beat, and then, with a trace of outrage, "DeVoy?"

Jem still couldn't blush on command, but he ducked his chin and mumbled, "I had to be sure."

"Jesus Christ." DeVoy patted himself down. A moment later, he produced an envelope, from which he drew out a photo. He passed it to Jem. The photo was a bad quality close-up of a bird. A pretty bird. Something tropical, Jem guessed. He didn't mind birds, but his joke about the hawk and the owl hadn't been far from the truth. After a few seconds, DeVoy said, "How about it, Mr. Zachary? We got a deal?"

"Well," Jem said.

"Now come on. That's the one you wanted. You said scarlet macaw, and that's what you're getting. And look, it's a chick, so you're going to have this guy for a long time. So, how about it?"

"I don't know." Riffing was one of the things Jem did best, when he could stop listening to the front of his brain and just…flow. It was like someone plugged him in, like all the parts of him that were normally dark lit up. And right now, he knew the role he was supposed to play. He'd been DeVoy plenty of times, and he knew what the other guy did, knew how it drove you crazy when you wanted to close the deal. "This is all weird," Jem said. "I don't feel good about this."

"Man, what's weird? Look, I've got this bird. You want this bird. That's business. He's going to a good home, right? That's what I care about. That's the important thing here."

Jem hesitated. He shook his head. He was surprised the hairs on his arms weren't standing up. He was surprised, too, by how much he'd missed this.

"You're not going to get a better price. This is rock bottom. You're going to pay twice this if you go to anybody else."

The next part was the trickiest. The right duration of silence. Building in all the cues—the body language, the breathing, the microexpressions on his face—to suggest indecision, dismay, struggle.

"Ok," Jem finally said.

DeVoy's relief was visible. "All right."

"Ok," Jem said. He was talking himself into it. He was a guy buying a bird, and he was telling himself it was ok. "Yes, God." He gave a little laugh. "Let's do this."

"All right, man. All right. Now, you got the money—"

"I didn't—" This was one of those times when blushing on command would have been really useful. "I didn't bring it with me."

DeVoy opened his mouth and snapped it shut again.

"I didn't know—I mean, I thought—" Jem shrugged. "I can get it. Today. Tonight, I mean."

"Unh-uh. You think I'm driving out here again? The deal was—"

"I could meet you." That was the best and worst part about riffing; even Jem didn't know what was going to come out of his mouth. "Later. With the money. Come on, man. I fucked up; what do you want me to say?"

For a long moment, the babble of voices from the hall rode over both of them. Then DeVoy said, "The Cottonmouth Club. Don't fuck up again."

Jem offered up a watery smile in thanks, and DeVoy snatched the photo back. Then he pushed his way out of the vestibule and disappeared into the crowd.

After a ten count, Jem left the vestibule and merged with the stream of people. Easy. Simple. In a few hours, it would all be over. And then, once he had what he needed, he'd take it all to Tean. Proof. And Jem would let Tean have all the credit, of course. There'd probably be a commendation from the city. Maybe even something from the association. Some kind of award. He could see Tean smiling already.

3

"Dr. Leon!"

The young man with the smartphone—dark hair, brown skin, remarkably good looking—was the conference's official photographer. Or social media manager. Or something. And he refused to give up.

But Tean also refused to give up, so at the next intersection, he broke left and picked up the pace. Thanks to Santaland's maze-like floor plan, another intersection immediately presented itself, and Tean turned again. He thought he heard distant swearing behind him.

As Tean hurried through the resort's corridors, he kept an eye out for Jem. His husband had been surprisingly unresponsive to the check-in texts Tean had sent throughout the day, and he'd flat out ignored Tean's invitation to dinner. Granted, the invitation had been last minute; that morning, Tean had thought Jem would prefer not to be dragged to an interminable meal with Tean's colleagues, who would, in spite of Tean's best efforts to steer the conversation to something Jem wanted to talk about, end up gossiping about other members of the association, or debating technical questions, or reliving grad school days. And although—or perhaps because—the first day of the conference had been enjoyable for Tean, he felt guilty at the thought of Jem spending more hours on his own. But when Tean had suggested Jem join them, and he promised to keep the dinner short, Jem simply hadn't responded.

Which might be, a part of Tean's brain observed, because he's in trouble.

Tean squashed the voice and went back to scanning the faces streaming past him. The hallway he'd chosen led back to the lobby, with its plastic Santas and plastic reindeer and, today, a roboticized Mariah Carey singing through bursts of shrieking static. Not that anybody could hear anything, of course. Not with half the conference thronging the room, drinks in hand, shouting to be heard, everyone trying to find the group they were waiting for.

"Dr. Leon! Dr. Leon!"

Tean ducked, but not before he saw out of the corner of his eye the young man with the phone. He'd emerged from a different hallway, and now he started across the room, forcing a path through the crowd. He was short, which meant he disappeared in the crowd of bodies, but he seemed relentless, and Tean didn't have much hope.

He did a quick glance for Missy, praying she'd be waiting and ready to leave for dinner. He didn't spot her in the sea of faces. When he checked for the persistent young man, Tean realized he'd lost him. He swore under his breath (and not one of the nickel-and-dime ones that Jem liked to tease him about) and sought cover.

He found it, temporarily, behind a group of men, where he could watch the lobby for Missy and, he hoped, stay out of sight. One of the men was big, dark haired, and pale. The next had a golden tan and a swimmer's build. The third had strawberry-blond hair worn longish, with a beard that he was currently scratching—probably, Tean guessed, as an excuse to cover his mouth.

"—not arguing with him, John."

The one with the swimmer's build nodded and looked like he was trying not to sigh.

"I'm simply pointing out that if he's going to deduct points for the use of the passive voice—"

"In April," the bearded man said.

The big man fixed him with a glare and continued, "—it would be prudent to remove that same construction from the assignment handout."

"Would it help," the bearded man asked, "if I told you I'm giving Colt those points back? He got an A for the semester. He'll have a slightly higher A if I give those points back. There, presto chango. He has received those points back."

"The points are immaterial," the big man said.

"Bullshit," the swimmer coughed.

The big man paused to give him a look. The swimmer and the bearded man shared a lightning-strike grin.

"It's an easy fix," the big man said, swinging that look back to the bearded man. "For example, instead of 'it would be prudent,' you could say, 'you should remove.'"

The bearded man made an agreeing noise. "While we're on the topic of easy edits, Emery, maybe we should talk about that version of the Lord's prayer I heard last Sunday."

"Please don't get him started," the swimmer said.

"I've never heard so many swear words peppered in before. And in a church, no less."

"In the first place, motherfucker, that horse's ass pastor asked me—" the big man began.

"Am I allowed to have a beer this weekend?" the swimmer asked. "I think I need a beer."

"You're certainly not allowed to have any gummies," the big man said. "In case you've forgotten what happened last time."

At that moment, of course, the conference's social media manager-slash-photographer-slash-(whatever that robot was called, the one Jem made Tean watch all those movies about, the exterminator, maybe?) appeared again, saying, "Theo, I'm going to lose my mind. Have you seen—hey!"

Tean shot off into the crowd.

The lobby was clearly not a refuge. He checked his phone as he scurried into the Santaland labyrinth again, lifting his head to smile and nod at conference-goers he knew—or who had been in the same panels as he had. No messages from Jem. Nothing from Missy. A glance over his shoulder showed him the young man jogging after him, so Tean decided he'd better jog too.

Two turns and cutting through what was clearly some sort of service corridor landed Tean in a part of the resort he recognized, although he had no idea how he'd gotten there. He hurried to the next intersection. One of the hotel bars was located—yep, right there. Complete with walls, and dim lighting, and, just to reinforce how important this fact was, walls. Conference-goers filled the tables and booths and pressed up to the bar, shouting orders. Margaritas seemed to be in high demand—well, everything seemed to be in high demand when you turned a bunch of veterinarians loose for the weekend—and the bartenders laughed and joked and slung drinks as fast as they could.

Tean slipped between the knots of bodies, offering small waves of acknowledgment to the people he knew, working his way into the next section of the bar, where a wall would block him from sight. Around him, the usual chaos of a conference bar unspooled. A red-faced woman shouted, "A penguin," like it was some kind of punchline, and her companion, a woman with a faux hawk, snorted her drink in laughter. A harried-looking girl who might have been barely eighteen shouldered past Tean with a tray of appetizers, the smell of cheese curds and marinara sauce trailing after her. A group of what Tean thought of as the old school of wildlife vets—middle-aged white men in pseudo-hunting apparel, including ridiculously impractical boots—grouped up around a two-top, one of the men attempting to do a turkey call in spite of his obvious inebriation.

In one of those swirls and eddies that carry people through crowds, Tean suddenly found himself facing an empty table. He dropped down into a seat, glanced at the men seated at the table next to him—one of them blond and muscular, in a Hennessy Landscaping tee, jeans, and heavy boots; the other slender, with long chestnut hair drawn up in a bun, and smelling unmistakably of cannabis—and took out his phone. Then he did a double take because the slender man was wearing what appeared to be pink Crocs (which Jem had refused to let Tean buy, even when the brown ones were on sale), purple tights, and an enormously oversized black t-shirt that showed a stick figure humping the words YOUR FEELINGS.

The slender man caught Tean's gaze and brightened. "I'm blending in."

The blond man snorted.

"Something to eat?" the harried girl asked, hovering next to Tean's table, the now empty tray under one arm.

"Oh," the slender man said, "you should have the cheese curds. We had the cheese curds—well, North had the cheese curds, but he didn't share with me—"

"You said you didn't want any," the blond man said. "You shoved that anti-dairy council pamphlet in my face."

"But even though North didn't let me have any, on account of he's keeping me waifish and frail until he puts a baby in me—"

The blond man choked on his beer.

"—they're really good, well, I think they're really good. In part because I could sense that they were good. Psychically, I mean. But in part because North made this noise when he ate one, and it's the same noise he makes when I use my finger to—ah!" At that point, he started screaming, probably because the blond man was trying to rip one of his nipples off through the baggy black t-shirt.

"Uh, no," Tean said to the waitress. "Still waiting for someone."

She was gone before he'd finished speaking.

"Now I'll never be able to get that areola embroidered," the slender man was moaning as he massaged his chest.

"We never should have come here," the blond man said. "We should have said no to this fucking job as soon as they mentioned this fucking place."

"We love this place! We have good memories of this place!"

Tean tried to block out the argument as he typed a message to Missy, asking her to meet him in the bar instead of the lobby.

"We don't have any good memories of this place," the blond man said. "This place is your fucking wet dream because you got to spend a day with your non-sexual soulmate."

"John-Henry isn't my soulmate, Emery is. And I never said non-sexual."

"Meanwhile I've got to relive the waking nightmare of walking into this fuck-fest with you and hearing you talk about your spiritual vulva clamping down."

Tean dropped his phone.

By the time he'd recovered it, the slender man was halfway through his rebuttal. "—and I didn't say my spiritual vulva was clamping down. I said if I had a spiritual vulva, it would be spasming."

As though that had somehow resolved the argument, he turned a triumphant look toward the table of women next to them. One of them stared back, mouth agape, the ruin of a half-chewed pretzel forgotten.

"What is he, a magician?" That was the voice of the big man from the lobby, and it came from the hallway outside the bar.

"Emery." That sounded like the bearded man.

"Well, he keeps saying he disappeared, like he's going to saw himself in half. Have you checked—"

"Maybe you can catch him tomorrow." That sounded like the swimmer.

Tean sank down in his seat.

"He's the last one. I've emailed him, like, eighteen times asking for a photo, and he hasn't replied, and the conference organizers begged me to do a publicity post with these speakers, and he's the last one." That was definitely the young man with the smartphone. "I almost had his picture, but—"

"He disappeared." That was the big man again, voice dry.

As though conjured—perhaps, a small part of Tean's brain suggested, by a magician—the young man with the smartphone appeared in the opening. He did a quick survey of the bar and turned, and a moment later, he was gone.

Tean let out a breath. He let a full minute pass and slid out of his chair.

The couple next to him was arguing again.

"Because," the blond man said, "what the fuck do you think 'platonic' means? It's the same fucking thing as 'non-sexual.'"

"Not if you count psychosexual—"

Tean didn't exactly run. But he did have a better understanding of why that two-top had been miraculously unoccupied when he'd found it.

On his way out of the bar, he bumped into Missy. She let out a surprised laugh as they steadied each other.

"That bad?" she asked. "I know we've got a mixed crowd, but I didn't think it would drive you to drink."

"No, no," Tean said, shuffling toward the lobby, hoping she'd pick up on the body language. After a moment, she did, and he wondered if there was a polite way to ask her to walk faster. Jem would know. She was still looking at him, waiting for an explanation about the bar. The best he could come up with was, "I thought I saw someone."

"Oh, speaking of which, did you see—"

But before she could finish, a man loomed up out of the crowd. He was one of those white guys who tanned well, so blond his hair almost looked white from the sun, and the shirt he'd chosen, and the way he rolled his sleeves, put the definition of his chest and arms on display. It took Tean a moment to process what he was seeing: the Auburn City Police Department patch, the holstered gun, the badge.

"Ms. Bennett?" he asked. "Missy Bennett?"

Missy blinked, looked at Tean, and looked back. "That's me. I'm sorry, can I—"

"We'd like to talk to you." The man nodded over his shoulder to another officer. "In private, please."

4

The rental, a 2019 VW Jetta (white, even though Jem had asked if they could get a different color), carried Jem out of Auburn and into the rolling hills of central Missouri. Dusk settled in the trees the way flocks of birds came together, and limestone gleamed when the headlights swept across it. He fiddled with the radio and couldn't get anything except some country stations, but not the good kind of country, so he messed around with his phone until he got some Kacey Musgraves playing whenever the Maps app wasn't telling him to turn.

As he drove, the world got smaller, shrinking to a dark shell at the edge of his lights. The heat had lessened, but not by much, and even with the AC blasting, Jem felt sweat threatening to break out again on his temples. Where the highway cut through the hills, the raw faces of granite and limestone hemmed him in, and when he left the hills, trees lined the sides of the road, branches arching, until he felt like he was shooting down a tunnel. In Utah, unless somebody put up a building, you could see pretty much across the valley—until you hit a mountain, in other words. Here, Jem couldn't see shit. He wondered what you were supposed to do if you got lost. If your car broke down, for example. If you didn't have mountains to tell you which way was east or north or south or west. He wondered about the thick, smothering green. He wondered about snakes.

But most of that happened on one side of his brain, while the other side was busy planning for what lay ahead. Get the proof. If possible—if Jem were lucky—get the bird. And then get out. Simple. The best plans were always simple.

A little voice at the back of his head, a responsible, civic-minded, kind, and unfailingly patient voice, which sounded a little like the doc, was asking if this was really the best idea. So, Jem played that picture for himself again: Tean's surprise, Tean getting a commendation, maybe an award. He'll be glad, Jem told himself. And there was another thought, one he couldn't quite bring himself to touch, although he was aware of it at the lowest level of consciousness: He'll be proud.

The Cottonmouth Club was a low, ramshackle building on the corner of a dead crossroad. It had corrugated panels for walls, and more of the same for its roof. In places, slapdash paint suggested an effort to keep the structure standing. A single light, swimming with moths, illuminated the gravel lot, and a pole with an empty frame suggested signage that had decayed or been taken down or been stolen. Better days, Jem thought. The name of the bar was written on the side of the building, though some of the letters were missing. They'd discolored the panels where they'd hung, so when the VW's headlights splashed across the galvanized steel, Jem could spell out the words for himself.

At the door, he showed a fake ID—one of the ones Tean didn't know about—to the cue-ball bouncer by the door. Probably not necessary. Jem wasn't sure the guy would have carded him, but it didn't hurt to be proactive. Jake Benning from Wyoming was visiting a cousin, Jem decided. To buy stock. That made sense; they had to run horses around here somewhere. The bouncer didn't care about any of that, of course. He waved Jem in, and that was that.

Inside, the club was almost as dark as the night outside, with only a few pendant lights oozing brownish light that did nothing to push back the gloom. A long bar dominated one wall, with bottles filling the shelves behind it. Tables held the usual suspects—a man in a stained undershirt; a four-top of glassy-eyed college bros; a chinless pair of men Jem thought might be father and son. Booths lined the wall opposite the bar, with sagging curtains that could be drawn to provide the illusion of privacy. Def Leppard pounded over the speakers. A few blocky TVs above the bar showed grainy images of what Jem took to be soft-core porn, but the real show was the stage at the far end of the room.

A spotlight picked out the pole at center stage, where a skinny girl in a bikini bottom hung upside down. Jem took her for young, but after a moment, he thought maybe she was just thin—drugs, or an eating disorder, or both. She slowly slid down the pole, her tiny breasts defying gravity and her eyes empty, until her head bumped the stage. A poochy guy was humped right up against the stage, with a spray-on tan and rockabilly hair. When he reached out to fondle her, a gold cross the size of a remote control swung out on its chain.

Movement at the periphery of Jem's vision made him turn, and he spotted DeVoy peering out of one of the booths. Jem nodded and moved over, and no sooner had he sat down on the sticky vinyl banquette than a waitress appeared. She gave him a tired, marionette smile that Jem realized, after a moment, was supposed to be suggestive—to go along with the skirt that barely covered her ass and with hair chemically cooked until it was blond.

"We're fine," DeVoy told her over the music, and she nodded and shuffled away. Then his gaze swung back to Jem. "Took you long enough."

"Sorry." Jem didn't have to pretend to be curious; he poked his head out of the booth's enclosure, caught a whiff of puke clinging to the velvet curtain, and gave the club another look. As he watched, a heavyset guy in a biker's cut passed a bag of what Jem thought might be meth to a white man with hair like a cotton swab. "Hey, this place is a little rough. Are you sure—"

"Do you have the money or don't you?"

"Well, yeah, but—"

As Jem reached for his wallet, DeVoy lunged across the table to grab his arm. "Not here, dumbass!"

"Hey!"

DeVoy released him and sank back onto the banquette, holding up both hands—truce, not quite an apology.

"This feels messed up," Jem said, sliding an inch toward the edge of the booth. "Forget it."

"Whoa, whoa, whoa!" DeVoy patted the air. "Now come on. You can't go running off now. We got a deal."

"What deal? You drag me out here to the middle of nowhere—"

"Look, man. You're here, right? You want the bird, right? So, chill." DeVoy waited, and when Jem didn't move, he relaxed. "I'm gonna grab the bird. The one I showed you, right? Pretty little thing. And you sit here. Have a drink if you want. In ten minutes, you meet me out back. I'll have the bird, and you'll have the money, and we'll both be happy. All right?"

Jem knew the right look: wanting to be tough, but uncertain, the veneer of aggression without anything to back it up. The way a scared guy would try to look if he found himself in a place like the Cottonmouth Club, if he didn't know how to back out, or if his pride wouldn't let him.

DeVoy grinned. "All right then."

Then he slid out of the booth, crossed the bar, and disappeared through a door to the side of the stage.

When he was gone, some of the knots in Jem's back loosened. He took a deep breath, pulled at his tee where sweat had bunched it under his arms, and tried to think.

The waitress passed again, and Jem ordered a Keystone Light. He thought maybe that was called irony, but he also thought if Tean had been there, he would have scrunched up his forehead and explained — or tried not to explain — that it wasn't technically irony. The woman came back faster than Jem expected, and he gave her cash and shook his head when she asked if he wanted anything else. Peeling himself from the vinyl, he shifted to the edge of the booth for a clear view of the bar. The curtains blocked him partially from sight, which gave him an ideal way to observe the rest of the room. He sipped at the Keystone Light. The beer was mild, with a hint of the mineral-metallic flavor Jem associated with some other light beers. It was smooth, you could say that. Of course, tap water was plenty smooth too.

The too-thin girl on stage had been replaced by a taller, full-figured woman who, when she turned in profile to twerk, Jem realized was pregnant. The college bros, minus one, seemed to have lost interest, but lots of men in the crowd had perked up. Jem noted a few women mixed in among the faces; he'd been in strip clubs before, and he knew women were more common than lots of people believed, but these didn't look like bachelorette parties or cougars on the prowl. These were hard-faced women in worn clothes, most of whom stared at their drinks and seemed oblivious to the music and catcalls and the representatives of the male gender who were making jackasses of themselves.

One woman drew Jem's eye because she was laughing, glancing at the stage with no apparent self-consciousness before returning to the group of men and women she was sitting with. She was sharp jawed, and although it was hard to tell in the ugly yellow light of the club, Jem thought she was pale. Her blond bob was gelled back, and she wore a mechanic's jumpsuit. Where a name should have been, the patch sewn onto the chest read FUCK OFF. She seemed to sense Jem's gaze, sitting up straighter, scanning the room, and Jem drew back into the privacy of the booth.

What to do about DeVoy? Jem touched the pocket of his jeans, where he kept the telescoping antenna and the barrette. He didn't have to check the paracord with the hex nut; it was a weight around his neck, the metal flat against his chest. Go out there? Have some fun? The thought caught Jem by surprise, and his first reaction was to remind himself that this was about someone trying to sell exotic animals, about someone doing something illegal, something Tean would have found abhorrent. But now, with Nelly singing over the club's speakers, with Jem's blood pumping faster as his mind played out scenarios, he couldn't pretend this was about Tean. Not completely. In part, at least, it was because of the boredom. And in part, if

Jem were totally honest with himself, because he missed this. Missed the shadiness. Missed the chaos. Missed being good at it. Missed, in a way he hadn't fully formulated to himself until now, a world he understood.

A man broke up laughing at a table beyond the curtain of Jem's booth, and another man shouted over him in a hillbilly twang, "Swear to Christ, man: sixteen and tits like a hog."

Jem peeked out at the club again. The dancer had come down from the stage and was now grinding in the lap of a green-faced kid. The boy couldn't have been much older than twenty-one, and if his coloring were any indication, his buddies had been plying him with drinks—and probably more than drinks—all night. A birthday, maybe. Or maybe he just couldn't hold his liquor. As Jem watched, the boy leaned forward and puked all over the dancer. She screamed and slid off him to land heavily on the floor.

It was all over in a matter of minutes: the cue-ball bouncer tossed the kid out of the club, a fiftysomething woman in jeans and a polo came out to clean up the puke, and the screaming dancer was escorted backstage by a guy with zero neck. Another girl came out—Black, with a weave that hit her at the small of the back, and white tassel pasties she was already using to good effect.

For one last moment, Jem debated: leave, or go around back and find DeVoy. The rational part of him said leave. The part of him that sounded like Tean told him to leave. The smart, sensible, responsible thing to do was to leave.

But a question nagged at Jem: why exotic animals? Why a bird? Because of the conference? Because the town was full of people like Tean, people who loved animals? But that only raised other questions. How had DeVoy known to target them? How had he known enough about exotic birds to trap a potential buyer?

The responsible thing was to go home.

A wordless cry of protest made Jem scan the room. It took him a moment to spot the disturbance: a girl being strong-armed toward the door behind the stage. She wore a tight dress with cut-outs to expose part of one breast, her stomach, her hip. The man forcing her toward the door was another of the no-neck variety. It was obvious she didn't want to go, and it was obvious, too, that she was on something. Watching the guy maneuver her with practiced ease made the hair on the back of Jem's neck stand up.

Something—a sixth sense, maybe—told Jem he wasn't the only one watching. He spotted a clean-cut guy in a t-shirt and jeans who was tracking the girl as she was forced out of the room. And then Jem spotted the second man—blond, big, with a MAGA hat and a ragged denim vest—who was watching Jem. When the girl cried out again, Jem tore his eyes away from the man, but he was too late. The girl was gone.

And then the hillbilly laughed again. "Swear to Christ, man: tits like a hog."

All the voices in Jem's head snapped off, and he slid out of the booth.

It took him a moment to spot the gambit. The big guy in the biker's cut was coming back from the bathroom, and he was moving with that wired, twitchy energy of somebody who'd just hit the pipe. Jem took out his wallet, dug out a twenty, and then launched himself out of the booth. He dropped the bill on the floor as he passed the table with the two redneck jerkoffs. When he passed the biker headed in the opposite direction, he twisted his body to give the man plenty of room to pass.

Then he turned around and called, "Hey."

The biker spun around, fists tightening, eyes wide. Whatever he'd smoked, it had him good and amped up. Jem displayed open hands and smiled. Then he threw a look at the jerkoffs.

"I think you dropped some money," Jem shouted over the music. "That asshole is picking it up."

The biker turned. He saw the fallen twenty that Jem had dropped. The rednecks had enough time to flush, push their chairs back, struggle to get out of their seats. One of them said, "Wait a minute—"

The biker broke a chair over the closest guy's head, and he went down like Jem saw in the movies sometimes. The second guy tried to throw a punch, but he got himself tangled in the legs of his chair, and all he managed to do was fall forward and sprawl across the table. The biker crashed into him, and both men—and the table—went down.

Screams and shouts erupted throughout the club. The biker's friends decided to join in, and more fights broke out. A redhead behind the bar was screaming, "Donny! Donny! Somebody get Donny!" Jem focused on the door behind the stage and ran.

For the first fifteen feet, his path was clear. Then a big, bearded guy loomed up in his path, swinging a bottle at Jem's head. Jem deked him, cut right, and the big man stumbled as someone punched him in the back. Another guy swam up at Jem out of the brownish darkness, this one with a knife. Jem kicked a chair into the man's path and jumped onto the stage. The Black girl had her back to the wall, her eyes wide as she tried to get her feet under her—she'd broken a heel, a distant part of Jem noticed. Jem sprinted past her toward the door. He risked one last glance back at the brawl. He'd lost sight of the clean-cut guy who'd been watching the girl get forced behind the stage. But he spotted the blond man, the one who'd been watching Jem: he had his back to the wall, facing off with one of the college bros. He'd lost his MAGA hat, and he was saying something to the bro. The bro swung, and faster than Jem could track, the blond man popped him in the face. The bro fell into one of the chairs, face slack, and didn't get up.

When the blond man started to look around again, Jem ducked through the door behind the stage.

On the other side, another cue-ball guy was rushing toward him, already shouting, "You can't be back here —"

Jem cut him off. "Donny? Where the fuck is Donny? They told me to get Donny out there."

The guy's eyes widened, and he surged past Jem.

And then Jem was alone, and when the door fell shut, the sounds of the fight dropped to a series of buzzing thumps.

It was brighter back here — not by much, but enough that you wouldn't trip over the loose carpeting or walk into a wall. Several of the doors were marked DANCERS, and behind them, Jem could hear women's voices. He skipped these for now. He moved down the hall, found a utility closet, where the fiftysomething woman was rinsing a sponge out in a sink. Jem gave her a nod and shut the door again and kept moving. He stopped at a door that read MANAGER. Yellow light and the sound of TV voices suggested an occupant, but he didn't hear anything that sounded like the girl who had been forced back here, and so, after another moment, he kept moving.

The next door was locked — no deadbolt, only a latch. Jem dug out his wallet, found his scratched-up UCCU debit card, and slipped it between the door and the jamb. He loided the lock on the first try, and the door popped open. The smell of cold concrete and steel and motor oil seeped out.

Voices from the direction Jem had come made him step through the doorway and pull the door shut behind him. He listened over the thud of his heartbeat, but the voices didn't seem to be moving toward him, and then, after several long moments, he couldn't hear them anymore.

When he turned on his phone's flashlight, it gave barely enough light to make out the shape of the garage: a rectangular box with two roll-up doors, the walls made from the same corrugated steel as the rest of the structure. Shelves lined the walls, filled with supplies — paper towels, cleaning solutions, tampons, condoms, toilet paper. One of the roll-up doors was raised, letting in night air and the hum of crickets, and in the bay behind the door, a white panel van sat, its engine ticking as it cooled.

Jem moved toward the van, but he stopped again at the sound of a sole scuffing gravel. Then a familiar voice muttered, "I'm going to kill that cracker-ass motherfucker." Jem held himself still, trying to gauge the sound. DeVoy must have been close, perhaps just on the other side of the roll-up.

Shouts erupted at the front of the club—the indignant, outraged cries of drunks with wounded pride. DeVoy swore again, and steps moved away, the sound of crunching gravel fading slowly as he went to investigate.

When the sound of DeVoy's steps had been swallowed up by the shouts, Jem jogged to the van. He tried the front passenger door, and it opened. Stink—garbage and something rancid and a hot, animal smell— rolled out, and he pulled his tee up over his nose. A flattened McDonald's bag lay in the footwell, with a crushed Big Mac box and a cardboard fry sleeve.

From the back of the van came a sudden whirring sound, the thrum of metal, and then a clatter.

Jem jerked back from the van, swearing. He caught himself. Then he worked the paracord off from around his neck, looped it around his fist, and let the hex nut bounce against his thigh. He drew the telescoping antenna from his pocket and held it in his other hand. The noise came again—the rattle, clatter, whir. His brain took him to a pet store. A bird, or birds, in a cage.

Letting out a shaky breath, Jem yanked on the handle of the van's sliding door. It opened easily, running silently on its track. In that first moment, the interior of the van was a dark, gaping mouth. The ambient light from outside did nothing to break it up, and when the bird—or birds— thrashed again, the sound activated something prehistoric in Jem's brain. Goose bumps ran up his arms. He lifted the phone and brought the flashlight to bear on the darkness.

Cages sparked and glittered under the light—copper-colored wire, stainless steel, some round, one as big as a doghouse. Dark eyes gleamed back at him. They were all inside cages—that was the first, automatic thing his brain checked—and then one of the birds, a bigger one he didn't recognize, spread its wings and made a furious noise, and Jem took a step back. He steadied the flashlight, wiped his mouth, and let out a choked noise that he supposed was a laugh.

"Holy God," he muttered.

After another moment to steel himself, he climbed into the van. It rocked under him, and its poorly maintained suspension groaned. The birds chittered and shuffled and battered themselves against the cages.

"It's ok," Jem murmured. "I'm not going to hurt you."

He snapped photos of the cages. As the initial mixture of surprise and fright faded, he got a clearer look at the van's contents. The cages were stacked along the driver's side of the van's cargo compartment, and they'd clearly been bolted to the metal floor. That was interesting, since it suggested this wasn't a one-time operation.

Cardboard boxes filled the rest of the van. Jem opened the first one and found bottles—small plastic ones, the kind vitamins and supplements came in. Printed labels covered each bottle, but something about them struck him as unprofessional. The font was part of it. And the layout. And the quality of the print job. Jem hadn't ever run that big of a game before, nothing on a scale that involved manufacturing, but he recognized shit when he saw it, and he was looking at shit. He ignored what he took for Chinese characters and took his time with the English words, making sure he got them right. Powdered rhino horn. Tiger bone. Pangolin scales. One vial with a sealed top had something liquid inside it, and Jem had no desire to open it and discover what leopard bone wine smelled like. He would lie, he decided, if Tean ever asked him how long he looked at the dried tiger penis, but he couldn't help himself: he stuffed the plastic packet in his back pocket.

In the next section of boxes, he found drugs. They were still in prescription vials with the childproof tops, still with the labels on them. He found Cymbalta and Valium and Viagra. He found Vicodin and Percocet. He found Xanax, prescribed to Sally English, and when the bottle rattled, he shoved it in his back pocket.

The third box held small plastic totes, and when Jem opened these, he found IDs. State-issued non-driver IDs. Driver's licenses. Social Security cards. Passports. Most of the passports, Jem noticed, were foreign. Lots from Cambodia, Thailand, Laos.

Another, smaller box, held jewelry: chains, rings, necklaces.

Part of his brain, the part that had kept him alive this long, the part that was always alert, sent up a ding, and Jem wrestled his attention away from the IDs. It took him a moment to understand what had set off his internal alarm: silence. The shouts from the front of the club had died down. Any minute now, DeVoy would be coming back.

Jem grabbed a few of the IDs and a handful of the jewelry, and he pocketed all of it as he slid out of the van. His heart was hammering now, and he could smell the flop sweat building on his body. He eased the door shut. One of the birds squawked indignantly, and it sent an electric jolt through Jem. He moved around to the back of the van to snap a photo of the license plate, but it was covered in mud. He'd used that trick a few times himself. Grimacing, Jem snapped a photo anyway—at least you could tell it was a Missouri plate.

As Jem stood, a key rattled in the door that led into the club. Then it opened.

Jem darted behind the van, into a well of deeper shadow. He pressed up against the metal skin of the building. His legs were shaking, and it took all his focus to keep himself still, to keep the tremors in his body from working their way into that thin sheet of corrugated steel.

Voices moved into the garage.

"—came back here during the fight," a man was saying. His voice was hard, but he sounded young to Jem. "I saw him."

"And I'm telling you, I didn't see anything." That was DeVoy. "I was smoking. Nobody came out this way."

"What is your fucking van doing in the fucking garage?"

"Nothing, man! I needed a place to park."

The silence that came after was hot and snarled. And then, in a different voice, the man said, "You want to tell me what kind of dumb shit you're pulling?"

"Nothing!" DeVoy's laugh rippled with nerves. "I swear to God!"

The silence lasted longer that time. DeVoy's breathing was a little too fast.

"You sure about that? Because this is not the place to do dumb shit. This is a legitimate fucking business. Do you understand that?"

"Come on, man! I fucking told you—"

The sound of the blow was soft and stinging—a slap, Jem guessed. His legs were shaking harder, and sweat dripped into his eyes, stinging. He wiped his face on his shirt. The corrugated steel was cool and flexed restlessly at his back.

"Get it out of here," that hard, young voice said. "And don't bring your shit around here again."

Footsteps clipped toward the club again, but Jem barely heard them. The panicked part of his mind played out DeVoy's route to the driver's seat of the van: he'd walk around the back of the van and run right into Jem. Jem eased himself up from the steel panel, wincing as the metal relaxed back into its original shape, at the slight sound of release. He had to get out in front of the van, had to get out of the garage—

The phone in his hand buzzed, and in the silence, the sound was unmistakable.

"What—" DeVoy began.

Steps slapped the concrete, racing toward Jem. The owner of that other voice didn't waste any time, it seemed.

After an instant of shock, Jem was already running. That was what you did when your cover was blown. He twisted sideways to clear the gap between the van and the roll-up door's track, and then he was out in the night air, with the humidity and the gnats and the stink of garbage from an overflowing dumpster and the skunkiness of weed. Security lights cut wedges out of the darkness, making patches of gravel incandescent. The loose stone crunched under foot; with every stride, it shifted and slid, threatening to pitch him face first onto the ground.

Chips of stone sprayed into the air, ahead of Jem, inches to his left. The boom of the gunshot came a moment later, thunderous in the silence.

At the corner of the building, Jem skidded into a turn. In front of the club, many of the vehicles were gone—a consequence of the brawl, Jem guessed. A big guy with a beard was holding the door of a truck, helping a woman with batwing arms into her seat. They were both staring, their attention obviously drawn by the gunshot.

Another shot cracked the air behind Jem.

He sprinted for the Jetta. He jammed the keyless start button before his butt had hit the seat, and as the car purred to life, he hammered the shifter into reverse. Another shot came as Jem reversed, the car slewing across the loose stone in an arc that almost brought Jem crashing into the cars behind him. Then he hit the shifter again, and the Jetta lurched forward, carrying him out of the lot.

5

Tean had given up on pacing. He'd given up on sitting. He stood in the Santaland lobby, phone clutched in one hand, and was useless. Totally, perfectly useless.

Of course, he was in good company.

"I'm sure everything's all right." Kristin, Missy's friend who had been planning on going to dinner with them, had stuck with Tean since the police officer had taken Missy for questioning. "I'm sure she's fine."

"I have a terrible feeling about this," Heather the animal psychic said. She'd shown up in the lobby, announcing that she'd been drawn by psychic danger. Kristin had told Tean in an aside, though, that she'd seen one of Heather's friends recording a video of Missy being led away by the police. Heather put her fingertips to her temples and frowned. Maybe, Tean thought, her abilities worked like broadcast television. Maybe she needed a bunny-ear antenna.

Rod snorted. Tean had seen him earlier, at Rod's one-man "panel," which had mostly consisted of him boasting about his success with the cat sanctuary, interspersed with a few softball questions from people who were clearly his friends—or at least his sycophants. And, of course, interrupted magnificently by his spat with Missy. Rod had joined them in the lobby without any explanation. Now, he eyed Tean and said, "You don't have to stick around if you don't want."

It was at least the fourth time he'd said it.

"No," Tean said, but he heard the strain in his voice. "I'll wait."

With most of the conference-goers occupied either by dinner, drinks, or last-minute preparations for their paper or panel, the Santaland lobby was practically empty. As the minutes dragged past, it took on a nightmarish quality. Nat King Cole blatted on the blown speakers. A Starbucks cup perched on the trim of Santa's sleigh. The Christmas trees drooped, and tinsel fluttered in a draft, and one flickering section of lights seemed to be communicating in Morse code.

Tean checked his phone again. Still nothing from Jem, and it had been over an hour since that first, frantic text, not to mention all the others since.

He tried another one: *Are you ok? Where are you?*

"If you've got something better to do—" Rod began.

"I'm staying," Tean snapped.

A woman in a blazer and a polka-dot skirt crossed the lobby toward them, her gait somewhere between a half-hearted run and a power walk. By the time she reached them, her cheeks were red, and she was huffing slightly. She nodded slightly to Kristin and Heather and asked, "Have any of you seen Yesenia?"

Tean shook his head. Rod snorted. Heather touched her temples again. Maybe there was a titmouse near Yesenia, and Heather could contact her that way.

"Sorry," Kristin said. "I haven't seen her today."

The woman let out a despairing noise. "Dr. Trevino is furious. She says she won't stay in a normal hotel room. She says she has to have a suite."

"Well…" Kristin said, and she turned a hopeful look toward Tean, of all people.

"It doesn't matter what she wants," Heather snapped, dropping her hands from her temples. "She's a guest. She might be the keynote speaker, but we invited her. If she doesn't like it, she can leave."

"Maybe the resort would be willing to upgrade her room," Tean said. "We can ask."

Rod shook his head, his mullet swaying against his collar. "I'll take care of it. Tell her I'll get her settled."

The woman beamed a smile at Rod before scurrying off again.

She'd barely disappeared when a young guy rushed up to them. He was buttoned up in a three-piece suit and wringing his hands (which Tean didn't know if he'd ever seen outside of a movie before), and his voice was high-pitched and femme when he said, "Where's Dr. Alvarez? Have you seen Dr. Alvarez?"

This time, Kristin and Heather traded a look.

"Don't know, son," Rod said.

"But I need her! An entire panel of herpetologists got into one of the fountains, and they're making the elves do inappropriate things! They're going to get kicked out of the conference!"

"You might remind them—" Tean began.

"Now, hold on," Rod said, holding up a hand to Tean. "I'll handle this. Son, you go take a few pictures, and then you tell them you're forwarding those pictures to the chancellor or president or whatever you want to call it at their universities. And tell them to put the elves back, or I'll have something to say about it."

The young man kept wringing his hands, his gaze fixed on Rod.

Rod clapped his hands once. "Go on, now. Get!"

The young man bolted.

Kristin snagged Tean's sleeve and leaned in. "I haven't seen Yesenia all day."

"Neither have I."

"And it's been—well, it's been a mess. Right?"

Tean didn't answer. He wasn't sure that he'd call the conference a mess, but it had certainly suffered its moments of disorganization. Now that Kristin called his attention to it, a mental list began to form: equipment missing from multipurpose rooms; water stations with no water; hotel staff trying to clear a ballroom so they could set up for a Bat Mitzvah. Every conference had its share of disorder, of course, but this one did seem…well, worse.

He offered a shrug in response to Kristin's question.

Before either of them could say more, another man jogged across the room toward them. He was one of the stocky, bluff-faced guys who seemed overrepresented in the profession, and he wore a khaki shirt that was vaguely reminiscent of Boy Scouts. As he craned his head for a look around the lobby, he asked, "Seen Yesenia?"

"Is there a sign or something?" Tean muttered.

"No," Heather said. "We haven't seen her."

"Because Anika and Wes are having it out about multipurpose room seven. Anika says Yesenia told her she could set up for tomorrow's panel, and Wes said he's supposed to have the room in the morning for his roundtable."

"You've got to be kidding me," Kristin said, rubbing her forehead.

Rod puffed up again. "Tell them we had to make some changes to the conference program. Tell them both to sit quiet until they get a new draft."

"But—" the Boy Scout began.

"And if they don't like it," Rod said, "they can talk to me. You tell anyone who wants to know, I'm handling things while Yesenia is indisposed."

The guy nodded, relief creasing his face, and he hustled off again.

"Yesenia isn't indisposed," Kristin said. "And you're not in charge."

Rod ignored her, his gaze fixed somewhere over her shoulder. But a moment later, he said, "Somebody's got to do something. Or do you want to leave things like this, everybody running around, the whole lot of them like chickens with their heads cut off?"

"That's not the point—"

"I think she's dead," Heather said. The expression on her too-thin face was hard for Tean to read—a grotesque imitation of distress, perhaps. "Missy probably killed her."

Tean stared.

Kristin made a choked noise.

Rod laughed.

"I'm sorry," Tean said. "What?"

"It makes sense," Heather said. She shivered and chafed her arms. "Feel that? That's death."

"That's air conditioning set to an unethical—and financially irresponsible—sixty-seven degrees," Tean said. "What do you mean, she's dead? And why would Missy kill her?"

"She's not here, is she? Yesenia, I mean. Nobody's seen her all day."

"We don't know—" Kristin began.

"And then the police show up, and they take Missy off for questioning, and the ether—"

Rod burst out laughing again.

"Is this funny to you?" Tean asked.

"You'd better believe it is, son. The whole thing's a goddamn joke."

Heather drew herself up. "It's not a joke. And I'm not making things up. Did you know Missy and Yesenia had a huge fight yesterday?"

"They had a disagreement," Kristin said.

Tean nodded. "Missy mentioned—"

"A disagreement." Heather made a face. "I've never seen anything like it. I thought Missy was going to attack her right there—jump on her, go for the throat."

Rod smirked and looked away.

"They were screaming at each other," Heather continued. "Well, Missy was screaming. Yesenia was just Yesenia—talking the way she always talks, like she doesn't care who you are or what you think. But she knew what she was doing. Everything she said, it wound Missy up more and more. She kept screaming and screaming."

"Missy wouldn't have—" Kristin tried.

"And when Yesenia finally left, Missy said she wished Yes was dead."

Tean had known—and been married to—Jem Berger long enough to know embroidery when he heard it. "Is that really what she said?"

Heather flashed him a startled look. Her shoulders shrank. "Well, I mean, not exactly."

"What did she say?"

"Oh, I don't know. It was the same general idea. 'The world would be better off without you.' Something like that." Her tone took on an edge. "I'd say that's pretty much the same thing."

"Not necessarily," Tean said. "The world would be better off without any of us."

"Rod got in a fight with Yesenia too." Kristin's cheeks were red, and the words tumbled out. "It doesn't mean anything; people fight all the time. There's no way Missy would kill Yesenia. Tean, you've known Missy forever. Tell them."

"I think we're jumping to a lot of conclusions," Tean said. "Yesenia might be sick, like Rod said. She might have had a family emergency, and she had to leave."

"Without telling anyone?" Heather said.

"And the police could be talking to Missy about any number of things. She might have had a death in the family; the police could be notifying her in private."

"He didn't look like he was telling her a cousin died," Heather said. "He looked the way cops look when they bust you." Color tinged her wasted cheeks, and she mumbled, "On TV, I mean."

"I thought you were drawn here by psychic danger." Rod's voice lilted into mock-spookiness at the end. "Or maybe it was a vision, huh? That's how you saw him?"

Heather glared at him.

With a chuckle, Rod said, "I guess I'd better go take care of things. While Yesenia is indisposed." To Kristin, he added, "You feel free to step right up, miss, if you think I'm doing it wrong."

Kristin opened her mouth, but Rod was already sauntering away.

"Tean?"

When Tean turned, Jem was jogging across the lobby—coming, Tean noticed, from the direction of the elevators.

Tean asked, "Where have you been?"

Jem opened his mouth, and then the expression on his face changed, and he asked, "What happened?"

The evasion registered at the back of Tean's mind, but only distantly. He told Jem what he knew: Yesenia's absence, Missy being taken by the police, Heather's insinuations.

"I don't really think she killed her," Heather put in. "It's the spirits, sometimes they—"

"Did you check Yesenia's room?" Jem asked.

Overhead, Nat King Cole died a staticky death, and John Lennon picked up—voice distorted and sounding like one of Yoko Ono's side projects.

"That's where we should start, right?" Jem nodded in answer to himself. "Instead of thinking she ran away or disappeared. Simplest explanation first: she's sick, like Rod said, or she fell, or something."

"Ok, yes," Tean said, "that's a good idea, but—"

"Be right back."

A few minutes later, Jem and a chipmunk-cheeked white woman in a red Santaland uniform left the front desk. The woman was carrying a keycard, saying, "—if it's a wellness check, of course." Jem waved for Tean, and Tean shot Kristin and Heather a look.

"One of us should stay here in case somebody comes looking for Yesenia again," Kristin said, giving a meaningful look at Heather.

"I'm not staying," Heather said. Her wattle swung from side to side as she shook her head, and she started off toward Jem. "I'm being summoned by the spirits."

Tean tried not to sigh.

Kristin, however, made no effort not to roll her eyes.

Hurrying across the lobby, Tean had almost caught up with Heather when a group of men entered the Santaland lobby. They came in through the automatic doors that connected to the parking lot, and they didn't look like vets or biologists or even Santaland elves—not unless elves had taken to wearing a lot more leather and living rough. There were four of them, and they moved like a pack.

Heather spotted them too, squeaked, and abruptly changed course. She cut away from Jem and hurried—practically ran—toward the closest hallway.

"What—" Tean began.

"The ether!" Heather said without looking back, waving one hand for him to go on without her.

When Tean reached Jem, he said, "I don't know what that was about—"

"You know what?" Jem asked, hand on Tean's nape, steering him toward the elevators. His gaze flicked over the men near the door before settling on Tean. Blue eyes. The color of a summer squall. He grinned, but it only touched his mouth. "Let's keep moving."

"Do you know those guys?" Tean asked, twisting for another look.

Jem's hand forced him—gently but firmly—forward again. "I do not. But I don't like the look of them."

The Santaland woman gave them a glance and sniffed. "Two of those are the Rangel boys."

"A little faster, please," Jem murmured, and with his free hand, he took her arm and hustled the three of them out of the lobby.

The elevator came when the woman—her name tag said Daisy— pressed the button, and Jem practically threw them inside the car. Santaland only had three floors, and Daisy pressed the button marked with a two. The doors slid shut, and then the elevator began to inch upward.

After what felt like five minutes, Jem said, "Are you kidding me?"

"It's for our older guests," Daisy said. "Some of them don't like it moving too fast."

"I could have Spider-manned my way up the building faster than this."

"Jem," Tean said, "what—"

"Nothing. It's fine. Everything's fine."

But some emotion Tean couldn't name tightened Jem's expression. After a moment, he reached up and removed Jem's hand from his nape, and then he laced their fingers together.

Jem gave him a compressed smile, barely more than a line, but he squeezed Tean's hand once.

An eternity later, they reached the second floor. When they stepped out into the hall, Daisy turned left, and they followed her past several rooms. Then she stopped and knocked on the next door. Silence answered them.

"Ms. Alvarez," Daisy called, "are you in there? This is Daisy with Santaland. We're just making sure you're ok."

The silence drew out for another few seconds, and then came a heavy thump and the sound of running steps.

"Open it," Jem snapped.

Daisy stared at him.

"The key!"

She inserted her key into the card reader. The light flashed green. Tean reached for the handle, but Jem got there first, pressing into the room. He released Tean's hand and reached into his pocket where, no doubt, he was carrying some of his weapons. Some things never changed.

46

"Hey," Jem shouted, "stop right there—"

Then he ducked as something came flying across the room. A can of spray paint. It landed on the floor, and Jem rushed forward again.

"Go get security," Tean said, pushing Daisy toward the elevators. Then he moved into the room after Jem.

As soon as he cleared the threshold, a mixture of foul smells reached him: paint, feces, urine, overheated body. It was a standard hotel room, with a king bed, a dresser, a TV, a desk. A sliding glass door led to a balcony. It looked out on a strip of grass and then dark water. The Lake of the Ozarks, maybe. Or the reservoir. Tean had gotten turned around, and he wasn't sure what he was looking at. He only had a moment to process the sight of the water—the saw-teeth of light rippling in the dark, his brain suggesting the reflection of hotel lights; farther and higher, a flash of red, probably an aircraft warning light on the other side. Then his attention narrowed to the woman crawling over the balcony railing.

She was tall, olive skinned, with dark hair and dramatic sideburns. He recognized her: this was the woman who'd been screaming as security hauled her bodily from the resort. Between her teeth, she was holding an envelope. For a moment, their eyes met, and Tean looked into a wild, unseeing energy that made him suspect this woman was mentally ill. Then she released the rail and dropped.

"Jesus Christ!" Jem shouted and sprinted toward the balcony.

Tean hesitated, taking in the rest of the room. The dresser and desk had clearly been rifled, with drawers hanging open and clothes and papers scattered across the floor. On the walls, spray-painted words read, LIAR and TELL US THE TRUTH and, the letters jagged with the same trembling energy Tean had seen in the woman's eyes, BIRDS AREN'T REAL. The coverlet on the bed was darkly wet, and a heap of feces marked the center of the mattress.

"Son of a bitch," Jem said as he poked his head back into the room. He made a face and put his hand under his nose. "She's alive, in case you're wondering. It's not that far of a fall. She must be half gazelle because she bounded away."

Tean nodded. Then he took out his phone and started recording. He took in the walls, then the dresser and desk, then the bed. Jem crossed to the bathroom. The door was open, and he stuck his head inside. When he pulled back, he gave a single shake.

Then Jem's head came up, and he moved toward the door that led to the hall. As he passed Tean, he gave him a push that sent him toward the balcony, and he drew the paracord from around his neck.

"—magically unlocked by my magic," a voice said in the hall.

The door swung open, and a blond man stepped into the room—big, muscular, wearing the same landscaping tee that Tean had seen when he'd sat next to him in the Santaland bar earlier. He hadn't noticed Tean and Jem because he was turned back toward the hall, saying, "It wasn't magically anything. It was open when we got here, which you'd know if you weren't playing bait-and-tackle in a public hallway."

The second man Tean remembered from the bar, the slender one with the bun of chestnut-colored hair, drifted into the room while hitching up his purple tights. "Oh, bait-and-tackle sounds amazing. I could be a simple, uh, carp, and you could be the rough-around-the-edges fisherman, and you'd have these callused hands because you've spent so much of your life alone and jerking off—"

"I have calluses because I work for a living, pansy-ass. Jesus fucking Christ. Not that you'd know—"

"And then one day the carp and the fisherman meet, and the carp doesn't mind that the fisherman's hands are gross and knobby and sometimes it feels like he's using sandpaper to, um, twist—"

"Shaw," the blond man said when he saw Tean and Jem.

"Well, you do a lot of twisting, which is fine, but sometimes the carp would like to be stroked—"

"Shaw!"

The slender man's head came up, and he took them in. Then he beamed. "North, you're not going to believe this, but you know how my magic magically unlocked the door?"

"Who the fuck are you?" the blond man—North—asked.

"Who the fuck are you?" Jem asked.

"I'm King fucking Kong," North said. "What the fuck does it look like? Answer my fucking question."

"Donkey Kong," Jem said with an edge in his voice Tean hadn't heard in a long time—and, if he wasn't wrong, the hint of suppressed excitement. "I played that."

"Why don't we all calm down—" Tean began.

"That's my psychic." The slender man—Shaw—grabbed North's arm. "The one I was telling you about. The one who connected me to the puppy even though it was long distance and there were all those extra charges. And it was worth it, North, because the puppy told me that if we would stop feeding him so much cheese, the evil spirit that makes him bark right in my ear when I'm trying to sleep after, um, meditating—"

"I'm not going to ask you again," North said.

"Animal psychic?" Tean asked.

The set to Jem's shoulders looked slightly embarrassed, but he kept his gaze fixed on the men in front of him. "You're the one he was talking about," Jem said. "The one whose noodle is past al dente."

"Oh, well," Shaw said, "that was really only a one-time thing, and it was private, you know, animal psychic-client confidentiality—"

"Motherfucking traitorous piece of shit," North said, directing a furious glance at Shaw. "I was sick! I had a fever!" Then he stopped, and with what looked like an effort of will, drew himself back together. His gaze resettled on Jem. "All right, we'll do this the hard way."

Jem didn't say anything, but Tean recognized the coiled energy of his body, the way his free hand dipped toward his pocket.

"Let's not do anything hasty," Tean said. "We can explain—"

"North," Shaw said.

"I'll deal with you later," North said.

But Shaw grabbed his arm, turning North toward the door and, at the same time, moving them further into the room. Tean tugged Jem backward, giving the other men space to maneuver. The muscles in Jem's back were hot and tight, all that potential violence trembling with a kind of molecular frenzy. But North and Shaw seemed, for the moment, to have forgotten Tean and Jem. Their attention was fixed on the door.

At that moment, the four men from the lobby stepped into the room. Up close, Tean formed a clearer impression of them. They were all white, and their ages ran from late twenties into hard forties or early fifties. One of them might have been pretty five years ago, a kind of white trash Ryan Gosling. The next was older, with a goatee of graying stubble. He wore wireframe glasses, which he removed and folded with one hand. The third looked a little like a tee-ball coach Tean remembered from childhood, with his dad haircut and double chin—but you had to overlook the tattoos scrawled across his knuckles. The fourth was a killer. Tean had seen the look now, knew it—the thousand-yard stare under slicked-back hair.

For a moment, Tean was sure the men's attention settled on Jem.

"Fucking hell," North muttered. "This is your fault. I wanted to go to Disney World."

Then the killer pulled up his shirt. Blued steel showed behind his waistband, and he reached for the gun.

6

Jem moved when he saw the gun. He launched himself forward, paracord in one hand, the other slipping the telescoping antenna—pried from the back of an old RCA television years ago—out of his pocket. At the edge of his vision, he noticed the big blond fucker, North, shoving Shaw toward the balcony, shouting, "Get him out of here." Then Jem's focus tunneled to the fight.

He swung with the paracord first. The beauty of paracord was that if you bought the good stuff, it stretched at least thirty percent of its length, and it could hold over a thousand pounds of static weight. If you got a long piece of it and you tied a hex nut to the end and you built up some speed, you could do some nice damage, and you could do it from farther away than people expected.

So, while the one with the slicked-back hair was still pulling his gun from his waistband, Jem whipped the paracord once and let the hex nut fly. It cracked against the man's hand, and Jem thought he heard something break. The man screamed, and the gun dropped to the floor.

That was when North kicked the one with the dad haircut in the knee. Dad dropped, squealing.

Jem extended the antenna with a snap of his wrist and slashed at the pretty one. The antenna whistled through the air, and the pretty one stumbled back, crashing into Slick-back. Jem turned on the fourth man, the older one with the goatee. If you fought fast and lowdown and dirty, the way Jem liked to fight, a lot of the fight was over if you managed to hit first. Three of the four were already out of the fight.

But he wasn't fast enough, not quite.

Goatee charged into Jem, a knife coming up. That was a killing move, designed to bring the knife up under the ribcage. Jem whipped the paracord at him, but he hadn't had time to build up speed or to aim, and it whapped uselessly against the man's side. With the distance between them closed, the antenna was useless, and Jem dropped it. He twisted, felt something tug at his shirt—the knife, his brain screamed—and threw an elbow. He caught only air. Goatee, on the other hand, got a shoulder into Jem, and the force of the blow threw Jem back. He lost his footing and fell, and he landed between the wall and the bed.

For a moment, Jem couldn't breathe, and black specks whirled in front of him. The sounds of the fight were distant, buried under his brain's screams for oxygen. Tean, Jem thought. Tean.

Somehow, he got to his feet. The black spots danced and thickened, and he tried to suck in air. Tean needed him. Tean. The knife. Tean and Shaw, who looked about as substantial as a piece of cottonwood fluff, in his purple tights and his pink Crocs.

Jem glimpsed out of the corner of his eye North fighting with Slick-back—North clearly had the upper hand, and Slick-back was barely able to stay on his feet as North rained down brutal, heavy, clubbing blows with one fist, the other hand holding Slick-back upright by the shirt. The hotel room seemed enormous now, the flood of adrenaline stretching everything out into unreal dimensions, and it took an eternity for Jem to scan the room and find Tean and Shaw.

And then all he could do was stare as Goatee lunged with the knife.

Shaw had put Tean behind him, and it was clear he'd been trying to cover Tean as they made their way to the balcony, where they could escape. But Goatee had caught up to them, and although the physical distance wasn't much—four or five feet as the scarlet macaw flies, a crazy part of Jem laughed—the bed was in the way, and time was the real bitch. Time, dilating in the chemical rush of adrenaline. Everything taking so much longer than it should have. The knife coming up toward Shaw slowly. It would go through that big baggy t-shirt like it was nothing. It would go up under the ribcage, into the heart and lungs.

And then Shaw reared back, the movement so smooth it looked boneless, and spun something from his hand. The telephone handset, still attached to the coiled cord. The cord stretched and flexed just like the paracord, and the handset whipped in a perfect arc, a real beauty. It cracked Goatee in the face, and his nose broke in a spray of blood. Then Shaw leaned forward, grabbed Goatee by his short scruff of graying hair, and yanked his head down to knee him in the face.

Goatee crumpled like an empty bag.

North's shout drew Jem's attention. Pretty Boy had finally worked himself up for the fight—or, more likely, had realized he wasn't going to be able to lie low and let the others do the fighting for him. He had a gravity knife, an ugly little leaden smear in the lamplight, and he slashed wildly at North as he pressed his attack. North retreated, shielding himself with a pillow from the bed. Feathers spilled out from the gashes the knife had left, filling the air.

Jem had lost the paracord and the antenna in the fall. He glanced around, settled on the clock radio and yanked its plug from the wall.

Pretty Boy pressed North back until the bigger man was cornered. The pillow sagged between his hands, most of the stuffing gone—feathers drifting on invisible currents as they settled on the dresser, the desk, the bed.

Raising the clock radio, Jem slid across the corner of the mattress, picking up a few feathers of his own along the way. He landed easily on his feet, came up behind Pretty Boy, and slammed the clock radio into the side of his head.

Pretty Boy stumbled back with a shout, and Jem caught his arm. He slammed it against the desk twice before Pretty Boy's fingers sprang open and the gravity knife fell. When Pretty Boy thrashed, Jem let him go.

The four men clustered at the doorway—Goatee, whose nose was a swollen bloody traffic light, was supporting Dad Haircut, who was hopping on his good leg and moaning; Slick-Back cradled his broken hand; and finally Pretty Boy, who probed his puffy ear, his shoulders hunched.

Jem waited for some classic bad guy stuff, but the four men shuffled out of the room, and then it was over.

North threw the pillow aside and turned to Shaw, asking questions in a low voice. Jem barely noticed; he was moving toward Tean, already hearing himself forming their private versions of the same inquiries.

"I'm fine," Tean said, catching his hand. "Are you—"

Jem rubbed his chest. "Surprised me is all."

"Oh my gosh," Tean said, pulling Jem into an embrace. "You could have been killed."

"It wasn't a magic spell," North said. "It was a fucking pillow, and would it have killed you to do something besides stand there and watch?"

"I was being a bodyguard," Shaw said. "Like Whitney Houston."

"No, she wasn't the bodyguard—" Jem began.

"Don't," North snapped at him. "For fuck's sake, is everyone in the universe determined to give him exactly what he wants?"

Shaw beamed and opened his mouth.

Before he could say whatever he had planned, though, voices came from the hall.

"We need to go back to the lobby and call the police," a man said.

"I don't think that's necessary," another man said.

"I don't care if you think it's necessary, Emery. Somebody beat the shit out of those guys, and I don't want Auggie wandering around up here—Auggie, come on."

A third man said, "Ree, maybe he's right."

"No. If I have to hear one more time about this disappearing vet, I'm going to shove a pencil in my ear."

"You have got to be fucking kidding me," North said in an underbreath, and he pulled out the desk chair and dropped into it.

Shaw was actually quivering with excitement, touching his hair, checking himself in the mirror.

A fourth voice said, "The lady told me he was up here to check on Yesenia. If he's not with her, I promise we'll call it a night—"

That was when four men reached the doorway to the hotel room. One of them big and muscular, with dark hair and eyes the color of straw. One of them built like a swimmer, with a golden tan and perfectly mussed blond hair. One of them with a bro flow pushed back behind his ears and a seriously good beard. One of them shorter than the others and clearly younger, with a crew cut and the first hint of a disbelieving smile.

"What the fuck took you so long?" North asked.

The big man in the doorway glowered at them: the expression was automatic, like the snap of a shutter. "What the fuck are you doing here?"

"Oh, Emery," Shaw said. He tried to get to the door, but North caught him by the waistband of the tights—and, in the process, left him three-quarters of the way to bare-assed. Shaw fumbled with the tights, but his gaze stayed fixed on the doorway. "I knew you'd come. See, I magically summoned you with my magic—"

"No," North said, "he didn't, because there's no such thing as magic."

At the same time, Emery was saying, "There's no such thing—" But he cut himself off and gave North, of all people, a furious look.

Shaw was still talking. "—and then you came, and I just need to give you one hug, but I'm caught on something, these tights—well, it might be a curse. Did you see any witches?"

"No way," the shorter man said, grinning as he brought up his camera.

The one with the bro flow and beard groaned.

The one with the swimmer's build was smirking. "Your soulmate is here, Ree."

"In the first place," the one with the straw-colored eyes said, "the concept of soulmates—"

Shaw was clawing at North's hand and whimpering.

"Oh for fuck's sake," North muttered and released him.

Shaw catapulted across the room and crashed into the man at what Jem guessed had to be close to Mach 1. Emery rocked back.

"I got a photo of it," the shorter man said, training his camera on them. "Emery hugged Shaw back. It's official."

"We're officially leaving," the one with the bro flow said, taking the shorter man by the shoulder.

"Do you have any idea what's going on?" Tean asked.

Jem shook his head, but he was surprised to find he was smiling. Shaking, too, as the adrenaline left him cored out. But the men had a good vibe, and he could feel the edges of it.

The man with the straw-colored eyes was trying to get free of Shaw's embrace, while Shaw was trying to wrap his legs around him, spider-monkey style.

"No, don't worry about me," North said, sprawling in the chair. "I almost got killed while this horse's ass played with his doodle and watched."

"Yeah, about that—" the one with the swimmer's build gave Jem and Tean an assessing look. "What happened? We saw some guys—"

"Enough," the big man growled, forcing Shaw off him. Shaw landed with a thud, caught himself, and rebalanced. The big man gave him a furious look. And then with a kind of helplessness in his expression, seemed to cast about for something to say. He settled on the shirt, the one with the stick figure humping the words. "That's offensive. Telling people to fuck their feelings goes against all the work we've been doing as a society to escape the psychologically devastating effects of toxic—"

"Toxic masculinity!" Shaw said at the same time. Over his shoulder—to Jem, of all people—he said, "We finish each other's sentences all the time."

Jem's smile slid into a grin. Most of it was the fresh helplessness on the big man's face.

He was trying to build up steam again with "—and, at the same time—"

But Shaw spoke over him. "And it's not telling people to fuck their feelings. It's telling them to make sweet, gentle, nurturing love to their feelings. With their penises."

Tean choked on his spit.

"With their penises," North muttered. "What are they going to use, donkey brains? Their pinky fingers?"

"Oh, the pinky finger can be highly erotic, like that time you—"

Shaw cut off abruptly when North sat up in the chair.

"No, keep going," the shorter man said. "I want to hear this."

"Do you want to grow up to have pubic hair?" North asked. "Because if so, quit fucking encouraging him."

A flash of anger, hot and serious, flashed across the younger man's face. The guy with the bro flow tightened his grip on the younger man's shoulder and said something in a low voice.

A voice from the hall broke the moment.

"What in the seven hells is—get out of my way!" In contrast to the words, the man's voice had an easiness that, combined with the confidence in it, made the tone close enough to pass for friendly. Jem had heard that voice before. Guards used it. Some cops used it. People who liked bullying, who knew they could get away with it and the world would still smile on them, they used it.

Apparently, the big man knew it too. He was already pale, but as Jem watched, the color drained from his face. He turned, and the movements had a shuffling, zombielike quality, as though the signal from brain to body was coming from a long way off.

The man in the doorway stopped. He had a nice tan, and his blond hair was almost white from summer sun, and the jeans and the Auburn Police Department uniform shirt showed off a hard body, which was probably why, Jem guessed, the jerkoff was wearing a size too small. Shock painted his face for a moment as he stared at the big man. And then he said, "Emery?"

The blond man, the one with the swimmer's build, held himself tightly, and his face was a mask. He'd sensed something, probably some more finely tuned version of the tension that Jem had picked up on, and whatever it was, it had put him in fight mode.

But all the big man—Emery—said was, "Fuck off. Right now."

The guy in the Auburn PD shirt shrank inside his shirt. It only lasted a moment, the way his shoulders curved and he sank down. Then he looked like one of those car wash inflatables, puffing himself back up, a nasty grin cutting across his face. "Well, well, well. Emery Hazard. Didn't think I'd run into you."

"I won't tell you again," Emery said. "Fuck off."

But the cop, whoever he was, made a show of peering past Emery, looking into the room. "Now, what do we have here?"

"Officer—" Tean began.

"Chief. It's chief, pal. Chief Cassidy."

"Oh," Shaw said, "North's middle name—"

"Shaw," North barked.

Shaw shut his mouth.

"I've got eight guys mucking around in a murdered woman's bedroom," Cassidy said. He wrinkled his nose. "And made a fucking pigsty of it. What the hell am I supposed to think about that?"

"Don't overexert yourself," Emery said.

The nasty smile hooked at the corner. "I think you'd all better come into the station and explain yourselves."

"What do you mean, a murdered woman?" Tean asked. "Did something happen to Yesenia?"

Jem shook his head.

"No, I want to know—" But Tean cut himself off and let out a long, hard breath.

At Cassidy's instructions, they moved out into the hallway, where a uniformed officer watched them. She was Black, hair buzzed, and young, and she stood there like a statue when Cassidy left them.

Before long, Cassidy was back, accompanied by another officer and, this time, Missy. She was a wreck: eyes red, face puffy and streaked with snot, looking small with her hands cuffed behind her back. The officer was carrying something in an evidence bag, and Jem thought he saw the rust of dried blood. They stopped at the bank of elevators.

"Missy?" Tean called. He took a step, and the Black officer put a hand on her service weapon. Tean stopped, but he shouted, "Missy?"

She glanced over at the group of men, and for a moment, nothing registered in her face.

"No talking," Cassidy said.

"Tean?" Missy said.

"I told you no talking."

"They said—"

Cassidy shoved her, and Missy stumbled forward. She started to fall and caught herself.

"You piece of shit," Emery called at Cassidy.

But the shove, or the fall, or something had shaken words loose for Missy, and as Cassidy strong-armed her toward the elevator, she called, "They're saying I killed Yes. They're saying I killed her. There's a t-shirt, they said. In the reservoir. And that poncho in my room—"

She was still shouting as Cassidy herded her into the elevator car, and then the doors slid shut, and she was gone.

7

The Auburn Police Department had its headquarters in a one-story cinderblock building fronting a small harbor, just south of where the lake met the dam. The station was painted white, with a flat, built-up roof, and it had its name in stenciled-on black letters. The hardware on the front door looked like it had come from a church jumble—antique and mismatched, and probably worth about seventy-five cents.

Inside wasn't much better. Every cramped inch of the main room huddled under aggressive fluorescents. Desks were shoehorned into the available space. Trays were choked with paperwork, and ancient computers looked like they'd last been updated during the dot-com boom. At least one of the deputies was a smoker, the stink of tobacco strong. A window A/C unit churned the air sluggishly, fluttering its little plastic streamers, but all it did was recirculate the smell of cigarette smoke and mildew and Pine-Sol.

Tean and the other men were directed to a single row of chairs, their ripped vinyl upholstery patched with duct tape. There weren't enough chairs, but that didn't matter. The big man, Emery, refused to sit, ignoring the man who was clearly his partner. He paced on the narrow strip of linoleum instead, and his partner stood with his back to the wall, arms folded, and watched. Shaw sat on North's lap, looking miserable as North rubbed his back. The man with the longish hair sat, and the conference's photographer sat, and Jem and Tean sat, and then there was nothing to do but wait. Jem took out the Goosebumps paperback he'd had folded in the back pocket of his shorts—*Night of the Living Dummy* had become a favorite, and, Tean guessed, a comfort read. Tean considered the tiny side table with its old magazines—*Field & Stream* from May of 1993. The art of stalking trout. America's bird: the truth about chokes, load, safety, and calls. Big bucks by bike.

"That's my new business model," Jem whispered.

In spite of himself, Tean managed a smile.

"It's going to be ok," Jem said. "It's a misunderstanding."

Tean shook his head.

"Everything's going to be fine," Shaw said, although he sounded as miserable as he looked. "Emery's going to fix everything. Right, Emery?"

Emery didn't seem to hear him. When Shaw opened his mouth again, North laid a hand flat on his back, and Shaw closed his mouth slowly.

"Do you know what the rate of wrongful conviction is in Missouri?" Tean asked.

Jem's eyes were a storm of blue, but he didn't look away. After a moment, he shook his head.

"Nobody does," Tean said. "That's the whole problem. Most people who are wrongfully convicted don't have the means to prove their innocence."

"Or they weren't wrongfully convicted," Emery said, the words low and thrumming with the potential charge of his anger. "How about that?"

Tean shot him a look, but after a moment, he shook his head and sank back into his seat.

"Missy's going to be fine," Jem said. When Tean stayed silent, Jem added, "We're all going to be fine. We just need to ride this out."

"Ride it out," Emery muttered. "Jonas couldn't find his ass in a paper bag. If he thinks she did it, it's because there's so much evidence that even he can't fuck it up."

"Hey," Jem said, but Emery didn't seem to hear him.

Tean sank lower into his chair. His mind kept going back to the hotel, to when he had moved toward Missy, the way the officer had put her hand on her gun. This wasn't Salt Lake City. This wasn't Utah. There was no Ammon he could call if things got bad. If things got bad. That made a laugh knot in his throat. There wasn't much *if* about it.

"Did you know seventy-jillion percent of Missouri police officers get their first arrest wrong?" Jem whispered.

"That's false," Emery said without slowing his pacing. "Seventy-jillion isn't a number, much less a percent."

But Tean fixed his attention on Jem. Jem gave him an encouraging nod, and after a moment, Tean let the reins slip. He'd been working on this. He'd been trying not to. For the girls. And, if he were being honest, for Jem, although Jem, for the most part, rolled with it.

"Did you know that Missouri has the eleventh highest rate of police killings in the United States? I looked it up before we left."

"Of course you did," Jem murmured.

"And Missouri police officers are rarely held accountable for those killings. Last year, only one officer was charged with murder in connection with a fatal shooting, and he was acquitted."

"Maybe it was a good shoot," Emery said. He stopped his pacing and stared at them. "Did you think about that?"

"The rate of police killings in Missouri is five times the rate in Utah," Tean said. "And it's almost double the national average."

"Hey," the younger guy said in a worried tone, "you're ok. You don't need to freak out."

"Where are you getting those numbers?" Emery asked.

"Ok," the blond man said, pushing off from the wall.

"Maybe police in Missouri face a higher rate of violent offenders. Did you think about that?"

"Come over here."

"No, John, I'm having a conversation."

"You're picking on him because you're upset about something else; for heaven's sake, Ree, you gave me almost the same speech about police killings last week. And you're going to feel bad about how you're behaving later. So, let's cut out the middleman, and you and I walk over here, and you can savagely whisper your counterarguments in my ear."

"Savagely whispering counterarguments is the title of Theo's sex tape," the younger man said. Then he squeaked and rubbed his leg where, Tean guessed, the man with the longish hair had pinched him.

When Tean checked Jem's face, he was surprised to see a grin.

Jem tucked it away, expression serious again as he asked, "And?"

"And if we don't get murdered by police officers in this hick town," Tean said, "we'll likely be arrested and convicted."

"Community service," Jem said. "Picking up trash. You know I wanted to work on my tan."

"No, we'll be convicted for tampering with evidence. Or destroying evidence. Or aiding and abetting."

"Chump change."

Tean shook his head. "Felony charges, minimum. And the girls—"

Jem made a warning noise.

The girls were off limits, so Tean corrected course. "And we won't be getting fresh air and sunshine. We'll be in a cell, probably for the rest of our lives, and eventually you won't be able to stand being around me, not for that long, and you'll drown me in a fresh batch of toilet wine, or you'll turn your toothbrush into a shiv, or you'll use the bedsheet to make an improvised hangman's noose—"

"I don't know how to tie one with rope," Jem pointed out, "much less a bedsheet."

"You'll figure it out."

"I don't want you to be disappointed."

"And it'll take days before they remove the body because they'll want to teach you a lesson. And that's how our story is going to end, with you killing me because of overexposure, and me murdered with cheap prison linens."

"That's ridiculous," Emery said in a louder voice. The Black deputy, watching them from one of the desks, startled in her seat. "No, John, I will not be quiet. The term 'prison linens' is misleading because linen is much too costly and unable to stand up to the wear and tear of use in a penitentiary, and even ignoring the fact that they'd never incarcerate husbands together—"

"Thank God," the blond man murmured.

"—it's statistically impossible that you two would end up in the same cell, much less for the duration of your sentence, and that's still leaving out time that you'd spend in the dining hall, the library, the recreation yard, etcetera."

"Did he say etcetera out loud?" the younger man said.

The one with the longish hair shushed him.

"We're having a conversation right now," said the blond one—John, maybe? "You and I. About Jonas Cassidy."

Emery shot him a dark look and opened his mouth. Then he seemed to think better about it, and he allowed himself to be led away—well, as far away as possible in the stamp-sized station house.

In a quiet voice, Jem said, "I would love to be your bunk-mate-slash-toilet-wine-hookup-slash-prison girlfriend, but it's not going to come to that."

Tean was running his finger up his nose before he caught himself; this pair of glasses, which Jem had given him, stayed firmly in place. He hadn't caught himself doing that, trying to push them back up, for a long time. He set the thought aside and took a moment to consider what he wanted to say.

"Jem, there's no way Missy could have done this. I don't care about a t-shirt and a poncho."

"Bloody poncho," Jem said.

"Even so, there's no proof that's Yesenia's blood. For heaven's sake, there's no proof Yesenia's dead."

"You're looking for her too?" North asked.

"No," Shaw said, "I summoned them psychically."

Then he squealed when North pulled his hair.

Jem, for some reason, was grinning, so Tean answered, "Why are you looking for her?"

"Because someone hired us to follow her."

"And because I had a premonition—" Shaw began, but he cut off, trying to defend himself as North reached for his hair again.

"What do you mean someone hired you?" Jem asked. "Watch her do what? Why?"

North and Shaw traded a glance. When Shaw gave a tiny nod, North said, "The board of trustees for that animal safari place she runs? The one down by Cape Girardeau? They think she's embezzling."

"And grifting," Shaw announced proudly.

"And all sorts of other financial shit."

"Including bribes for development deals." Shaw was rubbing the patch of hair North had pulled. "You know she's building another park, right?"

"That's good," Jem said to Tean. "That means it could have been somebody else."

Before Tean could respond, Emery broke away from his whispered conversation with John and threw the group a look. "Of course it was someone else. As I told you, Jonas couldn't kick a tire down a hill; he certainly couldn't find a murderer." He seemed to consider this and added, "Not someone who actually committed the murder, anyway. I imagine he'd be quite effective at locking up innocent people."

"Oh my gosh," Tean whispered.

"That's maybe not the most helpful thing to say right now," Jem said, and for the first time in a long while, Tean heard an edge in his voice.

"Why not?" Emery said. "It's the truth."

"Ok," John said and rubbed his forehead. "Take it down a notch."

"And there were those other guys," the younger man said, sitting forward in his chair. "We saw them leaving her room after you kicked their asses."

"Auggie," the man with the longish hair said.

Auggie ignored him. "I got them on camera."

"You did?" Jem asked.

"Well, yeah. I was recording everything because I couldn't get, um, Dr. Leon to hold still for an official picture—"

"Hmm?" Jem murmured to Tean.

Tean shot him a dirty look. "I was busy."

For some reason that made Auggie smirk, and his expression only got wider when Jem said, "I'll find some time in his schedule. Tell me when you want the photo, and I'll personally make sure he's ready and available."

Auggie held up his phone. "But it could have been those guys, right?"

"Auggie," the other man—presumably, his partner—said again. This time, there was no mistaking the warning tone.

"Stop interrupting him, Theo," Emery said. "His hobby is proving useful for once."

"Oh my God," John said under his breath.

"I'm not sure," North said. "About those guys. I think they were there for something else."

"Or someone else," Shaw said. For some reason that made color rush into Jem's face, and Tean made a mental note to ask why. Jem looked like he might be about to say something, only before he could, Shaw continued, "I'm a natural-born witch—well, North is a natural-born witch too, but he can only divine if handbags are genuine or not. Oh wait, actually, now we're both wizards. Well, North is more of a wizard and I'm more of a mage—"

Emery was making a growling noise that, if it had been an animal vocalization, Tean would have placed somewhere on the spectrum between distress and aggression.

"Maybe you can tell us later—" John tried, stroking Emery's arm.

"So," Shaw said over him, "I was thinking what if it was like that. Because I cast a charm to find us more friends, because we always try to make friends and then somebody—" This was said with a great deal of eye-rolling and a fond tone. "—won't stop talking about beers and cars and sports and he makes them watch TV for like four hours straight, and nobody else is allowed to talk even during the commercials—"

"It was a fucking Super Bowl party," North put in.

"—and an ungodly amount of cheese: cheese curds, cheese dip, cheese nuggets—"

"Hold the fuck on. I've never in my life had anything called a cheese nugget."

"—and then our friends—" There was that tone again, and Shaw even patted North's cheek as he beamed at him. "—never come back."

"Because the Super Bowl happens once a year, Shaw, and it's not my fucking fault I have a job and responsibilities and—and I don't always have time to call the guys up to hang out."

Shaw mouthed, "The guys," to Auggie, who immediately dissolved into giggles, face pressed into Theo's shoulder.

"Anyway," Shaw said, "maybe this is like the time I tried to put some tingle back in North's dingle, only then it was too much tingle, and he thought we had to go to the doctor, and I said let's try some ice, and then I got out the sandwich press and thought maybe that would subdue the evil tumescence—"

"It wasn't an evil tumescence. You put a hundred fucking milligrams of Viagra in my beer and took advantage of me! I should have the sheriff throw you in jail for assault, you monkey-dick piece of shit."

"What is happening?" Tean asked Jem.

Jem was trying to cover a huge smile with one hand. "I have no idea, but I'm into it."

"You get used to it," John said. "It starts to roll over you, and then, after a while, you don't really notice anymore."

Emery's growling noise got louder.

"Unless you're Ree," John added with a sigh.

"It's not like that," Emery snapped. "It's not like any of what you just said. There's no such thing as magic or psychics or—" He tried to master himself, and in an icy voice, he said, "Stop talking."

"Maybe I should weave a compulsion charm so that I can only speak when spoken to," Shaw suggested.

North started to laugh, tried to disguise it as coughing, and failed totally.

"This is your fault," Emery said to him. "You encourage him."

Shaw sat there, looking like butter wouldn't melt in his mouth, and said, "Maybe the compulsion charm would be tailored to you, so I could only speak when you spoke to me. It would work because we're soulmates."

North fell apart laughing.

When Emery opened his mouth, John squeezed his arm and said, "You're giving him what he wants."

So, Emery snapped his mouth shut, which for some reason only made North laugh harder.

Tean watched all of this like he was seeing it through an oil slick. He could sense the humor, the affection, the good-natured antagonism—the vibes, as Jem would have called them. But his brain kept coming back to Missy, to the panic on her face. Jem noticed, of course; he rubbed Tean's back.

Auggie was sitting up, peeling himself away from Theo, when he caught sight of them, and he said, "Oh shit." For a moment, uncertainty chalked his face, and he kicked North's boot. Then he mumbled, "Sorry. We, uh, we kind of got carried away. She's your friend, and it's serious—" Then he sat up straighter and held up his phone. "You said nobody's seen Yesenia all day? Let me see if she popped up in any of the photos I took. That might help, right?"

Tean nodded, but even that expression felt distant.

"Thanks," Jem said.

"Could I talk to you?" Theo said quietly, the words clearly meant for Auggie alone.

"I'm reviewing some conference footage on my phone," Auggie said. The words were painfully neutral. "That's all."

"Yes," Theo said. "Exactly. That's all."

For some reason, that made Auggie bring his head up and level a challenging look at Theo. It lasted only a moment, long enough for discomfort to prickle in Tean's belly, and then he went back to his phone. Theo, looking miserable, pushed his hair back with both hands and shook his head.

"I'm Jem," Jem said, touching his chest. He wrapped a hand around Tean's knee. "This is Tean."

"What does that name mean?" Emery asked.

John shushed him. "John-Henry Somerset," he said. He wrapped his arm around the bigger man. "Emery Hazard."

"North McKinney."

Shaw straightened up on North's lap. "Kingsley Shaw Wilder Aldrich."

"Auggie," he said without looking up from his phone.

The man with the longish hair was silent for a beat too long before he finally said, "Theo."

"How do you all know each other?" Jem asked.

North rolled his eyes. Shaw quivered, bright eyed with excitement. Emery made a disgusted noise. John-Henry said drily, "Long story. You're both here for the wildlife conference?"

"Tean got invited," Jem said. "He's, like, a guest of honor."

"I'm not," Tean said. "I'm speaking on a panel, that's all."

"He's being modest," Auggie said, still focused on his phone. "They were super excited to get him."

"I knew it!" Jem half-shouted. When Tean shot him a look, he lowered his voice, but only barely. "I totally knew it!"

"They weren't super excited—" Tean tried.

"Yes, they were," Auggie said. "They told me to get a million photos. They want photos of you eating and talking and laughing. I think you're the unofficial poster boy."

"No, I—"

"Oh my God," Jem whispered with what sounded ghoulishly close to glee.

Face heating, Tean tried a diversion. "You're—you work with animals too?"

"I work with a dog who won't stop pissing in my kitchen," Emery said. "What's that profession?"

"Oh," Shaw raised his hand, "dog whisperer, dog piss whisperer, dog piss boy, dog piss slop boy—"

He tried to say more, but North got a hand over his mouth.

"Our son bought us tickets to attend," John-Henry said. "For Father's Day. He knows Emery likes, um, informational events—"

"Didn't he make you go to a pen convention once?" Auggie asked distractedly.

"It was not a pen convention—" Emery began.

"But," John-Henry said over him, "Colt didn't realize it was a professional conference." Amusement lacing his voice, he added, "Turns out, that doesn't really change anything for Emery."

"All I said was that the panel on zebra mussels was both engaging and entertaining—" Emery stopped and set his jaw. "I will not be baited into this conversation again."

"A panel on mussels," Theo said and rubbed his eyes.

"It actually was a good panel," Tean said. "All three of the speakers were very funny."

Silence. The kind of echoing, reverberating silence Tean associated with bottomless holes. Jem looked marginally horrified.

"Thank you," Emery said in a tone of complete and utter vindication.

Jem covered his eyes. John-Henry rubbed his forehead again.

"He's going to be unbearable for a week," North said.

"Please don't," John-Henry muttered.

"She's not in any of the photos," Auggie said. "I've got a couple of short videos, and she's not in those either."

"That doesn't prove anything—" Emery began.

At the same time, Tean said, "That doesn't necessarily mean—"

Auggie rolled his eyes.

"When's the last time she shows up?" North asked. "In your photos, I mean."

Auggie checked his phone again. "Yesterday afternoon. I did some publicity stills in the lobby."

"So, we start there," North said, "figure out the last time anybody saw her."

"What we should do," John-Henry said in an even voice, "is answer the questions from the police, and let them do their jobs."

Theo held out a hand. "Finally."

Emery snorted. "Good luck with that."

"You know this guy?" Jem asked. "Cassidy?"

Shaw squirmed on North's lap. "I really feel like I need to mention that North's middle name—"

But Emery cut him off with "I know him."

"And?" Jem asked.

"And he's the chief of police in this town—" John-Henry said.

"A dubious distinction, considering it's a position hired out to politicians and people-pleasers," Emery said. Then a scarlet fringe brightened his cheeks. "And, of course, occasionally to properly qualified candidates."

"Nice save," John-Henry said.

"What's your beef with him?" Jem asked. "You say he's no good at this; how do you know him?"

Emery opened his mouth, but when John-Henry shook his head, he made a face. "It's a long story."

"Where have I heard that before?" Jem muttered.

"But he's arrested the wrong person," Tean said. "Can't you tell him? It wasn't Missy; she never would have done something like that."

Emery and John-Henry traded a look. "I understand how you feel," John-Henry said, "but you've got to understand, in a murder investigation, there's always someone who thinks it's impossible their friend or family member could have done something terrible. I'm not saying your friend is guilty, but if there's forensic evidence—"

"But that evidence is wrong," Tean said. "Or it's been planted. They haven't even done a DNA test."

Unhappiness etched John-Henry's face, and he didn't reply.

"Well, it doesn't matter if your friend killed her or not," North said.

Shaw wriggled around to look at him.

Blushing, North mumbled, "I mean, it matters, but not in terms of our job. We're supposed to be investigating Yesenia Alvarez. The way things look right now, that means finding her and figuring out if she's even still alive."

"Someone broke into her car," Shaw said.

North glanced at him, a startled look fleeting across his face, and then said, "Actually, yeah. Someone did break into her car. Or tried to, anyway."

"How do you know that?" Tean asked.

"Because we were trying to break into it," Shaw said.

"There were scratches around the passenger window," North said. "Somebody used a slim jim to get inside. Somebody who either didn't know what they were doing or didn't have steady hands."

"Did you get into her car?" Auggie asked.

North snorted.

"North is very good at breaking into cars," Shaw said. "Just like he's very good at sex. One time, he told me all you have to do is stick it in and wiggle it around—he was talking about breaking into cars, but I pointed out that's how he does sex too—"

Shaw cut off with another cry, massaging the dead arm North had just given him.

"The car," Emery barked.

North gave him a long, cool look before speaking. "The car," he said slowly, "was fucking filthy. The footwells. The seats. Animal hair everywhere."

"What kind of animal hair?" Tean asked.

"How the hell should I know?"

"I could summon up an ectoplasmic reproduction," Shaw offered. When North glared at him, he said, "But I won't because nobody defended my honor against North, not even my soulmate—"

"Don't say it," Emery said.

"—Emery Hazard."

Emery fixed him with a death stare. Then, holding out a hand to Auggie, he said, "Let me see the video of the men who went into Yesenia's room." Auggie passed over his phone, and after a minute, Emery grunted. "The younger two are the Rangel brothers; I thought I recognized them. Quinn and Colin. They're dumbasses."

"You know them?" Tean asked.

"I know who they are. They're pieces of shit stuck to the heels of the Ozark Volunteers."

When Tean glanced at Jem, Jem shook his head.

"They're the neo-Nazi-lite brigade of this charming little asshole of the world," North said.

"Less Hitler," Shaw said. "More incest."

"I was going to say, 'Less Hitler, more goat-rape.'"

"But that doesn't make any sense. We don't even know if they have goats."

"That's not the point—"

"Much less if the sex was consensual."

"Consent? That's the least of their worries—"

"Oh, you should always worry about consent, North."

"Knock it off," Emery said. "This woman, Yesenia, she's missing. Someone broke into her car. Four men entered her room, clearly prepared for violence."

"And the woman," Tean said, looking to Jem for support. "There was a woman in her room when we got there."

"What woman?"

Jem frowned. "We saw her yesterday; security was dragging her out of the resort. She was screaming about something."

"Oh," Auggie said. "Her!" He took his phone back from Emery, swiped a few times, and held it out so everyone could see the screen. On it was a picture of the woman from Yesenia's room—there was no mistaking the sideburns.

"You know her?" Jem asked.

"No, but she's cuckoo. She's gotten dragged out two or three times already, always makes a huge scene."

"She wrote something on the walls," Jem said, glancing at Tean.

Tean frowned. "Something about birds. And the truth."

"Birds aren't real," Shaw said.

Tean blinked. "Yes, that's it."

"She's right," Shaw said. "They're not."

Tean decided to let that one go for the moment.

Emery, however, did not. "What do you mean, birds aren't real?"

"They're not real." Shaw shrugged, glancing from face to face. "You didn't know that? There's no such thing as birds. They're just drones, you know, the kind the government uses to spy on us."

"That's ridiculous. Birds are..." The big man seemed to struggle for a moment.

"Birds?" John-Henry suggested.

Emery shot him a look and then, to Shaw, said, "Birds are animals. Biological organisms."

"Much better," John-Henry murmured.

"Would you like to contribute your expertise," Emery asked Tean, waving one hand wildly, "whatever that might be?"

"I'm not sure what to say," Tean said. "Birds are real?"

"It's less compelling when you say it like a question," Jem told him. "You should say it like it's a fact. Like you really believe what you're saying."

"It's not so much a question of belief—"

"Like this, 'Birds are biological organisms. Their class is *flap-a-wingicus*.'"

"No—" Tean began.

And at the same time, Emery said. "Their class is Aves."

"Don't worry, Emery," Shaw said. "Lots of people don't know birds aren't real. You've been indoctrinated your entire life by Big Bird—literally. Why do you think that children's show has an enormous yellow bird for its mascot?"

"He saw something on TikTok," North said. "Cut open every fucking pillow we had."

"For the feathers?" Theo asked.

"Who fucking knows? We have memory foam."

"But there could have been feathers," Shaw said. "That was the important part."

"I've had a kink in my neck for a motherfucking month, in case anybody cares."

"So," Auggie said—and the poor kid actually held up his hand. "I'm going to jump in here. Birds Aren't Real is, um, real. Like, in the sense that it's an actual movement. But it's, like, a joke. A parody of conspiracy theories. It's—"

"I swear to God, John," Emery said, "if I hear one more Gen Z-er use the word ironic incorrectly, I'm going to commit murder."

Auggie threw Theo a look, and Theo said, "It's satire."

"Oh." A little color came into Emery's face. "All right, then."

"So, this woman," Tean asked, "the one in Yesenia's room, she—what? Fell for it? Believes it's actually real?"

"Like me," Shaw said proudly.

Auggie shrugged. "No idea."

"More importantly," North said, "is she the one who took a dump on the bed?"

"I could try to find her on social media," Auggie said. "I'm pretty good at that."

"No," Theo said, sitting forward. "You're not doing that. He's not doing that."

"I'm on my phone all day anyway," Auggie said. And then, in a lower voice that was clearly meant for Theo alone, he added, "And it's my decision."

An ugly flush rippled through Theo's face, and he looked away.

"That would be helpful," Jem said.

"But we don't want to cause any problems," Tean said, his gaze sliding from Auggie to Theo.

"We want to help," Auggie said. "We're good at finding people."

"Then do me a favor," North said, "and find Yesenia while you're at it."

Auggie shrugged. "I can see if she's posted anything. I can look at Missy's stuff, too, if you tell me what to look for."

North grunted. "While iCarly does his thing, Shaw and I are going to do some real detective work and track her down. If she's alive, your friend goes free. If she's dead, we still get paid."

"And if she's dead," Shaw said, "I can probably contact her spirit on the astral plane and find out who killed her."

"You don't have to help us," Tean said.

"Why not?" North said. "We're looking for her anyway."

"Besides," Shaw said, "you saved North's life."

"Excuse me?" North said.

"With the knife. When you were trying to fight the bad guys with a pillow."

"He didn't save my life, thank you very fucking much. I was handling that situation."

Shaw cocked his head. And then he made a soft, understanding noise.

"No," North said.

"Of course you were handling it," Shaw said. "You were handling it so well."

"Do not do this. Do not placate me."

"You were swinging that big, bad pillow at those men. And you were backing up really fast. And then you got yourself wedged in that corner, and I'm sure it was all part of your plan."

"I did have a plan, for your information."

"And it was so brave how you let Jem swoop in at the last minute and smash that guy on the head while you distracted him."

For a moment, North breathed through his nose, his color rising.

Shaw beamed at him. Then he patted North's head.

North's breathing took on a ragged quality.

John-Henry shook his head. "I think we're all forgetting that there's due process and an official investigation." To Tean and Jem, he said, "I understand that you want to help your friend, but you've got to be open to the possibility that she did actually do this."

"Thank you," Theo said. "Doesn't anybody else see how crazy it is to rush into this? Let the police do their job."

"That's a fucking terrible idea," Emery said. "Unless you prefer to allow an innocent woman to be arrested, prosecuted, and imprisoned for a crime she didn't commit. Is that what you'd prefer, Theo?"

"Of course not—"

"Then it's strange to hear you suggesting a course of action—"

"Ree," John-Henry said. Emery took a deep breath. John-Henry said, "I think you're letting your feelings about Cassidy affect your judgment."

"And I think I'm the best judge of my own state of mind. Which of us, John, is better suited to evaluating Cassidy's investigative capabilities?"

"You need to think about your tone," John-Henry said, "and about how you're talking to me."

"You, because you've seen him in person for a few minutes, total, in your entire life, or me, because I was his partner for months?"

John-Henry set his jaw and stared at Emery.

After a long moment, Emery dropped his gaze and mumbled, "I apologize."

"We've got an inside track," Jem said, hand on Tean's shoulder. "We can talk to people at the conference, ask about Yesenia, see if there's anyone else who'd want to hurt her. If this happened, it's got to be related to the conference, right?"

"Not necessarily," Emery said, some of the edges knocked off his voice. "I told you I recognized those brothers. They're local, and I don't know what connection they'd have to the conference. We could look into that. Ask around."

When Emery looked over at John-Henry, the blond man sighed and nodded, rubbing his forehead.

"Ok," Jem said. "That's it, then. We've got a plan?"

He looked at Tean, and Tean felt the old helplessness rise up. But he nodded and said, "We've got a plan."

"We're the fucking A-Team," North said sourly.

Auggie glanced at Theo.

"Mr. T, this team of ex-special forces—" He stopped. "It's not worth explaining."

"Got it," Auggie said. "Like, someone today might say the *Avengers* movies."

"Auggie," John-Henry said with a pained note.

Auggie's grin was surprisingly wicked. "Or the Jimmy Timmy Power Hour."

"I don't even recognize the words coming out of his mouth sometimes," Emery said. "Do you?"

Theo's face, though, was a thundercloud, and he didn't respond.

"First of all," North said grudgingly, "dope reference. Second of all—" He fixed Auggie with a dirty look. "—we're the fucking Avengers." He gestured to the chief's office at the back of the building, where the sound of movement suggested Cassidy's return. "Now we sit around with our dicks in our hands and wait for Chief Buttwipe to let us go."

"Don't count on it happening soon," Theo said. "He brought us here to question us. Not that we have anything to do with this. Not that we should have anything to do with this."

The latter was clearly meant for Auggie, and the younger man seemed to brace himself, his whole body tight.

Emery smiled, a savage slice of white teeth. "I think I can give him something else to occupy his attention."

John-Henry groaned and buried his face in his hands. "I'm going to make Colt bail you out. How will that feel, making your son learn how to post bail?"

"It should be a valuable life skill." Voices moved closer to the door, and the knob rattled. "Especially considering his wastrel boyfriend."

"He's been looking for an excuse to use wastrel ever since he watched a documentary on the Dust Bowl," John-Henry said.

"*Raisins to Raisins and Dust to Dust?*" Tean asked.

Emery glowered at him.

"That thing was, like, eighteen hours long," Jem said. "I swear to God I died for a few minutes in the middle of it."

"It was three hours long," Emery said, "and it was exceptionally informative. And why did you watch it? It has nothing to do with animals."

"Believe it or not," Tean said, "I do have other interests."

"Clown fires," Jem said.

"What—" John-Henry began to ask, then stopped himself with a grin that, a moment later, Jem mirrored.

"Oh, I love clown fires," Shaw said.

"Fuck me," North said. "Somebody just fuck me right now."

"That'd be the day," Emery muttered.

Struggling to sit up, North managed, "Excuse me—"

Then the door to the chief's office opened, and Cassidy emerged. A uniformed officer appeared a moment later, guiding Missy toward a hallway—presumably, Tean decided, where the cells were located. Cassidy scanned the group of men, and a gleam of something—amusement, satisfaction, fun—darted across his expression.

"Well, gentlemen, why don't we start—"

"The primary question," Emery said, rounding on him, "is did this pissant town hire you because they wanted an ingrown anal hair as chief in order to make the rest of them look better by comparison—"

"Sweet Jesus," John-Henry said.

North and Shaw were already giggling uncontrollably.

Theo scratched his beard.

"—or was it because your incompetence and stupidity make you an ideal patsy for whatever dirty shit is going on around here? Take your time before responding, Jonas. I remember that polysyllabic words are difficult for you."

It only got worse, Tean quickly learned, from there.

8

That night, Tean crashed when he and Jem got back to the resort, and they slept late—well, late for Tean, which was still early for Jem. The conference itself continued according to its normal schedule, which meant Tean's day was tied up with panels and coffee meetups and the annual IHCPA business meeting, which was even more boring than it sounded. Tean made Jem promise not to do any investigating without him, and while Jem was responsive to texts all day, and he always had a plausible explanation for what he was doing—reading, swimming, watching TV—Tean knew his husband, and he knew that any of those explanations might have covered something dangerous, something Jem was trying to protect Tean from.

The day's proceedings carried Tean almost to the evening social, and he barely had time to rush back to their room, shower, and change. He was pulling on his khakis when Jem let himself into the room, gave him a single glance, and said, "No, sir."

"What—"

"Drop trou, mister, and put on the clothes I laid out for you."

Tean eyed the outfit on the bed: some kind of cream-colored polo shirt that also managed to look like a sweater; light-wash jeans; and white sneakers.

"I didn't realize those were for me."

"Well, they are. And I spent time picking them out. So, get changed."

A different tack: "The sanctuary will be dirty, so I should probably wear—"

"No," Jem said, grabbing the Keens from where Tean had left them by the door. "I'm hiding these until tonight is over. Sneakers."

"Jem!"

"What?"

"We're going to be late."

"Then get your ass out of those khakis and put on your nice clothes while I shower."

Tean stared at him.

"And give me a kiss," Jem said.

Tean gave him a kiss.

"Are you ok?" Jem asked, fingers hot on Tean's nape when they separated. "Last night was a lot."

"I'm fine. Well, I'm not fine. Nobody's fine. We're all ticking time bombs, our bodies accelerating toward cell death while we poison our planet and create irreversible climate change that will cause catastrophic death and destruction to most of life as we know it."

"Right. Want me to suck you off?"

Something went down the wrong way, and Tean had to clear his throat a couple of times.

Jem smirked as he shucked his t-shirt and shorts. He was half hard when he peeled off his boxers, and his dick bobbed.

"You did that on purpose," Tean said.

"Tick-tock, babe. Offer still stands."

"Go take a shower. We have to hurry."

Jem rolled those nicely muscled shoulders, palmed his dick, and laughed when Tean threw a towel at him.

Tean changed into the clothes Jem had picked out, and he had to admit that even though the shirt looked like a polo that was also a sweater, and it seemed wildly impractical for summer in this part of the world, it was actually…great. It was silk, and it was breathable, and it looked good with the jeans. It was one more of the endless list of things Jem had done to make his life better over the last few years, and, as usual, one of the things Tean had assured himself would be silly or unnecessary or wasteful.

When Jem came out of the shower naked, with a few beads of water catching rainbows on his shoulders, Tean said, "I changed my mind about the blow job."

"Too late," Jem said, rifling his suitcase. "Go get the comb wet, please."

"But it's not off the table completely, right?"

Jem threw him a smile, the big one, with his crooked front teeth exposed, and went back to searching for clothes.

Because he was Jem, somehow he was dressed and looking perfect by the time Tean returned from the bathroom. He looked completely at ease in a loose white Henley so thin it was almost see-through, which he'd rounded out with blue trousers and suede loafers (no socks, of course).

"Are you wearing underwear?" Tean asked.

"You have to buy me a drink to find out." Jem beckoned for the comb, and taking it, he turned Tean around. This was an old routine for them now, and he had Tean's hair subdued in a matter of minutes. He took longer with his own hard side part, and after a few rounds of "Just a minute," Tean started jingling the car keys.

"You're definitely not wearing underwear," Tean said as Jem drove them out of the Santaland parking lot. "I can see your penis."

"Aww, shucks, Doc."

And, of course, for some reason Tean was the one who started blushing.

Mid-Missouri Big Cat Sanctuary—Rod's cat sanctuary—was hosting that evening's cocktail hour, which would be followed by a tour of the facilities, followed by (inevitably) more drinking. It was located north of the Santaland resort, on a bend in the reservoir's shoreline. Tean had done some research on the sanctuary during a particularly boring session that day; Rod owned hundreds of acres, and as Jem and Tean drove closer, it became clear that Rod was intent on marking his property. A chicken-wire fence ran along the boundary, with signs every hundred feet that said MID-MISSOURI BIG CAT SANCTUARY and PRIVATE PROPERTY and NO TRESPASSING and DANGER! BIG CATS!

"Doesn't want people on his land," Jem said. "Kind of strange when you rely on paying visitors."

Tean nodded, but he said, "Well, I'm sure he doesn't want lawsuits. And he's probably tired of dealing with people sneaking into the sanctuary. Local kids, people who don't want to pay the admission fee, activists."

Jem raised his eyebrows.

"Don't get me started," Tean said with a laugh.

Jem didn't say anything, but he wrapped a hand around Tean's knee, and they drove on in silence.

Their drive onto the property gave Tean a chance to assess the sanctuary. It was close to what he expected: a gravel drive that led to a central parking lot, dirt service roads with deep ruts, dust from daily traffic coating everything in a reddish-brown drift. The buildings had plywood siding painted what Tean thought of as conservation department brown, with three-tab shingles that looked like they should have been replaced ten years ago. In the distance, the cat enclosures were visible: black-rust skeletons of cattle panels and sheet metal, and farther, the ruddy glimmer of water. A lake, Tean guessed, where the enclosures converged. An ideal— and common—layout.

Several hotel shuttles were parked in front of what was clearly the central building. Unlike the other structures, this one had board-and-batten siding with barn-red paint, a patchwork steel roof, and small, serviceable windows that suggested economy and function—probably the former first, then the latter. Conference-goers mingled on a neatly sheared swath of lawn, and while many of the attendees wore semiformal outfits—jackets and ties, or summer dresses—equally as many wore everyday clothes. A woman in olive-colored bib overalls and a Duluth Trading Company t-shirt passed a glass of white wine to a woman in a t-shirt, jeans, and enviably sturdy-looking hiking boots. Her trucker hat said *Live, Love, Rescue* in what Tean thought of as Etsy font. A man in a sand-colored work shirt and khakis was trying—struggling might have been a better word—to find something in the pocket of a utility vest. Another man, heedless of the heat in a long-sleeve Carhartt shirt and shiny nylon field pants, fanned himself with a fishing hat.

"That is a godawful amount of brown," Jem said to himself as he parked the Jetta. "What is happening right now? Have these people never been to a cocktail party?"

"They're comfortable."

Jem paused with his hand on the gear shift. "I hope I'm not hearing a tone."

"I'm comfortable too," Tean hurried to say.

Jem's blue eyes could look quite stormy sometimes.

"Very comfortable," Tean added.

"This is a professional event."

"Yes, and—"

"And it's important to me that my husband, who is extremely handsome, look his absolute best."

"I appreciate that, but—"

"Which means not wearing khaki, and not wearing his Utah DWR polo, and not wearing his twenty-year-old Keens."

"I understand, and what I meant to say earlier was—"

"Or brown, Tean. No brown! Look at all that brown! I mean, hell, they're all vets, aren't they? Have they ever heard of a peacock?"

Tean had to stop at that one. A chuckle slipped out, and then Jem was laughing too, both of them laughing a soft, awkward laugh after the tension of the quasi-argument. It slowly eased and opened up until it felt real, and then everything was ok again.

When they'd both quieted, Tean said, "Thank you for picking out nice clothes for me."

Jem accepted a kiss on the cheek, but he said, "No more brown."

"You realize lots of animals use colors to find mates."

With a grunt, Jem fixed Tean with a look. "You're already taken."

"I know; I was only saying—"

"Good," Jem said. He adjusted himself, and it was much more, um, graphic without the underwear. Then he caught Tean's eye and smirked.

"Oh my gosh," Tean said, and the words sounded a little choked as he fumbled for the door handle.

But getting out of the Jetta didn't improve things; the fresh air was, well, not so fresh. It smelled like fresh-cut wild onions and animal scat, like citronella-scented fuel from the guttering tiki torches, and the heat was a crushing, sweaty fist that clamped down on every inch of exposed skin. Sweat broke out everywhere, immediately.

"I changed my mind," Jem said. "I don't want to be a supportive spouse."

"I guess I should have seen that coming."

"I want to lie in an ice bath, naked, and watch *90 Day Fiancé*, and never go outside in this swamp ever again."

"Your, uh, you know, would probably freeze."

"Like a freezie-wienie. No, a wiener pop. Hey, that might be fun."

"It wouldn't be. It would be agonizing. There would probably be necrotic tissue, diminished, uh, engorgement, skin grafts."

"The engorgement would be fine, thanks."

Tean scowled at him. "I thought you were going back to the resort. I thought you weren't going to be supportive."

"And to answer your question, I assume you'd come in occasionally to warm things up. And feed me bonbons."

Tean sighed and started across the lawn.

"Is that a yes about the bonbons?"

"I'm getting a drink. I'm going to get drunk."

"What about wiener-pop sex at regular intervals? No, ma'am, not you, but I'm flattered."

Tean ducked his head and walked faster.

Tinkling laughter suggested that Jem had, once again, gotten away with it. Whatever *it* was. And however he managed to do it.

At one of the cash bars, Tean bought himself a Coke, and he got a local IPA for Jem—something called 4 Hands. The slushy sound of shifting ice came from behind the bar, and when the bartender—a young guy with a thin mustache—set the cans in front of them, condensation beaded on the aluminum.

Tean and Jem moved to the side, to allow the next thirsty veterinarian to step forward, and they found a quiet spot along the side of the welcome center. For several minutes, Tean watched the conference-goers circulate. Some of them had already grouped up, a phenomenon Tean was familiar with from other conferences. Other attendees fluttered around—either because they were genuinely social, or, more likely, because they saw the opportunity for networking. A fair number lurked at the perimeter, many of them alone; before Jem, that would have been Tean. Then he thought of Missy, and Hannah, and other friends who insisted on dragging him out of hiding, and he realized that wasn't quite true.

Thinking of Missy brought a fresh wave of worry. Last night, under the fluttering aggression of the fluorescents, still reeling from the fight in Yesenia's room and Missy's arrest, Tean had seen no problem in the idea of working with six total strangers. If anything, he'd been grateful at how quickly the plan had coalesced, at how their various interests had aligned.

Twenty-four hours later, though, reality had settled down on his chest, a weight Tean couldn't dislodge. He didn't know those other men. He certainly had no reason to trust them. Yes, the two who had found them in Yesenia's room, North and Shaw, seemed to be telling the truth. And yes, Shaw had saved Tean's life when that man had come after them. And, if Tean were being honest, he had a hard time believing Shaw, in particular, was capable of concealing a secret agenda, much less a nefarious alter ego. None of the men had struck Tean as untrustworthy—and, more importantly, they clearly hadn't set off any of Jem's alarms, and Tean trusted his husband's judgment about people.

"That's a lot of thinking happening over there," Jem said.

Tean gave a half-smile. "Sorry."

"Don't be sorry. Want to tell me what's going on?"

"It's—" For a moment, Tean fell silent again. Then it all spilled out. "It's silly, isn't it? I mean, this is a joke. The A-Team?"

"Totally. The Avengers is a way better name. Oh! Or we could call ourselves the Justice League."

Tean shook his head.

Squeezing his shoulder, Jem leaned in. Tean caught a whiff—citrus and stone, skin-prickling—and the hoppiness of the beer floated on Jem's breath. Tean had a hard time remembering before Jem, when the smell of beer had meant something else to him. "I know what you meant. You've got to stop thinking about it like that."

"How am I supposed to think about it?"

"You've got four sets of people who want different things. Right now, those different things overlap, so it makes sense to work together. When they don't overlap anymore, we go our separate ways."

"I don't know what Auggie wants." Jem opened his mouth, and Tean rushed to add, "Besides my picture."

Jem cracked a smile. "It seems like he wants a spanking."

A laugh slipped out of Tean. "Jem."

"What? Theo's a zaddy, and Auggie knows he's pushing his buttons." Tean laughed again in spite of himself. Rubbing Tean's shoulder, Jem said, "Look, it feels crazy if you think of it too big, like, 'We're going to save Missy and find Yesenia's killer.' So, start small. We've done this before, right? We can do it again. Right now, all we need to do is learn as much as we can from people at the conference. Starting with Rod."

"Because he's a suspect. Because he might have killed Yesenia and framed Missy."

"Well, Yesenia was going to build her next safari around here. I wouldn't be too happy if I were Rod. Although at least Rod has tiger kittens, so I guess that's ok."

"Cubs. Or whelps." When Jem stared blankly, Tean added, "Not kittens."

"I'm going to call them kittens."

"And he doesn't have any; certified sanctuaries don't breed animals. That's kind of the whole point, actually."

"You're telling me there's not one goddamn kitten in this whole place?"

"Cubs," Tean said. "Ok, let's go look for Rod."

But they couldn't find Rod. At first, that didn't seem too strange; it was a major social event for the conference, and if Rod wasn't busy talking to other conference-goers, then he was probably dealing with the logistics of the cocktail party or had been drawn away to deal with sanctuary business. So, Jem and Tean circulated, chatting with the other people in attendance, leading the conversation to Yesenia or Missy or Rod—all easy topics, considering the events of the last day.

They talked to a man in a VIETNAM VET trucker hat who spoke in a way that made spit bubble between his teeth. "She's supposed to fix everything," he said. "Like something needed fixing. How's she going to fix anything if she goes running off when her period hits?"

"Charming," Tean muttered as Jem steered him away.

"I gave him your phone number," Jem said. "He wants to connect on LinkedIn."

"He probably does want to connect on LinkedIn. He's probably going to add me as a friend, and then he'll post something inappropriate, and then my boss will see it, and I'll get fired. Guilt by association."

"Probably," Jem said and licked his ear.

Wiping at the saliva, Tean skittered away. "Jem!"

A woman with an eyepatch and fine-lined scars raking her forehead stared at them.

Jem laughed. "What?"

"Go away," Tean said, giving Jem a shove.

"He tastes even better than he looks," Jem told the woman.

Her one eye got bigger.

Tean gave Jem another shove. "This is a work event. You're acting crazy tonight."

"Come on, I was goofing around."

"Go goof around somewhere else," Tean said and stalked away.

He made it ten yards before he looked over his shoulder, and by then, Jem was slinking through the crowd, shoulders stooped. Tean wiped at his ear again. First the almost-fight about the clothes at the hotel, then Jem's eruption when they got to the party, now this. For a moment, Tean almost went after him. But Jem didn't look back, and after another moment, Tean turned his attention to the party.

For the next hour, Tean made his way through the crowd, and with every minute that passed, he was reminded that this was exactly when he needed Jem most. His conversations stalled or petered out or, in rare occasions, exploded. Universally, they failed to provide anything useful. He talked to a man with a tattoo of a 1965 Mustang on his neck—Tean knew it was a 1965 Mustang because the man made a point of telling him—who wanted Tean to, quote, "go for a ride with him in the dark," after Tean had mentioned once—once!—the inevitability of cell death. A woman in a Stars-and-Stripes jumpsuit held him captive for fourteen minutes and twenty-seven seconds talking about the differences between ferrets and stoats, ignoring Tean's every attempt to steer the conversation back to Yesenia. A sweaty, red-faced man in a vegan leather jacket became agitated when Tean pointed out the statistically higher odds of dying on a toilet in Missouri. That was when Jem hooked Tean by the sleeve, pulled him away, and pointed up toward the welcome center, where Rod had just emerged from a side door.

"Oh, shit," Tean said.

"That's a quarter in the swear jar."

"It's your swear jar because the girls made it for you, and anyway, it's full. Jem, he's got Kristin."

Tean didn't point, but he nodded again in Rod's direction. He had emerged from a door farther down on the welcome center, and he was towing Kristin around the corner of the building. Away from the party. Away from the guests.

Jem moved after them, killing his beer as he walked and then tossing the can into a nearby recycling bin. His hands dipped into his pockets. The set of his shoulders was sloping, a kind of feigned easiness, and he smiled at someone in the distance. He was a liar, he had told Tean on many occasions, and his whole body was the lie. Tean hurried behind him.

As they reached the corner, Rod's voice reached them: "—poking around in there, huh?"

Kristin said something too soft for Tean to hear.

Jem turned the corner first, and Tean was only a few feet behind him. The welcome center's bulk plunged this side of the building into shadow, and although the heat only lessened marginally, the gloom reminded Tean that the day was ending quickly. Kristin, in a ruched, dusty-blue maxi dress, had her back to the wall, and although Rod wasn't touching her, he stood close enough to bracket her, using proximity to pin her in place. The height difference between them was even more exaggerated, and there was no doubt Rod was using it to his advantage. He was wearing what Jem liked to call shit-kicker boots, dirty jeans, and a Death Angel t-shirt with the sleeves cut off. A silver belt buckle, about the size of a CD, weighed down the front of his pants.

"There you are, Kristin," Jem said. His easygoing voice was part of the lie. "Don't be mad; Tean drank your beer. God, we've been looking all over for you. Oh, hey, man. What's up?"

Kristin stared at them, terror blanking her expression. Her glasses were askew, but if she noticed, she gave no sign of it.

Rod, on the other hand, took them in with a slow, calculating assessment. He didn't step back, but he did shift his weight to his heels, altering the shape of the space between him and Kristin. "We're having a private conversation."

"I don't think we met," Jem said, moving forward again, hand outstretched. "Jem Berger."

"Son, you need to go back to the party."

"I'm his other half. Normally I'd say better, but—" Jem stepped into Rod's space, hand still out for a shake.

Rod reached to grab Jem's arm.

Tean hadn't seen this particular move from Jem before, but it didn't surprise him; his husband was a voracious learner, and YouTube and TikTok were bad influences. Jem's hand, the one he'd stretched out for a shake, flattened. He drove the heel of his hand forward, into Rod's solar plexus. Rod staggered back, a wheezing gasp escaping him. Tean had once heard a mule deer in breech make the same noise.

Hands on hips, Jem considered Rod for a moment. Then he hooked him by the heel and shoved, and Rod landed on his ass, his head cracking against the board-and-batten. He gave Kristin a considering look and said, "Tean?"

"Are you ok?" Tean asked.

Kristin blinked. She glanced down at Rod, and when Tean touched her elbow, she startled.

"Why don't you come over here?" Tean asked.

"I'm not—I'm—" She seemed to become aware of her glasses at that moment and straightened them. "I'm fine. I'm sorry; I'm really fine."

"I know," Tean said.

Rod writhed on the ground, still trying to suck in air. Jem was watching him with the same bemused fascination on his face as when the girls had decided to give Scipio (and Tean) princess makeovers.

"He wasn't—he didn't do anything," Kristin said, but she followed Tean a few feet away from Rod. "He wouldn't have done anything." Then the question followed: "Would he?"

"Kristin, what's going on?"

"I went inside." Color tinged her cheeks. "I know I shouldn't have, but I thought—I don't know."

"Why did you go inside?"

Kristin shook her head.

"Kristin, what were you doing in there?"

"I went inside to look around."

The lie was so bad even Tean could hear it, and when he tried to catch Kristin's eye, she ducked her head. He glanced at Jem, who shrugged.

"Trying to steal my shit," Rod gasped, hand clutching his Death Angel shirt. "And that's assault, you stupid son of a bitch."

"I may be stupid," Jem said, "and I may be a son of a bitch, but if you get up again, I'll put you back down. And I'll use my belt, which Tean would not like, mostly because I'm not wearing underwear. God damn it, and now you made me tell him, and I said not until he bought me a drink."

Rod rubbed his chest, blinking watery eyes.

"Technically, I did buy you a drink," Tean said. "If it makes you feel better."

"Oh." Jem scratched his beard. "Yeah. Ok."

A nervous giggle escaped Kristin.

"I think you both need to tell us what's going on," Tean said. "Whatever it is, it looked serious. Yesenia is missing, and Missy is in jail, and something messed up is happening."

"I want to go," Kristin said.

"Too bad," Jem said.

But Kristin wrenched her arm from Tean and took a step back. "I wasn't doing anything wrong. I wasn't doing anything. I was looking around, and he—he grabbed me."

"Kristin," Tean said, "I don't think you're telling us everything—"

"I'm going to go," she said, her voice taking on a strangely artificial tone, as though everything were all right—or would be, if she could just make herself sound chipper enough. "I'm going back to the party. You can't stop me."

"Interesting theory—" Jem began.

But he cut off when Tean shook his head.

Kristin pranced backward, and a moment later, she spun and darted around the side of the building.

"Great fucking job," Rod wheezed. "You let her get away."

"Don't worry about her," Jem said. "Worry about me."

Rod made a hacking noise, and it took a moment for Tean to recognize the sound as a laugh. Sitting up, Rod did something with his head, flopping his mullet into place. Then he took a longer, deeper breath. "Well, son, you fucked up, you surely did."

"I'd like you to tell us about Yesenia," Tean said. "About your relationship with her, when you last saw her, about the parks."

"You aren't going to like prison, buddy boy." Rod looked up at Jem. His thin lips peeled back to expose small white teeth. "A fancy guy like you, they'll turn your asshole inside out."

Jem glanced at Tean.

"What was your relationship with Yesenia?" Tean asked again.

"My relationship." He hocked a wad of brownish spit onto the ground. "You know something? You came onto my land. You were invited. And then you assaulted me."

"You were threatening a woman," Tean said. "You became aggressive when we attempted to defuse the situation. My husband was defending himself, and his use of force was reasonable. I don't think the police will see any need to charge him. You, on the other hand, have more to worry about."

"I wasn't hurting her."

"Bullshit," Jem said.

"What was your relationship with Yesenia?"

"What's it matter? They arrested someone, that's what I hear. Case closed."

"No, not case closed. Not when the police learn about Yesenia's plan to build a second park in Osage Beach. That's not far from here. Not when they realize that put you in competition, and what that might mean for your business. I think when they learn about that, they're going to take a long, hard look at you. They'll forget all about Missy."

Rod sneered. He put a hand on the wall, gave Jem a wary look, and got to his feet. He gazed past them, and Tean fought the urge to look. The sneer faded slowly from Rod's face. When he spoke, his voice was hard but even. "It's not a business; it's a sanctuary."

"I've heard that one before," Jem said. "I've even run that game before, a version of it."

But Rod only raised his eyebrows. "It's the truth. You know how I got this land?" He only waited a beat before answering his own question. "It was my dad's land. His dad's land. He—my grandpa—did a little of everything. Some corn. Some sheep. Horses. Then they built the reservoir, and bang, half his land was underwater. Sure, they paid him, but he didn't care about the money. It killed him. Heart attack."

Jem and Tean traded a look.

"Dad, on the other hand. Well, Dad did care about the money. He had big plans for that money. Was going to drink it all away or die trying. You've never seen such a hoosier piece of trash. When he wasn't ass-up, sleeping off a drunk, he was buying every redneck toy you can imagine. Four-wheelers. A boat, of course, never mind Grandpa would have died before he went out on the lake. Jet skis." A hint of an unpleasant, self-conscious smile curled the corner of Rod's mouth.

"A tiger," Tean said.

"Oh yeah. Not that hard to get, believe it or not. Dumbasses do it all the time. They get a cub, and for a while, it's fun. Then the cat gets too big, and it gets dangerous, and they've got no idea what to do with it. They chain it up. Or they shoot it, and half the time, they do a shit-poor job at that like they did everything else. Dad thought it was fun to let that cub chase me. Got the scars still. On my back. On my legs. Cub didn't know any better, of course; thought we were playing. But boy, that gave Dad something to laugh about."

In the silence that followed, the hub of voices from the party seemed miles off. The shadows were deeper, dancing where the flames from the tiki torches bent in the breeze. The smell of Jem's cologne and the beer mixed now with a sour body smell from Rod.

"I read about your sanctuary," Tean said. "You've got all the appropriate certifications and authorizations. You pass every inspection with flying colors. You take good care of these cats—as good as anyone can while keeping them in captivity."

"You read about that, huh?" Rod gave a tiny, screwed-down laugh. "You got me in your sights, I guess. Gonna prove I killed Yesenia." He was silent again, and when he spoke next, his voice had a planed-down quality. "I got smarter than that dumb cat, and after a while, Dad lost interest in the game. He had other things to make him feel better about his fucked-up life. He'd drink. And when he drank enough, it was everybody else's fault. And everybody else was me and my mom. And if it was somebody else's fault, somebody else needed to be punished."

"Lots of people grow up with pieces of shit for parents," Jem said. "You're going to have to come up with a better sob story."

Rod cocked him a look that Tean couldn't decipher. Then he smiled — that little curling one, like a devil's tail. "He whaled on us for years," Rod said. "And the first time he went after the cat, I shot him. How's that?"

Off in the dark, one of the big cats yowled, the sound old and ancient, like the world's first heartbreak.

Jem's eyes cut to Tean, but he spoke to Rod. "What's that got to do with anything?"

"Just this: I take care of my cats. I take care of my land. I take care of what's mine. It's a sanctuary first, not a business. You've got to understand that." He waited, letting the lull drive the words home. "As for the rest of it, you've got it all wrong."

"What did we get wrong?" Tean asked.

"Yesenia. The safari park. Yeah, she was talking about building one. She came to me, told me about it. I said fine, do whatever you want. You know why?"

"Because you're running a sanctuary," Jem said, "not a business."

Rod gave a short laugh. "Because she would have been good for business."

"What do you mean?" Tean asked. "She would have been competition."

"Competition. Do you know what kind of animals she had? Birds, giraffes, antelopes. Cats are a whole different beast, pardon the pun."

"So, what?" Jem asked. "You think people are more interested in cats than a wildlife safari? Or you think you're going to draw a different crowd?"

"I think the same people who will pay a hundred bucks per car to drive through one of her parks, they'd be thrilled to get a two-for-one deal, pay a little bit extra, and come see the big cats when they were done." Rod watched them and shook out his mullet. "Her park would have made things better, understand? More visitors. More volunteers. If she's dead, well, I got fucked too."

Tean tried to analyze that, to probe it for an inconsistency or inaccuracy. When he checked Jem, his husband gave a tiny shake of his head.

"Can I go now?" Rod said, slapping dust from his jeans. "I've got a party I'm supposed to be at."

"You don't think that's in bad taste?" Jem asked, nodding at the t-shirt.

Rod pulled at the Death Angel tee, and a smile split his face. "Well, we don't know she's dead, do we?"

Together, Tean and Jem took a step back, giving Rod room to leave. He ambled away, his stride almost a swagger, like he was the one who'd knocked them on their asses instead of the other way around.

"Whatever was going on with Kristin," Jem said, "it didn't sound like he was mad at her for wandering around his welcome center."

"No," Tean said. "It didn't."

Jem was silent for a beat. "He's like a dog, you know? Wants to pee on everything. Don't you get that vibe?"

Rod's voice rose over the sounds of the party, and a chorus of laughs answered him.

"He's certainly determined to be a part of IHCPA," Tean said. "I wouldn't be surprised if he tries to get elected president."

"Want to see what he's got in there?" Jem asked, cocking his head at the welcome center. When Tean didn't answer right away, Jem added, "Around this side. Away from the party."

Tean gave a nod, and they started around the building, heading away from the sound of voices, the clink of glasses, the twang of some old Johnny Cash song picking up. He was trying to place the song—his mom loved Johnny Cash—when everything happened fast.

As they came around the side of the building, movement made Tean bring his head up, and he had just long enough to see two men hurrying around the corner toward them. Their paths carried them on a collision course with Jem and Tean, and in that slice of a moment before they crashed into each other, Tean recognized them as two of the men from Yesenia's hotel room: the one with the dark, deadly eyes; and the younger, good-looking one.

Then they collided. One of the men shouted, and Jem let out a furious noise, and Tean hit the ground hard. His glasses flew off. Blind, he rolled away from the sound of struggle, hands brushing the grass as he searched for his glasses.

Then a foot came down between his shoulder blades, and the muzzle of a gun jabbed him behind the ear.

9

Jem held his hands in the air. The paracord dangled from one; the antenna drooped in the other. He tried not to do anything, tried not to breathe, even. Because the man with the thousand-yard stare had a big revolver pressed to the back of Tean's head.

"I'll do it," the man said.

On the other side of the welcome center, a woman squealed—the sound outraged and titillated at the same time. A fresh chorus of laughter. The Johnny Cash song cut off, and Kacey Musgraves came on.

"Drop them."

Jem dropped the paracord and the antenna. They made soft sounds as they landed in the calf-high grass.

The one with the gun nodded to the other man—brothers, Jem thought; Emery had called them brothers, and Jem could see it now—who was holding a hand to his bloody nose. His ear was scabbed up and still looked a little puffy where Jem had gotten him with the clock radio the day before, but there was no satisfaction in seeing injuries, new or old; Jem's one responsibility was to keep Tean safe, and now there was a gun to his head.

"Up," the man with the gun said. He held the gun awkwardly in his left hand, Jem saw now, and his right hand was wrapped in a crude—and filthy—cloth bandage. "And don't try anything funny." Then he eased his boot up from Tean's back.

"I need my glasses," Tean said. His voice was even, but a static charge of nerves ran through the words. "I won't be able to walk."

"Give me a break."

"He needs his glasses," Jem said.

"Open your mouth again," the one with the thousand-yard stare said to Jem, and he adjusted his bandaged hand without seeming to realize it, "and I'll shoot him in the knee."

"Please," Tean said. He was a mess: dust and grass stains had ruined the cream-colored silk of the sweater polo, and his hair, like a fugitive, had seen its opportunity and taken it—somehow it now stood up all over the place, back to its normal crazy bushiness, as though Jem hadn't ever touched it. "I'm going to slow you down without my glasses."

"My dose," the pretty one said, which Jem figured was probably supposed to be *nose*. And then, words growing shrill, "He broke my dose!"

"Find his glasses," the one with the gun said.

"I'm bleeding!"

"You got shit for brains? Find his goddamn glasses so we can get the hell out of here."

The pretty one had big, wounded eyes, and he tried to search for the glasses by crouching, keeping one hand on his nose, and tilting his head back—which meant he was looking at the sky instead of at the ground, and patting the area around him helplessly. After half a minute of that, the one with the gun growled, "God damn it, Colin," and kicked Tean in the ribs.

Jem growled, but he managed to stay still. For now.

Tean only grunted and scrambled sideways, and the one with the gun—Quinn, Jem thought; Emery had said Quinn and Colin, so if the pretty one was Colin, then the one who had kicked Tean, the one Jem had to kill, must be Quinn—grabbed Tean's glasses from a clump of grass and thrust them at him. A moment later, Tean had them settled on his face, and he blinked and looked around until he saw Jem. When their eyes met, Jem gave him a tight nod. It will be ok, he thought, trying to send the words. I will make sure you're ok.

The doc understood, of course; Tean's dark eyes softened, and he even offered a new moon of a smile.

"Up," Quinn said again, kneeing Tean in the back.

Tean steadied himself and stood.

"We're going for a walk. You first." That part was for Jem. "We'll come along behind you, nice and slow."

Jem nodded.

"That way." Quinn pointed toward a scraggly line of trees, where the ground began to drop toward the reservoir.

After another nod and a quick check of Tean, Jem started off. He heard steps behind him, recognized Tean's easy way of moving over land, even land he wasn't familiar with, and the heavier steps of Quinn, and then—

"Watch where you're going, dumbass."

Jem turned his head enough to see Colin recovering his balance. The younger man still had his head tilted back, and he said, "You're supposed to do this so it stops bleeding."

"Who cares if it bleeds? Can you be a man about one goddamn thing? Stop it from bleeding. Jesus Christ, Col. Put your head down and walk a straight line. Hey, I didn't say stop walking!"

The only good part, Jem thought as he resumed walking, was that if he died in Missouri after being captured by Tweedledee and Tweedledum, nobody would ever learn about it in Utah. His reputation would be intact. Nobody would ever know the final humiliation of these two rednecks getting the upper hand because Jem had taken a kick to the jaw in the tussle, because that fraction of a second when he slowed down had been enough.

He pressed the thoughts down and focused on the situation at hand. He still had the barrette, but he needed to be close to use that. Or the tube sock, but for that, he needed rocks—and, more importantly, time. If they put them in a car, maybe. If they put Tean in first. The barrette to the throat, and then take the gun. Maybe. Or if he could get them talking. But Quinn's threat lingered, and Jem wasn't ready to risk it. Not yet.

At Quinn's instructions, they followed a dirt road for a hundred yards. Dusk was rushing in, darkness swallowing everything: the cat enclosures, the outbuildings, the pinned-up silhouettes of trees. The sounds of the party had faded to a buzz in the distance. At first, Jem thought the noise, the slap and murmur of water, was his pulse. Then, through the trees, he caught sight of the stirring restlessness of the reservoir, the slight chop of the breeze.

"Here," Quinn said.

Jem turned where the road branched and an older section cut through the trees. He made it another ten yards, into the deeper darkness under the canopy. And then he stopped and had to fight a giggle that swelled up in his throat.

The Jeep was white, glimmering in the twilight. A soft-top, probably twenty years old. And leaning against it, dressed—improbably—in summer-weight navy trousers and a crisp white button-up, was Emery Hazard. His eyes glittered in the dying light, and Jem thought of autumn fires, of aspen leaves drifting like embers, and a chill ran over him. It was impossible to miss the holster on his hip or the big cowboy revolver.

"Hello, dumbshits."

That did it; the giggle slipped out. Only a tiny bit before Jem could stop it.

The best Quinn could come up with, apparently, was "Hey!"

Colin echoed him a moment later: "Hey!"

Emery didn't roll his eyes, but nobody could have missed his disgust.

"I'll shoot him," Quinn said, and Tean made a noise that Jem thought meant Quinn had jabbed him with the gun. "Get the hell out of here! Right now! Or I'll shoot him!"

"It's obvious you're going to shoot him," Emery said as he picked up his phone from the Jeep's hood. "You've got a gun pressed against his head," he said as he placed a call and put the phone to his ear. "What was I supposed to think? You're giving him a haircut? Lord knows he needs one."

That giggle slipped out of Jem again.

"Shut up," Quinn said.

"I cut his hair, actually," Jem said.

"Yes," Emery said into the phone, "I want to speak to the manager." To Jem, he said, "Have you ever heard of clippers? Number two."

"We like his hair. We like it just the way it is."

Tean cleared his throat. "I don't, actually. In case it matters."

"Yes, I'll hold," Emery said into the phone. To Jem again, "Try a high and tight, next time. Or a crew cut. God, John and Auggie should be telling you this. Anything, really, so he doesn't look like such a hippie."

"Didn't you hear my broder?" Colin shouted through the bloody nose. "He said get—"

"Get out of here, yes, I heard him."

Grass rustled as Quinn shifted his weight behind Jem. "Who are you calling?"

Emery cocked an eyebrow.

"Who are you calling?" Quinn asked again, louder, and this time, Jem could hear the uncertainty in his voice.

"The Cottonmouth Club," Emery said. "Well, more specifically, I've asked for the manager of the Cottonmouth Club."

The silence spread like a flash-freeze, and Jem thought he could hear the air crackle.

"We don't—" Quinn began.

"Don't embarrass yourself," Emery said. "I followed you dipshits out there today. So, I'm going to ask for the manager, and I'm going to tell him I've got the Rangel brothers, and they're pissing me the fuck off, mostly because they're so fucking incompetent that spending my time like this is a fucking disgrace. And I'm sure the manager will tell me he doesn't know what I'm talking about, and then he'll run like his ass is on fire and tell his boss, and the next time you two crawl out of whatever septic tank you live in, somebody'll put a bullet in your head."

The change in Quinn was the way the air changed before a lightning strike. Jem couldn't see him, but he must have moved because Emery said, "Point that thing at me, and I'll kill you."

Quinn's breathing quickened, and then Tean grunted and stumbled into Jem. Jem caught him, trying to balance both of them. The sound of the Rangel brothers beating feet filled the night. By the time Jem and Tean were standing steady again, the brothers were two black dots, the night swallowing them up.

When Jem looked back at Emery, he said, "Don't they need their Jeep?"

"They'll skulk around until we leave. I'm tempted to slash their tires because they ruined my day."

"What if—" Tean made a weird noise that Jem realized, a moment later, was supposed to be a laugh. "What if they hadn't run away? What if he'd tried to shoot you?"

"Then I would have shot him first. Or, more likely, John would have shot him in the back."

Brush whispered among the trees, and when Jem craned his head, John-Henry was emerging from the deeper shadows, picking at a twig that had gotten caught on his sleeve. He wore a pale linen suit over a blue shirt that looked like linen as well, and when he glanced up and smiled, Jem wanted to do a mental eye roll.

"You know, if I looked like that," Jem whispered to Tean, "I could rob Zions Bank with a Tootsie Roll."

Something that might have been surprise flittered over Tean's face, and then he smiled, some of the tension in his body unwinding. "You're very handsome."

"Yeah, yeah."

"You're the handsomest man I've ever met."

"At least I don't have those little lines around my eyes."

"What are you two whispering about?" Emery asked.

"Nothing," Jem said.

"Crow's feet," Tean said.

Emery shot John-Henry what must have been a meaningful look, and John-Henry's easygoing expression reassembled itself into chagrin, with a dash of amusement.

"See?" Emery asked.

John-Henry ignored the question and looked at Tean and Jem. "Are you all right?"

"Fine," Jem said.

"Would you really have shot them in the back?" Tean asked.

"I don't think it would have come to that," John-Henry said, which Jem recognized wasn't exactly an answer. "Ree?"

Emery grunted and flapped a hand dismissively.

"What are you two doing here?" Jem asked.

"Saving your asses," Emery said. "Was that unclear?"

Jem opened his mouth, but Tean squeezed his wrist, so he changed what he'd been about to say into "I meant how did you end up here?"

"He also meant to say thank you," Tean said. "We're both grateful."

"We've been following those two all day," John-Henry said.

"Dressed like that?" Jem asked.

With a laugh, John-Henry shook his head. "We thought they were going to the party; we had bags in the car, so we changed."

"Then I saw your Three Stooges act," Emery said, "and we had to pivot."

Tean glanced in the direction the brothers had gone. "Why were they here? Were they coming after us?"

"I don't think—" John-Henry began.

"Not unless they were staging the worst surprise attack in the history of the world," Emery said. Then he frowned and added, "If you omit North Korea's failed gambit in 1950."

"I will," Jem said, "but only this time."

For whatever reason, that made Emery nod.

John-Henry, on the hand, gave Jem a closer look. The blond man was handsome, sure, and on top of the good looks, he carried an air about him—authority, yes, but also a kind of unflappable confidence. Jem's first thought was businessman—money, and the certainty that, because he had money, the world would shape itself to his liking. Easy pickings, in other words. But the eyes were wrong. John-Henry had cop eyes, and now that Jem knew what to look for, he had a cop look too—the hair, the posture, even something about the way he walked. And right then, those cop eyes were considering Jem with an uncomfortable degree of scrutiny.

"So, you do this for fun?" Jem asked. "Follow shitheels around when you're on vacation?"

"A surprising amount of the time, unfortunately," John-Henry murmured. "It seems like we have to leave the country to have a real vacation."

"Don't be dramatic," Emery said. To Jem, he said, "Obviously not."

"Here's the thing, though," Jem said. "We appreciate that you showed up—"

"Saved your asses," Emery said.

"—and last night, taking the heat from Cassidy, that was righteous. But we don't know you, and I'm starting to get a little wigged out that you're so eager to help a couple of strangers."

"What he means—" Tean began.

"Is it easier to believe that I want to fuck over Jonas for personal reasons?" Emery asked.

John-Henry rubbed his forehead.

"Maybe," Jem said.

"He was my partner when I was police in St. Louis." As soon as Emery said it, Jem could see it in him too—the cop eyes, most of all, although his dark hair was longer than most cops, and he carried himself differently than Jem expected. Didn't act like a cop, a part of Jem's brain registered, and that sent up a warning flare. "He was dirty. When I confronted him, he dumped it on me. That's how I ended up in a steaming pile of shit called—"

"Home sweet home," John-Henry said.

Emery set his jaw and, after a moment, said, "Yes. Precisely."

"And you?" Jem asked.

"You might not have gotten the vibe yet," John-Henry said, "but right now, I'm along for damage control."

Emery snorted, and in spite of himself, Jem cracked a smile. But a moment later, he said, "You're cops."

John-Henry fixed those cop eyes on him again, but he had a best-buddy smile when he said, "That's right."

"Recovering," Emery said.

For some reason, that made John-Henry roll his eyes.

"And you?"

"I'm a wildlife vet," Tean said.

"We know," Emery said, but his eyes didn't leave Jem. "Your paper on the effectiveness of coyote bounties had organizational weaknesses, and I'll need to conduct more research, but I think I caught at least two factual errors."

"Er—" Tean shot a confused look at Jem. "Thank you?"

"What about you, Jem?" John-Henry asked, and you had to have spent a lot of your life knowing cops, knowing them from the other side of things, to know this was a cop question, and a cop was asking it, and cop eyes were watching you, waiting for the tell.

Jem Berger was good at a lot of things, and one of the things he was best at was bullshitting. "Real estate."

John-Henry waited a moment, and when nothing more came, he made a noise that could have meant anything.

Standing up from where he'd leaned against the Jeep, Emery broke the silence. "Well, I'm not sitting around here until those two bags of dicks come back. They know we're following them now; they'll either go to ground, or they'll get nervous and fuck up. My money is on fucking up."

"I don't understand," Tean said, running a hand through his hair. Jem winced internally; the movement only made Tean's hair wilder.

"They've got shit for brains," Emery said in the tone of someone explaining something very simple. "They know I'm following them—"

"No, I meant, I don't understand why they came here. At first, I thought they were after us—because we'd run into them in the hotel, I suppose, although I still don't understand why they were there."

Jem kept his face as smooth as he could. John-Henry's eyes cut toward him, and Jem pretended not to notice, his attention on Tean.

"But if they weren't coming here to find us," Tean continued, "I don't understand why they were here at all."

"Rod's a creep," Jem said. "He's got a lot of smooth answers, but he gives me a weird vibe. I bet they were coming to see him."

John-Henry's gaze lingered on Jem. A half-formed question was written on the blond man's face.

"Why would they come to see him in the middle of a public event?" Emery asked. "Why not arrange a meeting? Or if that wasn't possible, why not wait until everyone else had left?"

"I don't know," Jem said. "Do you have a better explanation?"

"Of course. They were here to steal veterinary supplies, most likely to treat their injuries from the fight. Painkillers, I suspect. And then whatever else they could score."

"In the middle of a party?" Jem asked. "Isn't that what you said? Why not wait?"

"Because they're shit-for-brains and they're hurting."

"Maybe that's why they came here to see Rod, because they're morons and they didn't think about waiting until the party was over."

Emery's straw-colored eyes were cool and distant, and he gave a single, dismissive shrug, as though the argument—conversation—were no longer interesting. A prickle of a flush ran through Jem. He was distantly aware of Tean squeezing his wrist again.

"The important part," John-Henry said, "is you're ok. I know this is personal for you; you care about your friend, and you want to make sure she doesn't get convicted of a crime she didn't commit. But whatever happened to Yesenia, there are clearly some dangerous people involved." He offered that best-friend-next-door smile. "It might be better if you stayed at the resort. Lie low. Don't put yourself in danger. You don't know what you're getting in the middle of. Ree and I will see what we can do, and if there's a way you can help, we'll let you know."

Jem tried to anchor himself to the feeling of Tean's hand around his wrist. He tried to make himself be here, now. But as his adrenaline ebbed, the fear came creeping in: the collision with the Rangel brothers, how quickly things had gone wrong, the gun to the back of Tean's head. And now this, to stand here, listening to this, being talked to like this. Like he was dumb, the way he felt when he drifted among the conference-goers. Like he didn't know anything about this. Like he was a sheep instead of a wolf.

It might be better, Jem thought, if you go fuck yourself.

"In other words," Emery said, "stay out of the way and don't make our job harder than it needs to be."

"It's not that simple," Tean said. "Last night, we agreed —"

"Maybe you can do something about this," Emery said, gesturing broadly at the shadowed bulk of the sanctuary. "Get it shut down or something. One less fucked-up atrocity in the heartland. You'd think an organization of people dedicated to habitat conservation would at least pretend to care about shutting down a shithole like this."

It took a lot to anger Tean; he was, on the whole, the most patient, compassionate person Jem knew, and he hated conflict. So, Jem found it darkly satisfying to see the tightening in Tean's mouth, the way he put his shoulders back, the clenched fists at his sides. It was obvious he wanted to say something. It was also obvious he wasn't going to do it. Not without a nudge.

"Actually," Jem said, "you're wrong."

Emery's sunset eyes flicked to Jem, almost amused. "Excuse me?"

"You know what?" John-Henry said. "We're all tired —"

"You don't know what you're talking about," Jem said. "Does he, Tean?"

Tean held himself rigid, refusing to look at Jem.

"Go on," Jem said. "Tell him."

"Tell me what?" Emery asked. "Tell me that it's humane to keep animals in cages, in a place they were never meant to be, like exhibits in a freak show?"

"That's not what it is," Tean said, the words brittle with nerves and coming a little too fast, a little too loud.

"Of course it is."

"Ree —" John-Henry tried.

"No, it's not." Tean swallowed, and when he spoke again, he had his control back—voice professional, modulated, calm. The only hint of his anger was that his voice was a little deeper than usual. This was Tean, the wildlife vet, in his element again. "I understand your point. In a perfect world, taking animals out of their natural habitats and placing them in enclosures like this, especially for our own entertainment, would be cruel. But this isn't a perfect world. These cats are trafficked to America by people who have no regard for their well-being. They're bred here in captivity, without any oversight. People buy them as pets, and then they get scared, or they get bored, and they abandon them. They can't be returned to their natural habitats; they don't know how to live there. Places like this— sanctuaries that are inspected and certified—do their best to provide a good quality of life in the face of tremendous obstacles. These cats are not in cages, and they're not unhappy, and they receive food and veterinary care. To try to take an imaginary moral high ground instead of acknowledging the complicated realities, both ethical and logistical, of dealing with these cats is either willfully blind or intellectually disingenuous."

The frost-freeze silence crackled through the summer night again. Emery's face was flushed, his chest rising and falling furiously, feet set wide.

"We're going to go," John-Henry said in a low voice, taking his arm. "Leave it—"

"No," Emery said, yanking his arm free. He drew another deep breath, and when he spoke, his voice was tight. "All right."

"All right?" Jem asked.

"All right?" John-Henry said.

Tean hunched his shoulders and folded his arms.

"I acknowledge that my comment was an oversimplification. You are...not wrong. I apologize."

"Now maybe you should fight him," Jem told Tean.

Tean turned on him, horrified.

"Jesus," John-Henry muttered. "It took me thirty years to get to 'not wrong.'"

"Perhaps, John, if you presented your arguments more cogently instead of, for example, trying to convince me that Colt should be allowed to grow his hair out because, quote, 'It's his hair, and he can look like Shaggy from Scooby Doo if he wants to' —"

"Ok," John-Henry said. "Now we're leaving. For real."

"But what about—" Tean began.

"We'll hang out a few miles down the road and see if the Rangels take us anywhere interesting." He gave Jem one final, considering look. "I meant what I said: it's in your best interest to focus on keeping yourselves safe. Don't leave the resort."

Jem nodded and smiled—relief, exhaustion, gratitude. Some of it was even real.

John-Henry frowned. "We'll walk you back to the party."

"They'll fuck up," Emery said as they headed back toward the dome of light and sound on the other side of the welcome center. "The Rangel brothers, I mean. And when they do, we'll pin them to the fucking wall, and they'll talk."

Jem nodded, making his face optimistic, hopeful. But he had an idea what the Rangels would tell them: about the guy who'd wanted to buy a bird, the guy who'd broken into a van and seen a lot of shit he wasn't supposed to see. A guy they'd followed back to Santaland and cornered in Yesenia's room. A guy who wasn't connected at all to Yesenia's disappearance or Missy's arrest. And what would Tean say when it all came out?

"They'll lie," he said. "People always lie."

Emery and John-Henry traded a look, but neither of them said anything.

They left Tean and Jem at the fringe of the party, where tassels of light fluttered against the darkness, and the brocade of voices and music and the distant, plaintive cries of big cats gave the night texture. Then, together, Jem and Tean walked back to where they'd been attacked, and Jem recovered the paracord and antenna from where he'd dropped them.

"All right?" Jem said, breaking the silence between them.

Tean nodded. But he didn't look all right: even in the half-light, shadows hollowed out his eyes, and tension Jem hadn't seen in a long time pulled at his face.

"I'll be faster next time," Jem said. Tean looked at him, so Jem clarified, "I won't let that happen again."

He didn't know what to call the look on Tean's face, but after a moment, Tean nodded.

"So," Jem said, "what now? Go back to the resort and be good little boys like Emery and John-Henry told us?"

"No. Not while Missy's still in trouble." Tean was silent for a long moment, and in the dark, with the party like a TV backdrop, the silence had the sense of movement, the way water looks still but runs fast. "I know we should let the police handle it. Emery and John-Henry seem to know what they're doing, and they're going to look into this. For all we know, North

THE FACE IN THE WATER

and Shaw are going to find Yesenia tonight or tomorrow, and it'll all be a misunderstanding."

"A misunderstanding didn't put that bloody poncho in Missy's room."

"That's what I don't understand," Tean said. "Why would she have it in her room?"

"Are you asking because she's not an idiot in general, or because it makes no sense to leave a bloody t-shirt in the reservoir and then bring another piece of incriminating evidence home?"

A gleam of a smile. "I should have known you'd think of it too."

With a soft laugh, Jem said, "Never mind. Give me your big speech. Tell me the sequence of events doesn't make sense or something like that."

"None of it makes sense."

"No."

After another of those silences, Tean said, "I guess I'm trying to say that I know we shouldn't be doing this. I mean, Emery and John-Henry aren't wrong. We're in way over our heads."

Jem's phone buzzed, and he glanced down to see a Facebook friend request from August Paul Lopez. He looked back at Tean. "Is this the part where I'm supposed to tell you we're going to do it, God damn you, and don't try to stop me, and you can have my badge, but you can't have my gun?"

"What?"

"You'll have to catch me first, copper."

"Wait, I thought you were a copper. What kind of badge were you turning in?"

"You know we're not going to stop trying to prove Missy is innocent. I know we're not going to stop. So, what are we doing?"

Tean thought about that for a while. "Feeling guilty about doing the right thing? And also struggling with my social conditioning to do what authority figures tell me to do? And maybe a little bit of waffling because I'm scared and I don't want anything bad to happen to you because we were trying to help one of my friends?"

"God," Jem said, appraising his husband, "maybe I'll wear the hat."

"Huh?"

"The cop hat. And the belt, maybe. With the cuffs jangling."

Even in the dark, even under the brown of Tean's skin, the blush exploded like fireworks.

"Maybe then you'll do what I tell you."

The blush deepened, but Tean said, "Grunting and saying, 'yeah, uh huh, oh' isn't exactly an instruction manual."

"I could write you an instruction manual if that's what you want."

Tean started walking toward the parking lot.

"It would have pictures. No, diagrams. It would have diagrams. Wait, we haven't even talked about where we're going."

"I'm going to get my bag from the car, and I'm going to look for something I can use as a weapon, and then I'm going back to that party and asking more questions until Rod kicks me out or somebody tells me something useful."

Jem's phone buzzed again as he trotted after Tean. This time, it was Instagram - @aplolz was requesting to follow him.

When he caught up with Tean, Jem said, "Penis. And butt. And the whole body, but like the one you see in art books."

"The Vitruvian man? What are you talking about?"

"The sex manual I'm writing for you. Those are some of the diagrams." His phone buzzed again—August Paul Lopez wanted to add Jem on Snapchat. And then again when Auggie followed him on Twitter. His handle read, *Auggie is open for profile reviews*. A DM popped up a moment later.

Need to talk.

Then another: *Now.*

Then a third: *Theo says I need to tell you this is Auggie from last night* and then a skull emoji.

Jem grinned.

"What?" Tean asked as he opened the Jetta's door.

"I honestly don't know. You know the pretty kid from last night?"

Tean's bushy eyebrows went up.

"Oh please," Jem said. "You were thinking the same thing. We all were. He's got a jawline like a fucking razor blade."

"Uh huh," Tean said.

"He wants to talk," Jem said as he typed in his number and sent it to Auggie.

"About what?"

Jem's phone buzzed and as he answered, he said, "Let's find out."

"Find out what?" Auggie asked.

"You know it's kind of insulting that Theo thought I couldn't figure out who you were."

"Right? Thank you."

A disgruntled noise suggested Jem was on speakerphone, so he set his call to speaker as well and said, "He knows there are pictures on those profiles, right? Like, he knows I can see you?"

"Don't get me started."

"Auggie," Theo said. He had a nice little wallop of authority packed behind the name. Not a cop. Maybe money. Zaddy's got coins. Or maybe just big dick energy, but not the asshole variety.

"We found her."

"What?" Tean asked.

"Who?" Jem said.

"Una." Auggie's grin shone through his voice. "Una Marchesi. Born in St. Louis, Missouri, on June 17, 1996, at Barnes-Jewish Hospital, currently living with her parents and unemployed, ardent believer in the Birds Aren't Real movement, and no longer taking her anxiety medication because, quote, 'They were using it to control my brain.' Oh, the 'they' in that sentence is the same they who were using birds to spy on us."

"The girl from Yesenia's hotel room? You found her?"

"Hold please," Auggie said.

A moment later, a photo came through on Jem's phone. The image showed the same olive-skinned woman Jem remembered from the hotel room—the same dark hair and dark eyes and sideburns. She was smiling at something off camera, and she looked less…well, erratic.

"Holy crap," Tean said.

"I know, right?"

"Don't encourage him," Theo said, and it was one of those things that sounded like a joke and then less and less like one the more Jem played it back in his head.

"I'm good," Auggie said. "I don't need encouragement; I already know it."

Theo answered with a sigh.

With a laugh, Jem said, "He's cute when he's like this, huh?"

"He certainly thinks he is," Theo said, and this time, the affection in his voice was clear. Then he grunted and said, "Jesus, Auggie, my ribs."

"How did you find her?"

"It wasn't that hard," Auggie said, and the pride in his voice was strangely endearing. Jem's mental outline of the younger man began to take shape: probably had older siblings, distant parents. Daddy issues was too easy and too throwaway a phrase to mean anything, but there was a reason he'd chosen an older partner. He liked being good at things. He liked being the object of attention. But not in a way that was annoying. Jem did a quick revision: it wasn't annoying yet. "I had her picture from the conference," Auggie continued, "and then I joined some Birds Aren't Real groups on

Facebook. It wasn't that hard. I just posted her picture, one with the hotel security taking her out of the resort, and asked if anyone knew her."

"And that worked?" Tean asked. "It seems like a group of paranoid people who believe in conspiracies wouldn't be willing to identify one of their own."

"Oh, yeah, they didn't want to. So, I got on a dummy account and answered my own question, said her name was Clarice Starling. People couldn't wait to correct me."

Jem burst out laughing.

"I said don't encourage him," Theo said, but wry amusement gave the words a twist.

"Is Clarice a friend of yours?" Tean asked.

"Oh my God," Jem said.

"Oh my God," Auggie said. "You're as bad as Theo."

"Excuse me," Theo said. "I'm the one who introduced you to *The Silence of the Lambs.*"

"Yeah, but that's only because your deep well of cultural knowledge, acquired from years and years of experience—"

"Because it came out before you were born," Theo cut in.

"You're going back on your schedule," Jem told Tean. "At least one movie every week from the golden age."

Tean looked like he was trying not to make a face. "No one has ever considered the Nineties the golden age of anything."

"Except parachute pants," Auggie said. "And I'm going to tell you this, knowing it probably won't mean much to you, but I found a picture of Theo wearing parachute pants—"

"For a Halloween party," Theo said. "Because of MC Hammer. When it was topical."

"—so if you want to see it, I can totally send it to you."

"What are parachute pants?" Tean asked.

"Remember those jeans you found for a dollar nineteen at DI? The ones where your whole body fit into one leg?"

Auggie burst out laughing. "Wait, what?"

"They were fine when I wore a belt," Tean mumbled.

"Those," Jem said, "but nylon."

"I'm sending it right now—" Auggie began.

"Auggie, we need to get going," Theo said, voice tightening. "We agreed on a phone call. Now you're dragging it out."

A fractured silence followed. Some of Jem's mental outline of Theo began to take shape as well. The big picture seemed to be that he was an asshole.

"Yeah, sorry," Jem said. "If you can send over whatever you have, that would be great."

"No," Auggie said, the word subdued. "We found her. Like, we're parked a hundred yards behind her."

10

The sign read Chickweed Farm, and it was fifteen minutes south of Auburn, set on a bluff that overlooked the bones of the Ozarks. Limestone, Tean corrected himself as a pair of headlights swept over the stone below them, and it flashed with sudden brilliance. Not bone.

Jem slowed the Jetta at the sign, and they rolled forward for another twenty yards, following the drainage ditch and, beyond it, the wire fence that marked the edge of the property. A breeze tugged on the long stalks of Indiangrass, and when one of them brushed the fence, sparks sprayed out into the darkness. Jem swore and jerked the wheel.

"Electric fence," Tean said.

"The Mid-fucking-west," Jem said, rolling his shoulders. "How many poisonous snakes live here? Don't answer that."

The Audi was half-hidden in the brush on the opposite shoulder, and Jem turned them in an easy half-circle and pulled up behind it. Weeds crunched and rustled against the undercarriage. In that final moment, headlights picked out twin silhouettes in the car ahead of them. Then Jem killed the engine, and Tean opened his door.

A breeze carried the faint smell of chicken manure and dusty grass and hot tar. The farm itself consisted of several shadowed bulks against the night sky: pole-frame barns, Tean guessed, as well as smaller sheds that would be used as workshops or to store equipment. A few acres of pasture were thick with grasses tall enough to hit Tean above the waist, their seed heads heavy and bobbing as the wind shifted. A frame house was set off at a distance, a solitary window on the second floor enameled with yellow light.

From the little Tean had been able to read on the drive over, it was a working organic poultry farm, selling direct to consumers, although a few local grocery stores carried their chickens. He couldn't find anything suspicious or noteworthy. It was, from what he could tell after that short search and this first, nighttime impression, a poultry farm like any other.

Except, a part of him said, Una is here. And she was in Yesenia's room. And that must mean something.

Gravel crunched under Jem's footsteps, and Tean followed him to the Audi. The dome light went on as they approached, and the window went down, and Auggie stuck his head out. For some reason it surprised Tean to see Auggie behind the wheel, Theo riding shotgun. Auggie smiled, drew his head back into the car, and the simultaneous thunks came as he unlocked the doors.

Tean got into the seat behind Auggie, and Jem sat behind Theo. The two men had changed into dark tees and jeans, probably because they hadn't packed their official sneaking-around clothes. Crumbs and wrappers littered the seat, and when Jem wiped a spot clean, Auggie said, "Sorry."

"Don't apologize," Jem said. "You should see our car when the girls are done with it. How many do you have?"

Auggie opened his mouth, but Theo said, "I'd like you to tell them about Una so that we can go."

For a moment, Auggie grimaced—the expression etching his face for only a moment and then gone, but leaving behind a trace, making him look older. He nodded. "So, like I said, she was pretty easy to find. And once I did, I took some time to dig around in her social media." He unlocked his phone and passed it back. Tean reached for it, but with a quick smile, Jem intercepted it. He scooted over so they could look at it together, his thumb sliding easily over the glass as he scrolled through Una's Facebook profile.

"You can see she posts a lot," Auggie said, "and a lot of it's not, um, cogent."

"Cogent," Theo muttered.

"What?" Auggie said with a half-laugh. "It's not. Plus it's an SAT word."

Not cogent was putting it mildly, in Tean's opinion. Jem didn't linger over any of the posts, but it was clear that they'd been written in a stream-of-consciousness style that didn't lend itself to, well, concision.

—*motherfuckers watching everything I do everywhere I go finding out everything I know went to the store tonight saw one an owl I think it was an owl it was supposed to be an owl its eyes I swear to God it was sent to track me followed me right up to the store thank God don't want to think about what it would have done if I'd been there they're always watching don't know who to trust have to kill them nothing else will stop them*—

They were all like that: seemingly spontaneous posts that channeled Una's fear and rage.

"She's crazy," Jem said.

Theo grunted.

"What's that supposed to mean?" Jem asked.

Tean touched his knee, and Jem rolled his eyes.

"She might be mentally ill," Theo said, his voice even, almost detached. "But belief in conspiracy theories isn't a mental illness, not in itself."

"You're the expert, huh? What are you? A doctor?"

"No," Theo said.

At the same time, Auggie said, "Actually, yes."

"I'm not a doctor," Theo said.

"He's got his doctorate. In English literature."

Jem wrinkled his nose. "What do you do with that?"

"Tell teenage boys not to sit on each other's laps, mostly," Theo said drily.

"He's only saying that because he had Colt and Ashley in class," Auggie said with a smirk. "Wait, do you know Colt and Ash?"

"You teach high school?" Jem asked.

"It's not just Colt and Ash," Theo said to Auggie. "Ninth-grade boys can't stop touching each other. It's enough to make me want to join a monastery."

"I don't understand what we're supposed to be looking at here," Tean said.

"Keep scrolling," Auggie said. "You'll see it."

As Jem slid his finger along the phone's screen, he said, "Sorry, but what makes a high school English teacher an expert on conspiracy theories? Is that, like, your hobby?"

Auggie burst out laughing. The sound was bright and full of life, and it washed away the last of that darkness that had etched his face. Theo grinned seemingly in spite of himself, and when he relaxed, it was easier to see what might have drawn Auggie to him: the dark blue of his eyes, crinkling now at the corners; the prominent cheekbones; the thick beard that Tean knew, without Jem having to say anything, Jem was worried might be better than his own.

"Theo's hobby is reading," Auggie said. "Oh, and breaking things and then making me hire someone to come fix them."

"I do not break things," Theo said, "and I certainly don't make you hire people to come fix them."

"We had this old window unit that didn't do jack shit. The summer after I graduated, Theo took the whole thing apart."

"I was fixing it."

"Pieces everywhere."

"I'd watched a video!"

Both men laughed for a moment. When their laughter stopped, Auggie's eyes came to Tean, and a strange uncertainty charged the air—as though Auggie felt he had exposed too much in that moment.

Tean heard himself say, "Jem tried to fix my toaster once."

Jem paused scrolling through Una's feed to look up, his face stricken.

"Well," Tean said, "more than once."

"You rat bastard traitor," Jem said.

Fighting a grin, Tean said, "He never actually took it apart. Well, he never actually fixed it either."

"How dare you?"

"But he was fixated on this screwdriver, like that was the problem."

Auggie started laughing first, and then Tean. Theo joined in a moment later, although more reserved, and Jem was last, finally cracking a grin as he tried to scowl at Tean.

This time when the laughter faded, the energy in the car was different. Theo shifted around, angling his body toward them for the first time. The concern in his face was transparent as he said, "Look, I'm sorry about your friend. And I'm glad Auggie was able to help, but I don't think the safe, responsible thing to do—"

Auggie coughed, "Dad," into his fist.

A crooked smile zigzagged across Jem's face.

But Theo didn't smile. He drew a deep breath and seemed to try to calm himself. "I'd like our part in this to be over. If there's something else we can do—if you need us to do some research, for example, then we'd love to help. But not this."

This, Tean intuited, meant being out in the dark, sitting in the car, watching an organic poultry farm while a potential murderer did who knew what to the birds. It meant the danger of involving themselves in trying to find a murderer when the police weren't interested in doing their jobs. It meant, Tean understood—because he had felt an echo of what he saw now on Theo's face—putting Auggie in danger, or letting Auggie put himself in danger.

"Of course," Tean said. "Jem, let's go."

"Wait, you didn't even see it," Auggie said, and he threw a look at Theo. He reached back, took his phone, and made several quick passes with his finger. When he held the screen out toward them, Tean saw the post that must have caught Auggie's attention.

I emailed THE BITCH again, and she ignored me AGAIN. I'm done waiting for her to do THE RIGHT THING and be a DECENT PERSON. She's a BITCH and she's always going to be a BITCH and I'm going to do whatever I have to do to show the world that she's a liar. She's part of the problem. People like her are the reason NOBODY IS SAFE. If she won't do THE RIGHT THING, then I only have one option left. TRUTH is unstoppable, which means I'm unstoppable. See you at IHCPA, BITCH.

It had been posted the week before the conference.

"Jesus Christ," Jem said.

"Are we sure she's talking about Yesenia?" Tean asked.

"Yeah, the further back you go, the more there is." Auggie pocketed his phone. "In some of the early posts, she calls Yesenia a bitch, and then, after that, it's always just 'the BITCH' in capital letters. I'm guessing Yesenia must have blocked her, because I can't find any posts from Una on her Facebook page. But I get the feeling Una wasn't lying about contacting her."

"See you at IHCPA," Tean said.

Jem shook his head. "Any clue what she's doing here?"

"Killing chickens," Theo said, and it was impossible to tell from his tone if he was joking.

"There's nothing on her social media profiles about this place," Auggie said. "She does videos on TikTok, and she's got Instagram and Twitter, but it's all versions of the same thing—reposting material from Birds Aren't Real, as well as her own, um…content."

"Batshit rants," Jem said.

Auggie flashed a grin and nodded.

"All right," Jem said. "Sounds like we've got our killer."

Theo shifted in his seat, but he didn't say anything.

"What?" Jem asked. When Theo didn't respond, Jem said, "She clearly has a thing for Yesenia. A fixation, or whatever you want to call it. She showed up at the conference, like she promised. There's all that weird shit about being unstoppable. I mean, you can't tell me that's not a threat."

Theo didn't say anything.

"Will you just tell him already?" Auggie said. "Or I'll do it for you, and I'll do a bad job, and you'll have to jump in and correct me."

After a long moment, Theo said, "You'd do a bad job on purpose. Your memory is perfectly fine."

"It's because I'm young. And virile. I've got a mind like a steel trap, not one that has gone mushy like the oatmeal a certain someone eats every morning to—uh, you know what? I forgot what I was saying."

Theo fixed him with a look for a few long heartbeats. Then he glanced at Tean and Jem. "People who believe in conspiracy theories aren't typically violent."

"And you learned all about this by being a high school English teacher," Jem said.

"I learned a few things by teaching a unit on conspiracy theories for the last five years and reading a lot—and I mean a lot—of terrible research papers. And no, Jem, I don't consider myself an expert on it. I'm simply telling you what I know. Then we're going to leave. If you don't want to hear what I have to say, we'll skip to the next part."

Auggie opened his mouth, but Tean spoke first, "No, please. Whatever you know could be helpful."

Jem made a discontented noise, but he quieted when Tean nudged him. Tean considered his husband for another long moment. It wasn't like Jem to react this way to people—to create friction, to antagonize. Oh, sure, Jem could be a little shit when he wanted to, and he knew how to get under people's skin, to make them too angry to think clearly. But ninety percent of the time—ninety-nine percent of the time—Jem's way of engaging with the world was to smile and nod and charm everyone around him. So, what Tean couldn't figure, staring at him now, was why Jem seemed to have his back up about Theo.

Then Theo spoke, and Tean turned his attention back.

"People who believe in conspiracy theories," Theo said, "are typically...let's say, open to those ideas for a few common reasons. Most of them are experiencing some degree of anxiety, which, I recognize, can be a mental illness. They're also typically isolated. That doesn't necessarily mean they're loners living off the grid, but they feel alone, lonely. And many of them feel disconnected from society at large—like the world has moved on, or they've been disenfranchised or marginalized or otherwise decentered from the world they knew."

Jem opened his mouth, but he shut it again when Tean nudged him and said, "The conspiracy theories provide a sense of community."

Theo nodded. "Exactly. A particularly tight sense of community, similar to what you see in cults—the belief that you are part of an exclusive group, with access to special knowledge. And, of course, conspiracy theories often offer an explanation for why the world is the way it is. Those explanations are a kind of...palliative, I guess."

"It's not their fault," Jem said grudgingly.

"Yes," Theo said. "That's a very good way of putting it. Conspiracy theories validate these people's feelings that they've been left behind, but they also explain that phenomenon in a way that makes someone else responsible."

"And you think this is how Una feels?" Tean tried to play it out in his head. "This is why she became a…a believer, I guess, in Birds Aren't Real?"

"I think none of those traits suggests violence."

"Ever heard of the Unabomber?" Jem asked.

"I didn't say that no one who believes in conspiracy theories is capable of violence. I'm saying that belief in conspiracy theories doesn't, on its own, suggest mental illness or a predisposition toward killing someone."

"Right," Jem said again, "Unabomber."

In the weak light, Theo's jaw tightened. Tean nudged Jem again, and Jem ignored him.

"Are we done?" Theo asked.

Auggie looked helplessly between his—well, Tean wasn't sure if Theo was his husband or his boyfriend—between his partner and Jem and Tean.

"You followed her here?" Tean asked.

Theo jerked out a nod.

"How?" Jem asked. "Did you teach a lesson on that in school too?"

Even Auggie caught it this time, his eyes widening slightly. "Hey, we know what we're doing. Believe it or not, we've found people before. People nobody else could find. We're good at it."

"That's not what he meant," Tean said. "It's been a long day. A long couple of days, actually. Right, Jem?"

The silence limped past. "Right."

"We called around to motels in the area," Theo said. "We described her. We had a whole song and dance. Once we found the motel where she was staying, Auggie insisted on confirming that she was actually there before we called you." His tone suggested how he felt about that. "Of course, when we got to the motel, she was leaving, so we followed her here."

"And she didn't notice you," Jem said. "The paranoid conspiracy theorist."

"No," Theo said, finally baring the edge in his voice. "Unless this is an elaborate ruse. Either way, you can discuss it with her at your leisure. Auggie, let's go."

"Hold on—" Auggie began.

"No, Theo's right," Tean said, opening the door. "Thank you both so much. Jem?"

The struggle played itself out in Jem's face. "You did a good job."

Theo made a disgusted noise and stared out the windshield.

Looking miserable, Auggie sank into his seat. "Her car's up the road. We can keep watch while you check it out."

"That isn't what we agreed," Theo said.

"We won't be doing anything," Auggie said in that low voice couples use when they're trying not to argue in front of others. Tean had used it a few times himself. "We'll be sitting here in the car, exactly the same way we're sitting here now."

"We agreed—" Theo began. Then his gaze came up to the rearview mirror to catch Tean's, and he said, "Would you excuse us, please?"

Face hot, Tean slid out of the Audi and shut his door. A moment later, Jem's thumped shut.

"That was the politest way anyone has ever told me to get the fuck out of his car," Jem said as he joined Tean.

They started up the road in the direction Auggie had indicated, looking for signs of Una's car.

"What was going on back there?" Tean asked.

"What?"

"The way you were acting. How you talked to Theo."

"You heard him. He learned about conspiracy theories in school?"

"Jem, they're trying to help us."

"They're amateurs."

"We're amateurs. That's what Emery and John-Henry said to us at the party, and they weren't wrong."

"Emery and John-Henry don't know us. And we don't know them, Tean. We don't know any of them. You should remember that."

"What does that mean?"

Jem took a deep breath. When he spoke, he slung an arm around Tean's shoulders, throwing Tean off balance on the next step before their strides merged. "We both should remember that. Just because they say they're helping us doesn't make it true. People believe what they want to be true. Or what they're afraid will be true. Let's not make that mistake."

In the distance, a rooster crowed, which was one of the many disappointing realities of animals that Tean had encountered; the whole crowing at dawn thing was nonsense. The damn birds crowed around the clock.

"So far, these guys have helped us. We're here, aren't we? And John-Henry and Emery saved us."

"We could have handled that." But when Tean looked at him, Jem blushed and shrugged.

"And North and Shaw took our side at the resort," Tean said.

"What else were they going to do?"

"Jem."

He smiled, and the expression looked sad on his face as he pulled Tean closer. "You, Teancum Leon, are a very smart—"

"Not that smart."

"—very hot—"

"Not really."

"—very good guy."

"I'm not that good. I told that man at the party some, uh, facts I'd learned about Missouri, and I knew he wasn't going to like them, and I told him anyway."

Jem's real smile glowed in the darkness. The moonlight fell into the slight gap between his front teeth. "Hit me."

"Did you know that in 2017, a man died in Missouri after being hit by a deer?"

"I thought there were a lot of deer around here. I thought hitting a deer was kind of normal."

"No, he was hit by a deer. The deer ran into him."

"Oh. How does that—ok, I guess."

"And he was on a toilet."

"Wait, but—"

"In his backyard."

Jem scratched his beard. His voice sounded off when he said, "In his backyard?"

Tean nodded.

"Damn," Jem said.

"You want to know the worst part?" Tean asked.

Jem nodded, still scratching his beard.

"I didn't source it. It might not even be true. But he was such a—such an ass, and I let myself get annoyed."

Jem cleared his throat, but his voice still sounded strange when he said, "You didn't source it, huh?"

Tean shook his head.

"Oh my God," Jem whispered.

"Do you have something stuck in your throat? Because you don't sound normal."

In answer, Jem kissed the side of his head.

"That doesn't really address my question," Tean said.

Jem opened his mouth to say something and then pointed. A moment later, Tean saw it through the brush: the gleam of chrome.

They found the car behind a thick, tangled brake of honeysuckle. It was a Ford Escort that had to be twenty years old, and the bluish-green paint was peeling like a sunburn. Tean turned on his phone's flashlight and directed it through the windows. Dirty clothes and plastic shopping bags covered the back seat, along with travel-sized toiletries, a box of Cheez-Its, a twenty-four pack of Lifewater (down to seven bottles), and what was unmistakably a five-gallon safety can, the blue-steel kind meant for gasoline or kerosene. When Jem tried the passenger door, it was unlocked, which answered one question but raised several more, and inside, it smelled like stale body odor and vinyl that had baked in a summer day.

"Ok," Jem said. "She's staying at a motel but more or less living out of her car, and she drives out to a chicken ranch in the middle of the night for…what?"

"Poultry farm."

Jem made a questioning noise as he crawled into the car.

"It's not called a chicken ranch. It's called a poultry farm. You could call it a chicken farm if they only raised chickens, I suppose."

"She left her purse," Jem said, a note of triumph in his voice. "Shit, hold on." Plastic rustled as Jem emptied some of the Walmart bags on the back seat. Then, after donning them as improvised gloves, he dumped her purse out on the driver's seat. Tean made his way around the car, trampling the knee-high prairie grass, and tried the driver's door. It opened easily, and he crouched next to the Ford to see what Jem had turned up.

Most of the list was what Tean would have expected: a partially crushed tampon, a pack of tissues that had clearly seen better days, receipts and scraps of paper, half a bag of M&M's. The credit cards and a driver's license were under the name Una Marchesi.

The only item that didn't belong was an envelope. Tean remembered that envelope. He'd seen Una with it as she escaped from Yesenia's bedroom.

Jem flicked a questioning look at Tean, and Tean nodded.

"Well," Jem said in an underbreath, "what'd you get, Una?"

He opened the envelope and shook it out on the seat. Photos, glossy four-by-sixes, slid across the upholstery. His phone began to buzz, and he made an annoyed noise, considered the bags on his hands, and then seemed to decide to ignore it. Tean leaned closer, angling the light of his phone to mitigate the glare on the glossy paper.

They were animals. A crocodile. An African gray parrot. A tamarin. A bat-eared fox. A macaque. A scarlet macaw. A capuchin monkey. A tiger.

"Hey," Jem said. "That's my bird."

Tean raised his head, his surprise at the statement transmuting into bewildered amusement at the outrage on Jem's face, when several things happened at once.

Headlights flashed down the road, in the direction they had left Theo and Auggie. Jem jerked upright. A horn blared, and Tean's head snapped toward the light and sound. A figure, nothing more than an outline against the light, was frozen at the edge of the honeysuckle brake. Tean had only a moment to process the general shape of the figure, the outline, and to decide, in that instant, it wasn't Una.

Then the figure turned and ran.

Jem scrambled out of the car and sprinted after the figure.

Tean shouted, "Jem, wait!" But Jem didn't slow. A moment later, the sound of a body hitting the ground came from the other side of the honeysuckle.

Tean fumbled the pictures back into the envelope, stuffed it into a back pocket, and raced after his husband.

When he reached the road, Jem was picking himself up, swearing a blue streak. A rut in the dirt road suggested what had happened. He tore off again, but by then, the figure had shrunk to a relatively darker patch against the night. Tean ran after them, but the figure had too much of a lead, and the darkness would make finding them impossible.

Then the door to the Audi opened, the dome light winked on, and Auggie darted across the road. He was young, and although his legs weren't as long as Jem's, he was fast. He sprinted after the fleeing figure. A moment later, Theo got out of the car, his movements slow and unusually stiff. He favored one leg, and as he ran, he bellowed, "Auggie! Stop!"

An uneven patch of ground made Tean stumble, so he turned his attention forward again. Auggie was in the lead, closing on the fleeing figure. Jem wasn't far behind, but it was clear that the fall had cost him, and now Jem's stride looked off, and he was losing ground.

Ahead, the hum of the electric fence made the hairs on Tean's arms stand up. As he watched, the fleeing figure threw themselves at the fence. Tean understood the decision as soon as he saw it; the electric fence wasn't like what you saw in movies, where an entire chain-link section was electrified and would kill you if you touched it. Most electric fences had a single line carrying the electric charge, which was mounted on insulated reels set low on the fence posts. The rest of the fence was plain old wire. As long as the figure cleared the electrified line, he — or she — would be fine.

Sure enough, the figure jump-stepped onto a mid-section of wire and launched themselves over the fence. Auggie duplicated the maneuver a moment later, and he whooped as he landed, the sound wild and full of excitement. He's so young, Tean thought with a kind of horror that was also wonder.

Jem repeated the move, but when he came down on the other side of the fence, he shouted, "Fuck damn shit hell fuck!"

Tean dropped down beside him a moment later, while Jem was still hunched over, massaging his ankle.

"It's fine," Jem said.

"When you fell—"

"It's sprained is all."

Tean glanced up. Auggie was a dwindling shadow. Behind them, in the distance, Theo's pained sounds were coming closer, but he wouldn't be fast enough.

"Go," Jem said.

"But—"

"I'm fine. Go!"

Tean ran.

He wasn't a runner by nature or by training; exercise, for the most part, consisted of long walks with Scipio, or hiking, occasionally mountain biking. But all of those activities used his legs, giving him muscle he wouldn't have had otherwise. He wasn't going to win any races, but when he needed to move, he could move.

Ahead, the pasture opened up, and beyond it loomed the hulking shadows of the poultry houses. The path the figure and Auggie had taken snaked darkly through the seed-heavy grasses, and Tean raced after them. Everything was so dark; Tean had been on lots of farms, and it took him a moment to wonder why the automatic lights weren't coming on. Farmers loved motion-sensor lights. But this was an organic farm, and part of him wanted to laugh when he made the connection. The birds needed a minimum number of hours of darkness, without any artificial light. So, he ran into the darkness, and a rooster crowed again.

Auggie shouted. The sound was wild, fueled by adrenaline, and it had all of a young man's challenge behind it. The darkness was too deep, and Tean could make out only the barest suggestion of the shapes ahead of him, but then the thud of bodies came, and he knew what had happened: Auggie had caught up with the fleeing figure and tackled them.

Then Auggie shouted again, and this time, the sound was different. Fight. Fear.

Tean pushed himself to run faster.

Metal glinted in the night.

Training took over. With some animals—not all, but some—the best thing to do if you were attacked was to make yourself as big and noisy as possible. Animals don't want to fight; fights might mean death, and even in victory, an injury could eventually prove fatal. So, the bigger and noisier you are, the less an animal is going to want to fight you. In theory.

So, Tean screamed, "Get off him!"

He couldn't do much about making himself bigger, not while he was running full out, but he screamed again, wordlessly, and he screamed some more. He screamed until his lungs burned and a stitch in his side made it impossible to scream any more.

And it worked. As Tean got closer, he could make out the shape of Auggie and the other figure wrestling on the ground, rolling through the ryegrass, flattening the stalks into a clear patch. At Tean's approach, the attacker sprang up.

Auggie grabbed at his attacker, but the movement was dazed and uncoordinated. But he caught something—a bag hanging off the figure's shoulder. For a moment, the attacker lurched back, caught by Auggie. Then fabric tore, the sound filling the night, and the bag came loose. The figure stumbled, threw a single backward glance, and sprinted toward the poultry house.

Tean skidded to a stop next to Auggie and crouched to inspect the younger man.

"Are you ok?"

Auggie nodded, but his voice unraveled. "They had a needle."

"Did they inject you with something? Did they hurt you?"

"No, no." Auggie seemed to struggle. "I hit my head. I—"

"Auggie!" Theo roared behind them.

"Stay here," Tean said and sprinted after the fleeing form.

For the next ten yards, the attacker's shadow wove back and forth in front of Tean. Then, as they entered the deeper darkness cast by the poultry house, the shadows melded together, and the figure was gone. Tean kept running. The shock of his feet hitting the earth ran up his legs; the staccato of those hard, clapping steps echoed in the night's stillness. The tall grass whispered against him. Like silk. Like razor blades. The compact humidity of the Midwestern air was so dense it was almost solid, packed in around his chest until he couldn't tell if he was still breathing, and sweat stung his eyes. Then the darkness of the poultry house swallowed him too.

For a moment, he was blind. A moment later, as his eyes adapted, he could make out the dark solidity of the poultry house's panel walls, and the deeper darkness that marked ruptures in the steel: openings in the structure.

Taller, rectangular ones that were doors for humans. Smaller, squarish ones that were popholes for the birds—access to pasture was another requirement for organic poultry farms. Tean headed for the closest door.

When he stepped inside, a wall of sensation met him: the drone of an industrial fan that circulated air through the poultry house; the stink of ammonia and rotten eggs and straw and hot animal bodies; soft noises of discontent from the chickens—clucking, fluttering wings, a lone, disgruntled squawk.

The sound of running steps came from deeper in the poultry house, and Tean started after them. He made it two strides before he hit something. His brain processed several details simultaneously: metal catching him at the knee, the sloshing sound of water, the initial resistance and then give as something heavy started to turn over under the force of the impact. He decoded it without really thinking about it—a drinker, the catch-all name for any device used to water the poultry. Tean stumbled, trying not to overturn the drinker, and his ankle hit wood. A perch, his brain told him. Straw slid under foot. He windmilled, trying to stay upright, and for a moment, he caught his balance. Then the white sneaker that Jem had insisted he wear came down on something soft. Meat. But no squawk, no eruption of wings.

Tean landed on the soft meat thing, scrambled away, the lights in his head all flicking to panic. It took him a moment to gather himself. Farther down, wings flapped, chickens bocked, and wood slammed against wood. One of the popholes, a distant part of him acknowledged. I lost them.

Hand shaking, Tean found his phone and turned on the flashlight. Sleepy chickens stared back at him, feathers ruffled, pacing nervously on perches, scratching at the straw and dirt. He swept the light back and forth until he saw the body.

He'd seen Una Marchesi twice when she'd been alive. In death, she seemed smaller.

After a moment, he checked her pulse and breathing, but it was perfunctory, and the tremors in his body were already stilling. She was dead. When he turned her head, he found where part of the skull had been caved in. Only a trace of blood, he noted with dazed detachment. The scalp hadn't been lacerated.

"Tean?" Jem's question was a shout as he lurched through the doorway.

"Here," Tean said. And then, before Jem could ask, "I'm fine."

"Jesus God." Jem limped through the straw, and when he crouched to hug Tean, Tean turned into the embrace. He ran a hand through Tean's hair and squeezed him.

"Is everyone ok?" Auggie asked a moment later, as he and Theo stepped into the poultry house. His gaze settled on Una. "Oh God."

The dim light from Tean's phone did little to illuminate the men, and the shadows that shifted and passed over Theo's features made Tean think of statues and firelight. "Is everyone ok? You've got a concussion."

"I don't have a concussion."

"They could have killed you."

"Theo, I'm fine."

Theo didn't say anything; his face said enough. He massaged his knee as he peered into the darkness. His other hand, gripping the strap of what appeared to be a fanny pack, tightened until his knuckles popped out.

"Is that her?" Auggie asked, voice small.

Tean nodded. He tapped Jem's arm, and Jem released him. "Someone killed her. She was struck on the side of the head — a single blow, I think."

Theo threw him a look.

"No," Tean said, "I'm not sure; I'm not a pathologist. But we do some forensic work with animal attacks, and anyway, it's not like it's rocket science in this case."

"Why would someone kill her?" Auggie asked.

"Good question," Jem said. "What's that?"

"What? Oh. He — she?" He looked at Tean.

Tean shook his head. "I don't know."

"They were wearing that," Auggie said and shrugged. "I grabbed it when they were trying to get away." A smile slipped across his face. "As soon as they heard Tean screaming like a lunatic, they tried to run. They got away, but they left this behind."

Jem motioned for the bag, and Theo handed it over — but only after a look at Auggie, waiting for Auggie's confirming nod. That was interesting, Tean decided, although he couldn't be sure why.

When Jem opened the bag, light gleamed on several hypodermic needles and syringes. Two small vials were nestled with the syringes. Somehow — improbably — he'd kept hold of the plastic bags he'd been using as improvised gloves, and he donned them again now. He extracted one of the vials, glanced at it, and held it out for Tean's inspection. He repeated the process with the second vial.

"Well?" Auggie asked.

Theo was still rubbing his knee. "What are they?"

"Detomidine hydrochloride," Tean said. "And ketamine hydrochloride." Jem returned the vials to the fanny pack as Tean crouched next to Una. When he touched her, she was still warm. It took him a moment to find the injection site on her arm. It was a ragged puncture wound with some tearing. She'd been surprised. Maybe she hadn't even seen the needle coming. She'd pulled away. Only by then, it had been too late.

"Tean?" Jem said. "What's wrong?"

"It's a large animal sedative." The roar of the industrial fans filled his ears. It seemed to be getting louder and louder, and he had a hard time hearing himself talking over it. "Detomidine. They use it for horses. Ketamine is often administered with it, to speed the onset."

For a moment, the rushing emptiness of the fan was everything.

"Shit," Jem said under his breath.

"So..." Auggie said.

"So," Tean said, dusting his knees as he stood, "whoever killed her has veterinary training."

11

"We can't just leave her," Tean said as Jem urged him into the passenger seat. On the other side of the Jetta, Theo and Auggie watched, their faces set like sympathetic mirrors. "Not in there with the chickens."

Jem traded a look with the other two men. All he said, though, was, "Let's get away from here. Then we can figure out what we want to do."

"No," Tean said. "We need to tell the police what we saw."

"You saw how well that went last time," Jem said. "If we call up the local yokels, we're going to spend the night in a cell. The four of us." In a lower voice, he added, "Tean, what do we know? Someone—maybe a man, maybe a woman—killed Una and ran away. We can tell them that when we make the call anonymously. We left the fanny pack. We left the drugs. The police will find them. That's it, that's everything. Now can we please go?"

"You're ok with this?" Tean asked across the hood of the car. "Both of you?"

To Tean's surprise, Theo looked again to Auggie for the decision.

"We should call Emery," Auggie said.

"I don't think you understand the concept of get the hell out of here," Jem said.

"He's not wrong," Theo said. "We should call Emery and John-Henry. They're police. Well, Emery used to be. But John-Henry is the chief of police."

Something flickered in Jem's face, something too fast for Tean to catch.

"They'll know what to do," Theo continued.

"And if we need them to, they can tell Chief Cassidy anything we need him to know," Auggie said. "Emery's a private investigator. And John-Henry has done law enforcement around here for a long time. They both have contacts; they can tell the chief that's how they learned anything we want them to pass on."

Jem looked at Tean.

THE FACE IN THE WATER

Tean got in the car.

They drove back toward Auburn and Santaland in silence, with only the thrum of the tires and the grayish brilliance of the headlights carving tunnels in the darkness. They found a Mr. Fuel and bought a disposable cell phone with cash, and Jem called in Una's body when they were driving again.

"How bad is your ankle?" Tean finally asked when they reached the city limits. Pole-sheds sprang up. A U-Haul lot. The Auburn Electric Co-op. A Cenex, its windows papered over with ads for disposable vapes. In the parking lot, a girl in a sports bra and Daisy Dukes was jamming the gas nozzle into a tank over and over again with rhythmic enthusiasm. Everything lay under a dirty shroud of light pollution. Everything looked like a movie set.

"Not bad."

"I want to take a look at it."

Jem made a noise that could have meant anything.

"You shouldn't be driving," Tean said. "Pull over and I'll drive."

"Tean, I twisted my ankle. I didn't have a foot amputated." They drove another quarter mile in the ashen-orange darkness. "I'm sorry, by the way."

"What?"

"I know you're disappointed in me because we left her. Because I said we should leave her. I know that's—that's not what you would have done."

A little laugh escaped Tean. "It is what I did."

"You know what I mean."

They drove some more. Tean removed his glasses, and as they drove out of the city, Auburn slid away behind them like a greasy smear. Darkness came after.

"I'm not disappointed in you. I'm—I'm angry. At this whole situation. At the incompetence and the idiocy and the hatefulness. It's horrible. And it's not fair, not to any of us, least of all Una and Missy. And it's not right."

Jem reached over and took his hand.

"Do you know that the Lake of the Ozarks is man-made?" Tean asked.

Jem shook his head, an ember of a smile glowing in his expression. "Is this headed where I think it's headed?"

"There were towns down there. Farms. Homes. And they dammed it up and flooded it. I mean, in theory, it was to create hydroelectric power, but people knew what they were doing. They knew they were creating valuable waterfront property. They knew they were creating—I don't know, a recreational area."

"Disney World."

Tean huffed a laugh in spite of himself. "A little. Yeah. And they didn't care. They didn't care about the people who were forced to relocate. They didn't care about the animals who would die, or the habitats destroyed, or any of it."

"How much time did you spend reading about this before we came?"

"And now, fifteen million people come every year."

"Was this just for cocktail party stories, like the guy who died on the can? Or was there something else going on?"

"And they use a million gallons of gasoline every day, Jem. Every day. That's as much gas as ten thousand cars."

"But," Jem said, lips quirking, "they're having fun, and part of being human is living a full, happy existence. And somebody would have used that gas anyway."

"They're not all having fun. On average, ten people die every year."

"They died doing what they love."

"I doubt that, since they primarily died from drowning."

"Up until then, I mean. Although I guess some people might love drowning."

"Ten deaths. That's how many people die each year from shark attacks. Only these people aren't dying from shark attacks. They're dying because they're drunk and they're stupid and they're—they're fucking around in this fucking lake that was never supposed to be here."

Jem squeezed his hand. The AC hissed in the vents, and Tean's drying sweat left him feeling sticky. He plucked at his shirt. In the passenger window, his reflection chased him.

"First thing," Jem said, "and I know this isn't the time or place, but your swearing has really improved. Like, next level."

Tean tried to twist his hand free.

Laughing softly, Jem held on. "And second thing, you're right. I know you're right—and you know I know you're right. People are stupid. People are greedy. They do the dumbest shit, not thinking about who it'll hurt—not even if it'll hurt them—because they want something. So, preach it. I'm all ears. But I think maybe you're not mad at the dumb rednecks who fall off their boats and get their dicks sliced off by propellers."

"That wasn't in any of the scenarios I described."

"It was implied. I think—"

"No, it wasn't."

"I think," Jem said again, a little more firmly this time, "you're upset because of Una, and because of Missy, and because there's some systemic-level shittiness happening in this part of the world."

Tean rubbed his eyes and let his head rock back against the seat.

"I learned systemic last week," Jem added quietly, "and I've been waiting for a chance to use it."

"It was perfect," Tean said and wiped his eyes again.

"Hey."

"No," Tean said, his voice thick. "You're right. I'm not mad at those stupid, selfish people—I mean, I am, but for different reasons, and not right now. I'm mad at this stupid police chief. And I'm mad that nobody else seems to care. And I'm mad because I'm scared, and it's easier to be mad than scared. And I'm mad because I feel so helpless."

Jem stretched across the seat to kiss Tean's cheek.

Tean accepted the kiss and then pushed him away. "Do you know how many people die each year from distracted driving?"

"Hm?"

"Last year, over three thousand people—Jem!"

Jem released the wheel, turned, and propped his chin in his hand as he listened to Tean with a suspiciously interested expression. The Jetta began to drift. "Don't leave me hanging. How many people exactly?"

"We're going to crash!"

"You were saying something about distracted driving."

"You have to hold the steering wheel, you can't—" Tean reached for the steering wheel, but Jem got in his way. They were halfway across the double yellow line now, and headlights appeared in the distance. "Jem, there's a car coming!"

"I just want to hear one truly horrifying statistic about distracted driving so I'll learn my lesson."

"We're going to crash. And we're going to die. And the girls are going to grow up without parents, and whoever adopts Scipio won't let him lick nacho cheese from his whiskers like you do, and you and I will probably be burned beyond recognition in the inferno."

"I've always kind of wanted to be cremated." They were three-quarters of the way across the line, and the headlights swelled as they rushed toward them. "Hey, maybe we can be in the same urn? They'll have to mash up some of the bones that don't burn, I guess, but I bet they can make us both fit."

"Jem!"

"One distressingly soul-crushing fact."

"The cost of distracted driving every year is more than the National Institutes of Health's annual budget!"

Jem hooked the wheel, and they glided back into their lane, and a moment later, a Mack truck blew past in the opposite direction. A horn blared, and then everything was darkness and silence again.

Tean pushed his hands through his hair. He did it again. He realized he was bent halfway over like he was trying to catch his breath, and he sat up, readying himself for a really good shout.

And Jem was grinning at him, slouched in the seat, one hand lazy on the wheel. "Feel better?"

"No!"

Jem's grin got bigger.

In spite of himself, an answering smile broke out on Tean's face. The wildness of it, the hint of ferocity, everything whetted by adrenaline. He was startled to hear himself laugh. When he got control of himself, he tried for a severe, "You're insane."

"I love you," Jem said. "And we're going to figure this out."

Tean settled back into his seat and spent the rest of the drive trying to figure out why he was still smiling.

When they parked, he said, "I love you too."

"I know," Jem said.

"Thank you."

He had one finger through the keyring, and when he spun the keys, they chimed and slapped into his palm. "Stick with me, kid." Then he got out of the car.

"I'm older than you," Tean said.

Jem shut the door. It sounded like he was laughing.

Tean wondered, as he went after his husband, if there were any statistics on men dying of heart attacks because of their significant others, with no comorbidities. Maybe medical science could use him as the first.

As they crossed the Santaland lobby, a blonde in a sundress was trying to force a child to stay on one of the plastic reindeer while she took a picture. "No, sweetie, stay on Rudolph. Stay on Rudolph. Ride the reindeer. No, no, no, sweetie, stay—"

"You know that headband you got at Christmas," Jem said, "the one with the reindeer antlers?"

"I didn't buy it. You bought it. And you made Scipio wear it, and he hated it."

"He loved it. He got a million pets at the park because of it. Anyway, did you bring it with you?"

"Why in the world would I have brought it with me?"

"I had an idea for a game we can play tonight. It's called ride—"

"No," Tean said.

Jem smirked and opened his mouth.

"No," Tean said again.

"Right," Jem said, and something about how his smile spread made heat curl in Tean's belly. "That one is seasonal; we'll save it for the holidays."

Medical science, Tean thought. There had to be a study somewhere.

Although the smirk had faded, Jem still looked very satisfied with himself as he wagged his phone at Tean. "Auggie says we're meeting in one of the multipurpose rooms. Ready to get yelled at?"

Tean made a face as they started down the hallway.

"Hey," Jem said, the playfulness stripping away from his voice. "Watch what you say in there."

"What?"

"They're both cops."

"Ok."

"So, be careful."

"But we didn't do anything wrong."

Jem's smile was mirthless. "Cops have a funny way of seeing things sometimes."

"I don't understand. Do you want me not to tell them something? If you don't trust them, then we shouldn't be working with them at all."

"No," Jem said. "That's not—just be careful, that's all."

Tean frowned. The set of Jem's shoulders was tense, the muscles drawn tight. Under the resort's bright fluorescent lights, for the first time Tean noticed dirt and grass stains on Jem's shirt, and his limp seemed even more pronounced. As though sensing Tean's attention, Jem cast him an oblique smile. His shoulders fell back and down, loosening, and his body opened up, and even his limp faded to almost nothing—although Tean could see what it cost Jem, the strain showing around his eyes. Just like that, between one step and the next, Jem was a different man. He mouthed, *Careful*, and then he opened the door.

On the other side of the room, Emery stood clutching a fistful of pages that appeared to have been torn from a notebook. Shaw stood opposite him, beaming, clutching a notebook with the tattered edges of pages visible. Today's outfit was a pickle-colored velvet tee and matching joggers. His shirt had the word *Queenie* embroidered in lime green across his chest, and his headband, wristbands, and leg warmers were the exact same shade as the embroidery.

"—never in my life," Emery roared, "ejaculated!"

John-Henry, in the front row of seats, rubbed his forehead.

North sat with his big boots kicked up on the back of a chair, grinning. He looked like the only thing he was missing was popcorn.

Behind Tean, Auggie said, "Um."

"Great," Theo muttered. "That's our cue to go."

Jem, of course, was fighting a giggle.

The multipurpose room looked like any of the others being used by the conference. Rows of stackable chairs with minimal padding faced a portable screen, along with a table and chairs for the presenters. A projector on an AV cart was dark and silent. Plastic cups waited on a table near the door—the water carafes, apparently, had been retired for the day. Music filtered in from the hotel hallway, playing softly. It sounded like something from *White Christmas*, only if the composer had written exclusively for the jazz flute and had done copious amounts of cocaine. Was there a psychosexual dream sequence in *White Christmas*? Tean tried to remember. That didn't sound right.

"Ree," John-Henry said.

"And furthermore," Emery said, stabbing a finger at Shaw, "I do not own, and have not ever owned, quote, 'crotchless panties that displayed the splendor of his manhood.'"

"That seems like a good stopping point for this conversation."

"Wait," North said, "he's got more."

"And if I did," Emery continued, "I certainly wouldn't wear them on a roller coaster, where the likelihood of snagging an appendage or an orifice would be dramatically higher."

"An orifice," Jem whispered.

Auggie muffled a laugh in Theo's shoulder. Even Theo's normally stern expression relaxed somewhat.

"Ok," John-Henry said, "now we're done."

"You will cease and desist writing this—this—"

"Tripe," North suggested.

"Tripe! And you will never include me in your pornography again."

Shaw nodded enthusiastically throughout the tirade. So enthusiastically, in fact, that some of his hair fell free from its bun. "Right, of course, definitely. If I could—"

But when he reached for the pages Emery clutched, Emery yanked them out of reach.

"I was going to show you," Shaw said, "it's not even about you, Emery. And it's definitely not pornography. It's an epic love story—"

"Platonic," North said.

"An epic platonic love story, and it's about two totally fictional characters named Shawn and Emerson—"

Emery's growl reached a new level of intensity.

"Emerson Blizzard," North said to no one in particular.

"Thank you, North," John-Henry said as he stood and made his way down the aisle. He stepped between Emery and Shaw, eased Emery's fingers open, and took the pages. Then he passed them to Shaw and said, "Enough teasing for a little while."

Shaw opened his mouth. Then a hint of red came into his cheeks, and he grinned sheepishly and bounded off toward North.

"And you," Emery said, turning toward Jem and Tean. "What the fuck did I tell you?"

"We were just—" Jem began.

"I told you to stay the fuck out of the way while we handled this!"

"Who the fuck are you to tell me anything?"

John-Henry placed a hand on Emery's chest, but he shot Jem a look. To Emery, he said, "Take it down a little, love."

Emery's face remained a thundercloud, but he nodded.

"Are you all right?" John-Henry asked.

"Fine," Jem said sourly. "Thanks for asking."

"We're not fine," Tean said. "A woman is dead. Jem hurt himself—"

Jem made a vexed noise.

"—and Auggie hit his head; he may have a concussion. I think Theo did something to his knee."

"No concussion," Theo said, his hand on Auggie's nape. "And my knee is always stiff after I've sat for a while. How bad is Jem's ankle?"

"I need to look—" Tean began.

"Fine," Jem said a little more forcefully.

Tean started to respond to that—the tone, more than anything else. He forced himself to stop.

"Why don't you start from the beginning?" John-Henry said.

"And explain," Emery added, "why you did exactly the opposite of what we told you."

It emerged in a jumble: Tean beginning the telling, with Auggie jumping in to explain what he'd found about Una, and then the chaos of the chase through the dark. Several times, Emery shook his head and looked away, and John-Henry's expression was tight. North and Shaw traded looks, and both men grew serious in a way Tean wasn't sure he'd seen before.

When Tean reached his description of the prescription vials and the syringes, Emery broke in to say, "Detomidine is used by vets."

"Yes," Tean said.

"He was about to say that," Jem said. "He's a vet; do you think maybe he should tell you what vets use?"

"Jem," Tean said.

"Why do I need him to tell me?" Emery said. "I already know."

"Did you also know—" Jem began.

"Jem," Tean whispered.

With what looked like an effort, Jem shut his mouth, but an ugly flush rode his cheeks.

After a moment, North said, "This whole place is full of vets."

"I think what North is saying," Shaw said, "is Big Ag—"

"Jesus Christ," North said under his breath.

"—and Big Vet and Big, um, Bird—"

"Thank you all so fucking much," North muttered.

"—have made it possible for lots of people to have access to those drugs," Shaw finished with a victorious note, "not only trained and licensed veterinarians."

"My point," North said in an aggrieved tone, "is why are we surprised Yesenia was probably killed by someone at the conference?"

"Because—" Tean wanted to say, These are my people. But that would have sounded childish; the logical part of him knew, better than most, that anyone could commit murder under the right circumstances. But it was one thing to believe that some random Missouri hick could kill two women; it was another thing to believe that someone at the conference, someone who was educated, someone who shared, at least at the most general level, Tean's values—someone like Tean, in other words—could do something like this. "Because of the local connection," he finished lamely. "Those men, the ones Emery knows."

"The Rangels," Emery said, "will work for anybody. I want to take another look at the owner of that cat sanctuary; I know you talked to him, but he seems like our most likely suspect."

"I'm not sure he is," Tean said. "He had every reason to want Yesenia alive." And then Tean had to explain, for the rest of the group, how Yesenia's wildlife safari would have benefited the cat sanctuary.

"I'm part cat," Shaw said in the tone of someone imparting crucial information. "Or I was a cat in another life. Oh, Jem! Maybe you can contact my, um, inner cat? Astral cat? A regression! Maybe you can do a regression!"

"You sleep all day, knock things over so I'll have to pick them up, and you love putting your leg behind your head and trying to lick your own balls," North said. "You're already a fucking cat. What the fuck is a regression going to do, make you shit in a box?"

"Actually, I was reading an interesting story about litter boxes in schools—"

Emery was making that growling noise again, but Theo, in a slightly rushed tone, said, "I don't think we have anything to add, so Auggie and I are going back to our room."

"But why kill Una?" Auggie asked. "Isn't that the question we should be asking? I mean, either the killer followed her out to the chicken ranch—"

"Poultry farm," Tean corrected absently.

"—or they lured her out there. Actually, that seems more likely—she wouldn't know this area well, but if the killer knew who she was, if he posed as someone else from Birds Aren't Real, it wouldn't have been hard to convince her to vandalize the chicken ranch."

"Poultry farm."

"Good questions, Auggie," Theo said. "Can we go now?"

"Either way," Auggie said, "the killing must have been premeditated. There's no way Una and the killer were both randomly wandering around the same chicken ranch, and the killer just happened to drug her and bash her head in."

"Excuse us," Theo said, and then, voice flat, "I want to talk to you. In private. Now."

Auggie looked miserable, but underneath the misery, Tean caught traces of grim resolve. The two men moved to the back of the room, and their conversation began in heated whispers that weren't quite loud enough to make into words.

"He's not wrong," Emery said. "Why kill this woman? She was paranoid, hyperfocused on Yesenia in connection with these conspiracy theories, and she had a history of socially transgressive behavior. She'd be an easy patsy. If your theory is correct—" He glanced at Tean. "—why not frame her instead of your friend?"

Tean shook his head. "Maybe he or she doesn't know the people at the conference well. Maybe framing Missy was convenient."

John-Henry shook his head. "Whoever did this, they broke into Missy's hotel room to plant that evidence. Unless he was wandering the halls with a bloody poncho and she just happened to leave her door open, it wasn't convenience. The killer chose to frame Missy; the question is why."

"Who cares why?" North said. "We need to focus on what's important."

"My Emerson and Shaw story. I mean Shawn."

"Good Christ," North said in an undertone. More loudly, he continued, "Someone killed that woman tonight. The best reason is because she was a threat. So, that's one avenue of investigation—figure out what she knew, or what she had, and why that made her a threat to the killer. There's also the people at the conference. Our suspects, although that makes it sound like we're playing a game of Clue, for fuck's sake."

"I've played Clue," Shaw said. "One time, Emery and I played all night—"

"No," Emery said, "we didn't."

"We played it while you were dreamwalking—"

"No, we didn't," Emery snapped.

"—and Molly Ringwald and Richard Nixon were cheating—"

"What the fuck is going on?" Jem whispered to Tean.

Tean shook his head.

"Enough!" Emery shouted. "No more comments!"

Shaw shrank down, eyes wide, but Tean thought he detected a hint of a smile.

"We spent most of the day on the Rangel brothers," John-Henry said. "We followed them to a place called the Cottonmouth Club, which looks, pardon the language, like a real shit hole. Later, they were prowling around the cat sanctuary, and they went after Jem and Tean. I think our focus needs to be on them."

Jem shook his head. "I don't think that's the best approach."

John-Henry's attention on Jem was a little too keen for Tean's liking. "Why not?"

"What about the other people at the conference? Kristin was acting strangely, right, Tean?"

"She and Rod got into some kind of disagreement," Tean said slowly.

"She was trying to get into a restricted area of the welcome center. She does veterinary anesthesia. Maybe she was looking for supplies she hadn't brought with her."

Tean opened his mouth and shut it again.

Shaw raised his hand.

"No," Emery barked.

"One thing," Shaw whispered.

"No."

"One little thing."

"No."

"Your mouth is saying no," Shaw said, "but your eyes are saying yes, so I'm going to say it anyway."

"That's his fucking idea of consent, by the way," North said. "Try telling him you've got a headache when he's drilling his boner into your leg."

"We spent all day trying to figure out if Yesenia was alive. She doesn't have any new charges on her credit card—"

"How do you know that?" Emery asked.

"Because her password is password one two three four five," North said.

"And nobody at the conference has seen her. The resort staff hasn't seen her. None of the plastic Santas have seen her, even after exhaustive psychic probing."

"Ignore that," North said. "Nobody engage with that."

"But," Shaw said, "we did see somebody break into her car."

"You already told us that," Emery said. "For the love of Christ, if you waste my time again—"

"We told you somebody had tried to break into her car," North said. "Clean the shit out of your ears. Tonight, we saw somebody try to break in. Well, she did break in, so I guess it wasn't really trying."

"You saw her?" John-Henry asked.

"Who?" Emery asked.

North took out his phone and pulled up a picture. When he displayed it, Jem made a scoffing noise, and Tean shook his head.

"Heather?" Tean asked, although there was no mistaking her in the picture. She stood at the rear passenger door of the vehicle, holding a piece of metal she had worked behind the window. Her face was turned toward the camera as though she were scanning for witnesses.

"The animal psychic?" Jem said. "Are you kidding me? She's, like, a million years old."

"She was pretty spry tonight," North said, pocketing his phone.

"What did she say when you confronted her?" Emery asked.

"First of all, motherfucker, maybe I wanted to see what she was going to do. Maybe Shaw and I just hung back and watched."

Emery snorted. "In those boots?"

North sat up, dropping his feet from the back of the chair, his face coloring.

"North," John-Henry said.

For a moment, North seemed to fight an internal battle. Then, words stiff, he said, "She got away."

"She got away?" Emery asked. "How the fuck did she get away? On her fucking scooter?"

"Hey!" North shouted.

"She got away by setting North on fire," Shaw said brightly.

Tean looked at North. Jem looked at North. Emery pinched the bridge of his nose, and John-Henry sighed. In the lull, the furious whispers between Auggie and Theo were a snakeskin noise.

"You have got to be fucking kidding me," Emery said. "This is amateur hour, John."

John-Henry rubbed his shoulder.

"You two," Emery said to North and Shaw, "managed to get yourselves set on fire during a fucking stakeout."

"Emery, wait—" Shaw said.

"And you two, regardless of the fact that you have no fucking idea what you're doing, keep poking your noses into everything after you've been told not to."

Jem's face darkened, and he balled his fists.

"And you two," Emery shouted toward the back of the room, "fucked up our best—and so far, only—chance at finding this killer."

"We're in the middle of a conversation, Emery," Theo said.

"Flashing your fucking headlights?" Emery asked. "How about next time, you do a hula dance on the roof of your fucking car?"

"Jem wasn't answering his phone," Auggie protested. "The killer was going to catch them."

"The good news," Shaw said, "is we didn't get totally set on fire because I'm a pyromancer, well, just a baby one right now, but I channeled the flames away from us."

"Pyromancer," North said. "He fell asleep with a jay one time and set his own dick on fire."

John-Henry held up a hand before Emery could speak. In a surprisingly tight voice, he asked, "North?"

"When we saw her splashing kerosene on everything," North said, not meeting anyone's eyes, "we tried to stop her. She was obviously trying to destroy evidence. I didn't expect her to throw the kerosene at me."

"And you definitely didn't expect to catch on fire so quickly," Shaw said in what must have been meant as a helpful tone.

"Are you hurt?" John-Henry asked.

THE FACE IN THE WATER

North made a face and shook his head. "Still have my fucking eyebrows, but I lost my favorite tee."

"He has a million favorite shirts," Shaw said. "This one was Lowell's Landscaping. It was gray. They're all gray."

"The L's looked like lawnmowers; it was fucking awesome. Sue me for thinking it was fucking awesome."

"Imagine what I'll be able to do after I finish Master Hermes's advanced pyromantic and pyrokinetics course."

North rolled his eyes. "Shaw put the fire out with the extinguisher I keep in the car, but she got away while we were, uh, busy."

"This Heather woman," Jem said, touching Tean's arm. "That's who we should focus on, right? I mean, she was obviously trying to get rid of something in Yesenia's car. Do you know her? What's she like? What's her deal with Yesenia?"

Tean shook his head. "I've never met her before."

"But that's who we should focus on, don't you think? John-Henry? Emery?"

"I'd certainly like to know what she was looking for in Yesenia's car—" Emery began.

"The photos." Tean sat up and checked his back pocket, where he'd shoved the envelope they'd found in Una's car. Paper crinkled under his touch. "Una took them from Yesenia's room."

"What photos?" Auggie asked.

Theo's silence practically vibrated, a low-frequency buzz to it, but Tean registered that at a distance. He hurried to the presenters' table at the front of the room, shook the photos out of the envelope, and separated them, as best he could, using the envelope so that he wouldn't have to touch the photos with his bare hands. The other men gathered around the table, although Theo hung back so far that Tean wasn't sure if he could see anything.

"Animals?" Auggie said.

Shaw's hand hovered over the macaw, not quite touching. "He's beautiful." Then he glanced at Jem. "He looks a little like your soul."

"What are we looking at?" John-Henry asked.

"Is that a capuchin monkey?" Emery asked. "A crocodile, a tiger. Jesus Christ."

"Why did Yesenia have these?" North asked.

Theo cleared his throat. "Why did Una have them?"

It took Tean a moment to realize they were all looking at him. "How should I know?"

"We don't expect you to know," Emery said. "We expect you to use your professional fucking judgment and give us a best guess."

"That's a lot of pressure—" Jem began.

"Let him answer," John-Henry said quietly.

"I don't know," Tean said. He scanned the pictures again, and his eyes came to rest on the scarlet macaw again. The brilliant colors. The strong horizontal bands. An infinitesimal smile tugged at the corner of his mouth, because now that Shaw had said it, he could see Jem in the bird. Color-block t-shirts. Everything so bright and alive. Some of the fear and tension that had locked his brain since the encounter at Chickweed Farm dissolved, and his mind began to move again. "Many of these animals are highly sought after. Not all of them, but many of them are among the most trafficked animals in the world."

"Ok." John-Henry gave a confused laugh. "What are we talking about? A gang of animal smugglers?"

"People pay money for these things?" North said. "Go to a fucking zoo. You want an animal, I've got a dog you can have."

"He's mad because the puppy and I had a slumber party," Shaw said.

"That's what you're calling it? A slumber party? You doped his cheese with Benadryl and wrapped him in a blanket so he couldn't get away from you. I woke up at two in the morning with him scratching at the door because you ate some of the drugged cheese too and he needed to go out."

Shaw raised his chin. "Friends don't let friends do Benadryl alone."

"Animal trafficking is frequently linked to terrorist organizations, human trafficking, arms dealing, and drug smuggling." Emery rubbed his chin. "The Ozark Volunteers might be expanding."

John-Henry gave that laugh again, but he cut off at the look on Emery's face. "You're serious?"

"Who are the Ozark Volunteers?" Jem asked.

"Imagine Jeff Foxworthy doing a standup routine about neo-Nazis," North said drily, "and you've more or less got it."

"Is that possible?" Tean asked. "Could Yesenia have gotten on their bad side? If she was investigating an animal trafficking operation—"

"Or benefitting from one," Emery said. "We don't know how she got those animals for her safari park, do we?"

"What kind of money are we talking about?" North asked. "I mean, birds, hell, even a tiger. How much money could they be making?"

"Enough money that drug cartels and terrorist organizations find it worth their time," Emery said drily. "The entire business, from top to bottom, involves the worst pieces of human shit you can imagine. The irony is that only the ones at the top make a fortune. The ones at the bottom, the locals? They don't get hardly anything. All these people stripping their country of its wildlife for a few fucking bucks."

Tean shook his head. He caught himself and tried to stop, but it was too late.

"Something I got wrong, Dr. Leon?"

"We should focus on this connection," Tean said.

"No, you looked like you wanted to say something."

"Yesenia had those pictures for a reason. Una took those pictures, and we can assume she had a reason as well."

"The birds," Theo put in.

Tean shot him a grateful look. "Yes, that seems likely. And it also seems likely that, if someone is trafficking animals in the area—perhaps this group you mentioned—they'd have someone on their staff trained in some rudimentary veterinary practices."

"Why not just shoot her?" Auggie asked.

"He's right," North said. "Why inject her with something at a chicken ranch—"

"Poultry farm," Tean said, unable to stop himself.

"—and then bash her on the head? Everybody in a hundred miles owns at least one fucking gun. If she's a problem, why not shoot her? And why the frame job?"

Tean glanced around. He was surprised to see John-Henry staring at Jem. Jem, for his own part, slouched in his seat, playing with the part in his hair, but Tean knew him well enough to recognize the coiled readiness that meant Jem sensed a threat.

"How did she get the pictures?" Shaw said. "I mean Yesenia. If she had a source among the traffickers, or if we can figure out how she learned about this, that might give us another angle."

"The fucking Ozark Volunteers," Emery said.

John-Henry asked, "What do you think, Jem?"

Blinking, as though the question had woken him, Jem gave a tired smile. "Oh, I know when I'm out of my league. I'll let the pros handle this one."

"I think you could help us a lot. For example, the Cottonmouth Club seems to be involved somehow. The Rangel brothers visited there while Ree and I were following them. And when Ree called the club, the Rangels panicked."

Jem shook his head. "The Cottonmouth Club?"

He was so good, Tean thought, that unless you knew him, had known him over years, you wouldn't have seen the glitch. And something opened inside Tean, a wide, yawning darkness, because he knew his husband was lying.

"That seems like a good place to start," John-Henry said. "Tell us about the Cottonmouth Club, Jem."

Jem's smile was the right degree of uncertain, the right mixture of worry and amusement—like this might be a joke, and he wasn't getting it. "I've never been to the Cottonmouth Club; we got here on Thursday."

"Jem," Tean said.

Jem flicked him a look, and it was like old transparency layers, the kind they'd used with overhead projectors when Tean had been in school. This Jem, the liar, on top, superimposed over the blurry other Jem, the real one, looking out at Tean and begging for help.

"I'm still not clear," Emery said to Tean, "in what regard you believe I was incorrect in my assessment of animal trafficking."

"Um, maybe not right now, Emery," Auggie said.

John-Henry hadn't moved. He had intensely blue eyes—a kind of perfect, ocean blue—and they were locked on Jem. "One more chance," he said, so quietly that Tean barely heard him.

Jem spread his hands. He gave a tiny laugh. He looked around—the nonverbal equivalent of *What gives?*

"Ree," John-Henry said.

"A dancer at the Cottonmouth Club told us you were there Friday night," Emery said. "Dr. Leon, I can source those numbers—"

"Emery, Christ," Theo said.

"I don't know." Jem held out upturned hands. "I wasn't there."

John-Henry shook his head.

"Come on," Jem said. "I'm blond. I've got a beard. Average height. That's not exactly an unusual combination. Hell, if somebody saw us from behind, they could get you and me confused, or Theo."

"North," Shaw said softly.

"What are you talking about?" North straightened in his seat. "He was at the Cottonmouth Club?"

"It's been a strange couple of days," John-Henry said. "And one of the strange things is that you and Dr. Leon showed up, and this woman died, and your friend got arrested, and you haven't been able to stay out of things since."

"Hold on," Auggie said. "Aren't we jumping the gun a little?"

"Jem," Tean said. That darkness stretched wider inside him. It was like a pool of water. If something fell, the ripples would spread, rings of them rippling outward. He felt like he had to hold himself very still. "What are they talking about?"

"I don't know," Jem said. The hint of anger was just right. Confusion bleeding into frustration and fear. The best lies, Jem liked to say, were the ones that were true. "I wasn't at the Cottonmouth Club."

Emery snorted.

"What kind of evidence do you have?" Theo asked. "You're putting a lot of pressure on him because a dancer described a blond man at the club."

"The fuck were you doing at the Cottonmouth Club?" North asked, voice rising.

"Everyone's getting so angry," Shaw said. "We all need to calm down."

"I wasn't at the club," Jem said. "I don't know what you want me to say. I was at the resort the whole night."

"We came here for the conference," Tean said, and even though it was true, he felt like he was lying. "And then Yesenia, and Missy—I don't know what you're accusing us of."

John-Henry sat back and glanced at Emery. Face unreadable, Emery pulled a folded piece of paper from his pocket and tossed it onto the table. It landed next to the animal photos: a sheet of copy paper, with a cheap color inkjet image. A photo—more accurately, a security still. Of Jem. In the background, a bar was visible, and a woman was frozen mid-spin on a pole.

Tean looked at Jem. He saw the lie already weaving itself together.

"Now just a second," Jem began.

"You lied to me?" Tean said.

"Of course not."

"I thought—" What almost came out was, *I thought we were done with that*. Tean managed to stop himself, but not before hurt sparked in Jem's eyes. "I asked you where you'd been. When you came back, when I texted you after Missy got arrested, I asked you what you'd been doing. And you lied to me."

"I didn't lie to you." But now it was like all those layers of transparencies, all those superimposed Jems, had gotten scrambled, and the lie was weak and obvious.

"What about that?" Tean nodded at the security still.

"I'm trying to tell you—"

"Did you do what they're saying? Did you go to that club?"

"Will you let me finish one goddamn sentence?"

"There you go, then," Tean said. "That's the answer. You did. You went to that club like they said, and you're still lying about it. The proof is right there, and you can't even tell me the truth right now."

"If you'd let me explain—"

Lurching away from the table, Tean shook his head.

"Dr. Leon," Emery barked.

"Tean, wait a second," Jem called.

Tean glanced back in time to see Jem start after him.

Theo stepped into Jem's path. "I think you need to answer a few questions."

"Get out of my way. Tean, please!"

"Dr. Leon, we're not finished," Emery said.

"I need a minute," Tean said. "I need some air."

"I said get out of my way," Jem said, hand dipping into his pocket, cocking his shoulder like he meant to drive through Theo.

"Sit down, Jem," John-Henry said.

"This is all wrong," Shaw was saying over everyone else. "Everybody calm down."

Jem's hand started to come out of his pocket.

"Jem," Tean said, and the shock in his voice must have transmitted itself, because Jem gave a furious shake and settled back onto his heels. After a moment, Tean said, "I can't do this right now. I'll—I'll be back."

"Where the fuck do you think you're going?" North shouted after him.

Tean slipped out of the multipurpose room and let the door fall shut behind him.

12

Tean couldn't go far; he knew that. He had left Jem, left him with strangers, with men who didn't trust him. Who had no reason to trust him. The opposite, in fact, since the proof of Jem's lie was right in front of them. A distant part of Tean's brain registered the reality that Jem might even be in danger; how well, after all, did Tean really know those men? What might they want from Jem, and what might they do if Jem resisted, fought back, did something reckless?

He had barely made it to the water cooler at the next intersection when he realized he had to go back. He turned around as John-Henry emerged into the hallway.

The blond man was still dressed in the linen suit he'd worn to the cat sanctuary, and he gave Tean a tired smile as he moved to join him. A nice smile, Tean decided. It might have been fake; people said Ted Bundy had been quite charming. But in that moment, when the hurt and disappointment and, beneath them, the fear were so great, Tean latched on to that smile.

"That was a lot," John-Henry said. "I want to apologize. I'm sorry it happened that way."

Tean shook his head.

"I didn't want to do that, if it makes any difference."

Tean thought about shaking his head again to that, but the effort seemed too great. He heard himself say, "You're separating us."

John-Henry cocked his head. The smile dimmed. But all he said was, "Nobody's going to do anything to Jem, but he did seem pretty upset. Of course, you seem pretty upset as well. I thought maybe you'd like to call him, and then he can go back to your room, and you can get some air."

"And someone will watch the room. And you'll watch me."

"Help me understand what's going on here," John-Henry said. "Why don't we start there?"

So, Tean called Jem. The breathing on the other end of the call was agitated, and Jem blurted, "I'm sorry."

"It's ok," Tean said, and that was his first lie of the evening. "Are you ok?"

"Fine. They're all giving me dirty looks, but nobody tried anything." He gathered himself like he was getting ready for a jump. "Are you ok?"

"Yes." And that was the second lie.

"Tean." The despair in that syllable said Jem, as usual, had heard the truth. "I fucked up. I'm sorry. I can explain it. Do I really have to tell you I didn't kill Yesenia?"

"What? No, no. Of course not. It was just…Jem, why did you lie?"

Over the call, Jem's breathing softened, and it felt like a long time before he answered. "Will you come back? This feels silly, talking on the phone like this."

"John-Henry wants to talk to me. And they want you to go back to our room."

"Fuck what they want. I want to see you. I want to make sure you're ok. They can't make us do anything."

"I told him I'd talk to him," Tean said, which was another lie. "Will you please go to our room? I'll be back in an hour. Less."

Jem's breaths rasped in Tean's ear.

"I'll be back in an hour," Tean said again, more firmly. "Please go to our room, and don't do anything—don't do anything I wouldn't do."

Another of those long moments stretched out. "Tean, I'm sorry."

"I know." Tean swallowed. "I'll see you soon."

He disconnected. John-Henry was gracious enough to look off into the middle distance, his expression neutral. When Tean cleared his throat, though, he glanced over and asked, "How are you doing?"

"Terrible."

John-Henry nodded. "Why don't we go for a walk?"

They left the resort, and for the first hundred paces, as they followed a concrete path along the embankment, Tean didn't recognize the kindness. But then his body began to remember how to move, and the smell of the lake and the honeysuckle registered, and even the heat, pressing against him like it was determined to wring every drop of sweat out of him, was a kind of relief. The pain pulled back a few inches, and then Tean had to try not to cry. They kept walking, and the stars were bright over the hills, the water was like that stillness inside Tean, that dark, waiting place ready to ripple whenever it was touched. They passed under a line of hickory, and a bird startled overhead—a big bird, its wings flapping, branches creaking and clacking as it cleared a path and flew away from Tean and John-Henry.

John-Henry swore, hand going to his hip. Then he gave a shaky laugh, and the linen jacket fell into place over his gun.

"Owl," Tean said.

"Yeah," John-Henry said. "God, that one was huge, right?"

"Probably not as big as you think. They're big birds, but at night, especially when they surprise you, they seem a lot bigger. And all those feathers, the wings—they don't help." Tean smiled, although it felt thin and diluted, like the starlight in the folds of the lake. "They're part of the genus *strix*. One of Linnaeus's names. It's the Latin word for these mythical vampire-owl monsters."

John-Henry gave him a long look. "Which is a kind way of telling me that people have been scared of owls in the dark for a long time."

Shrugging, Tean thought of that darkness inside him. "We're all scared of the dark. We're scared of places we don't know, and the dark is the fundamentally unknowable place. It makes what we do know unfamiliar. You can spend your whole life somewhere, know it inside and out, and at night, in the dark, it still becomes frightening, part of a world we don't know. Artificial lighting—in the sense of the kind of lighting we're accustomed to now—changed the world for humans. It let us reclaim the night as part of our world. Until, of course, the power goes out." His smile stretched, and he said, "Sorry; sometimes I forget how weird I am." He heard himself add, as though it were a kind of explanation, "Jem doesn't mind listening."

To his surprise, John-Henry grinned. "Someday, you're going to have to ask Ree about vampire stars."

"I think I'm having my usual effect on him. I'm not trying to argue, but sometimes I forget not everyone wants to discuss things the way I do."

"Are you kidding? He lives for that kind of thing. After you corrected him about the animal sanctuaries, I had to listen to all his counterpoints and rebuttals and outlines, everything he wanted to say to you. It went on for an hour, I swear to God. He's a little intimidated by you, but don't tell him I said that. It's the doctorate." John-Henry's gaze grew thoughtful. "How good are you at yelling?"

"Not…great?"

"You'll figure it out."

Tean had no idea what to say to that, so they walked in silence for another dozen yards.

"How long have you two been together?" John-Henry asked.

"We've known each other almost three years. We had…a rough start, I guess."

"You're married?"

Tean nodded.

"And let me guess," John-Henry said, "he's lied to you before."

The sound of their steps on the concrete seemed very loud in the darkness.

"Sorry," John-Henry said. "That's none of my business. I asked because—well, if you want to talk about rocky starts and bad behaviors repeating themselves, I'm kind of an expert." In the weak light, it was hard to tell for certain, but it looked like he blushed. "Ree and I went to high school together. I was not a good person. Actually, that's letting myself off easy. I was horrible. I was scared of who I was, and Ree was…not. So, I had to punish him for that. I tortured him, literally."

Tean turned, taking in John-Henry again. It was easy to see it: the remarkable good looks, the natural athleticism, the easygoing smile, the boy who would have been friends with everyone without even trying. Tean knew the type; Ammon was the type, or at least, shared some of those qualities.

"He forgave me," John-Henry said with a tight smile, "in case you're wondering. I'm still working on forgiving myself. Of course, then I turn around and do something downright shitty, so, like I said, bad behaviors repeating themselves. It doesn't mean I don't love him. And it doesn't mean I don't want to do better. I just screw up now and then." His smile broadened. "It helps that Ree has his own share of screw-ups."

The breeze picked up, dragging on Tean's hair, carrying the fishiness of the lake and something else—a mixture of body odor and cannabis that, for a moment, Tean thought might be John-Henry. Then the breeze settled again, and the stink faded.

"This is…not what I expected," Tean said.

Out across the water, the red aircraft warning light blinked on and off.

"Jem is such a good person," Tean finally said. "If you think he killed Yesenia, you're wrong. If you think he's trying to hurt someone, you're wrong."

John-Henry said nothing, and the silence became an undertow, dragging more out of Tean.

"I lost my temper." Tean rubbed one eye. "I hate losing my temper. He doesn't understand why I get upset, even though we've talked about it dozens of times. For him, it's all so…I don't know if easy is the right word, but things aren't so charged. For me, everything is charged. Fraught. I don't know how to turn it off."

"Maybe you could help me understand what exactly is going on."

Tean laughed. "That would be nice, wouldn't it? I don't know what's going on. I'll have to talk to Jem. If you want my guess, Jem went to that place because he thought somebody was an easy mark. Like—" He stopped himself.

"Like Shaw," John-Henry finished.

"It has nothing to do with intelligence. That's not what I'm trying to say. I'm sure Shaw is very smart. For heaven's sake, Jem can put one over on me as easily as he does anyone else. It has to do with knowing how people work, and it has to do with knowing how to make people want things, or be afraid of things, or…believe."

John-Henry was silent for a long time. "What else has he done? What are we talking about? The animal psychic thing seems harmless, but if you say there's more…"

When the wind picked up this time, the lake rolled against the shore, a sloshing sound like a kid shaking a mason jar.

"I'd like to go back now," Tean said.

"I think we need to finish this conversation."

"Jem didn't hurt anyone. And right now, he's terribly upset, and I need to make things right with him. That's all you need to know."

Frustration marred John-Henry's features, and as he opened his mouth, Tean braced himself for the argument.

Then the darkness behind John-Henry gathered, took on shape, and a figure burst out from the underbrush. In the ambient light, the baseball bat was barely more than a silhouette, a gleam of starlight on polished wood. Their attacker rushed up behind John-Henry, and even as Tean opened his mouth in a warning, he knew it would be too late.

He grabbed John-Henry and dragged him to the ground. They hit the concrete walkway in an explosion of breath, and the bat whistled through the air overhead. A man shouted, rage and frustration, and the bat swung through the night again, coming down toward Tean's head. Tean scrambled backward—a crabbing, scuttling motion on hands and feet. He had an impression of John-Henry rolling in the opposite direction. Then the attacker turned toward Tean again, and Tean forgot about everything else.

It was dark outside, but as Tean got to his feet, he could make out enough details to recognize Colin Rangel. Under a mask of shadows, he no longer looked young, and he'd lost his tired prettiness. He looked furious and petulant, with a bully's sneering satisfaction as he came at Tean with the bat. Behind Colin, another man moved toward John-Henry, who was still picking himself up, reaching for a gun that, Tean saw, he'd lost in the fall. Tean guessed this second man would be Quinn. Something crackled in his hand, a nasty, electric spark and pop, and for a moment, a jagged, violet current arced on the stun gun.

"Said don't kill you." Colin grinned—a smear of white interrupting the darkness. "Bring you back, you and your butt-buddy. Didn't say anything about hurting you, though."

He lunged, bringing the bat up over his head. It was one of those ridiculously overblown moves, so dramatic that it felt, for a moment, choreographed. His brain made the instant connection to every fight scene of *Buffy*, which was easy since Jem had made him watch all seven seasons. Then he realized that, overblown and dramatic and choreographed or not, the bat was probably going to break his shoulder when it connected.

Colin swung the bat, and it came down with that hiss of displaced air. Tean backpedaled, stumbled as he stepped on a branch, and caught himself. The bat missed him, but that rush of displaced air licked the side of Tean's face, hot and damp, and his body unleashed another flood of adrenaline. His vision narrowed to Colin and the bat. Tean readied himself to run, to lose his attacker in the trees as he made his way back to the resort. Then John-Henry let out a shout, and Tean realized, with the dark pull of despair, that he couldn't run.

Still moving backward, Tean caught sight of what had tripped him a moment before: a branch that had fallen across the trail. If Colin had noticed, he gave no sign of it; he advanced toward Tean, giving big, warm-up swings with the bat, like he was stepping up to home plate. He was still smiling. Tean wondered if Colin Rangel knew how to hit someone with a bat and not kill them. He had the feeling, as he looked at the nasty streak of a grin breaking up the darkness, that Colin might have a habit of getting carried away.

What Tean needed right then was Jem. Not because Jem would have thrown himself between Tean and Colin—although Jem would have done it, and without even thinking about it. Tean needed Jem because Jem would know what to do. All Tean could think about was how to scare off a mountain lion, or what to do if you stumbled across a bear. The problem was that Colin wasn't a mountain lion or a bear. If he was any kind of animal, he might have been a feral dog, only brave enough to attack something defenseless, or when he was with his pack. If Tean had a gun, or maybe even a knife, Colin would have run. Of course, Jem never carried a gun or a knife, and he still managed to take care of himself.

The plan crystallized in that instant. Tean dug into his pockets and came up with loose change and a hotel keycard. Colin brought the bat back again, putting his whole body into the swing. As Colin stepped forward, Tean threw the handful of change at his face. Colin closed his eyes instinctively and caught the stick with his foot.

The stumble was nothing, really. A moment when Colin was off balance. The bat whiffed harmlessly through the air, and Colin swayed. Then he steadied himself, planting his foot on the concrete again, his body compensating automatically for the disruption.

It was enough. Tean charged into the younger man, planted both hands on Colin's chest, and shoved. Colin rocked backward, arms windmilling as he tried to keep his balance. The bat clipped Tean's arm—bad luck more than anything else, Colin whipping the bat around as he tried to keep his balance. And then Colin passed the tipping point, and he fell. The lake seemed bright and open under the starlight, but the embankment was a steep drop into darkness, and Colin screamed as he fell. The scream went on for what felt like a long time, interspersed with thuds and the crack of breaking branches. Then the screaming stopped, but the sounds of his fall continued. Silence punctuated the end of the fall. No splash, a part of Tean's brain registered. No cries for help.

Then John-Henry shouted again, and Tean dragged his attention back to the fight. Quinn Rangel, with his slicked-back hair and his dead eyes, darted forward again. The stun gun in his good hand crackled, and he kept his bandaged hand tight against his chest. John-Henry dodged the attack. The blond man made it look easy, but frustration showed in his face as his gaze cut back toward Tean. It was clear that Quinn, now lacking the advantage of surprise, wasn't having any luck getting John-Henry with the stun gun. It was also clear that John-Henry wasn't willing to abandon Tean, but he couldn't get past Quinn.

Tean raised an arm to signal that he'd head for the trees, hoping that John-Henry would understand and withdraw, but before he could do so, Emery emerged from the trees. He came out from a stand of pines, moving quickly but without any apparent sense of hurry, and he was carrying a three-foot section of fallen branch. It looked, to Tean's newly acquired first-hand experience, about the same size as a baseball bat.

Quinn's head snapped sideways, his attention settling on Emery. For a moment, Quinn seemed indecisive. He shot a look at Tean, but if he was surprised not to see his brother, he didn't show it. Then he whipped his attention back to Emery again. By then, Emery had closed the distance between them to a few yards. The big man hadn't said anything. His face was pale, almost luminous in the starlight, and when he glanced at Tean, his eyes glinted like chips of amber fire.

The remaining Rangel brother broke and ran. Emery took two sprinting strides after him and hurled the branch straight at Quinn's back, like he was throwing a javelin. The blow caught Quinn between the shoulder blades — or that's what it looked like, anyway. Quinn stumbled. And then he went right off the embankment, just like his brother.

He screamed. Then there was a sound like a body striking stone, and the scream ended. For what felt like a long time, they listened to Quinn fall into darkness.

"Jesus," John-Henry said, his breathing fast, his face flushed. "Good timing, babe."

Emery grunted as he moved to the edge of the embankment and looked down. Tean hurried down the path, and by the time he reached them, Emery was stepping back, shaking his head.

"I'm not going down there," he said. "It probably wouldn't be too bad in the daylight, but I'm not breaking my fucking neck for those two brainfucks."

"That's a bad fall," Tean said. "They're injured, perhaps seriously. They might even have gone into the lake."

John-Henry gave him a strange look, but all he said was, "Ree's right. I don't want any of us risking ourselves going down there in the dark. I'll call from the resort, say I heard something while I was out for a walk. They'll send somebody to check."

Tean bit the inside of his mouth. After a few seconds, he nodded.

"What are you fucking doing when I'm not looking?" Emery asked Tean. "Sending up a signal flare for those pieces of shit?"

Tean let out a weird breath that he realized was kind of a laugh. "He said they were supposed to bring us back alive." And then the rest of what Colin had said came through. "I think he thought—I think he thought John-Henry was Jem."

Emery grunted again. "I always thought Colin needed glasses. Too fucking vain."

That weird laugh escaped Tean again, and he pressed his hand to his mouth to stop it.

"It's not that I'm not grateful," John-Henry said, "but what are you doing out here? I thought you were watching Jem?"

"I left Heckle and Jeckle in charge," Emery said. Then, settling himself to face Tean, he said, "I understand the argument that people in developing countries may choose to participate in animal trafficking because it seems necessary, but that willfully ignores the fact that many other people in those same countries choose not to participate in trafficking and find other sources of income. In fact, that kind of behavior is, over the long term, counterproductive to a nation's wealth and natural resources, and under no circumstances could it be considered ethical behavior from a Kantian framework."

Tean stared at him. Finally, he managed to say, "What?"

"You came out here," John-Henry said, voice taut, "to argue with him?"

"I came out here to finish a conversation using logic, reason, and hard evidence—"

John-Henry took Tean's arm and started him walking back to the resort.

"John, hold on."

"Keep walking," John-Henry said.

Tean nodded.

"John, the path is too narrow for me to—" Frustration laced Emery's voice. "If you'd trade places with me, I could finish explaining to Dr. Leon—"

"Mary, Mother of God," John-Henry said.

"Maybe we should walk faster?" Tean asked.

"If only it were that simple," John-Henry said.

But he did pick up the pace.

13

Their hotel room had been destroyed.

Jem flipped over a suitcase. He picked up an armful of clothes from the floor—his and Tean's, mixed together—and dumped them on the bed. He slotted one of the dresser drawers back into place. One of the assholes who had searched the room had smashed a lamp against the wall, and Jem carried the trash can under one arm and started picking up the biggest pieces.

His mind kept playing back those awful moments in the multipurpose room: John-Henry's fucking cop eyes, that fucking cop voice, that fucking cop's way of talking until you were in a corner and you didn't have a fucking chance. He dropped a ceramic shard that had once been part of the lamp, set down the trash can, and went to open the window. It didn't open, so he tried the balcony slider. That didn't open either, which didn't make any sense because it was a slider. The whole point was for it to open. He tried again. And again. And then he went at it, yanking on the handle in furious, repetitive jerks as his body heated and sweat prickled all over him. With a short bark of a yell, he shoved on the handle and released it. The door remained closed. In the half-reflection of the night and the glass and the room's dim light, he looked like he was swimming.

"It's locked," Tean said.

Jem wiped his forehead as he turned. Tean stood just inside the room, door shut, behind him, arms folded across his chest. A dark mark on one arm, where the sweater polo's sleeve rode up, looked like a bruise starting to form.

"You have to unlock it first," Tean said gently.

Jem nodded and wiped his face again. When Tean's gaze moved, taking in the room, Jem said, "I didn't—it was like this." His voice sounded thick, and he didn't recognize himself in it.

Tean's response was to walk across the room, still hugging himself. Most of the light was behind him now, and shadows shifted across his face, his shoulder, his arm. Was it a bruise? That seemed very important in the moment.

Slipping past Jem, Tean fiddled with slider's handle, and a moment later, the door opened on its track. A wall of lukewarm air pressed into the room, sticky against Jem's skin and smelling like mulch and water and old cigarette smoke. Fresh sweat popped on his chest like fireworks.

"Is that better?" Tean asked. Then he touched his glasses like he wanted to resettle them and blurted, "I'm sorry for how I reacted. I shouldn't have shouted at you. I definitely shouldn't have—have left you with them."

"You're sorry?" Jem asked. "I'm a fucking moron. I'm sorry. I'm the one who fucked up." He tried for a smile, but it felt like it canted, like it might slide right off his face. "All they did was give me dirty looks and walk me back here, so you don't have to worry. They didn't even beat me up or anything."

For a moment, there was nothing but the sound of water, and the simmering heat closing like fingers around Jem's throat.

"Do you want to talk about it?" Tean asked.

"I want to keep saying I'm sorry. Like, a million times. Does that count as talking about it?"

A smile worked its way to the surface, and somehow, the worst of it was over. Jem cleared the clothes from the bed, sweeping them into one of the empty suitcases. He squared up the mattress. He straightened the comforter. His face grew hot when he realized he was smoothing the wrinkles out with one hand, and he wondered, if he were in one of those old-fashioned books Tean sometimes read, if he'd be laying down a handkerchief next, or whatever shit those guys did.

Jem did a little flourish, and Tean's small smile rose to the surface again as he sat. He held out his hand, and Jem took it and sat, and their knees bumped.

"So," Jem said, dropping his eyes to the carpet again, "I shouldn't have, you know, done that. Running that game, first off. Although how I was supposed to know Shaw would end up being a private detective, I have no idea. He literally fell out of his underwear while we were talking." He struggled with how to explain the rest of it: hearing everyone call Tean Dr. Leon, and seeing the posters and the conference programs, all those names with impressive initials behind them, all the words that Jem had to stop and sound out, and even then, they didn't mean anything to him. Feeling like he'd walked through the wrong door, and everyone was staring at him, even though he knew that was all in his head. Feeling like they knew, somehow, that he didn't belong here. Didn't belong with Tean, maybe, in particular. "There was this guy," he finally said, "in a Sonic the Hedgehog t-shirt. And I was trying really hard to be good."

The rest of it flowed, more or less, and he told Tean all of it: DeVoy, the pictures, the mixed motivation of wanting something interesting and the belief that Tean would want to know about someone trying to sell exotic birds. Jem managed to stop short of saying, *I thought you'd be proud of me,* but only barely. Then the Cottonmouth Club, his skin crawling by inches, the girl they'd forced, stumbling, through a door to a back room, the van.

"Like I said," Jem finished, "I fucked up. And when you asked—I wasn't trying to lie to you. I mean, I was, but not because I wanted to lie." His eyes felt hot. "I guess it doesn't matter why."

Tean adjusted how their fingers wove together. His free hand stroked Jem's arm, brushing the blond hair there lightly.

"Could you say something, please?" Jem asked. "Anything? How's your swearing? Have you been practicing?"

"I'd be lying if I said I wasn't—well, unhappy, I guess." Tean's nails scritched lightly at the sensitive skin on the inside of Jem's arm. "I don't like that you lied to me, but I understand it's more complicated than that, and things got out of hand. And I don't like..." Voices came from the hall, filtering through the door, a babbling enthusiasm that told Jem the biologists had gotten into the appletinis. "I mean, we've talked about this."

Jem nodded. The drunken biologists passed their room, words and laughter fading, and Tean was still waiting. "I'm sorry," Jem said.

Tean shook his head.

"It was a one-off, I promise. I did something dumb. I'm not going to do it again."

"I should have known."

"What's that supposed to mean?"

"Did something happen?" Tean asked.

"You should have known what?"

"Did someone say something to you? Did someone make you mad?"

"What are you talking about?" Jem squared up on the mattress to face Tean. "I told you: it was a one-off."

"But I should have known! You read about it all the time, about spouses knowing what their partner is thinking, about finishing their sentences."

"That sounds fucking awful, if you ask me."

"You read about how they're across the country, or halfway around the globe, and they know when something bad happens."

"Boring," Jem said. "That's not our jam. We like a little variety."

"Some husband is out working on his tractor, out of sight, on the back forty—"

"The back forty," Jem said and tried not to rub his temples.

"—and the tractor tips over, falls on him, pins him—"

"Maybe he should have set the safety blocks a little better."

"—and he's stuck there, with massive internal bleeding, unable to get help—"

"Think about it this way," Jem said. "He's a busy guy, right? He's finally got a few quiet minutes to sit and decompress."

"He's not going to decompress; he's going to decompose."

"He's a farmer. He probably likes that. Circle of life, all that stuff."

"No, he hates it. He wanted to be a librarian, only his stern and demanding puritanical father made him take over the family farm, and now he's going to die. He's going to hemorrhage out. Or maybe the internal bleeding isn't that bad, and he's going to be pinned there, in the cold—"

"What time of year is it? Maybe it's spring. Maybe it's a beautiful evening, and the fireflies are out."

"—and the birds are going to peck out his eyes, tear off his nose and his ears, until wolves or coyotes come along and tear out his throat—"

"A real St. Francis kind of situation, huh?"

"—only back home, his partner knows. She has this sudden sense of danger, and she rushes out to the back forty with—with Bessie, their mule—"

"This scenario is getting eerily detailed."

"—and they pull the tractor off him, and they get him to the doctor, and he's all right."

"You didn't talk about the mountain of medical bills," Jem said. "What about the inevitable foreclosure on the farm? That evil bank guy from the old Christmas movie? And the guy and his wife end up living on the streets, selling their bodies, only nobody wants them because they're the human equivalent of beef jerky? Oh, and maybe the guy makes his wife into soup— during the Depression, everybody loved soup."

"What are you talking about?" Tean asked.

"What are you talking about?"

"I'm talking about—about us!"

In spite of himself, Jem felt a small smile hook his lips. A moment later, a hint of amusement creased the corner of Tean's mouth.

"What's going on?" Jem asked. "You're not upset because we don't have a psychic bond. You don't even believe in psychic bonds. So, what's really got you cranked? Are you mad at me because I ran a game? Are you angry because I did something illegal or unethical or whatever? Did you finally reach your breaking point because it's embarrassing to drag me around and…and explain me, I guess?"

Tean sat up a little straighter. "Jem, is that what you think—"

"Is it about the lying? Because I've tried to be good about lying. I mean with you, anyway. And I know I should have told you, only everything happened so fast, and the last couple of days have been a blur."

"Hey, hold on." Tean took Jem's hand. "I am not embarrassed by you. Well, I mean, that time you tried to get the barber to give you a *Fresh Prince of Bel Air* haircut, that wasn't the most comfortable moment of my life."

"I have the jaw for it. I could pull it off."

"I love you. You're so smart and talented and funny, and you put up with—with Bessie the mule."

That smile hooking Jem's lips pulled bigger.

"I am not embarrassed by you," Tean said again, scooting closer until their legs were pressed together. "I'm proud of you, of everything you've accomplished, everything you do for our family. I'm proud that I'm privileged enough, fortunate enough, just plain, um, damn lucky to have you in my life." Dusky color rose under the soft brown of Tean's cheeks. "I've been bragging about you for the whole conference, although I'm never going to admit that if you try to tell Hannah."

"Ok," Jem said. His eyes stung, and he whispered, "Swear jar. That was only a nickel one, though."

Tean kissed him, and Jem, after a moment, cupped the side of Tean's face and kissed him back.

"I am mad," Tean announced when he sat back.

Jem groaned.

"I am," Tean said. "I'd be lying if I said I wasn't. Lying has been a big problem for us in the past, Jem. It's—" He paused, and he looked like he was groping for the right word. "It's scary to me, to know that you can do it again. Did do it again. Because it was easier for you. That cost us so much before."

"I know. I swear to God, I know. I'm not going to do it again." Jem heard himself, and then he gave a shrug, unable to help the wry sharpness of his voice as he added, "Which, of course, is what all liars say every time. Including me."

Tean drew a deep breath. But if he was going to follow that thread, he changed his mind. "I'm also not happy that you took a risk like that."

"I wasn't in danger."

THE FACE IN THE WATER

"Especially without telling me."

"Tean, come on. This is the redneck butthole of the country. I can handle myself."

"Jem, something could have happened to you! Anything could have happened to you! You told me they cornered you behind a van, and they saw you, and then those men tracked you back to the resort!"

After a glance at the door, Jem made a lower-your-volume gesture with his free hand. "Ok, but—"

"No buts! Someone attacked me tonight. They thought—I don't know, it was all so fast."

"Someone attacked you? What do you mean, tonight? At the sanctuary—"

"No, here. Tonight. When I—when I went on that walk. They must have seen John-Henry from behind, mistaken him for you."

"Are they blind?"

"That's what I said," Emery said through the door.

Tean opened his mouth, but Jem said, "Holy God, Tean, are you ok?"

"He's fine."

"This is kind of a private conversation!" Jem shouted back.

"Then maybe you should consider using what my daughter, who is in preschool, knows is called an 'inside voice.'"

"Ok," John-Henry said, words muffled by the door. "Come on."

"They might be plotting—"

But his voice faded, presumably because John-Henry was shepherding him away.

"Are you hurt?" Jem asked. Then he remembered the shadow that might have been a bruise. "Your arm." He slid onto his knees, taking Tean's arm in both hands, and he turned it. The mark was above the elbow, still red, starting to darken. "Oh Jesus."

"Jem, it's fine."

"Does it hurt? Do you need ice?"

"It's nothing; it doesn't hurt." Jem opened his mouth, but Tean said, "Jem."

It cost Jem a lot to swallow, to surrender everything he wanted to say. The sting in his eyes was worse.

"Stop it," Tean said, fingers brushing at Jem's hairline. "It's not your fault."

"It is. It's exactly my fault."

"That's not what I'm trying to say. I'm trying to say that you took a risk. And I know you're smart. And I know you're competent. You're so good at everything you do—"

"I'm not very good at *Jane* fucking *Eyre*."

"Maybe you don't have to work your way through the entire AP Lit suggested reading list," Tean said, and for some reason, that brought a huge smile to his face as he continued to brush back Jem's hair. "My point is that I got angry because I was scared. And I don't like you lying and stealing—"

Jem rolled his eyes.

"I don't!"

"Yes, sir."

Tean fought a losing battle against another smile, and it was obvious when he spoke that he was trying to make his voice firm. "I don't. It's unethical, and it's immoral, and the cornerstone of civilization is—"

Jem gathered Tean's hands and kissed his fingertips. "I'll be good. I'll try so hard to be good."

For another moment, Tean smiled at him. Then the light in his face winked out, and he said, "Do you know what I thought, when—when that came out, when John-Henry wouldn't stop asking you, and you—" He stopped. Apparently, Jem's behavior had been awful enough that he couldn't even bring himself to describe it.

So, Jem nodded. To spare them both.

"What if something had happened? To you, I mean."

"You'd be fine," Jem said, but his voice was husky. "That twink at the afterschool program practically dropped his panties for you last week."

Tean wrestled a hand free and cuffed Jem—not hard, but not totally a joke either. "I don't like that kind of thing."

"Ok!"

"I don't like you joking around about that stuff!"

"I give up! I yield! Where's the white flag?"

Tean glared at him for another moment. Then his face softened. "I would die—"

"No dying."

"—like that farmer under his tractor—"

"No, Bessie would find you."

"—being eaten alive by crows and wolves and coyotes and—and ants, possibly raccoons—"

"Kind of an *Animal Kingdom* version of Golden Corral, I guess."

"—if anything happened to you. I love you so much, I would die if I lost you. Probably."

Jem couldn't help it. The grin burst out.

"Well, I don't know for sure," Tean grumped. "From a scientific standpoint."

"That's ok. I can accept probably."

For a long, quiet moment, Tean looked at him. The sound of the lake came through the open slider, and the smell of water, and that muggy blanket of heat weighing down every inch of exposed skin. "I would die," Tean said softly. "But it's more than that, Jem. We have two girls depending on us now. It's not just us anymore. I feel like a hypocrite saying that, because I know I'm the one who wants to learn the truth about Yesenia. But—but I can't do this on my own. You can't take risks, not without talking to me, not without telling me. I need you." He swallowed, and for the first time, tears slid down his cheeks. "And I know I'm at fault too. I know I—I owed you more than what I showed you tonight. More trust. More loyalty. It's hard for me, when everything from the past comes back like that, but you deserve better. And I'm going to work harder on showing you how proud I am of you. How proud I am that you're in my life, that you're willing to put up with all of my—my bullshit, and that you do it with a smile and with so much kindness that most of the time, with you, I feel normal, and that's something no one has ever given me before. I'm going to make sure you never feel like you're anything less than special and wonderful and perfect for me."

Jem reached up and thumbed away the tears. Tean's ragged breathing made him tremble.

"We'll both do better," Jem said. "How about that?"

Tean nodded.

"And I'm getting that Fresh Prince haircut."

Tean closed his eyes.

"I'm not going to be deterred by one small setback."

"Oh my gosh," Tean whispered.

"Deterred is a good vocab word."

More tears spilled down, but Tean gave a watery laugh and nodded.

"And don't think I missed that 'bullshit.' Swear jar."

This time, the laughter sounded solid.

"Because they're clearly finished, John," Emery said from the other side of the door. He knocked hard, the sound covering part of what he said next. "—don't have time to wait around while they fish each other's dicks out."

Tean's eyes bulged a little.

"To be fair," Jem said, "I was about to fish your dick out."

It was fun, after years together, to still be able to make him look so horrified.

Emery was knocking again by the time Tean reached the door. The big man gave him a cursory look and said, "A number of NGOs and non-profit organizations exist that are willing to compensate local poachers and traffickers at equivalent rates for doing conservation work."

"Did you look that up?" Tean asked.

"I'm sorry," John-Henry said. "He got bored, and he has his phone."

"It's a valid point," Emery said to his husband. To Tean, he said, "Well?"

"Uh, you're right?"

Emery didn't exactly puff up, but he did stand a little straighter, and he pushed past Tean with a satisfied grunt.

"Thanks," John-Henry said as he came into the room. "I'm going to be dealing with that for a week."

When John-Henry's eyes came to rest on Jem, Jem met his gaze. One thing he'd learned early—before Decker, although Decker had reinforced the point—was that staring matches, pissing contests, death glares, those were all stupid, bullshit moves. So, Jem smiled, shrugged, let one side of his mouth cock up, pure ruefulness.

"God," John-Henry said. Then he laughed. "You really are good."

Jem shrugged again, a real grin this time.

"Good at bullshit," Emery said.

"Thanks," Jem said.

"It wasn't a compliment."

"Imagine if he taught Colt how to do that shrug," John-Henry said.

"Thank you, John. Thank you for fresh fodder for my nightmares."

"I'm sorry about earlier," John-Henry said to Jem. "It's been a weird couple of days, and I had to ask. Are we good?"

"We're good."

"Bump his fist," Tean said. When Jem shot him a look, Tean added, "That's what you do with your friends."

The look on John-Henry's face almost made Jem lose it.

"He's serious," Jem said, stretching out a fist. "You have to learn to roll with it."

"Will you bump his fucking fist already so we can get on with this?" Emery asked. Then, to Tean, he said, "Name five reliable sources that I can use in future arguments about animals."

The look on Tean's face taught Jem that yes, he could actually be pushed even closer to the brink.

"Yeah," John-Henry murmured as he rapped knuckles with Jem. "I know what you mean."

14

They all settled down for Jem to tell his story again, this time with Emery and John-Henry as an audience.

"Where are the other guys?" Tean asked. "Should we wait for them, so Jem doesn't have to say it all again?"

"Auggie and Theo are having a conversation," John-Henry said, and his tone suggested it was anything but a friendly chat. "North and Shaw—"

"Are hunting for a leprechaun to fuck," Emery said sourly.

Jem burst out laughing.

"It's not a joke," Emery said.

That made Jem laugh harder.

To Tean's puzzled expression, John-Henry said, "Emery's joking. Well, it's not a joke. One time Shaw—never mind, it's a whole story. They went back to their room once Emery and I got back from our walk. I think it's just us."

"So," Emery said, "tell the fucking story."

When Jem had finished, Emery said, "How stupid are you?"

"Moderately," Jem said. "I couldn't read until I was in my twenties. Tean had to teach me."

Emery opened his mouth. A scarlet fringe ran along his cheekbones, and he shut it again.

"Good Lord," John-Henry muttered. In a stronger voice, he said, "You took pictures of the birds?"

Jem nodded and opened the photos on his phone. John-Henry looked through the images first, then Emery, and then Tean.

"Well?" Emery asked.

"I don't know," Tean said. "This bird—" He indicated the one that was most visible. "—looks like an African gray parrot. They're highly trafficked and quite valuable. I can't tell about the rest, not from these photos."

John-Henry was silent for a moment. "You said you grabbed some of the stuff in the van. Can you be more specific?"

"Um, some of the IDs," Jem said. "Some of the animal stuff—a tiger penis, that kind of thing."

"A tiger penis?" Emery asked.

"A dried tiger penis."

"That doesn't make it any better."

"They're a commonly trafficked object," Tean said. "I read an excellent identification guide from the National Fish and Wildlife Forensics Laboratory on distinguishing real tiger penises from fake."

No one, it turned out, had anything to say to that.

"Anything else?" John-Henry finally asked. Then, dryly, "The drugs?"

Jem scratched his ear. "Um, no?"

"Uh huh." John-Henry looked around, taking in the state of their room. "I'm guessing you didn't do this yourselves."

"Wait," Tean said, "you think someone was looking for what Jem took?"

"It's obvious, isn't it?" Emery asked.

"Not to me," Jem said. "Because I'm a moron, remember?"

The red in Emery's cheeks deepened.

John-Henry looked a warning at Jem, but all he said was "Did they take anything?"

"Nope. I might be a moron, but I'm not stupid enough to hide a take in my own hotel room."

"That's a high bar to set for yourself," Emery muttered.

"Is that really what we think is happening here?" Tean asked. "Those guys showed up in Yesenia's room for reasons totally unconnected to her murder?"

"They were looking for me," Jem said. "I saw them in the lobby that night; they must have followed us to her room."

But Emery was already shaking his head. "That doesn't mean anything."

"I told you—" Jem began.

"I heard your version of events. Yes, it's possible that this man DeVoy, or someone connected to him, sent the Rangel brothers and their friends to bring you back. In fact, that seems to be correct, based on what happened tonight with John and Tean. But it would be a mistake to assume that these events are completely separate from the murder."

"Yesenia had those photos of trafficked animals in her room," John-Henry said. "That means we've got an overlap, not a coincidence."

"They were at the cat sanctuary," Tean said slowly, trying to think his way through events. "And they weren't looking for us, I don't think. They seemed as surprised as we were."

"Slightly less surprised, I'd think," Emery said, "since they managed to hold you at gunpoint."

Jem rolled his eyes and shot Emery the bird, but he said, "But we talked to Rod. Yesenia's death is bad for his business. I mean, we both thought he was, well, telling the truth, I guess."

"How scientific."

Jem gave him the bird again. "And you checked out the sanctuary; you said it's legit."

"I suppose he could have bribed the inspectors," Tean said. "I don't know. There are a lot of possibilities. But it does seem strange, them showing up there."

"At this point," John-Henry said, "we're not going to eliminate any possibilities. Someone is still trying to cover their tracks. That's got to be why the killer targeted Una tonight. We've got to move fast before we lose our shot at this."

"Meanwhile Jonas is pulling his pud in the station house," Emery grumbled. "This is technically a vacation, John. This is supposed to be my Father's Day present."

"Then you can stay and attend the panels tomorrow."

Amber eyes widened. "Are you out of your mind?"

With a quiet laugh, John-Henry stood and stretched and held out a hand to his husband.

"What's next?" Jem asked. "Heather? She tried to burn Yesenia's car. Or do we go back to the cat sanctuary and try to see what those guys were looking for? Or maybe check out Kristin? I know she's your friend, but the anesthesia angle is…weird. We could try to track down DeVoy's original buyer, but all I have is the first name Zach and a description; I'm not sure how far we'll get. Or you could look at what I scored from DeVoy's van."

"I do want to look at that stuff, but I think we have something time sensitive to do first." John-Henry grinned. "We're going clubbing."

"This is his dream," Emery said, scowling at Jem. "Thanks so very fucking much."

"Costume change," John-Henry said. "Meet in the lobby in ten. And Jem, please don't try to sneak out before us. We're a team now."

Chagrin filled Jem's face, and a protest began to form.

For some reason, that made John-Henry laugh.

"Looks kind of like Colt, doesn't he?" Emery said.

"That time you found the vape pod in his hoodie."

"I do not—" Jem began.

But by then, the two men were out the door, and Emery pulled it shut behind him.

"—look like whoever that is," Jem finished to Tean.

Tean pushed his hand through his hair. "I hate team sports."

15

In the lobby, Jem decided that while John-Henry might have a cop's eyes, and he might have a cop's assholish personality lurking under the boy-next-door charm, he definitely knew how to wear a t-shirt. And jeans. And God damn it, the Adidas were actually pretty dope. The tattoo sleeves, though, were the real surprise. Vanilla cop got a little more interesting.

Emery had changed clothes too, into a similar getup of jeans and tee, although Jem wondered if Emery had picked the ass-strangling cut or if that had been John-Henry's idea. Either way, the man had a serious rump.

Jem had opted for neon-green Puma shorts and a sleeveless black Nickelodeon tee (it was mostly characters from *Hey Arnold!*), although he'd done the mature thing and worn his ROOS instead of flip-flops. He'd also opted for one of his more respectable trucker hats: black and white with red letters, it had the Wienerschnitzel logo in front and then I HEART WIENERS. Tean, on the other hand, looked miserable in jeans and a white tee; Jem had already caught him twice trying to tuck in the t-shirt, and it looked like Tean was considering giving it another shot as soon as Jem got distracted.

"Five bucks say his balls fall out the first time he takes a full step," Emery said. "Did you have to tape your dick to the inside of those things?"

"Yes," Jem said. "Want to borrow them?"

Emery's expression tightened with annoyance.

The perpetual sound of Christmas music swelled, and then faded, and then in the silence of the empty lobby, a distorted voice blatted over the blown speakers, "That was *Christmas on Death Row*. Next up, the Reverend Horton Heat gives his take on a classic."

"I don't understand," Jem said.

"Big surprise," Emery muttered.

"Is it a radio station? Is that what we're listening to? An all-Christmas, year-round radio station? Or does the resort have their own DJ?"

"Jem," Tean said.

"I need to know what's going on. These are important questions."

"We'll take two cars," John-Henry said. "When we get there, I want Tean to stay in his car with the engine running. Tean, if you see someone matching DeVoy's description leave the building, follow him. Otherwise, you don't get out of the car for anything; if anyone approaches you—anyone that's not us—leave and call Chief Cassidy."

"He might be busy," Emery said, "with a corncob up his asshole, so feel free to call anyone more useful: the fire department, a stray dog, a floating turd."

"Ree and Jem are going inside," John-Henry continued as though Emery hadn't spoken, "where Jem will check to see if DeVoy is in the building. If he is, we'll try to flush him out; Ree, you'll cover Jem in case someone notices him. If he's not there—"

"We wait and break in later," Emery said. "It's not a complicated plan, John."

"What are you going to do?" Tean asked.

"I'll be waiting out back," John-Henry said, "in case DeVoy gives everyone else the slip."

"It sounds suspiciously like loafing," Emery said.

"My husband, everyone." John-Henry nudged Emery toward the door. "Here we go."

In the Jetta, Jem and Tean drove in silence. Jem tried the radio, but after scrolling through static and cowboy country and then the droning, nasally call for donations from a pastor, he turned it off again. In the light from the dash, Tean looked exhausted. He was trying to tuck in his shirt again, one hand on the wheel.

"We don't have to do this," Jem said, reaching over to tug the shirt free from Tean's waistband again. "We can tell them we changed our minds. You were right, what you said back at the resort. We've got other people depending on us."

Tean's quiet was a held breath, and they drove over the rolling hills, past the cut faces of limestone and granite, the headlights slicing wedges out of the night: the dazzle of quartz when the headlight struck the gravel shoulder just right; the woven branches of the canopy; a stick-like bundle of movement that Jem guessed was a fox. Tean was trying again with the shirt.

"Do you think we should stop?" Tean asked.

"We can stop."

"No, I mean—do you think we should? We should make these decisions together."

"These decisions about investigating murders?" Jem asked, but his light tone fell flat. After a moment, he said, "No. No, I don't think we should leave it. Something messed up is happening, and Missy shouldn't have to pay the price for it. But I'm also not the responsible one."

"I think you're very responsible. You make the girls' lunches every night."

"That doesn't carry as much weight when I find you've taken out all the good stuff in the morning."

A smile rolled across Tean's face and then was gone. "That's just fine-tuning. They don't need quite so many candy bars." After a pause, he said, "I don't want you to get hurt. I don't want anyone to get hurt. But I also don't want Missy's life to be ruined. That seems like pretty bad math; all these people I care about, and I'm putting you and the girls at risk, and on the other side of the scale, it's only one person."

Jem reached over and tugged on that wild, bushy hair. "I think we both think we need to do this."

Tean sighed and nodded. "Fine, but Jem, you can't go in there. They've got a picture of you. They're looking for you."

"We talked about this. If anybody else knew what DeVoy looked like, I wouldn't go. But we don't have any other option. Plus, I've got this spiffy wiener hat."

"Don't you dare joke about this. This is dangerous. This is serious."

Giving Tean's hair another tug, Jem said, "We'll be careful. It's going to be fine."

Another sigh. Another nod.

"And it looks better untucked."

"Jem."

"You're not a Greaser. You're not a Shark or a Jet. You're not the Fonz."

"Plenty of people wear their shirts tucked in."

"Yes, they do. But not white t-shirts with jeans."

"If I had a belt, it would look fine."

"Untuck it, please."

"It's more respectable this way."

"Respectable really isn't the vibe of this evening."

"I look stupid!"

"Teangelus Mahina Leon!"

"This is ridiculous!" But he untucked the shirt, yanking it out in big, dramatic movements. "Nobody cares whether I tuck in my shirt at work!"

"Holy Jesus, you've been tucking in your polos?" And then a realization struck. "After you leave the house?"

Tean must have sensed the trap because he hesitated. "No."

"I'm calling Hannah."

"You misheard me."

"I'm waking her up. This is a national emergency."

It was stupid stuff. But by the time they reached the Cottonmouth Club—when Tean was arguing his Constitutional right to tuck in or out any article of clothing he wanted, whenever he wanted—the high-wire tension in his body had loosened, and he looked more like Tean and less like a stressed-out crazy man who had jumped behind the wheel of the Jetta. Which was, after all, the whole point. Sometimes, stupid worked.

The Cottonmouth Club didn't look any different from the night before: the rambling building of corrugated steel panels, the quilted layers of paint, the empty sign holder, the missing letters with their patina of dirt spelling out the name of the club. Lights made dirty yellow blocks behind the tinted windows, and music pulsed, giving the club its own heartbeat. It was hard to tell, with the melody distorted by the volume and the rattling bass, but Jem thought the song might be "Milkshake," by Kelis. It had certainly brought plenty of boys tonight; the gravel lot was full.

When Jem slid out of the car, Tean said, "Please be careful."

Jem nodded.

"But my level of careful. Not your level of careful."

Jem nodded again.

"Do you have your tools?"

"I'm going to close the door now."

"Don't eat any of the food. Hold on, I can send you a link about *Staphylococcus aureus*—"

"I love you," Jem sang softly and then bumped the door shut with his hip.

As he left Tean behind him, though, his phone buzzed. Jem pretended to check it and gave his husband a thumbs-up for confirmation.

John-Henry and Emery were already waiting for him when he reached their Mustang.

"Ready?" John-Henry asked.

"As we discussed in the car—" Emery began.

"Great." John-Henry hesitated, and for a moment, the cop eyes looked out at Jem again, as though he might say something else. A warning, probably. Cops loved warnings. But then he just jogged off toward the side of the club.

For a moment, Jem and Emery traded looks. Then a truck rolled into the lot, headlights bouncing, and Emery shifted his weight.

"I guess we'd better split up—" Jem said.

"You go first," Emery said at the same time.

With a nod, Jem broke for the door. His last glimpse was of Emery pacing, pretending to read something on his phone. Or, since he was Emery, probably not pretending.

Inside, a wall of cool and light and odor met Jem. The air conditioning must have been working overtime, a respite from the muggy stillness of the evening outside. The club smelled like a deep fryer with oil that needed to be changed, and like body spray and cheap synthetic fabrics. It made Jem think of clothing growing warm from friction, of chafing bodies. It made him think of a rash. The lights were dim, but in contrast to the near total dark of rural Missouri, they still made Jem blink as his eyes adjusted. The club was as he remembered it: the bar, the tables, the private booths. TVs showed grainy footage of half-dressed women. On the stage, a topless woman in a silver bikini bottom paraded with heavy, Bride-of-Frankenstein steps. Tonight, Kid Rock had gotten bumped by The Scorpions and all their empty promises.

Jem stepped away from the door to let a heavyset man in overalls pass, and he used the movement to hop onto a stool, positioning himself as far from the bar and the stage as he could, where the club's yellowish light was weakest. Someone had been showing his picture around the club. Someone had been asking questions. That meant he couldn't walk up to the bar, couldn't ask a waitress for a beer. Not without taking a risk. If anyone else had seen DeVoy, he wouldn't be in here at all, but that was the problem about being a sneaky shit—it caught up and bit you in the ass eventually.

For a couple of minutes, Jem stayed where he was. The Scorpions gave way to Katy Perry. An iron-haired woman in a black apron held up a finger to Jem, like she'd get to him in a minute. A man stuffed bills into the dancer's bikini bottom, and she leaned over him and pretended to squirt milk from her breast into his mouth. Jem was grateful for the distance; he could pretend, to himself anyway, she was pretending.

Then he spotted DeVoy. He sat with a man Jem recognized from his first visit: the spray-tan guy, the one with the giant cross around his neck. DeVoy looked worse for wear—he was fidgeting, talking rapidly, casting blind, nervous glances around the room. It was hard to tell in the club's gloom, but it looked like one eye was swollen. Probably, Jem thought, because someone had knocked DeVoy around for being a dumbass. Not a good time to approach him, Jem decided. Not sitting in the middle of the club.

When Emery came through the door, Jem glanced at him the way he'd check anyone who came through the door, the kind of automatic assessment and dismissal—the rookie move would have been to ignore Emery completely, and Jem wasn't a rookie. Then Jem let his gaze drift back to the middle distance, where he could watch DeVoy while pretending to watch the stage. The waitress finally began to make her way toward Jem's spot in the back, and a knot tightened between Jem's shoulder blades. Before the woman could reach him, though, Emery intercepted her, snapping something that made the woman hurry toward the bar. Jem grudgingly chalked a tally in Emery's column; that had been fast thinking.

Settled on his stool, all Jem could do was wait until DeVoy left the spray-tan guy. As minutes ticked by and Katy Perry changed to Ariana Grande, other faces—familiar faces—caught Jem's eyes in the crowd. The sharp-jawed, blue-toned blond in biker leathers, holding court with a cluster of rawboned men and women who looked like they all might be distantly related. The square-jawed, clean-shaven guy Jem had seen on his last visit—a little bit like young-Mitt Romney-hits-the-gym. Two nights in a row, Jem thought. Well, well, well.

It took him a moment longer to find the big, blond action hero. The man sat in one of the private booths, the curtain partially drawn, and he seemed to be watching the crowd instead of the stage. When his head swiveled toward the back of the room, Jem leaned back on his stool and thought invisible thoughts. A moment later, his gaze moved on, and the fist squeezing Jem's chest eased.

Then DeVoy slunk out of his seat and scurried across the room, bent almost in half as he moved, the posture of a man who didn't want to draw anyone's attention. Jem slid down from his stool, pulled his hat lower, and started after him. DeVoy disappeared down a narrow hallway, and Jem picked up his pace. The bartender—a woman with a septum piercing and, to judge by how her vest fit her, other piercings as well—glanced at Jem as he passed. He thought she might have done a double take, but he didn't want to draw attention by looking back to check, so he ducked his head and went faster.

When he came around the corner, DeVoy stood less than five feet away. He had his phone in both hands, and he was typing something, fingers flying over the screen. He looked up, looked down, looked up again. Shock opened his face.

"Hey bozo," Jem said.

DeVoy ran.

It was a narrow hallway crammed between plywood walls, and from the reek, at least some of the doors opened onto what passed for restrooms. At the end of the passageway, an EXIT sign hung above a steel fire door with a crash bar. DeVoy sprinted toward it. Jem charged after him.

When DeVoy hit the door, it flew open. He turned his move into a spin and darted out of sight. The door started to swing shut. Jem caught the crash bar on his hip, felt the distant ping of pain that said he'd have a bruise, and clutched the side of the door to swing himself around it, following DeVoy's path. Gravel skittered under his sneakers, and for a moment, the loose stone might as well have been ice. But Jem's grip on the door stabilized him, and a moment later, he was planted again, and then he was running through the heavy drapery of the night's heat. DeVoy had twenty feet on him, and he was headed for the roll-up doors on the back of the club—the same place, a buried voice in Jem's head noted, where he'd gone the last time.

The closest roll-up door stood open, and as DeVoy jinked around the corner, he suddenly went flying. The thumping beat of the club's music partially swallowed the thud, the jangle of metal, and the cry of pain.

Jem kept running, for form's sake, and skidded to a stop at the opening to the door. John-Henry had his hands on his hips as he stared at DeVoy, who lay at the base of a set of metal shelves, surrounded by a fallen can of paint, a plastic-wrapped bundle of toilet paper, a roll of individually packaged condoms like a forgotten streamer from the world's saddest party. DeVoy moaned and stirred.

"Don't get up," Jem said and set one foot between his shoulder blades.

"Fuck happened?" DeVoy mumbled. His nose was clearly broken, and a long, bloody mark rashed one side of his face.

Still keeping his weight on DeVoy, Jem nodded to John-Henry, who squatted next to the fallen man and patted him down. John-Henry tossed a wallet, a vape, a phone, and a pack of Orbit gum (bubblemint, so, gross) onto the ground. John-Henry finished his search and gave Jem a shake of his head. Then he picked up the wallet and began going through it.

As the rush of adrenaline died, more details began to work their way to Jem's consciousness: the smell of motor oil, the stickiness of his bare skin, the relatively lighter rectangle on the floor of the garage, where the ambient light from outside reached. And then the more important detail hit him.

"Where the hell is the van?"

DeVoy moaned again.

"Hey." Jem jostled him with his foot. "Where's your van?"

"Fuck, man. Fuck."

"You're goddamn right. Where's your van?" He bore down, driving his weight into that spot between DeVoy's shoulder blades. "I'm asking you a question."

"Cadenas told me not to park in here!" When Jem eased up, DeVoy brought a hand to his face. "My nose, man. I can't breathe."

Jem scanned the garage, but the van didn't pop out of hiding. It had been a long shot, of course. Part of him had known that. But at the same time, it had seemed completely possible—if this was where DeVoy operated, if he had a hookup, the owner of the club, maybe the manager. Jem let the rest of the thought go unformed. He looked at John-Henry, unable to keep the frustration out of his face.

"DeVoy Foreman," John-Henry said. "License is valid, address in Warsaw. That's not far from here. A couple of hundred bucks. Phone is locked."

Jem made a gimme motion, and John-Henry tossed him the phone.

"Code," Jem said, toeing DeVoy with the sneaker again.

"I need a hospital or some shit."

"Code."

"You gotta let me sit up. I can't breathe."

"You're going to choke to death on your own blood if you don't give me the PIN to this fucking phone."

John-Henry rose to his feet, face fixed.

"Nine, nine, nine, nine," DeVoy said. "Come on, let me sit up."

A sole scraped the garage's concrete slab, and both John-Henry and Jem turned. Emery stepped under the roll-up door, those dark straw eyes already reviewing, calculating. "Let him sit up."

Jem opened his mouth.

"He's not going anywhere," John-Henry said.

After a moment, Jem set his jaw and stepped back.

As DeVoy scrambled into a sitting position, Jem unlocked the phone. It was an Android, the screen busted, with icons he didn't recognize. Once he was sure he had access to everything, he shoved the phone in his pocket and turned his attention back to DeVoy.

"All right," Jem said. "Let's hear it."

DeVoy touched his broken nose, flinched, and dropped his hand. Then, apparently possessed by a stroke of genius, he tore open the bundle of toilet paper and ripped several squares of paper from a roll. He wiped at his face, where the blood had slowed to a trickle.

"Hear what?" he mumbled from behind the paper.

"All of it," Jem said.

"Wonderful interview technique," Emery said.

"I'm handling this."

"Oh yes, I can see that."

"I told you to explain," Jem said. "Start with the animals."

DeVoy hocked a bloody loogie that barely missed Jem's sneakers.

"Here's the thing." Hands on knees, Jem leaned over DeVoy. "You tried to sell me a bird. And when I showed up, I found all sorts of interesting shit. You had birds stuffed in the van. You had IDs. You had drugs. Jewelry. So, when a woman disappears, and we learn she had pictures of the same kinds of animals in her room, I start to get curious. I'm going to tell you one more time to talk about the animals. The next time someone asks, you're going to be in cuffs, and you'll have a murder charge hanging over your head."

DeVoy was still clumping the toilet paper under his nose, and his hand stilled now. Outside, a diesel engine rattled to life, and someone gave a long, drawn-out cry of "Free pussy!"

After the sound of tires on gravel faded, DeVoy said, "What woman?"

"Yesenia Alvarez."

"Don't know her."

"Wrong answer," Jem said. "Face down on the ground, dumbshit. You can wait for the cops."

"Hold on," John-Henry said. He took out his phone, tapped the screen a few times, and came closer. When he held the screen toward DeVoy, it displayed a picture of Yesenia. "Her."

"Oh," DeVoy said. "Her. I know her. What happened to her?"

"That's convenient. You didn't know her. Now you do."

"Fuck off, man. I didn't know her name." DeVoy squinted—both eyes were definitely looking puffy now—and shrugged. "A friend put her in touch. Said she was looking to buy. She wanted something. A pet. I think that's what she said. It's been a while, you know?"

"Who's your friend?"

DeVoy shook his head and looked away.

"Let's try that again," Jem said.

But John-Henry held up a hand, like a warning, and Jem took a deep breath.

"Did she say anything about using those animals for a park?" John-Henry asked.

"I told you: she wanted a pet." DeVoy gave a tentative dab with the toilet paper again. "She didn't know what she wanted. She said a pet. So, I asked what kind, like a bird. She said maybe, but maybe something else.

Could she get a tiger? Could she get a chimp? I mean, that kind of thing. That's what I remember. I left her some pics while I went to get a drink. When I came back, she was gone. Took the pictures. I remember—I mean, I freaked. I thought she was a cop or a Fed or something, like it was a sting. But nobody came. Nothing happened."

"When was that?" Emery asked.

"A couple of months ago. Spring. It wasn't hot as balls like this, that's what I remember."

Jem tried to make that line up with the rest of the puzzle. What had Yesenia been doing in this part of the state a couple of months ago? Until now, he'd assumed that her connection to the animal trafficking had happened within the last few days, during her time at the conference. Now, though, DeVoy was telling him that she'd driven across half the state months ago, with the sole purpose of…what? Stealing some photos?

"She never contacted you again?" John-Henry asked.

DeVoy shook his head.

"She didn't come back and buy an animal?"

Another negative.

"Your friend," Emery said.

"Unh-uh," DeVoy said. "I'm not bringing him into this."

"That seems like a poor choice. Do you think he'd do the same thing for you? You're in trouble. The best way to get out of trouble is to help the shit roll downhill."

"He wouldn't roll, man. He'd shoot me in the back of the fucking head. Unh-uh. No way. You can take me to jail. Go on and take me. But if you do, I'm not telling you about the other lady. The one who got in a fight with that one."

John-Henry and Emery shared a look.

"I thought you didn't see her again," Jem said. "I thought Yesenia never came back."

"He asked me if she contacted me again. She didn't. He asked me if she came back and bought an animal. She didn't. But she was in here. I saw her, man. And she was mean."

"Go on," John-Henry said.

"That woman." He nodded at John-Henry's phone. "That one. She was in here a few nights ago."

"How many nights ago?" Emery asked.

"I don't know, man. Wednesday? Thursday?"

"She came to the Cottonmouth Club," Jem said.

DeVoy nodded.

"Why?"

"It's not like we had a conversation. She was in there, that's all. I was thinking maybe I should try to get the photos back. I mean, she wasn't a cop; when I saw her again, I could tell that wasn't her thing. She was sitting there, looking around. Then she smiled. Got out of her chair and walked right over to this white lady, this other lady just trying to buy something, you know what I mean?"

"Let me guess," Jem said. "You don't know what she was trying to buy."

DeVoy gave him a bloody smile.

"What happened?" Emery asked.

"The white lady was scared. They start talking real quiet, both of them, but fast. And you can tell this other lady wants to get out of there. She's trying to, but that lady—" He nodded to the picture of Yesenia on John-Henry's phone. "—she grabs her arm. They go outside together, and that's the last I seen of them."

"Doesn't sound like much of a fight," John-Henry said.

"You had to see it." DeVoy licked his lips. "She was in here tonight again. Brought her fucking TV like anybody wanted that piece of shit. Fucking desperate."

Jem dug out his own phone and did a quick search. A moment later, he found the website he wanted and, because luck was good tonight, a photo to go with it. When he showed it, DeVoy nodded.

"Fuck, man. That's her. That's her."

He showed the photo of Heather Weis, animal psychic and dog trainer, to Emery and John-Henry.

"Of course," Emery said in disgust.

But John-Henry grimaced.

DeVoy was looking from one man to another, clutching the bloody toilet paper, sitting forward like he meant to get up. "That's all, man. That's it. Now I got to go. My nose—"

"Hold on," Emery said.

"The animals," Jem said, "where do you get them?"

DeVoy flinched. For a moment, he was frozen, hand planted on the concrete, legs tensing like he might jump up and try to run again.

Then the door that connected the garage to the club's employee space— the same door Jem had used on his first visit—swung open. Yellow light fanned across the garage. The beat of the music swelled. And a man wearing a ski mask stepped through the doorway, bringing up a shotgun.

In that fraction of a second when the gun was still coming up, Jem's brain made the connection: the bartender staring at him, her uncertainty, her suspicion, a few minutes while she debated it, and then going to the club manager, or making a call, and then more minutes as a decision was made. The backlighting only gave him enough material for an impression: shorter than average, built like a man, bulky clothes. The shotgun barrel was matte, refusing to catch the light, barely more than another shadow.

Emery barreled into John-Henry, carrying both of them to the floor of the garage. He kicked one of the shelves hard enough to topple it, and it fell with a crash, spilling tools and cardboard boxes and plastic jugs of cleaner.

Jem processed that out of the corner of his eye, because as soon as he saw the gun, he started to move too. He spun toward the roll-up door, already putting on the speed, and immediately went down. Limbs tangled with his. A flurry of fists and feet, shouting. DeVoy, a part of his brain registered. DeVoy in a sheer panic, and they'd crashed into each other like two of the Three Stooges.

The gun boomed, and Jem waited for the pain, for worse. But nothing came. A moment later, he was free of DeVoy, scrambling to his feet. He charged for the roll-up when something caught his ankle. He went down again, glimpsed DeVoy clutching at his foot. Jem kicked, trying to get free. He had a glimpse of Emery and John-Henry barricaded behind the shelves. The man in the mask was swiveling toward Jem and DeVoy. The movement seemed almost comically slow, the gun coming up. Jem didn't need an explanation for why, momentarily, John-Henry and Emery had ceased to be the primary targets. Take the easy kill first. Then take your time.

Still on hands and knees, Jem kicked again, trying to shake off DeVoy. Hands grabbed his shoulders, and for a panicked moment, Jem twisted back around to fight off this new attacker.

"Come on!" Tean shouted, hauling on Jem. "Come on!"

A different kind of gunshot rang out, and Jem turned his attention—automatically, unable to help himself—to the sound. Emery had produced a pistol from somewhere and was firing blindly over his improvised barrier. The man with the shotgun swung back toward the attack and fired again. The boom echoed through the tiny garage.

Jem kicked again, and this time, DeVoy's hand fell away. Tean hauled him to his feet, and a moment later, the two of them emerged from the reek of gun smoke and hot metal into air that smelled like dog shit and prairie grass and gravel dust.

Behind them, DeVoy appeared under the roll-up door, eyes white with panic. The shotgun boomed again, and DeVoy dropped like someone had cut his legs out from under him.

"Emery!" Tean shouted. "John-Henry!"

"Go!" John-Henry shouted back. "Run!"

Jem grabbed Tean's arm, but Tean refused to be led. He shouted into the mouth of the garage, "I'm calling the police!"

"Get the fuck out of here!" Emery roared, and then gunfire exploded again.

Jem shook Tean by the arm, but Tean turned on him, wild eyed. "We can't leave them!"

Blood hammered in Jem's ears. Then he heard himself say, "For fuck's sake."

A jerrycan was tucked up against the wall next to the string trimmer. Jem sprinted over to it. He shook it, and gasoline sloshed inside. Unscrewing the cap, Jem carried it to the roll-up door. Then he laid the jerrycan on its side. As gasoline spilled out across the concrete, Jem gave the can a kick. It made a tinny noise of flexing metal as it slid across the slab toward the shooter.

The shotgun boomed again.

Jem spun to the side of the roll-up door, putting the wall between himself and the gun. Then he worked his lighter out of his pocket. He tried to roll a spark, but his hand was shaking. Adrenaline. Exhaustion. Fear.

Crouching next to him, Tean took the lighter. He ran the wheel once, and a flame danced. Without needing to be told, he bent and set the flame to the spilled gasoline.

Fire whooshed across the garage.

"Let's get out of here," Jem said, struggling to his feet. He and Tean ran, but Tean stopped after twenty paces, turned back, and watched.

Smoke drifted out of the garage. That much gas wouldn't have been enough to start a real fire—Jem knew that, not poured on a concrete slab like that, not without fuel to keep it going. But the point wasn't to burn down the club. The point was to—

John-Henry came first, emerging from the garage in a scuttling, crab-like movement that kept him low. Emery came next, a rearguard withdrawal, keeping his aim on the shooter inside the garage. Then both men seemed to recognize some kind of invisible signal, and they stood and sprinted.

"Now, dumbfucks," Emery said. "Run now!"

Jem and Tean ran.

16

Tean started shaking after they'd gone a mile. He white-knuckled the steering wheel as the road curved and cut along the side of a bluff. The headlights pocked the sheer stone face with dimples, divets, shadows. It made Tean think of fungus, the lines where rock had been drilled and blasted like gills. The tires drifted across the yellow line. The light and shadows drifted with them.

"Easy." Jem wrapped one hand around the wheel, and the Jetta slipped back into its lane. He smiled at Tean. "How're you doing over there?"

"Terrible."

For some reason, that made Jem's smile broaden, exposing those slightly crooked front teeth. "You look pretty good to me."

"I'm not. I'm dying. Probably."

"We're all technically dying. Dying is part of living."

Tean sat up a little straighter. "I meant in a more immediate sense. I'm dying right now. From fear."

"You? Nah."

Elbowing Jem away from the wheel, Tean said, "I am. I'm having a heart attack."

"Oh, ok."

"That can happen. Fear produces adrenaline. Adrenaline causes the heart to beat faster. The strain on the heart becomes tremendous, and it becomes unable to pump blood efficiently."

"Well, I mean, it's not a real heart attack."

"It can lead to death!"

"Ok, ok. It's very scary. It's a very scary heart attack. I mean, it's not a heart attack, but it's still very scary."

"It's terrifying!"

Aside from their headlights, the dark had closed around them completely. When they cleared the cut and left the shining walls of limestone behind, trees crouched at the shoulder of the road, branches plaited together overhead. There was no sign of Emery and John-Henry. No sign of anyone else following them. No sign of anyone anywhere.

"Are you dead yet?"

In spite of his best efforts, Tean gave up a smile. "How are you not...I don't know, freaking out?"

"Well, I was, actually. Remember? A few minutes ago? When I wanted to run like hell and you insisted on staying to help those guys, and I thought you were going to get killed, and then I'd probably go crazy out of grief, and I'd end up living on the streets, and eventually a john would choke me to death or something and throw my body in a river, and as I decomposed, little particles of me would drift down to New Orleans, and I'd spend the rest of eternity getting puked on by frat boys."

Tean drove a few hundred yards. He adjusted the rearview mirror. He checked Jem, saw Jem waiting to catch him, and looked straight ahead again.

"You're not supposed to say crazy."

Jem shrugged.

Tean fought and lost. "That's still one of the most romantic things you've ever said to me."

"I've got a very narrow target audience."

They followed the dark tunnel of the trees, and then the canopy parted overhead, and wheat fields unfurled under the starlight, and a big old buck startled and leaped a fence, and then he was nothing but a silhouette of antler tines and the white flash of his tail.

"Ok," Tean said. "I'm better now."

Jem kneaded the nape of his neck with one hand. With the other, he worked a phone out of his pocket. He placed a call on speaker. A moment later, John-Henry said, "You guys ok?"

Jem opened his mouth to speak, but the thunder of gunfire across the call stopped him.

In the background, Emery shouted, "Fuck you, you fucking existential excuse for a foot fetish."

"Are they chasing you?" Tean asked.

"What's an excuse for a foot fetish?" Jem asked.

"He's had a rough couple of days," John-Henry said. "Our friend from the garage is having a hard time shooting while he drives."

"Hard time?" Emery said. "He blew off the fucking mirror."

"We'll be fine," John-Henry said.

"Do you have any idea what that's going to cost?"

A grin sparked in John-Henry's voice as he continued, "As soon as we get to a straightaway, I'm going to drop him in my dust. You two?"

"Fine," Tean said.

Jem glanced at the rear window. "All clear."

"Get back to the resort and find North and Shaw. Better wake up Theo and Auggie too. Stick together until we get there."

"Back the fuck off, motherfucker!" Emery shouted, and then the staccato of gunfire hammered across the call. A moment later, it disconnected.

Letting out a breath, Tean looked at Jem.

"It's not my fault," Jem said. "This time."

"I know it's not your fault."

"Also, since I failed to report this earlier, you're a kick-ass wonder-butt. Did you know that?"

"I don't have any idea what a wonder-butt is, so, no."

"You literally saved me from certain death. You're my hero. You're officially the butch one."

"I always thought—I mean, considering our footwear—" Tean stopped himself. Barely. He forced himself to look straight out the windshield.

Then he couldn't stand not knowing anymore.

Jem was covering his grin, but amusement crinkled the corner of his eyes.

"I didn't—that's not what I—" And then Tean snapped, "Well, you started it!"

"I love you so much."

Tean sighed. "I know."

At that point, Jem had to kiss him on the cheek. Several times. Until Tean elbowed him away, actually.

"Seriously," Jem said, laughing as he fell back. "How did you know I needed my ass hauled out of the fire?"

"The gunshots were a good clue."

"Ouch." But Jem was grinning.

"And I have a general policy that if you're quiet for more than fifteen minutes, some sort of chaos is being unleashed."

"Teanarchy Leon! Double ouch!"

"Last time I followed that rule, you were trying to squeeze Scipio into that hot dog sweater."

"It's his Halloween costume."

"In July."

"We had to make sure it fit."

"And you were wearing your own hot dog suit."

"Because we had to match."

"And somehow," Tean said, "you'd gotten your zipper stuck to his."

"I was checking to see if they'd—no, I don't have to explain myself. And I cannot believe you came to us out of a place of judgment. I thought you were our savior!"

Tean smiled in spite of himself, but it flaked away after a moment. "Jem, we can't go back to the resort."

Jem's mouth flattened into a line, and he scratched his beard. "DeVoy said Heather was at the club tonight. Trying to pawn stuff. She's desperate, and she already believes she's a suspect. For heaven's sake, she tried to burn Yesenia's car."

"That sounds like someone who's about to run. This is what I'm talking about: we can't go back to the resort. Heather might not be there tomorrow. And we can't call the police—I mean, we can, but they've already decided Missy is guilty—"

"No, let's go back to the resort. Emery and John-Henry were right; this is too dangerous, and I want you with the guys."

The thrum of the tires made the silence vibrate.

"And you're going to go see her yourself?"

"Look—"

"No, you look. I just saved your life! I'm a—a wonder-butt! I'm not going to sit in a hotel room, listening to those two bicker about—about their pit hair while you confront a potential murderer."

Jem scratched his beard some more. "About their pit hair?"

"I don't know," Tean mumbled. "They're very confusing."

"Ok," Jem said.

"And I'm the butch one. You said so."

"Ok." A hint of a smile played behind Jem's beard. "I said ok."

Tean settled back in his seat. He wriggled his shoulders to work out some of the kinks.

"Oh my God," Jem said under his breath.

"What?"

"You wouldn't understand."

17

Heather's house sat behind a line of dogwoods at the end of an overgrown drive. Not far, Jem was interested to learn, from the Mid-Missouri Big Cat Sanctuary. They'd gotten the address by calling Kristin, who had looked it up in the IHCPA directory. One side of the structure humped up with a second story and a gambrel roof, while the rest was a plain old ranch, all of it covered in wood siding that desperately needed replacing. A lean-to against the side of the house held three push mowers and one rider, but the grass was still knee high. In front of the house, a massive CRT television lay on its side next to a minivan—presumably where Heather had dumped it after unsuccessfully trying to hock it. The back of the van was open, and shadows suggested dog crates stacked inside. Lights were on in half the windows, and Jem decided Heather might not live alone.

When Tean stopped the Jetta and shut off the engine, the sound of barking dogs filled the stillness.

Jem's first, automatic response was to tighten up. Then he breathed out, relaxed his back, spread his legs.

Tean, of course, hadn't missed anything. "Maybe one of us should wait. Keep the car running."

"Nice try, wonder-butt."

"Jem—"

"Meth?"

"Um, no thank you?"

"No, Mr. Responsible. I'm asking if you think she does meth. I've been trying to figure out what she's using."

"Did she seem like she was on meth?"

"I don't know. I've only seen her—what, once or twice?" His memory was good, but on their first encounter with Heather, he'd been more interested in the game she'd been running, the animal psychic thing.

"Something was definitely off. Maybe it wasn't meth. She didn't seem wired. Maybe oxy? God, I don't know. We're going to have to riff."

Tean made a face.

"I'm sorry, but do you have a better plan?"

"We ask her if she killed Yesenia and then we leave?"

"I'm getting out of the car now."

When Jem knocked at the front door, a chorus of howls and barks and yips erupted, and the sound of nails scrabbling on floorboards rushed toward them. Fear spiked again inside Jem before he could tamp it down: LouElla's basement, Antony's wide, manic eyes; the teeth snapping, closing, tearing.

Tean's hand settled at the small of Jem's back, and Jem let himself shiver, once, before pulling the pieces together.

Heavier steps moved toward them, and the door opened.

Heather looked worse than he remembered: her face sallow, her eyes sunken, the whiff of an old, unclean body seeping out through the screen door. She stared at them blankly for a moment, and then, in a questioning voice, asked, "Dr. Leon?"

"Hi, Heather. I'm sorry to show up like this. I know we don't know each other well, but I think we need to talk."

Heather shook her head. "I can't, I'm—Harry, no!"

A Corgi pressed past her to shove his nose up against the screen. He sniffed a few times, and when Heather hooked his collar and pulled him back, he barked. Another Corgi immediately took his place.

Oh my God, Jem thought. A pack of bloodthirsty Corgis.

"I can't," Heather was saying again, reaching for the door. "I'm sorry, but I have to go—"

"It's about Yesenia," Tean said.

Something in Heather's expression annealed. Her hand tightened around the door, and she started to swing it shut.

"We know," Jem said. "About the Cottonmouth Club. About all of it. So, you can either tell us, or you can tell the police."

She stopped, the door halfway to the frame.

"We just want to talk," Tean said.

He was the kind of person who could say something like that and mean it. More than that, he was the kind of person who could say something like that, and anyone who heard him would believe it.

Heather eased the door open. "You can come in, I guess. I've got to keep working."

As she wrangled the Corgis—Jem thought there were five or six of them, but he kept losing count—Tean slipped inside. He took the first wave of the assault on his shins, Corgis leaping enthusiastically against him, yipping and jumping and crashing into each other. A bunch of adorable dumbasses who had immediately fallen in love with Tean, like most animals. Jem stepped in behind him, and then the Corgi brigade rushed him too. It was easier with little dogs, to stand and let them paw at his legs and sniff and bark. Easier, too, when Tean reached back discreetly to squeeze Jem's hand.

They followed Heather into the house. It had knotty-pine paneling and honey-colored floorboards that needed staining. Forget-me-not curtains hung in the windows, white ruffles gray with dust, and the smell of dog and charred food and fish oil made Jem's stomach turn. In the front room, a large crystal—the kind Jem had heard witchy types call a wand—rested on a special stand. A smudge stick smoked where it had been abandoned on a ceramic dish. A wall ornament of raw crystals had a design that clearly meant something to somebody, and on the wall opposite, seven miniature swords hung in a crisscross pattern—the seven swords of Saint Michael, Jem thought. She even had a crystal ball—Jem had to twitch aside the piece of silk covering it, and when Tean hissed at him, he dropped the cloth back into place and hurried after them.

In the kitchen, cardboard boxes that had clearly been rescued from a supermarket—Pampers, Land O'Lakes, Best Value—were stacked everywhere, making a maze out of the remaining space. What looked like photo albums had been stacked in a Green Giant French-style green beans box. Puppy pads and boxes of Frosted Flakes competed for space in a Gold Medal flour box. A woman who was running, Jem thought, and didn't have any idea what to take. Not exactly a hardened criminal. Maybe not even all that bright.

The Corgis had lost interest in them by then, and Heather put them out on the screened porch. To lie in wait, Jem assumed, until the opportunity for a bloodbath presented itself. Heather opened a cabinet and began drawing out cookbooks and sliding them, one by one, into a milk crate.

"Are you leaving?" Tean asked.

"I'm moving in with my mother," Heather said. "She's sick. She needs the help."

"I'm sorry to hear that."

Heather went back for another armload of cookbooks. She was already breathing hard, and when she bent, she had to steady herself with one hand on the countertop.

"Can we help you?" Tean asked.

"No. I've got it all organized; I don't need anybody messing things up."

Jem watched her. She took a magnet from the fridge that said WIGGLY BUTTS CROSSING and put it in with the cookbooks. She took it out again and stared at it, like maybe it ought to go in a better box. The wattle of crepey skin trembled as she tried to get enough air, and she looked gray.

"Yesenia—" Tean began, but he cut off when Jem shook his head.

Jem weighed his options. What he could see of her now. What he'd seen in the living room. He said, "You're a bad liar."

Straightening up from a box, Heather glared at him. "Excuse me."

"You're a liar." He shrugged. "You're not leaving because your mom is sick."

"How dare you—"

"Because I've got the gift, just like you, and I'm sick of you wasting my time."

She stared at him. Her lips were slightly parted, the tip of her tongue visible, and her breathing sounded labored. Then she made a disgusted sound.

"You don't believe me?"

Heather waved a hand at him and started to turn back to the boxes.

"It's cancer, isn't it?" Jem said. "It's a cloud around your aura."

Tean shot him a look, and Jem waited for the disapproval, the frustration, the helplessness. Among so many other things, the doc didn't like lying. But lying was what Jem was best at, and right then, they needed something—anything. Because his bluff about the cops might have gotten them inside the house, but it wouldn't get them what they needed. Heather would have a story—a lie of her own, something to explain everything. A sick mom, for example. So, now Jem had to riff, and riffing meant the fact that she was an animal psychic. It meant the crystal wand, the smudge stick, the desperation she couldn't quite hide. Heather didn't seem to have noticed anything; she was staring at the box of cookbooks, and when she finally spoke, her voice was gravelly. "A year."

"How bad is it?"

"Bad enough." She put a hand to her side and pressed, and her face went glassy with pain. "I thought you wanted to talk about Yesenia."

"I don't think that's why I'm here," Jem said. "I think that's why I thought I was coming here, but now that I'm here, I think something brought me. Something led me to you. Do you know what I mean?"

She didn't answer. Her breathing sounded like a razor on a strop. "Prove it."

"What do you do," Jem asked, "when people ask you to prove it?"

Nothing changed in her face.

"I'll tell you about you," Jem said, and a shiver went through the woman. "How about that? You're a smart person, but sometimes you make choices that you know are dumb, and you do them anyway. You're brave and you're willing to stand up for what matters to you, but you also know when discretion is the better part of valor. You care about people, but you're not going to let them walk all over you."

It was called the rainbow ruse, and it was one of the best ways to start—you're brave but you're careful, you're smart but you make mistakes. Big, general statements that covered opposing qualities, so that no matter who it was, the statement rang true. The whole point was to get them saying yes, because once they said yes, they wanted to keep saying it.

Heather stared at him. Her nod was barely anything, the tiniest movement of her head.

"You were waiting for someone, weren't you? You knew someone was coming tonight?"

Another nod, a little stronger.

"And here I am." The next bit was a gamble, but Jem thought it was right. He was riffing, and he'd stayed alive a long time because when he riffed, he trusted his gut. The psychic credit could be a swing and a miss—if you told someone they had psychic gifts, the wrong person might laugh at you, and that ruined the whole read. But Jem thought about what he'd seen in the front room and said, "When I met you in the hotel, I saw the Archangel Michael standing behind you. I saw the seraphic eye on his forehead, and the wings that burned when they opened." He tossed in a veiled question; the more the mark filled in the blanks, the easier the read. "I don't know what it means, not entirely. Do you?"

"My grandmother had the gift," Heather whispered. "She said it looks different to different people. She said I had a witch's tooth on the roof of my mouth; that's how she saw it." She seemed to wrestle with something before blurting, "Can you see anything? I tried calling Delilah for a reading, but she won't pick up, and I packed the cards, and...well, can you?"

Jem nodded, trying to picture what a witch's tooth might look like—let alone how it could be on the roof of your mouth. Tean didn't look like he had much patience for fooling around, though, so instead of following up on that tantalizing piece of batshittery, Jem said, "Why don't we sit down somewhere more...receptive?"

She nodded, as though the question had been obvious, and led them to the living room. She touched the wand. She uncovered the crystal ball. She sat in a lumpy armchair with what looked like velveteen upholstery, directly under the seven swords mounted on the wall. After lowering the lights, Jem sat too, and Tean sat next to him, taking a sofa done in blue chintz—which served, from the amount of dog hair and torn fabric, as the Corgi brigade's chosen spot in the living room.

As Heather leaned forward, face eager, Jem checked Tean again. He still couldn't read anything in his husband's expression. He didn't know if that was good or bad. But he knew how he felt, that sense of a door opening in his brain, of someone moving to the front of his head, someone who was smarter, luckier—someone who never lost. In sports, they called it clutch. Tean had told him about a book and something called flow. Jem called it riffing, and it felt like light riding along his nerves, like if he turned his hand and looked close enough, he could see the glow under his skin.

"Give me a moment," he said, and he let his eyelids lower a fraction. Seconds ticked away. "I keep getting a sense of darkness. Something closing around you. The fingers of a dead man's hand."

"Oh God," Heather said. "Oh Jesus."

"I don't know what that means, though. I don't—" He'd been working on pauses. The pauses were as important as what you said, most of the time. "I don't even know if it's a man's hand."

"Saint Michael," Heather said, fumbling a medal out from under her shirt to kiss. "Protect me. I didn't do anything to her. I didn't do anything to that woman. I didn't mean to do anything."

Jem narrowed his eyes. Piercing the veil, maybe. Scrying. He thought they'd said scrying in a few episodes of *Buffy*. Maybe that was a little too much because Tean cleared his throat. Twice.

But one of the tricks—one of the good ones—was not to follow up too soon. If you came back to it later, after the mark had forgotten, they thought it had come from the cards or the tea leaves or the ether. So, instead, Jem asked, "You didn't want to start buying at the Cottonmouth Club, did you? There's something there. Something I can't quite make out."

Another long moment.

Heather wiped away a tear and said, "I had to. They wouldn't fill the script anymore. They've got these pain centers, and they say they can help, but they're as scared as anybody else these days. They don't want their licenses taken away."

"And you didn't mean for things to go so far, did you? Not with the Cottonmouth Club. Not with Yesenia."

This time, the tears came faster. "I told her it was Vicodin. I told her I needed it—it's medicine. And she shouldn't have been there, shouldn't have

THE FACE IN THE WATER

been in the club. She took it and—and she laughed. Everyone talks about what a nice person she was, or is, or whatever we're supposed to say. But she wasn't. She was a bitch. She took the bag, and when I didn't let go, she shoved me. Right outside the club. A couple of guys saw it happen, and they didn't do anything." She had to stop for a moment and press one hand over her eyes, the other back at her side, probing again. "You saw. At the resort, at registration. You saw how she treated people. She's gone, and everybody's acting like they're worried. But nobody's willing to say what she was: a bitch."

That was twice now she'd dropped Yesenia into his lap. Next to Jem, Tean shifted on the worn upholstery, and Jem understood his impatience. If they were interviewing her, if they were working this the way they had in the past—if they'd been cops, and for a moment, the memory of John-Henry's disturbingly blue gaze, those cop eyes, almost made Jem lose his flow—now would have been the time to ask. But that wasn't how this worked. And Jem hoped Tean would trust him enough to go along for a few more minutes. And he hoped Tean loved him enough to—to forgive this, although Jem wasn't even sure if that was the right word.

"I'm getting something else now," Jem said. "A kind of disturbance. There's a natural flow to the universe, a way energy moves through us, a pattern we're all connected to. You know this." Heather was nodding along eagerly, the wattle trembling with each movement. "What I sense is a place—maybe a few places—where that energy is snarled. These are confluences." He'd spelled that word out from a book, and he kept it in his front pocket now for games like this. "When they get knotted like this, it's because something has disrupted the natural flow of things."

"The cancer," Heather said, her voice breaking on the word.

Jem nodded, and he forced himself to sit up straight, to keep his face interested and serious and…mystic, for lack of a better term. He tried not to see Tean, tried not to remember he was there. Not for this part of it. "Of course. But there's something else. We're working our way backward, following the flow back to its source, and this is more recent. I get the sense of struggle. Conflict."

"The fight with Yesenia at the club," she said. "I told you about that. She took my medicine."

She took your pills, Jem thought, which wasn't the same thing as medicine. He made a considering noise. "This seems bigger. A bigger snarl, I mean. Something about money. It might be recently. Or maybe it's—it's in the future? It's so close it's hard to tell. Perhaps it's a decision about money." He didn't exactly say, You tried to hock your TV tonight, lady, but he thought it as loudly as he could and hoped she'd pick up on it and explain, oh, just maybe, why she was getting the hell out of Dodge.

Tean did another of those annoyed little wiggles, and Jem winced mentally, thinking about all the Corgi fur he was going to have to clean off the doc. Then Heather's breath caught in her throat, and Jem refocused as she began to speak.

"I didn't—I never told anybody about that."

Jem shrugged. He went for half-embarrassed, a slumping, sloping smile. "It's not me. It's the energy."

Tean coughed again.

"It was a decision," Heather said. "It was…it was trouble, like you said. A snarl. So much of my life was tied up in it. And I was—I was so mad."

"Money," Jem said. "I'm sensing money very clearly now."

Heather nodded, wiping her eyes. She was sick, Jem thought. And old. And tired. And in that moment, Jem felt sick and old and tired too. When he ran a game, he went for people who wouldn't get hurt—not really, anyway, not unless they deserved it. This was different. And Tean was here. Seeing all of it. Worrying. Worrying about Jem, probably, which was worse than if he'd only been mad or judgmental or indignant.

"She came with cash in hand." Heather stopped and cleared her throat. "Yesenia. She knew I needed the money. She came out here a few months ago to see the venue, and we met. I'd just been diagnosed. I was telling anybody who'd listen because I…" She gave a wet laugh, and it sounded more like paper being torn. "Because I didn't know what else to do, I guess. And then, last week, she showed up again. The pain was so bad." She stopped and shivered. "I barely had enough money to feed the dogs. There wasn't anything left over. I haven't worked in six months, unless you count twenty bucks here or there, a few of my friends who know I have the gift. I go to the emergency room if it's bad enough, and they'll give me something. But they send you a bill for that too. And then she was here, and she was offering cash. And the pain was so bad."

"What did she want?" Tean asked.

"The land." She raised the collar of her shirt and snuffled into it. "She said I could get a trailer somewhere. With the dogs. She said wouldn't that be better than dying in here by inches?"

"You own more than the house?"

"A few hundred acres." She waved a hand, repeating her gesture from the kitchen. "It used to be worth something. I sat on it, thinking it'd be worth more. Now nobody wants it; the boom is over."

"But Yesenia wanted it," Jem said.

"She's building that new park. You know what happened? I asked her if I could work there. When I got better, of course. And she said sure, that'd be all right, they always need someone to clean out the enclosures. That was after I'd signed, when she knew she could be a bitch."

"When she took your pills at the club," Tean asked, "was that before or after you signed?"

"After, of course. By then, I had the earnest money. I won't get the rest of it until the sale closes in thirty days, and that's the problem, isn't it? Because now I have to leave, and all that money's tied up in the internet, I guess." Heather was silent, shoulders drawing in. Her voice sounded tangled when she finally said, "She didn't need me anymore. She laughed. Said she was doing me a favor, taking the pills, like I was some sort of addict. I wanted to do her a favor. I wanted to smash her head in."

After the words, the only sound was the click of the Corgis' nails as they moved out on the porch. There was hardly any light in the room, and Jem thought maybe he shouldn't have turned them down so low. Tean's knee bumped his, and Jem's heart kicked into second gear.

"I didn't do anything to her," Heather said, her voice rough as she wiped her eyes again. "If that's what you're wondering. I busted up her car a little. Maybe more than a little." She laughed. "I set the damn thing on fire. I went there the first time thinking maybe she left my medicine there. She didn't, of course. Then I heard she disappeared, and Missy got arrested, and I kept thinking—I kept thinking she's dead, and I was in her car. Fingerprints. And all that dog hair." Her laugh sounded a little stronger this time. "I watch enough *Forensic Files*, you think I'd have the sense not to make things worse, but I kept thinking about that dog hair. They'd think it was me. And if they took me, there wouldn't be anybody left to take care of the boys. I figured if I burned it..." She stopped there, the rest of the sentence unspoken, and shrugged.

Jem nodded slowly. Heather seemed smaller now, her hourglass body shrunken inside its old clothes. She was staring at the floor, her hands restless in her lap.

"I guess that's why you came—"

"I have one more thing to say," Jem said. He left the couch and moved to sit on the coffee table in front of her. He held out his hands. In that moment, he was grateful for the gloom, grateful that his back was to Tean, that he couldn't see his face. After a moment, Heather took his hands. Her skin was crepey and soft, and Jem thought he smelled Jergens. He squeezed once, and Heather brought her gaze up to his. "I don't know if you're going to get better or not. Nobody knows, and nobody can tell you, so don't throw away your money. But I can tell you one thing. You've got good energy. You've got people who love you." From the kitchen came the sound of a Corgi scratching at the door. "You've got your boys. And you're a fighter. As soon as the sale closes, find yourself somewhere nice, and get every treatment money can buy. You've got Saint fucking Michael as your spirit guide. Who the fuck is going to fuck around with you?"

She laughed and turned her head, and for a moment, Jem could see the girl she'd been. When she looked at him again, her eyes glistened, but they were brighter than they'd been, her shoulders a little straighter, her hands clutching his a little tighter.

A knock came at the door: thudding, loud, longer than it needed to be. Asshole, Jem's brain said. And then, Cop.

Heather startled in her seat, and a breath escaped her—a wheezy, punched-out sound. "They're here."

"Who?" Tean straightened and shot Jem a look.

Jem shook his head, but he got to his feet and got his hands in his pockets. Antenna. Paracord. The first one through the door would be surprised.

Then a voice shouted, "Police! Open up!"

"No," Heather moaned. "Oh God, no."

"Is that Chief Cassidy?" Tean asked.

"Open this door right now!" Now that Tean had named him, Jem could hear Cassidy under the thick padding of cop aggression. "Heather Weis, open the door!"

"Jeez." Tean got to his feet and glanced toward the kitchen. "Not exactly a soft touch. Should we…" He left the question hanging, but his gaze strayed to the kitchen again.

Jem shook his head. "Heather, you need to open the door and carefully and calmly do whatever the police ask you. They're not your friends, and don't believe them if they say they are, but they won't do anything to you."

"You said a darkness was coming," Heather said, her pitch wobbling. "You said a dead woman's hand was closing around me."

This time, Tean did shoot Jem a look—but it was more rueful than accusatory.

"I know," Jem said, partly to Tean and partly to Heather, "but right now, we've got to deal with this situation."

"All right," Cassidy shouted from the other side of the door, "guess we're doing this the hard way!"

It sounded like he enjoyed the hard way. Maybe even preferred it.

"No," Tean shouted. "We're just having trouble with the lock."

Silence. Then "Who's in there?"

Jem got a hand on Heather's elbow. She wasn't all that old but right then she seemed twenty years older—and sick, and scared, and alone. He helped her to her feet, and she was trembling.

"It's going to be ok," Jem said in a low voice. "Remember the other stuff I said. Remember you're strong."

Heather wiped her eyes and nodded. She sniffled and took an uncertain step toward the door, but after a second step, and a third, her stride evened out. Cassidy was pounding on the door again, shouting. Heather opened it—it wasn't locked at all, Jem realized, and he almost laughed at Tean's lie—and Cassidy had to stop mid-swing, his arm still raised, looking like some horrible historical statue in a pose that should have been triumphant and, instead, came off as ridiculous.

"I'm Heather Weis." She crossed her arms and rubbed her elbows. "What's going on?"

Cassidy recovered his poise. He was wearing an Auburn PD polo that was molded to an admittedly must-be-admired body, and his white-blond hair looked freshly gelled. A couple of uniforms behind him were watching from the driveway: one, a chinless redheaded kid with something approaching worship; the other, the Black deputy from the previous night, who looked on without any visible expression.

"Ms. Weis," Cassidy said, "you're under arrest—"

Heather let out a choked noise.

"What?" Tean asked.

"—for destruction of property, arson, vehicle hijacking, and conspiracy to commit murder. That's only round one, so we'll see what else we can come up with." He grabbed Heather, and maybe he hadn't done an arrest in a while, or maybe he was showing off for the redhead, or maybe he just wanted a chance to use those muscles, but whatever the reason, he swung her toward the wall. It wasn't exactly a professional move under the best of circumstances, but Jem had seen it done, had had it done to him a few times, and he knew it was step one before the cop cuffed you, plus a nice way to remind you who was in charge. Unfortunately, Heather didn't weigh as much as one of Cassidy's usual perps, or the chief of police was out of practice, because she flew through the air and smashed face first into the wall.

"What is wrong with you?" Tean asked, working his phone out of his pocket.

"She stumbled," Cassidy said, a hint of color coming into his cheeks. The Black deputy's face soured, and even the redhead looked a little embarrassed. "You all saw she stumbled."

Heather's lip was split and bleeding when she reeled back from the wall, and Cassidy didn't try to force her up against it again. She started to cry, and Cassidy, who was working the cuffs off his belt, shrank down a little. He didn't exactly shout for backup or call for help, but it looked like his balls drew up by a few good inches.

Meanwhile, Tean was tapping his phone's screen. He was trying to find the camera, God bless him, and normally watching him get lost—twice—in the calculator would have been one of those things Jem found too precious for words. Right then, though, the hair on the back of Jem's neck was standing up as seconds ticked past and Cassidy's attention swung from the cuffs to Tean to the phone to the gore dripping down Heather's face.

"What's that?" Cassidy's hand dropped to his side, the cuffs now forgotten. "Hey, what do you think you're doing?"

Tean brought the phone up. By some miracle, he'd found the camera, and now he tapped the screen. It was a still photo, not a video, but that didn't stop him from announcing, "My name is Dr. Teancum Leon, and I'm witnessing—"

"Witnessing?" Cassidy moved faster than Jem expected, his free hand coming up as he stepped toward Tean. He swatted the phone out of Tean's hand, and it flew across the room. Tean took a step like he was going after it, but Cassidy shoved him into Jem, and Jem had to steady both of them so they wouldn't fall. In the meantime, Cassidy crossed the distance to Tean's phone. He brought his heel up and then drove it down. Glass cracked. He did it again. And then again. Then he kicked the phone and sent it skittering under the couch. When he looked back at them, he wasn't grinning. But Jem had known bullies—on the street, in the foster homes he'd cycled through, in every walk of life. He'd known them in Decker. And he knew the way bullies looked when they were happy. "You aren't witnessing nothing," Cassidy said.

Tean was shaking, and it took Jem a moment as he steadied him to realize that it was fury, not fear or surprise. "I don't need a video recording. I'll report you myself."

"Is that right? And how do you think that's going to go?"

No one spoke. The air was pulled from the room like a drawn breath. Jem realized which way things were going, and he used the cover of Tean's body to reach into his pocket for the hex nut. Go for the face, he thought.

Unless he reaches for his gun. Then you have to deal with the gun first. Not to mention the two uniformed officers outside with their guns.

"Chief?" The Black officer called. "Everything all right in there?"

"Everything's fine, Leah."

"I see a senior citizen who needs medical attention. Are we taking her to the hospital, or am I calling an ambulance?"

Cassidy straightened and opened his mouth. Then he stopped. After a moment, he grinned: big, wide, perfect white teeth shining.

"All right, Leah. Go on and take Ms. Weis to the hospital. You and Rodney go on and take her. I'll stay and deal with this situation."

Jem shifted his weight to the balls of his feet. He was surprised, distantly, to discover Tean was trying to shoulder him back.

"Chief," the redhead—presumably Rodney—called. "Somebody's coming."

Headlights bounced down the road, and slowly the car took shape like smoke congealing into silver: a black Mustang. Jem couldn't make out John-Henry or Emery inside, but he recognized the car. It rolled to a stop behind one of the cruisers, and Emery got out from the passenger side, already shouting up toward the house.

"Is Jonas in there?"

Cassidy's head swiveled toward the sound; Jem wasn't sure if he could see anything, not from where he stood inside the room, but it was clear from his face he recognized the voice.

"Jonas," Emery bellowed, "get your micropenis out here. What kind of redneck carnival of fuckups are you running? Kid," this last word was directed to Rodney, "get the fuck out of my way."

Rodney didn't get out of his way, and through the open doorway, Jem watched as Emery barreled past him. The kid tried to stop him. Instead, he bounced off Emery, stumbled, and landed on his ass. John-Henry, who had barely managed to get out of the Mustang by that point, winced.

"Sir—" Leah barked at Emery.

But Emery kept coming. Cassidy moved over to Heather, who was still trying to cover her bleeding lip with both hands. He took her wrists and pulled them behind her back—not gently, but not inappropriately this time either—and the cuffs snicked shut. He was standing in a straight line with the door, and he looked up and grinned as Emery stepped into the house.

"Are you fucking kidding me?" Emery asked, giving Heather a single, considering look and then turning his attention to Cassidy. "I knew you were incompetent, and stupid, and sexually underdeveloped, and I knew you were a dirty motherfucker."

"That's verbal abuse and public disorder and —"

"So I suppose it should come as no surprise —" Emery said over him — shouted, really. "—that you're also a thug and a bully who's only capable of obtaining an erection by making victims of people not strong enough to fight back."

Cassidy took Heather by the arm and started to steer her toward the door. He cast a quick glance back at Tean and Jem, and then he called out to his officers, "Leah, Rodney, arrest the four of them."

18

It was ten in the morning by the time they were released, and exhaustion blurred Tean's vision as he, Jem, Emery, and John-Henry stumbled out of the Auburn police station. The offenses they'd been charged with had been misdemeanors, but they hadn't been able to bail out until the morning.

The day was bright, the air above the asphalt already starting to shimmer, and Tean swore he could smell the tar patches starting to soften. He shaded his eyes and tried not to groan when he saw North, Shaw, Auggie, and Theo waiting in the Audi. They got out, and Tean was surprised—no, never mind, no longer surprised by anything—to see that Auggie slid out of the Audi backward so he could keep his camera trained on Shaw.

"—and that was how I got my seventh ingrown testicle hair extracted," Shaw said with a note of what might have been pride, "and I did it by myself because North wouldn't help me."

"Because it wasn't ingrown," North growled. "Because no one has ever, in the history of the world, had an ingrown ball hair."

"And my next ingrown hair—wait, how long have I been talking?"

"Twenty-three minutes and fifty-three seconds," Auggie said.

"Did I do it?"

"Close. You've still got a hundred and twenty-three days and change to beat the world record for a livestream."

Shaw seemed to consider that for a minute. "Ok, then instead of telling you about the other ingrown ball hair, I'm going to tell you about when North wanted that CBD cream—"

"Don't you fucking dare," North said.

"—for his, quote, 'creaky ass.'"

North's face was almost purple as he rounded on Shaw.

"Auggie," Theo said.

Auggie glanced over his shoulder, as though only now realizing Tean and the others had emerged from the station. He tapped his phone and shoved it in his pocket. "Sorry."

North directed a furious—maybe even murderous—look at Shaw, but he turned toward the recently released inmates (Tean needed a word like felons, only for misdemeanors), and choked back whatever he'd been about to say. Shaw, who was wearing what appeared to be some sort of extremely short cloak—and nothing else—tugged his cloak up and looked extremely pleased with himself.

"Why is he about to hang dong?" Jem whispered.

"It's called a chlamys," Shaw announced and hitched it up again. "I made it myself on account of time travel."

No one seemed to have an appropriate response to that.

"We thought you might need a ride," Theo said after a moment.

"So, the four of you rode together in one car," Emery said. "Brilliant."

Theo breathed deeply through his nose. "North parked up the block."

"And just for that, you're not riding with me, motherfucker," North said. He jerked a thumb at Auggie. "You can ride with iCarly."

"In the first place, iCarly was a girl—" Emery began.

"Wait," Jem said, and when Tean looked at him out of the corner of his eye, he recognized the shit-stirrer expression. "I thought iCarly was the computer."

"Then you are as stupid as I already suspected." Emery turned to face him. "Don't talk from this point on."

That other smile, the dangerous one, cut across Jem's face.

"Hey," Tean said. For a moment, that's all he had. Everyone looked at him. It took an extra second to summon up, "Don't talk to him like that."

"I'll talk to him however I feel like talking to him," Emery said.

"Go on," Jem said. "Keep talking."

"Ree," John-Henry said, laying a hand on Emery's shoulder, "we're all tired—"

Emery shook him off. "Are you going to do something about it?"

Jem's smile became a slash of teeth, predatory, amused. It made Tean think of a wolf.

"I'll do something about it," Tean said. "I'll tell you that I don't want to hear you talk to my husband like that after everything we've been through—"

"Everything you've been through? We finally had a solid lead, and you had to stick your cocks in it because you couldn't wait a few fucking hours!"

The shout echoed up the street. A white lady with a stroller who was coming down the sidewalk toward them turned and headed the opposite direction. An older guy with the perpetual flush of a drinker stared, fumbling his keys as he tried to get into his car. Two boys fishing at the tiny harbor looked like painted miniatures, motionless as something took the bait off their lines.

"She was going to run, dumbass," Jem said. "She was loading up her truck, and she'd have been gone."

"She had no money; where was she going to go? Think. Think with your fucking brains if that's not too much to ask."

"Emery," Auggie said, "calm down—"

Emery turned toward him, and Auggie shut his mouth. Theo's face darkened.

"I still think it's not fair," Shaw said, "that nobody but me cares about the fact that Chief Cassidy and North Cassidy McKinney—"

"Shut up!" Emery shouted at him. And then, to North, "Put a fucking muzzle on him. You two were supposed to find Yesenia, and you couldn't do one fucking thing right, as usual."

"What the fuck crawled up your ass and died?" North asked.

"These two," Emery said, pointing at Jem and Tean. "Here's my fucking problem."

Jem opened his mouth, but Tean planted a hand in his chest and said, "We're done here."

"But what about the investigation?" Auggie asked. "What about your friend?"

"That's over," John-Henry said. "We're finished. It's one thing to ask some questions, to follow the Rangel brothers around, to lean on them because things seem hinky. It's another thing entirely to walk into a firefight and to have my husband starting World War III with a neighboring police chief just because he—" He cut off. The strain of it showed in his jaw.

Emery pivoted. He put his hands on his hips. His dark hair had fallen over his forehead, and he stared out from behind the fringe. "Do you want to finish that sentence?"

"No."

"Do you have something to say about me?"

John-Henry met him with a glare. Then, in a low voice, he said, "Cut it out."

"If you believe my judgment has been compromised, it's your duty as a husband to—"

John-Henry held up a hand. Emery stopped, although it looked like it cost him.

"We're going," John-Henry said to nobody in particular. "We'll see you all...later."

He turned and stalked off, and Emery went after him.

"Fucking asshole," North said. Taking Shaw by the chlamys, he towed him up the street. "We're out of here."

"But we have other leads," Auggie was protesting. "We've got the vet angle. You're a vet. You can think like a vet, tell us how the killer thinks, what they might do next."

"That's enough," Theo said.

"But she's innocent. She didn't do anything wrong."

Theo gave him a look—a mixture of love and secondhand pain—and in that moment, Tean could see the age gap between the two men. Then Theo said, "We'll give you a ride back to the resort."

The street had emptied, Tean realized. They were the only ones left.

He nodded, and they got in the car.

19

Tean didn't drink—not much, anyway, and not in a way that could be considered recreational. Certainly not in a way that would render him unconscious. And he didn't use cannabis, in spite of the pamphlets that found their way onto his desk, and the articles that appeared in his inbox, and the links sent by text message with titles like "Fifteen Reasons to Start Taking Edibles." He was an old dog, in his own way, and although he didn't have any particular objections to alcohol or cannabis when used responsibly, he hadn't grown up that way, and the changes in his life were always going to be incremental.

But in their hotel room, trying to sleep as daylight cut through the blinds, he really wanted to get hammered.

Next to him, Jem's breathing was soft and even. Jem, of course, had passed out immediately. He slept the sleep of the innocent, of dogs and babies. He even dreamed a little like that, sometimes, the murmurs and tiny kicks. Not right now, of course. Not when he was totally exhausted.

A part of Tean circled the events of the previous night: watching Jem work, seeing again, firsthand, how easily Jem lied and faked and manipulated. They'd been together for a few years now. Tean knew all of it firsthand, to various degrees. But seeing it again—

He got out of bed. He showered and kept the water cool, even though the AC was on full blast, because it wasn't worth trying to figure out the secret combination for the faucets again. When he stepped out of the shower, his skin pebbled with the cold. He dried himself, and his hair immediately turned into a bushy mess that defied his every attempt to fix it—even though he was using the same serum that Jem used, the same comb that Jem used, even though he was doing everything the way Jem had showed him how to do it. He dressed in a pair of khakis and one of his DWR polos because he liked those clothes, because they were familiar, because that was how he'd dressed before he'd met Jem and because, most importantly, Jem was still asleep and what he didn't know would never hurt him. Then he let himself out of the hotel room and went downstairs.

The conference was wrapping up. The keynote speaker was presenting, and then there would be one final poster session, and everyone would go home. Presumably, that included Jem and Tean. The hallways and lobby of Santaland were empty. Plastic Santas and plastic elves and plastic reindeer peeked out at Tean from behind plastic Christmas trees and plastic snow and plastic lampposts. Yearly plastic waste could encircle the planet four times—and that was every year. It was hard not to feel like plastic Rudolph was a noose around the neck of the environment, drawing tighter with every passing second.

Tean found himself in one of the resort bars, this one themed like Santa's Workshop. It was empty except for a pair of middle-aged women who wore conference badges but were clearly skipping the last sessions. One of them wore a sun visor that said IN WINE, WE TRUST. The other one had on a t-shirt that said CALHOUN FAMILY VACATION—FAMILIES THAT VACATION TOGETHER, STAY TOGETHER. Although Tean had his doubts about the statistical probability of that statement.

He ordered a hard cider, and he felt a bit like a rebel because it was only eleven, and then he took it to the back of the bar and sat. After a couple of swallows, though, he pushed it away. His head was throbbing, and the world had that grainy texture that came from too little sleep.

Still sitting there—and contemplating how many years a plate of cheesy tots would take off his life—Tean didn't notice at first when Emery came in. One minute, he was alone at the back of the bar. The next, Emery sat on the other side of the room, phone pressed to his ear. He looked freshly showered, his hair dark and wet and combed, and he'd changed into a fresh t-shirt and jeans. If Tean wasn't mistaken, the t-shirt was Death Cab for Cutie, and it looked a little too small for Emery and washed to the point of translucency. Emery sat bent over the table, head in one hand, but his voice was even, almost upbeat.

"Everything's fine, Colt. Yes, we're having a wonderful time." He listened. He ran his hand through his hair, and frustration or discontent or something made his shoulders rise and fall once. "No. No, everything's ok. We just had a disagreement. Yes, I apologized. Yes, I told him I was sorry." A soft noise, almost like a laugh, escaped him. "Yes, I used those exact words. How was practice? And how's Evie? What are five things Ashley has done that you don't want me to know about?" This time, the sound was definitely a laugh. "It was worth a try." He listened again. "It's been excellent. Highly educational. It was the perfect gift, Colt. Thank you again."

His hand moved, and for a moment, Tean could see his face: the smile that seemed surreally gentle, the openness, the vulnerability. Gone were the anger and the condescension and the cold, implacable argumentation. "Yes, I'll apologize again if I need to. Tell Aileen hello." He didn't quite roll his eyes, but the expression was there in his voice. "She already knows I love her. Yes, fine, tell her anyway. I love you. Yes, I understand the double standard." And then, in a rush, "Ashley is not allowed in your room with the door closed."

The call must have disconnected, because Emery sat up and pocketed his phone. He sat there for another moment, running fingers through his hair, looking at nothing. And then he glanced over, and eyes the color of straw fixed on Tean.

Tean braced himself for the onslaught. The bartender was cutting up limes, and the rhythmic sound of the blade passing through the skin and hitting the cutting board kept time for the droning voices on some sports channel Jem doubtless would have recognized. A white lady in a Santaland uniform pushed a sweeper-vac down the hall, leaving a trail of tiny pieces of garbage behind her. The belt inside the sweeper-vac squeaked—or a gear squeaked, or a wheel, or something.

When Emery spoke, his voice was barely loud enough to carry across the room. "My son. Our son."

Tean nodded.

Emery didn't move. He didn't have a drink. He didn't have any food in front of him. As far as Tean could tell, he'd ducked in here to finish that call with his son, and now he was sitting there, staring at Tean. He didn't look good—the dark circles under his eyes, the exhaustion that looked more than physical. Some kind of bad blood with Chief Cassidy, Tean knew, although the details had never been made clear. Or perhaps the events of the last few days, independent of Cassidy. Or perhaps all of it. Or something else entirely.

At some unseen signal, Emery stood. He navigated the maze of tables, his path bringing him closer to Tean—and, at the same time, closer to the exit. Then he stopped. His gaze flitted to Tean again.

In that moment, Tean wished Jem were here, to talk, to smile, to ask all the right questions. All Tean knew was that Emery looked unhappy and worn out, and that was the kind of thing Jem was good at handling.

But the moment had lasted too long, and Tean heard himself saying, "Would you like to sit down?"

For a moment, it seemed like Emery might shake his head. Then he drew out a chair. He sat back in the seat, almost a slouch. His eyes moved restlessly toward Tean and away.

"Do you want a drink? Something to eat?"

Emery shook his head.

The bartender had finished with the limes and was drying glasses now. On TV, a commercial for a hemorrhoid cream showed people doing all sorts of things without any discomfort: sitting, stretching, squats.

"Christ," Emery said, "why not just show them taking a shit?"

A laugh—so nervous it bordered on a giggle—worked its way through Tean. A flicker of something creased Emery's mouth.

"How many kids do you have?" Tean asked.

Emery held up two fingers. "Colt is sixteen. Evie will be five in September." Some sort of internal deliberation must have happened because he added, "Neither one is mine biologically. We adopted Colt. Evie is John's from a previous marriage."

But, Tean thought, he'd said, *My son*. He'd caught himself. But that's what he'd said.

Aloud, Tean said, "John-Henry doesn't seem like the kind of person who would make that distinction."

"Of course not," Emery said. "Yet another piece of evidence I'm an asshole."

Tean picked up the cider and looked at the bottle. His head throbbed.

"I am...sorry." Emery shifted in his seat. "I've been out of sorts lately. So many surprises. So many things I can't control." It must have taken an effort, but he asked, "Do you have kids?"

Tean held up two fingers, copying Emery's display from a moment before. "Girls. We're fostering, but maybe..." He let that thread hang out there. "Sofia will be ten in October. Anahí is six."

Emery nodded.

"It's new," Tean said. And then, because he couldn't help himself, "We have no idea what we're doing."

A laugh rippled in Emery's chest. "Good God. Join the club. You had the pleasure of hearing my son give me relationship advice; you're clearly in good company."

That made Tean smile. "It sounds like you're close."

One of Emery's hands came up and traced the line of the table. It was a long few seconds before he said, in a different voice, "I love him very much."

And Tean sat and wondered and tried to figure out who was sitting across from him.

"John is disappointed in me," Emery said suddenly. He rubbed his eyes. "Again."

Tean thought about what to say to that.

"I'm sorry," Emery said. "You don't want to hear about that."

"No." Tean turned the bottle of cider. "I call him John-Henry. Should I be calling him John?"

"Everyone calls him John-Henry. Except Colt, I suppose. For a long time, he went by Somers, but...but that doesn't seem to fit him anymore."

Tean nodded.

"I shouldn't have said that." Emery sat up like he might push back his chair. "That was inappropriate."

With a shrug, Tean said, "I don't even know if Jem and I are fighting. I mean, we aren't. But yesterday was so weird. And last night. I don't know. I thought our lives were...different, I guess. I thought things had changed. And the past few days have brought up things I thought we were done with."

Emery grunted.

"John-Henry doesn't seem like he'd be disappointed in you."

"He is. He's too kind to say it, but he is. My...temper, for lack of a better word. My inability to go along. I know I should have kept my mouth shut. I know that—that taking my frustration out on you and Shaw and the others, I know it was wrong. I knew it at the time." The corner of his mouth quirked. "Although I still believe you were jackasses for going to see that woman on your own."

Tean blinked. Then a fresh smile crept out. "An elephant named Casey killed someone—an animal keeper—in 1989."

Emery's silence had a stunned quality to it before he struggled his way to a "What?"

"By doing a headstand on him. It wasn't the only time. In 1988, an elephant named—you won't believe this—Tinkerbelle did the same thing."

"Christ Almighty."

"And in 1990, an elephant named JoJo did it."

"What the fuck was happening from 1988 to 1990? Was this because of Reagan?"

"But in India, elephants that are required to work are given breaks, food and water, even a pension. They get to retire. Do you know how many people in the world don't have a pension? How many people in India don't have one, much less sufficient food and clean water?"

Those straw-colored eyes narrowed. "India is hardly the only country facing poverty and inequity. It's certainly not the only country that has privileged treatment of certain animals. Take the United States, for example, and the quality of life of pets—"

"No, no, that's not what I meant." Tean blew out a breath. "Never mind."

"What did you mean, then?"

Tean hesitated, but the question was startlingly intent, and he felt the answer being drawn out of him. "I don't know. I guess one way of thinking about it is that who you are, the kind of life you lead, how things turn out, all of it depends on where you were born, how you were raised, that kind of thing. That's something I've had to recognize with Jem. And with myself, if I'm being totally honest."

"And?"

"And, I don't know, all we can do is try to recognize that, and look for how it affects us, and try to rise above it when it isn't right."

"And?"

"And I guess, thinking a little more broadly, that injustice is everywhere, and all we can try to do is make it right in our little corner of the world. And hope things get better. Hope we get better."

Emery considered this. "And the world is a fucked-up place."

"And that."

"And don't stand under an elephant when she's doing a headstand."

"That might be a tad literal."

"Literal or not, it's a valuable lesson." Emery was quiet for a moment. "I suppose I'm the Tinkerbelle in that story."

"Not necessarily. I'm kind of a Tinkerbelle too. I mean, Jem is just so…wonderful. I want to say he's perfect, but that's not fair to him. We're all kind of Tinkerbelles, I guess. Doing our own thing. Thinking what we're doing is right, maybe even good. But we're doing it because we've been trained to do it. Or because we think we'll be rewarded. And no matter how hard we try, we hurt other people, even if we didn't mean to. I've done that to Jem. I guess, maybe, I'm still doing it."

Emery nodded. He sat back in his chair, rubbing his eyes again. The TV had gone back to two talking heads who were shouting over each other.

"Fucking Tinkerbelle," Emery said.

A laugh slipped out of Tean. "Fucking Tinkerbelle."

When a lull came on the TV, Emery fixed his gaze on Tean again. "Jem seems…complicated."

"That's putting it mildly. Although, to be fair, he could say the same about me."

"He's clearly intelligent. He's resourceful. He has a certain charisma. I don't trust him."

"Jem is devoted to the people he cares about."

"But he's not safe, is he? He's not…tame, for lack of a better word."

The question took Tean by surprise. The word was a surprise. He hadn't thought it before, hadn't brought the issue to himself in those terms. But he understood, in that moment, some of the internal workings that had been going on in the dark part of his brain. He understood what he'd wanted to be true.

"No," he said quietly. "He's not."

"But he loves you."

Tean rolled one shoulder.

Emery gave a laugh. "That wasn't a question. John says he's…well, the word he used is besotted, but you'll have to forgive him because he reads an ungodly amount of romance novels."

"I think he loves me. I love him. I think we're ok; I don't think—I mean, I think everything will work out. But it's been hard, the past few days. Learning things aren't…resolved, I guess. I'd believed—I'd hoped—we'd resolved everything."

Emery snorted. "You're talking to the master of unresolved emotional bullshit. You know what I'm starting to think? Heat death."

"Maybe this is what Jem feels like," Tean said. "Maybe this is exactly what it's like."

"The first two laws of thermodynamics: energy is always conserved, and entropy is always increasing. Eventually, the universe will reach a state of thermodynamic equilibrium. Everything distant, drifting, cold. All the energy in the universe spread so thin that it can't do anything. Heat death."

"I know what heat death is."

Emery seemed to ignore that. "That's resolution. Resolution is closing things off. Shutting things down. The end."

"Right, but that seems like an oversimplification and perhaps a conflation of resolution as I mean it, in relationship terms."

"Of course it is. But that doesn't mean I'm wrong. Life is messy. Life is a crazy fuckfest where you can die because an elephant did a headstand on you. And relationships are even messier. Resolving things is all well and good, but if you think you're going to resolve everything, forever, then you need to be in a relationship with a body pillow."

Tean thought about that.

"John is going to kill me when I repeat this conversation to him," Emery said, and he sounded strangely proud of himself.

"That is the best relationship advice I've ever gotten," Tean said.

Emery sat back, a tiny, almost imperceptible smile, playing across his lips. "Damn straight."

20

In the dream, everything was still ok. In the dream, they were back home, and the girls were playing in the living room, and Scipio was nudging his leg to get some of the breakfast sandwich Jem was preparing. In the dream, there were biscuits. In the dream—in all dreams—there was sausage.

Jem woke to Tean rubbing his leg. Jem made some suitable waking-up noises. He wiped his mouth and discovered a strand of drool connecting him to the pillow. He closed his eyes and fell back onto said pillow.

"Complete and total emotional resolution," Tean said, "is like the heat death of the universe."

"No," Jem said and pulled a second pillow over his head. "Go away."

Tean laughed quietly.

Then it registered. Jem took an experimental sniff.

"I brought you something," Tean said. Paper rustled.

"Is that sausage?"

Tean laughed again.

"Is that a sausage biscuit?" Sniff, sniff. "And hash browns." Sniff. "God bless you, and coffee?"

"I guess you'll have to open your eyes to find out."

"Never," Jem said in his most imperious voice, which was kind of groggy and raspy and all-around sleepyish still. But there was definitely coffee out there. And carbs, so many carbs. And sausage. So, Jem pulled the pillow off his head and blinked a few times. The McDonald's bag swam into view. Then Tean's worried face behind those big, dark glasses. Always so worried. "I changed my mind. I decided I'm alive."

A small smile tugged at the corners of Tean's mouth. "I'm happy to hear it."

"Did you get—"

"Yes."

"No, did you get—"

"Yes."

Jem let out an exasperated noise and made a gimme motion for the bag. "You won't even let me finish. What about—"

"I got all of it, Jem. I told the lady I'd give her a hundred bucks if she'd make every breakfast sandwich on the menu for me, even though it's not breakfast time, plus some hash browns." Tean shrugged, and suddenly he couldn't seem to meet Jem's eyes. "I know you like options."

For a moment, Jem stared at him. Then he said, "Come here."

"No."

"I want to kiss you one hundred and forty-eight times."

"I'd better not. I might have mono."

"I love you so much."

"You should love me a normal amount."

"I love you more than anyone in the whole world."

"What about Scipio?"

"I love you more than anything."

"What about McDonald's?"

"Your ass, right here." Jem pointed to a spot on the mattress. "Kiss. Here." He pointed to his lips.

Tean made a face, but he shuffled over to the bed. He sat. He kissed Jem once, and then he held still, his whole body stiff, as Jem bore him down onto the bed and covered him with kisses. He probably didn't get all the way to a hundred and forty-eight, but then, he had other things on his mind.

When Jem pulled back, Tean's glasses were crooked, and his hair was even more of a mess than usual, and he was breathing in a way that Jem found immensely satisfying. He brushed some of the hair down, but it sprang right back up again. He tried to smooth Tean's eyebrows, but they were back to ka-chow status. He smiled, and it was a question, and Tean gave him the old, familiar, worried smile back.

"Hi," Jem said.

"Hi."

"What's going on?"

"I'm currently pinned on a hotel bed while your McDonald's gets cold."

Jem held up a finger. "Don't do that. Don't use McDonald's to distract me. What's going on?"

"Nothing's going on."

"You're mad at me."

"No."

"You're disappointed. I disappointed you."

"What is it with men worrying about disappointing their partners? Why is that a theme today?"

Still straddling Tean, Jem squirmed forward a few inches. He tapped Tean's breastbone with a finger. "You didn't answer the question."

"Of course I'm not disappointed in you."

"Last night," Jem said. He fought the urge to hug himself. He kept his hands on his thighs. Kept his shoulders open. He tried to smile. "I know you don't like it when I do that. Scratch that. I know you hate it when I do that. Talk to people like that, I mean. Um, lie. I guess. And cheat. And steal. Maybe there's something in there about highway robbery?" His face heated. "I'm sorry; I'm saying stupid stuff because I'm nervous."

"Let me up," Tean said quietly.

"No. You're going to tell me you can't live with somebody who does that kind of stuff, and then I'm going to have to chain you to a pipe in our basement so you can't leave me, and I'll only let you out so you can go to work every day and be the world's greatest wildlife vet." He could feel the flames on his cheeks now. "Nervous. Sorry."

Tean was silent for a long moment. "That is the worst basement-prisoner plan I've ever heard. You'd let me leave the house every day for work?"

"Somebody has to bring home the bacon. Besides, you're not a basement prisoner. You're a basement sex slave. There's an important difference."

Tean's nose wrinkled. "How much sex?"

"Lots. Lots and lots. We'll send the girls to play outside every day when you get home from work."

"Why can't I be a regular prisoner? Why can't you just want to make my skin into a dress?"

"No deal. Hot, steamy, raunchy sex. Relentless sex."

Tean wrestled his glasses back into place and gave Jem a look. "What is going on?"

"That's what I asked you."

"And now I'm asking you."

A lopsided smile. "Nothing's going on."

"Jeremiah." And then, softer, "Talk to me."

"I don't know. I told you: last night, this weekend, everything. Forget it; I'm fine now. I'll eat a million breakfast sandwiches and my stomach will explode."

"Oh no." Tean thrashed and wormed and wriggled, but Jem didn't let him up. "You are not going to distract me with—"

"Your favorite thing in the world?"

"—that kind of talk. I thought we talked about this yesterday. I thought everything was ok."

"Everything was ok. But then—" Jem shrugged. He tried to hold back the question, but it weaseled out of him. "You're really not disappointed?"

Tean was giving him that look again. The one that was unbearably perceptive, the one that saw past the flash and dazzle, the one that made a part of Jem squirm and, at the same time, went through him like magma: low and dark and hot.

"I'm not disappointed," Tean said. "I know you did what you thought you had to do last night. I trust your judgment. More importantly, I trust you. You are Jem Berger. I know what you did for her at the end. I know what it meant to her, or I think I know." He took a deep breath. "What worries me, though, is that you've spent this weekend thinking...I don't know. That I don't value who you are. That I don't respect you, or that I don't recognize that you're exceptional and wonderful and the best thing in my life, to be treasured absolutely and unconditionally. That upsets me."

"Well, I didn't—I mean, that's not how I was thinking of it. Not really. I just thought..." He caught a flicker of a smile and slapped Tean's chest. "I don't know, dummy. You're so good! I don't know how to be good. Or smart. You're so much better than me in, like, every way! And if you say you're not good, I'm going to flip you over and spank you!"

"That kind of behavior is exactly why I'm better."

It took a moment for Jem to catch the grin—not on Tean's mouth, but hiding behind those damn glasses. "You asshole!"

"Bad language, too."

"All right, here we go."

But flipping Tean over turned into rolling around on the bed, and that turned into lying next to each other.

"I went easy on you," Jem said.

"Thank you."

"Because of your glasses."

"That was very considerate."

"I don't want them to end up like your last pair."

The smile curved Tean's cheek. "I'm not, you know. Disappointed. But I want to know...I guess I want to know why you think I would be. And why you're so hard on yourself, I want to know that too. You're such an amazing person. You're resourceful and resilient. You've overcome challenges that would have ruined the lives of other people."

"I'm reading *Night of the Living Dummy*, Tean. It's second-grade material."

"See? That's what I'm talking about. Why do you do that? Is it something I do? Or something I say? Because if it is, I want you to tell me. I love you, and I think you're amazing. If I'm doing anything that communicates a different message, I want you to tell me so I can stop doing it."

The quiet gathered in Jem's chest like an ache. He reached over and brushed some of Tean's crazy mane. After a while, because he owed him this much, he said, "Of course it's not you."

"It doesn't feel like an 'of course' kind of answer. You thought I was ashamed of you. You thought I was disappointed in you."

"Ok, well, the first part is because I'm a giant hormonal baby living inside the body of a slightly less hormonal adult male."

Tean took a moment to catch up. "You'll have to explain that."

"It's being here, I guess. It's not exactly my scene, you know? And I know you're smart, and I know you're this accomplished, educated professional, and you have a great career, and it's one of the things I love about you. But it's…I don't know. I'm here. And everybody else has done a million years of school, and they've got PhD behind their names, and they have all these interesting, intelligent things that make you perk up."

"When did I perk up?"

"And I know that's not me. I mean, are you bored all the time at home? Do you want to stick your head down the garbage disposal every time I talk about TV or movies or food?"

Tean sat up. The afternoon light reflected off the lake, throwing shifting skeins of light over him. He was silent for what felt like a long time until he said, "I could do without watching the *Buffy* season two finale again."

"How dare you?"

The smile appeared behind the glasses again.

"No," Jem said. "How dare you?"

Taking Jem's hand, Tean asked, "I didn't know you felt this way."

"I don't. I swear to God. I'd kind of…I guess I'd forgotten. How intimidating you are. I mean, it helps that I've seen your butt, but when we first met, you were so smart and educated and owned all these books without any pictures. Anyway, it hit me again. So, like I said, I'm being a baby. I'll be fine."

"I don't want to talk about work stuff at home. I want to talk to you about you. And about your day. And about Scipio, and about all the treats you gave him that you weren't supposed to, and why you had to split a hot dog because he was starving to death."

"Sometimes he has this look in his eyes, and I know he's going to die if he doesn't get a tiny nibble."

"And about the girls, and about the life we're building together. I don't want somebody to talk to about the trout numbers, or the elk lottery, or—"

"The Bigfoot cover-up."

"That doesn't come up as much as you think it does."

"That's part of the cover-up."

Tean hesitated. "If you've changed your mind about going back to school—"

"No." Jem knew it had come out a little too fast. He breathed out. "No. I mean, maybe one day. But not right now. And I promise, I'm fine. I just wanted you to know. I love our life together. I love how I feel when we're together. How you make me feel. It hit me this weekend, that's all. Summing up: giant baby."

Tean made a face at that. But he asked, "And the other part?"

"Hm?"

"You said there were two parts. The baby part, and another part. Or maybe several more parts."

The light rippled: across Tean's face, catching the lenses of his glasses, dappling his shoulder, his chest, the thin, wiry frame.

"Ok," Jem said.

Those bushy eyebrows went up.

"Don't divorce me. Please."

"Jem."

"What you said yesterday—the other day?—about our lives needing to change. I know that's true. And I'm not trying to excuse what I did, lying to you about DeVoy, or getting myself into that mess, any of it. I know you're right. But—" He tried to release the pressure gradually; instead, the force behind the words blew them out of him like the spray of a dam breaking. "I'm not different, ok? I'm the same guy you met. I'm the same guy you, um, fell in love with. I guess. If we're putting labels on it."

"We're married. That's the ultimate label."

"And I know we have the girls now, and I know I have a job, and I know I'm ancient and quivering and my bones are turning into powder."

"Why did I let you throw yourself a thirtieth birthday party?" Tean asked. "That's what I want to know."

"But I'm still a piece of shit, pardon the language. I lie. I cheat. I steal. I'm good at it. And it's fun. I mean, I don't even feel bad about it, not unless

I think about how disappointed you'd be. Most of the time, it's enough to do my job. I find ways to keep myself entertained selling houses, bullshitting people who think they can bullshit me, that kind of thing. But last week, there was this asshole in the Albertsons, and he was screaming at this poor girl about his catering order. So, I lifted his wallet. And I sold his credit card numbers online. And I used the cash in his wallet for those awesome parachute pants."

The light shifted. Shadows moved across Tean's face. Like clouds, Jem thought. When you're looking out over the valley and clouds roll in.

"What if you'd gotten arrested?"

Jem snorted.

"I'm serious. What if you'd gone to jail?"

"This is my point. This is the problem. I'm trying to be better. I've tried, really. But this is who I am. And last night, when we were with Heather, it was so…easy. And it was like part of me was awake that's usually asleep. I'm not doing a good job explaining it. But I know you don't approve of that stuff. And I know you wish I were different. And I want to be different—for you, for the girls. You're right; I know you're right. But I don't know how to change. I don't think I can change, not that much. I don't know if I can be who you want me to be."

Tean was silent for almost a full minute. Then he lowered himself to the mattress again. His breathing got funny, and he took off the glasses and folded them and wiped his face.

"Tean."

He scooted over to Jem and rested his head on Jem's chest.

"I'll do better," Jem said. "I promise. I swear to God. I'll see a therapist or something. I'll get hypnotized. You can make me do the dishes by snapping your fingers, and if you say the words Bob Sacamano, I'll bock like a chicken. Please don't cry."

"I'm not crying because I want you to do better." Tean turned into Jem's chest, drying his face. "Jem, why didn't you tell me?"

"I feel like that's a trick question."

To his surprise—relief—Tean laughed and touched his eyes again. "Ok. Fair." He was silent again, and the silence was different this time. Calmer. Slower, if that was a thing. Could silence be slow? This one felt peaceful. When Tean spoke again, he had stitched up his voice into something resembling calm. "You're right, of course. I don't…like that you do those things. I don't want to use the word approve because it's not my place to approve or disapprove. I'm worried about the risk: that someone will catch you, that someone will hurt you, that you'll be arrested. And yes, there's still a knee-jerk ethical reaction when I hear about you doing that kind of stuff."

"The old knee-jerk ethical reaction."

Tean reached up and pulled on his beard.

"Ow!"

With a tiny smile, Tean said, "I guess part of me is comfortable with the fact that your targets tend to be people who can afford it, people who are assholes, or people who…I don't know. Who receive some sort of benefit, even if your motives are different from what they believe. Heather's a good example. It didn't matter to her that you weren't there because of a psychic summons. She needed someone to help her, and you did that for her. I know that's oversimplifying, but part of me is…is willing to let go of that, I guess. Because that's your decision and your life, and it's not my place to pass judgment on that."

"You didn't have any hesitation about passing judgment on the breakfast I prepared for the girls last weekend."

"Syrup or powdered sugar, Jem. Not both. We want them to have teeth when they grow up."

"It's their right as an American to have tooth decay. I will die on this hill." Jem's mouth quirked. "Nervous again. Sorry."

"I don't want you to be different. Not at a core level. You're everything I could ask for in a partner."

Jem made a face.

Laughing, Tean said, "In a husband. I don't want you to change."

"Maybe some small things."

"Maybe."

"Maybe I could try putting Scipio's harness on when we go for a walk."

"Maybe."

"Maybe I could not use the toast knife in the peanut butter and get all the crumbs in there."

"Maybe," Tean whispered, and his eyes were full of tears. He blinked them away. "I don't know how to say this. I wish you hadn't had the life you had growing up. My heart breaks for that boy. But I love the man, and I feel like if I wish those things away, I'm wishing away part of you too. And I don't wish you were different. I wish the world were different. I wish we lived in a world where you didn't have to do those things. So, I'm going to do better too. I'm going to make sure you know how proud I am of you. How much I value you. How special and wonderful you are to me."

Jem nodded and traced the curve of Tean's ear.

"You've gotten better at cold reading," Tean added, still in that whisper.

Jem's answering smile was wobbly.

"And you're still one scary badass motherfucker."

"Swear jar."

"Emery asked me if you were feral."

The words startled a laugh out of Jem. "Did you tell him I'm housebroken?"

"Oh my goodness."

"But I still bite."

Tean rolled his eyes. But his voice was serious when he said, "I am so lucky to have you in my life. You're talented and funny and caring. You're generous and kind. You're also the only man who could put up with me, which suggests you might need to reconsider your own choices, perhaps raise your personal standards to an acceptable level."

"Are you kidding? You're a catch."

"Ha."

"You are! You know how to dissect a narwhal."

"I'm not sure—"

"And you catch a hundred poachers every day before lunch."

"No, that's not accurate."

"And you think I don't know when you do those life expectancy calculators for me and get really sad because I'm going to die before I'm forty."

"It's all those McGriddles. I had to email them and ask them to add a box to the form."

"You are so gentle and, even though you don't believe it, full of hope, and you see this broken world full of broken people and you spend every day trying to glue it back together."

Tean offered a tight smile. His eyes were shining again, and it looked like he tried to speak and then gave up.

"Go on," Jem said. "Tell me about heat death."

"It's silly."

"I insist."

"No, it's nothing."

"I'm dying to know. I'm literally going to die if you don't tell me."

"It's not even that good. You're going to regret asking."

"Teancum Mahonri Leon," Jem said, sitting up and dislodging him. "I have never once in my life regretted anything with you."

And with that, he bucked his hips and slid out of his boxers.

"What's going on?" Tean asked.

"You realize you're wearing all brown again. Is it a rule? Do they program veterinarians at birth to wear brown, and you automatically revert back to it if I'm not around to catch you?"

"You were supposed to be asleep. You were never supposed to know."

Jem reared back and gave the outfit a considering look. "You know that revs my engine."

"No, it doesn't. You hate it. You make me wear green. And blue. And — wait!"

But Jem didn't wait. He shucked the Keens, undid the button on Tean's waistband, and dragged the khakis down.

"Are you out of your mind?" Tean asked. "The curtains are open. It's daytime!"

Tean's briefs went next. His dick was hard, pointing at his belly.

"I thought I recognized you," Jem said.

"No, Jem, my shirt —" But the words became muffled as the polo came over his head, exposing the slender chest, the stripe of fur down the center, the dark nipples.

"Better start talking about heat death," Jem said. "You're running out of time."

"This is a work trip. We're not allowed to have sex on work trips."

"This is extra naughty, then. Work-trip sex, with the curtains open, in the daytime." He crawled forward to sit astride Tean's legs, his knees dimpling the mattress. Then he kissed Tean's jaw, nosed his head to the side, and bit his neck.

Tean moaned. His voice was syrupy when he said, "Jem."

"I told you I bite." He blew cool air over the spot he'd marked. "Heat death?"

"Every — everything slows down." That little stutter went straight to Jem's dick, and he rutted forward, seeking contact with Tean's body, anywhere he could find friction. "Energy dissipates. It's spread too thin."

Jem dragged his chin over Tean's collarbone, his beard raising a flame under the dusky brown of Tean's skin. Tean shivered and broke off another sound.

"And?"

"And — ah! Everything f-freezes."

That was when Jem took a nipple in his mouth. Tean rolled his hips once, and contact sparked between them. Jem pulled back, liking the ring of hot flesh that he'd raised on Tean's chest. "And?"

"And life is about resistance, friction, heat."

The last bit of that sentence turned into a wail as Jem dove down and took Tean into his mouth. He spent a little while there, Tean's hands tight in his hair with the familiar mixture of helplessness and desire. When Jem pulled back, he kissed the head of Tean's dick, and a full-body shiver ran through his husband.

"How cold are you feeling right now?"

Tean's pupils were huge. He looked—and even sounded, a little— drunk. "That doesn't make any sense. That's not how it works."

"Makes sense to me," Jem said with a crooked smile.

"No," Tean said, with deep-chested gulps, one final attempt. "You have to eat your McDonald's."

"New life rule," Jem said as he went down again. "Sex before sandwiches."

21

"It's less romantic," Tean said, fixing his glasses, "when you finish, um, what we were doing—"

"Porking," Jem said around a mouthful.

"—and you push me out of the way to get a sausage biscuit."

"Less is a relative statement. And it's a McGriddle."

Tean figured he should argue the point. But his body felt loose, almost boneless, and he was snugged up against Jem, and for some reason, the mixture of maple syrup and the smell of Jem's body was strangely comforting. Like home, maybe. Which was a sign of something, Tean was sure. That he needed help, probably. Or to be sent to a monastery. Or, most likely, a lobotomy.

"Bite," Jem said, and Tean accepted a bite of pancake-y, maple-y goodness.

Then he heard his own thoughts and decided to blame the sex. He couldn't be expected to think like a normal human being after that. Not for at least eight hours.

"Can we stay here forever?" he asked.

"Hannah might get grumpy after a few years. We told her we'd only be gone the weekend."

"What about faking our own deaths? We'll make sure the girls get our life insurance. Hannah will probably raise them better than we could."

"It won't be enough money. Sofia wants to do dance; we both have to stay alive so we can sell our kidneys." Unwrapping an Egg McMuffin, he glanced down at Tean. "What's going on with you?"

"We have to go back to reality."

Jem smirked and took a bite.

"No," Tean said.

He waggled his eyebrows.

"Not even close," Tean said.

He shrugged.

"The sex wasn't so good it transported me to some magical, alternate universe. The sex wasn't so mind blowing that I feel transformed, like I've entered an entirely new existence. The sex wasn't so good I can't even comprehend going back to the life I lived before I met you. Whatever you're thinking, that's not it."

"If you say so."

"It's just—I don't know. The girls have soccer practice. I have to go to work again. I never get to spend as much time with you as I'd like."

"The boning," Jem said.

"No. Sitting quietly on a couch. Watching TV. Not talking to each other while we fork down frozen dinners. Like normal, ordinary, healthy couples do."

It looked like Jem was grinning, but it was hard to tell because he was deep into the Egg McMuffin by now. After he finished the next bite, he said, "Yard work."

"I told you I'd mow the grass."

"No, I have to do it."

"You really don't."

"With my shirt off."

"You really, really don't."

"And selling houses," Jem said. "So I can be Daddy Warbucks."

"That's an interestingly dated reference."

"And we've still got that murder to solve."

Tean closed his eyes.

"Uh huh," Jem said. "Nice try."

"If I can't see you, you don't exist."

"There's a thought."

"All sorts of animals do it."

"How does that work for them?"

"The vast majority of them get eaten, I assume."

A gentle tap at the center of Tean's forehead made him open his eyes again. "It's been a hard couple of days," Jem said and proffered the Egg McMuffin. Tean took a dutiful bite. "But we're closer to the truth than we were."

"How is that, exactly?"

"Well, Una's dead."

Tean stared at his husband.

"I mean, that's important, right? The killer had to act again. That tells us something."

"I don't know if it tells us anything, Jem. Even the murders are different—or seem to be. Let's assume Yesenia's dead. Let's assume the blood-stained poncho planted in Missy's room really did have Yesenia's blood on it. That suggests a lot of trauma to the body. Physical violence. Enough of it for her to lose quite a bit of blood. Una, on the other hand—I mean, an injection, and then a blow to the head. Those don't even sound like the same killer."

"A blow to the head can bleed a lot," Jem said. "So, it could be the same guy. In fact, I'm sure it's the same guy. And I don't think we should get hung up on how he killed them. He's not a serial killer with an elaborate ritual."

"I never should have let you watch *The Silence of the Lambs* again."

"He's an evil piece of shit who kills people. That means he's going to kill people however he thinks he can get away with it. If we hadn't interrupted him at the chicken ranch—"

"Poultry farm."

"—he would have made Una's body disappear too."

"You keep saying he," Tean said.

"Statistically more likely."

Tean was quiet for a long moment. "It seems like the only people left are—I don't know, the Rangel brothers, or whoever they work for. I suppose it's possible they killed Yesenia for investigating their operation. DeVoy didn't seem to think so, but then he got killed, which kind of seems like a mixed message."

Jem brooded over the empty McMuffin wrapper for a moment. The afternoon light had shifted, and Tean was surprised to see the sun low over the hills, the water in the reservoir a crucible of molten gold.

"What do we know?" Jem asked. "Yesenia was kind of a bitch. She fought with Heather, manipulated her, and took advantage of her desperation. Stole from her too, but I don't think the sheriff is going to care about that."

"But it does tell us something about Yesenia. It tells us that she could be petty and cruel. She didn't want those pills. And she'd already taken everything of value that Heather had. She latched on to something Heather valued, and she took it because she could."

"Ok. And we know that whoever killed her wanted to frame Missy."

"Or frame somebody," Tean said, "and Missy was a convenient target."

"Either way, that doesn't sound like an international gang of animal traffickers. If Yesenia was becoming a problem for them, they'd figure out her routine, find the right opportunity, and put a bullet in the back of her head. Then they'd get rid of the body. The end."

"That definitely wasn't in *The Silence of the Lambs*."

"They wouldn't kill Yesenia and then drag bloody clothing all over town, leaving a trail of evidence everywhere they go. So, I think we're back to the amateur theory. This isn't a professional killer. This isn't a serial killer. This is someone who kills for personal reasons—greed, anger, jealousy."

"Jealousy? You think Yesenia might be involved with someone?"

"Who knows? I'm spit-balling. What about the vet angle?"

"What about it?"

"When we almost caught this guy at the chicken ranch—"

"Poultry farm."

"—you said the drugs he used, they're the kind vets use? Not what a people doctor would have."

"I've never used the words 'people doctor' in my life."

Jem jogged his knee. "That suggests our killer is a vet."

"Or anyone with the proper training."

"But there's a vet convention in town. And Yesenia has enemies. And she died here. That has to mean something."

Tean shrugged. "We tried that, remember? She had arguments with people, but nobody's going to admit to a blood feud now that she's disappeared, and we've already investigated anyone who seemed like they could bear a serious grudge."

"If you were a vet, how would you kill her?"

"What?"

"I'm serious. You've got the training. How would you do it?"

"I don't know. I've never thought about it like that."

"So, start thinking. You've got all these drugs. You know anatomy. You want to make someone disappear. What do you do?"

"Well, I don't, as you put it, drag DNA evidence all over the place."

"But you—the killer—you think you're smarter than everybody. You think you can point them in the wrong direction. Maybe you think you have to do it."

"Jem, I appreciate what you're trying to do, but I don't think I'm going to be much help."

"Give it a try."

"I am trying."

Suddenly, Jem cocked a grin at him. "Under what circumstances would a vet piss and shit on someone else's bed? Besides, you know, kink."

"That's not something a vet would do. It's not something a human would do. It's not even something an animal would do, not unless—"

He'd been rattling off the words unthinkingly, and now the tail of his thoughts caught up with him.

"Not unless what?"

"Not unless it was trying to mark its territory."

Jem frowned. "What?"

"Maybe we've been thinking about this the wrong way. Maybe we've been thinking about motive the wrong way. What if the killer murdered Yesenia like you said—because of some strong emotion? But it wasn't rage, not exactly."

"He was protecting his turf?"

"It's not unbelievable. Humans manifest territorial behavior in all sorts of ways."

"Ok, but what territory—"

Tean slid over to the pile of clothes on the floor and rooted around for his phone. Cassidy's stomping had cracked the screen, but it still worked. "The land. Heather's land."

"Heather didn't kill Yesenia. At least, I don't think she did. You heard her last night; she went all in on the psychic stuff, and if she'd killed Yesenia, she would have showed some sign of it."

"Not Heather." Tean pulled up the maps app, pinched, zoomed, panned, swiped. And then he held it out for Jem's inspection. On the screen, a pin marking Heather's house was only a few millimeters from a pin marking the Mid-Missouri Big Cat Sanctuary. "Rod."

22

It took them hours to get ready, to go over the plan, to be sure everything was in place, and by the time they arrived at the sanctuary, only a glint of the sun remained above the horizon.

In the last light of day, the cat sanctuary looked more run down than Tean remembered. The perimeter fence sagged, and the NO TRESPASSING signs were sun bleached and tattered. Rust stained the wire panels for the enclosures. A cougar slept on top of a cracked concrete block, and for a moment the sun seemed to pick out each individual tuft of fur, surrounding the big cat like a nimbus. A rut jarred the Jetta, and Tean pulled his attention back to the road.

When they reached the welcome center, the parking lot was empty. Tean parked the Jetta across several of the accessible stalls, front and center and facing out toward the exit, in case they needed to make a quick getaway. That made him think he sounded like a bank robber or a getaway driver or a wheelman. And the fact that he knew all those terms meant he'd watched Jem play way too much *Grand Theft Auto*.

"You're my wheelman," Jem said.

Tean groaned.

"What?" Jem asked. His laugh was a little too fast, the color in his cheeks a little too high. The hard side part was perfect again, and his beard was on point. His eyes were stormy blue squalls the way the sky would look through the rain.

"Nothing."

That made Jem laugh again.

They got out of the car, and Jem took the lead, loping past the entrance to the welcome center and following the side of the building. Tean came after him, glancing around. There had to be some staff at a place like this, even after hours. To keep people from making off with the cats if nothing else. But he still saw no other vehicles—no trucks that belonged to the cat sanctuary or to a contracted security company, not even a golf cart like a mall cop might use. The swampy heat felt like a wet cloth over his face, and sweat prickled under his arms.

When they reached a metal door near the back of the building, Jem produced a set of picks. He had the door open in thirty seconds, and he held it with his shoulder and stuck his head inside. After a moment, he beckoned for Tean to follow.

Inside, the air was cool and smelled like the air conditioning system, and a security light gave enough for them to see by. They stood in a narrow hall that could have been plucked from any low-rent office anywhere: drywall with a few dings and utilitarian gray paint; fluorescent panels; a water cooler with an empty jug; commercial-grade green carpet stained from years of traffic. Tean passed a pair of disposable gloves to Jem, and he started trying doors.

They found an employee restroom that smelled of old urine and even older urinal cakes, a tiny utility room with a furnace and water heater, a room filled with cardboard boxes, and discarded plastic wrap—a quick check of the closest box revealed hundreds of donation envelopes, the kind a visitor might pick up on their way out of the sanctuary. The next door Jem tried was locked.

"Give me a break," he muttered.

"What's wrong? Is it too hard? Can you open it?"

"Is it too hard," Jem said scornfully. "I could open this thing with my wiener. Hey, that's actually an idea—"

He opened his mouth in exaggerated pain when Tean poked him. Then he gave the door handle another considering look. He grabbed it, leaned into the door, and yanked. For a moment, the effort defined the muscles under his *Alf* t-shirt. Then the latch popped free from the frame, and the door swung open.

"Is it too hard," Jem said again.

"How was I supposed to know?"

"Also, I should get husband points for not saying 'that's what he said.'"

"There's no such thing as husband points."

"Like earlier, when I was doing that thing you like with my tongue—"

"Minus a hundred husband points," Tean whispered furiously and elbowed him out of the way.

The office could only have belonged to Rod. The space itself, even the furnishings, were all typical: the filing cabinets Jem would have described as jankety, the mismatched chairs, the particleboard desk. But the clues Tean expected were there. The size of the desk, for one, meant to dominate the room, meant to impress. And what covered the desk: the pelt of an ocelot, a scatter of big cat claws in a silver dish, the resin—Tean hoped it was resin— skull of a sabretooth tiger. Tean was sure Rod had an explanation. These were teaching devices, most likely. But the truth was, these were trophies. Rod might not use that word. He might not even think it. But that's what they were. Trophies like the photograph of Rod shaking hands with President Trump, circa *Home Alone 2*. Trophies like the photos of C- and D-list celebrities, of scantily clothed women and cars and regional superstars— one appeared to be a weatherman—lining the shelves behind the desk.

"Jesus Christ," Jem said. "Is this guy a nut-tugger or what?"

"I don't know. I have no idea what a nut-tugger is."

"It's exactly what it sounds like."

Tean shushed him and moved into the office to begin his search. Jem drifted over to the filing cabinets. The whole point of this visit—now, tonight—was to find the murder weapon. Tean was convinced—Jem, less so—that the killing had happened here, at the cat sanctuary. And the most likely place for that killing was in Rod's office.

In the first drawer, Tean found a letter opener as long as his hand. He held it up, trying to rake the light across it to catch any hint of dried blood. There were ways to detect blood even if it had been cleaned, but that wasn't an option right now, so he'd have to do the best—

"Put that back, son." Rod stood in the doorway. The Pantera tee still had its sleeves, and it was baggy on his whipcord frame, but Tean thought he detected a bulge on Rod's hip. Rod nodded at the letter opener in Tean's hand. "We don't want to have some kind of misunderstanding, do we?"

Tean laid down the letter opener. Jem rolled one of the filing cabinet drawers shut. The cabinet made a soft, metal boom. He glanced at Tean.

"What are you boys doing here?" Rod asked. "The sanctuary's closed. You're trespassing."

"Call the police," Jem said. "Chief Cassidy would love that."

A dry crook of a smile appeared on Rod's face and was gone. "I asked you a question."

"We're here because you killed Yesenia," Tean said. "And we're going to prove it."

Rod didn't laugh. His posture didn't change. The air conditioning came on again, and the tail of his mullet drifted on an invisible current.

"You killed her," Tean said again.

"That's something to say, all right."

"How'd you know we were here?" Jem asked suddenly.

At this, Rod tipped him the same dry smile. He spoke to Tean, though, saying, "I already told you. The new park would have been good for both of us. I didn't particularly like her, but I liked what she would have done for the sanctuary."

"Maybe," Tean said. "That's a reasonable explanation. But there wasn't anything reasonable about why you killed her. You killed her because this is your territory, and she was intruding."

In the silence, the whisper of air in the vents might have been Tean's imagination.

"That's what happened," Tean said. "Isn't it? It was one thing for her to build a park in Osage Beach. That's sixty, seventy miles away. But she changed her mind. She realized she could get Heather's land for practically nothing. She'd be right here, butting up to your sanctuary. She'd get all the Santaland traffic, all the business the resort does. For a long time, you've been the only option. And now she was here, and she wasn't going away. Not even after you terrorized her, breaking into her room, marking your territory. She wasn't the kind of woman to back down. That's why people wanted her as president of IHCPA."

"I pissed on her bed," Rod said. "That's what you're saying? And that means I killed her? Boy, you'd better come up with something better than that."

"That's a starting place. If they can get a sample, they might even be able to match your DNA."

"Bullshit. I'm a human being, not a dog pissing on a tree."

"Humans are as capable of territorial behavior as any other animal. Every society has laws and traditions that encode territorial behavior, manage it, civilize it. And, of course, to punish people who don't respect those boundaries. That's why people—and nations—fight over land that's worthless, and it's why we have things like the castle doctrine. That's why people put up signs warning against trespassing, like the ones you've got all over your property. Territorial behavior is at the heart of most organized sports, the way we talk about competition and struggle. Of course, like most biological traits, it's contingent on a number of factors. Most humans don't manifest it as…strongly as you do."

"Bullshit," Rod said again. "Why didn't I kill Heather then?"

"That kind of behavior, when an established neighbor is perceived as less of a threat, isn't uncommon in the natural world. There's even a name for it: the dear-enemy effect. It's one thing to share a border with Heather. You knew Heather, and you knew you didn't have anything to worry about from her. Yesenia, on the other hand, was new. And she was clearly a threat.

You started with trying to scare her—the vandalism to her room, the ritualized aggression when you saw her in public. When that didn't work, you had to take a more aggressive stance."

Rod's pupils were small and hard. Somewhere in the building, a soft ticking noise began.

"It's over," Jem said. "You might as well own up to it. The police are going to uproot your entire life. Once they start looking, they'll find enough to put it together. They'll check traffic cameras. They'll interview witnesses. They'll canvass neighborhoods and businesses. They'll find footage of you driving a route from here to the reservoir. They'll find people who remember your face, your truck. They'll find somebody from the resort who remembers seeing you in the wrong hallway."

"Like Una," Tean said. "That's what happened, isn't it? She broke into Yesenia's room, and she caught you."

"What he means is," Jem said, "she walked in on you literally shitting the bed."

"And then she had to go. She was paranoid, and she was a nuisance, but if she told that story, people would start asking questions. So, you lured her out to the poultry farm. It would have been easy; a story about a government cover-up, a chance to expose them, anything that she would have believed. And then you drugged her and killed her."

"If you hadn't dropped trou," Jem said, "you could have killed her right then, but she caught you in kind of a delicate situation."

Rod bared his teeth. Not a smile. Nothing exaggerated. His lips peeled back slightly, exposing a hint of craggy yellow. He didn't even seem to be aware he was doing it.

"You know what I keep thinking?" Jem slid one hand into his pocket, and at the same time, he leaned against the filing cabinet, propping himself up with one elbow on top of it—the movement designed to draw attention away from his other hand as he got one of his weapons. "I keep thinking about that story you told us. About your dad."

"It's over," Tean said, echoing Jem.

Rod's chest rose and fell under the Pantera tee. The cotton moved with him. The hint of definition at his hip, the blocky shape that had to be man-made—Tean couldn't decide if it was there or not.

"I don't think so," Rod said.

Jem's hand was a fist inside his pocket. "What does that mean?"

"You're full of shit. Both of you."

"The police—" Tean began.

"The police would be here," Rod said, "if they thought what you were saying was worth a drop of piss. But they aren't, are they? Let me guess: you went to that little cunt of a chief we got, and you laid it all out, and he told you to mind your own business. I went to the public forum when they introduced him, the mayor and the rest of the jack-wits. You know what they said? He had image. That's what they wanted in their chief: image. How the fuck about that?"

Tean drew a deep breath.

"Here's the thing," Rod said. "You don't have shit. You can't prove I did anything. I'm telling you I didn't do anything. You've got no evidence, which is why you're poking around in here after hours, trespassing."

"Someone will find something. You killed two women. They'll make a connection back to you, and you'll go down for them."

"Son—" Rod's gaze latched on to Jem. "—get your hand out of your pocket."

Jem didn't move, but his body communicated the coiled energy waiting to be released.

"What you two didn't think about," Rod's potbelly swelled as he chuckled, "is you pissed off some powerful folk. You do that, and you can't expect to get lucky forever. There's always somebody needing some extra cash. Want to know what it costs, keeping an eye on the two of you? A hundred bucks. Somebody sees you, makes a phone call. There's a hundred bucks."

"Bingo bango bongo," Jem said.

Rod's expression tightened. "Try something, boy, and my friends out here will make Swiss cheese out of you. And then we'll have some fun with your boyfriend. What do you think about that?"

Jem swallowed. It looked like he fought the movement, but his gaze cut toward Tean.

Tean gave a tiny shake of his head.

With a grimace, Jem released whatever he'd been holding in his pocket. He removed his hand slowly, and he displayed both hands, open, to Rod.

Rucking up the Pantera tee, Rod grinned. He unholstered the gun there—a scratched-up semi-automatic about the same size as the Jetta. He waved and stepped back. "Come on then."

Jem went first, and Tean followed. Waiting in the hall were three of the four men who had been hounding Jem since his first visit to the Cottonmouth Club. The Rangel brothers were there, looking worse than ever—Quinn with his slicked-back hair and dirty bandage on one hand, Colin with his torn ear, both of them scratched to hell and holding

THE FACE IN THE WATER

themselves like they had a few new aches after the fall they'd taken the previous night. Tean was surprised, a little, they were both alive. The third man was the one with the goatee, who had come after him and Shaw in the hotel room. Shaw had broken the man's nose, which was still impressively swollen, black and blue under a splint. His eyes were so puffy Tean wasn't sure how much he could see.

"We all told Dusty he ought to take the night off," Rod said, "but he had a personal interest in seeing the two of you again. And Boyd, well, the poor guy's using a cane. Needs knee surgery. He wanted to come too, but we told him no way."

"You never let him have any fun," Jem said.

Rod let out another short chuckle. "No, son, I guess I don't. Here we go, and don't try anything funny."

He marched them toward the door they had used to enter the building. When they emerged, the night was heavy with the water in the air, the humidity ringing the security lights with halos, and the smell of honeysuckle and the fresh-cut grass came in on every breath. Rod pointed them toward the cat enclosures, and as they hiked across the lawn, the three thugs spread out in a triangle. To cover an attempted escape, Tean concluded.

"You said powerful people," Jem said.

The sound of steps came back as the answer.

"That means these guys don't work for you."

"Stop talking, son."

"But that's what I don't get. If the animal trafficking didn't have anything to do with why Yesenia was murdered, why are these bozos here helping you tonight? Why would anyone give you a call and tell you we were on our way here?"

"Professional courtesy," Rod said.

"That doesn't make any sense either. Tean said he checked. The inspections and certifications all came back good. What, do you bribe them all? Is it all for show? And then you pay these guys to bring in cats when you need to change up the show?"

Another of those short chuckles. "You've got it all figured out, huh?"

It was the contempt in Rod's voice that made Tean turn it on its head. The tone that suggested how stupid they were, how blind, and Tean's natural stubbornness making him go back to the beginning and work the problem one more time.

"Oh my gosh," he said, and the frustration in the words was directed purely at himself.

"What?" Jem asked. "Did you forget your inhaler? He forgot his inhaler."

"Ok, that's actually not too bad of an idea. I mean, it's risky, but you like risky, don't you? That's part of the fun. How you prove you're smarter than everybody else."

Rod made an indeterminate noise.

"What?" Jem said. "What's he doing?"

"He's not buying the cats from them," Tean said. "He's selling." The scam unfurled itself in his mind as he spoke. "One of the things about cat sanctuaries is that they don't breed cats in captivity. Of course, that's kind of a problem when your business model relies on people paying money to see cats. So, I'm guessing Rod still does take in rescues, but he's also got a — what do you call it?"

"Side hustle," Jem said.

"It wouldn't be that hard. Make sure the pregnant females aren't around when the inspections happen. Or even better, every time a rescue comes in, you breed them. That way you can explain they were pregnant when they were taken in by the shelter. You set aside a few of the cubs for trafficking, and the others go into the sanctuary. I imagine that's one of the biggest draws, letting people see, maybe even handle, the cubs." And then more of it became clear to him. "Did Kristin help you with the births? Not to sell the cubs; I don't think she'd do that. I bet she thought she was doing a service, helping you with those pregnant cats you rescued. Only then she started to wonder. Is that what she was looking for in your office? Some kind of record?"

Rod spat on the ground in answer.

"For real?" Jem asked. "So, what? He kills Yesenia, covers it up, and then, when people start asking questions, he and his trafficking buddies decide they've got a common interest in making the problem go away." He looked over at Rod. "Are we on the right track?"

"You need to shut your mouth," Quinn said. He was holding a gun in his off-hand, and that thousand-yard stare went straight through Tean.

"Let 'em talk," Rod said. "They've got nothing else to do."

"Quinn said you have to stop talking," Colin said. The pretty boy—not so pretty after falling down the embankment at the reservoir—looked like he was on some sort of drug. His pupils were contracted in spite of the darkness, and a nerve jumped in his face as words spilled out of him. "If Quinn says you have to stop, then you have to stop."

Rod made a disgruntled noise, but he didn't press the point.

As the lawn gave way to the walking trails that connected the enclosures, the light faded behind them, taking the color with it. Each step raised little puffs of dirt that Tean knew, from his previous visit, was red. Tonight, though, out here, it looked black. Like he was throwing up tiny clouds of ash or smoke with each step. The smell of the lake reached him now, the scat that had cooked on hot concrete all day, the butcher smell that he guessed was the raw meat the big cats were fed.

Up close, the enclosures seemed much bigger than they had from a distance. Hog panels had been bolted together to create the walls—at least sixteen feet high, Tean guessed—and around the perimeter of the enclosure, a sheet metal roof stuck out at an angle, presumably to keep the big cats from climbing out. Farther back, where old-growth oak and hickory grew, was the lake. But his attention remained focused on the portion of the enclosure closest to the fence.

It was divided into three sections. The first was a safety gate, which was a small, transitional area with a second gate that allowed entry to the enclosure proper. The point of a safety gate was so that the keepers could enter and leave the enclosure without ever giving the cats a chance to escape. The second area was what Tean guessed was a feeding area that doubled as a holding pen. A guillotine door connected this to the main area, and for the moment, the door was down and closed. Light glinted on steel water bowls, raised to keep the cats from spraying in their own drinking water. In addition to a designated feeding area that could be controlled, it also offered a way to section off cats, or to keep them all corralled while the enclosure was cleaned or otherwise serviced.

The third area was the largest—the enclosure itself, where the cats could run and play. The trees and brush closest to the hog panels had been cut down, and in their place, a variety of elements had been added to entertain the cats. Concrete platforms and logs suspended from chains offered perches and cat walks. Hammocks at different heights offered more places for the cats to laze. Dark shapes among the maze of structures suggested toys, but Tean couldn't make them out at this distance. He started to pull his attention back when green embers, lurking in the dark, caught him. Old, genetic instinct panicked. Then his rational brain asserted itself: eyes. Tapetum lucidum, a tissue in many animals' eyes that reflected visible light back through the retinas. It helped them see in the dark. It also created the effect commonly known as eyeshine.

The eyes were low, almost subterranean, and then he understood: one of the underground dens. For a moment, the eyes seemed to be looking directly at Tean. Then the cat moved, and Tean lost it in the darkness. He thought of water buffalo, deer, wild horses. His pulse in his ears was hoofbeats, the sound of prey animals born to run.

"Did you see her?" Rod asked.

"Jesus Christ," Tean whispered.

Rod laughed. "That's Sita." They had reached the enclosure now, and he motioned Jem and Tean off to one side and began to open the lock on the outer gate.

"Who or what is Sita?" Jem asked.

"Bengal tiger," Rod said.

He stepped into the transitional space and opened the second gate. After doing something with a chain, he backpedaled quickly out of the enclosure. But nothing moved, nothing charged out of the darkness. Standing at the outer gate, one hand wrapped around a bar, Rod offered a sloppy, excited grin. Tean knew that feeling, the rush of danger, of taking a risk. He could feel the underbelly of that sentiment in the terror congealing in his bones.

"The thing about Sita is, she's a man-eater. Nobody knows how that happens. Most tigers are terrified of humans, don't want anything to do with them. But some of them, a switch flips in their brain. One day, they realize these monkeys in the funny clothes don't taste so bad. And they sure as hell don't put up much of a fight. After that, there's nothing you can do about it." He bared his teeth the way he had in the office. "The polite term is 'persistent predators of humans.'"

But Tean thought he knew how it had happened. He thought he knew why they'd never found Yesenia's body. Why there had been so much blood.

Jem shot Tean a look. It was a question, maybe a plea. Tean kept his face still and didn't answer it.

"Go on," Rod said quietly.

Tean didn't move.

A jagged laugh erupted from Jem. "You've got to be kidding me. I'm not going in there. You want me dead? You can fucking shoot me yourself."

"Son, if I shoot you, I'm not going to kill you. I might shoot you in the foot. I might shoot you in the knee. And then I'll drag you in there, and I'll let you crawl. Sita likes playing with her food."

Another of those lightning-bolt laughs tore out of Jem. He looked at Tean, who was still fighting to keep his expression blank, and then back at Rod. "What the fuck is wrong with you?"

"Go on," Rod said in that same tone. In the dark, his teeth were nothing but the rough outline of splinters and saw-blade edges.

"No—" Jem said.

But Tean caught his wrist. He swallowed. Then he nodded. He had to give Jem a shove to get him moving, but then they were inside the safety gate. Rod slammed the outer gate shut, and the bolt went home. Tean tried the gate, but it didn't move, and Colin gave a hazy laugh. Tean turned to inspect the inner gate. Rod had done what Tean had been afraid he'd done: he'd chained the gate open, so that Tean couldn't shut it again. That was smart; the whole purpose of the safety gate was to protect the sanctuary employees, and Rod didn't want that. Not tonight.

Jem's breath had a whistling sound to it, but when Tean looked at him, he jerked out a nod. "Fine."

Tean nodded.

"This is why people live in cities," Jem said. "You realize that, right? This is why we invented fire and houses and—and Agent Orange."

"At least it's not a dog," Tean said.

The laugh broke Jem up again for a moment. Then that strained composure reasserted itself. "No," he said, a hint of hysterical amusement underlying the word. "Nope, it's not a dog."

"We're going to run to the feed box."

Jem nodded, crouching next to the interior gate. He produced a tube sock from his pocket, shook it out, and grabbed a rock from the ground inside the enclosure. He dropped it into the sock.

As Jem continued the process, Tean pointed. "That guillotine door, the vertical slider, over there. See? And then we're going to get it open, and we're going to stay in there until someone comes to help."

Something moved in the dark: a bulk of muscle and razor-sharp teeth and claws. The green embers breathed to life again. Higher, Tean thought. Coming out of her den. He tried to run through what he knew—what little he knew—but it felt like sand pouring between his fingers. In the wild, a tiger wouldn't attack them, not like this. But this cat had been caged, perhaps for her whole life, and who knew what had been done to her, or what she might do if given the opportunity.

Jem's breathing accelerated, but he nodded in response to Tean's directions. His hand tightened around the improvised sap.

"I'll distract her—" Tean began, which was one of the stupidest things he'd said in his whole life, but he was saying it for Jem, so it was ok.

And then the sound of the engine reached them. It was throaty, almost growly, and it seemed to be moving toward them. A moment later, headlights flicked on, bouncing toward the enclosure across the uneven ground.

"What the fuck is that?" Quinn asked.

"Hey," Rod shouted. "Hey!"

"Quinn?" the older guy with the goatee—Dusty, Tean thought Rod had called him—said.

"What the fuck is that?" Quinn asked again.

"Stop!" Rod shouted, waving at the oncoming headlights.

A truck, Tean thought. And coming straight at them at approximately forty miles an hour.

"Motherfucker," Quinn said. He fired with the gun in his off-hand, and a moment later, Dusty followed suit. Colin hunkered down, and he seemed to have forgotten his own gun. The thunder of the shots drowned out the sound of the engine. The truck was nothing more than the headlights and an impression of movement: a mass of steel and fiberglass rushing out of the dark. Like the tiger, a distant part of Tean thought. Like we made our own tiger.

Glass cracked. The truck's wheels tore up the grass, threw clouds of dirt into the air, kicked up rocks that pinged against the hog panels. All of it seemed to be happening far away, like Tean was watching it on a movie screen.

Jem yanked him down, and a heartbeat later, the truck hit the side of the enclosure about ten yards away from them. The truck—Tean glimpsed the Mid-Missouri Cat Sanctuary logo on the door—plowed through the hog panel, humped over a tree stump, and crashed against one of the concrete platforms. The tires continued to spin, kicking up clouds of dirt as the truck tried to move forward.

Up the hill, two more sets of headlights sprang to life, and in the haze of the crossing beams, Tean could trace the outline of two vehicles. The trucks themselves were junkers, and he didn't recognize them, but he could barely make out Emery and John-Henry behind the open doors in firing stances. He couldn't see who was in the second car, but it didn't take him long to figure out who it belonged to.

"We're here!" There was no mistaking that voice. Or, for that matter, what appeared to be a rainbow unicorn shirt as Shaw poked his head out of the passenger window. He waved at Jem and Tean. "We're rescuing you!"

"You have got to be kidding me," Jem muttered.

"Drop the guns," John-Henry ordered from the Mustang. "Show me your hands!"

Rod and the other men traded looks. They didn't seem convinced.

"What the fuck took you so long?" Emery asked. "You were supposed to intercept them."

"The window lock was being a bitch." North's messy thatch of blond gleamed in the ambient light. "Next time, you can steal the trucks."

"Next time, use your own fucking car instead of worrying it might get scratched."

"Suck my ass, it's custom paint."

"Who the fuck are you people?" Rod screamed.

"We're their friends," Shaw said.

North and Emery opened their mouths simultaneously, like they might argue the point. Then something passed across their faces, and they stopped. Tean sat up. That ancient part of him was awake now, gathering and responding to sensory data the way it had been bred to do, the part that had kept humans alive in jungles and on the savannah and under the peaks of mountains.

In the darkness, something moved. And then Sita, a thousand pounds of fur and teeth and muscle, hurtled out of the enclosure.

23

Clear of the hog panels, the tiger bounded once, her body compressing as she gathered force, and then she leaped on Dusty. The man had time to scream before her jaws closed around his head. Her teeth tore into his neck, and blood, black in the night, fountained into the air. It made a soft patter as the drops hit the dry earth and were soaked up by the dust, while the dying man's feet beat a tattoo against the packed soil. The cat jerked her head once, and bone snapped. Dusty's feet went still.

"Fuck me," Jem said, and he wondered from a distance if he had just wet himself.

"The dart gun!" Rod screamed. "Get the dart gun!"

Colin screamed, a bit too late, and Quinn fired at Sita. Jem couldn't tell if the shot went home, but Sita yowled, and she released Dusty. She loped away from the enclosure, and the darkness swallowed her.

The hum of engines. The smell of blood and offal and gunpowder. In the distance, the sanctuary truck—which must have been on cruise control—was still trying to power through the concrete platform, tires skidding and spinning.

"Get on the fucking ground," Emery said.

"Kill them," Rod said.

Quinn glanced up at the pair of headlights. "There's four of them."

"Kill them, or that fucking tiger's going to kill all of us, get it?" Rod waved at the safety gate where Jem and Tean huddled. "Colin, shoot them. I've got to get to the dart gun."

Tean tugged on Jem's arm, and when Jem risked a glance, Tean nodded at the feed box again.

Then a UFO descended, playing Billie Eilish.

That was Jem's first impression, anyway. Farther down the enclosure, lights and music blazed to life. Lines of red and green and blue and white danced across the ground. The music was ear shattering even at a distance. Rod, Quinn, and Colin turned to look.

Behind Colin, Theo stepped out of the darkness, a baseball bat cocked over one shoulder. He swung, and the bat caught Colin in the back. Colin lurched forward. The gun flew from his hand and disappeared into the shadows. For a moment, it looked like Colin might steady himself, but then Theo hit him again: a big, brutal motherfucker of a swing. Colin went down.

The music was still thundering.

Colin had been standing behind Rod and his brother, and when he fell, neither man seemed to notice; their attention was still fixed on the two vehicles parked up the hill.

Auggie appeared at the exterior gate, a pair of bolt-cutters slung over one shoulder. He set the blades to the gate's steel wires and began cutting. Theo darted glances at him and back at Quinn and Rod, who were shouting over the music, arguing about something. The wires fell away easily under the bolt cutters, and Auggie already had half the gate's lower panel clear.

As he worked, Auggie was laughing uncontrollably. He shouted over the music, "Stole the lights and sound system from the resort!"

Jem looked over at Tean, who was watching Auggie work, and he had a clear view of Tean's mouth as he said to himself, *Holy shit.*

Swear jar, Jem thought.

Theo waved to catch their attention and pointed at the gate, where Auggie had cleared the bottom half of the door. Without waiting for Tean and Jem, Theo grabbed Auggie and pulled him into a run, the two men heading away from the light show and into the dark. Jem had a small moment, long enough to hope they knew about Sita, to hope they'd be careful. Then he was helping Tean through the mess of clipped wires. He followed him out of the enclosures in time to see Quinn pull the pin from a grenade. He did it with his teeth, probably because he was a dead-eyed drone who'd watched too many bad movies.

Then he lobbed the grenade at the vehicles parked up the hill.

A burst of gunfire came from above. Quinn broke right while Rod broke left. Colin still lay on the ground, writhing in pain, screaming but unable to make himself heard over Billie Eilish still singing "Bad Guy." Jem waved for Tean to follow as he tore after Rod.

Then the grenade went off.

Even at a distance, the boom was concussive, like someone had clapped a hand against the side of Jem's head, and the heat rolled over him like a wave. Glass shattered. Metal popped and tore. The headlights made a wall of light, and behind it, all he could make out was the silhouette of twisted metal.

God, he thought. Please let them be alive.

Then he ran faster.

Tean believed in exercise. Tean believed in meeting a minimum number of minutes that some group of doctors somewhere had decided was a good idea. Tean believed in walking at brisk speeds and in hiking as something recreational and not as something you were forced to do by your loving and wonderful and sometimes slightly demented husband. Tean, in that sense—maybe in every sense—was in much better shape.

But Jem was younger, and he was wearing sneakers instead of Keens, and he had accepted the grace of his savior Ronald McDonald, which meant he had actual fuel for his body instead of somehow surviving on one bean and a single flake of red pepper. Plus, he'd learned how to haul ass when he was a kid. There wasn't anything to teach you how to haul ass like LouElla coming after you with the antenna.

So, he hauled ass, and heartbeat by heartbeat, Tean drifted behind.

Jem kept his focus on Rod. The other man's stringy mullet flopped as he sprinted toward the welcome center. The dumbass boots had no grip on the lawn, and Rod must have spent half his energy staying upright, slowing down every time his feet were about to slide out from under him. Even at a distance, his breathing sounded labored. That little belly was slowing him down. Too much beer. Too much easy food. Too much time sitting around jerking off to tiger porn, or whatever a guy like Rod watched. The gap between them closed to twenty yards. Then fifteen. Then ten.

Something moved in the periphery of Jem's vision. He didn't look. He didn't want to look. If he saw those demon eyes following him, full of their green fire, he'd shit himself. While running. In a really sweet pair of shorts (palm trees and sharks on green plaid; if he had to pick a pair of shorts to die in and, presumably, wear forever as a ghost, these shorts would be at the top of the list).

But he did glance back, and Tean was charging along behind him, face grim with resolve.

The sound of metal on metal drew his attention. Rod had stopped at the welcome center's side door, hunched and favoring his side—probably a stitch—as he tried to work a key into the lock. He gulped for air, and his free hand white-knuckled the door jamb as he steadied himself. He missed on the first try, the key bumping off the lock and scratching along the face of the door. On the second try, he got the key home, and he jerked the door open.

He reached inside, fumbled with something, and drew out a moment later with what Jem took, at first glance, to be a rifle. Something about the shape was wrong, though, and a moment later he decided it had to be the dart gun. Rod fooled with it for a moment. Then his head came up, and his eyes widened when he saw Jem. He dropped the dart gun and went for the gun at his side, but the baggy Pantera tee was in his way, and for a single moment, he had forgotten about that.

It cost him. That moment let Jem put on the gas, and he bounded forward, closing the last of the distance between them. Rod rucked up his shirt, and his hand went to the gun. He got it free. He started to bring the muzzle up toward Jem.

Jem spun the sock once, building up speed. Then he struck. Cotton stretched. The loose jumble of rocks inside pulled on him, suddenly heavier than they'd been a moment before. Then they made contact with the side of Rod's head. Rod's eyes rolled back. His legs bent at the knees, and Jem had the thought that it looked like Rod was doing one of those dances, the Russian one, where you kick your legs out while you're squatting. Then Rod fell over backward, and the gun bounced on the grass, and he didn't move.

"Fucking piece of shit!" Jem shouted, only barely aware that the distance had decreased the volume of the music, only barely aware that he was screaming down into Rod's face. "Fucking take that, motherfucker!"

"Jem!"

Jem spun. Tean's face was white, his eyes wide. He was crouched next to the dart gun. A prickle climbed Jem's spine. He tried to breathe, but there wasn't any air, not anymore.

"Don't move," Tean whispered. "When I tell you, get inside."

The far-off beat of the music continued. Jem strained to hear something else: the padding of giant paws, the whisper of the grass, the rumble of a growl just being born. He'd seen *A Ghost in the Darkness*. That was lions, but still, the principle—

"Go!" Tean shouted.

Jem jumped over Rod's body, grabbed the door, and yanked it open. Then he stopped.

Tean knelt with the dart gun braced against his shoulder. He fired once, twice, a third time. Even over the music, the psst of compressed air punctuated each shot.

"Tean!" Jem shouted.

Tean scrambled to his feet and threw himself at the door. He might have made it if Rod hadn't been there, but he wasn't looking, and he caught Rod's legs with one foot, and he stumbled.

Sita surged out of the darkness. A demon, Jem thought. Humans had believed, for a long time, that demons took this shape. She was nothing but an impression of power, an outline of savage strength sketched against the deeper darkness of the night. Her eyes burned with green fire.

Jem lunged forward, caught Tean's shirt with both hands, and hauled him forward—up and forward, actually, pulling so hard that Tean's feet left the ground. They fell backward into the welcome center, and the door began to shut on its pneumatic closer.

Slowly.

A massive weight struck the door and hammered it shut.

Outside, in the dark, Sita roared her fury.

Another blow came, the thud of a massive body striking the door.

Metal squealed. Claws. Jem visualized those huge claws raking the door. He clutched Tean to him. Something primal had taken over inside him—the city boy had been scraped away, all the tricks and games gone, and what was left was the thing that knew only fire and shadow and the ferocity of teeth and muscle.

Then nothing.

Then a minute of nothing.

Jem held on to Tean. The shakes surfaced, and he rode them out, and he listened.

It was a long time before he believed the silence.

24

"The motherfucker got what he deserved," Jem said and took another drink of his beer.

"He got what he deserved," Shaw repeated at full volume, directing the words toward North.

North looked like a man about to commit murder.

It was Monday afternoon, and most of the conference-goers had abandoned Santaland—the conference was over, and while a few had stayed because of some ghoulish fascination, the resort still felt empty by comparison. In one of the hotel bars, Tean nursed a Diet Coke. North had pointed Jem to a local beer, and Theo and Auggie had gone that route as well. Emery had ordered a Guinness, of all things, and John-Henry had followed Tean's example. Shaw had come back from the bar with one of the refill pitchers, which he had somehow convinced the bartender to fill with Coke. At least seven times now, by Tean's count, he had called it his victory stein.

They had spent the rest of Sunday night and a fair part of Monday morning being interviewed by Jonas Cassidy. There had been a lot to explain: not only Rod's role in the deaths of Yesenia and Una, along with the land deal that had drawn Heather into the investigation and ultimately led to Yesenia's death, but also the connection to an animal trafficking ring, the fight at the sanctuary, Sita's escape, and the deaths of two more men. When the police had arrived, they had found Sita sedated. Before the drugs had taken effect, though, she had bitten down on Rod's neck. He had bled out before emergency responders had arrived.

"We should have checked," Tean said again.

"Fuck that," North said. "He was trying to kill you—"

"He said they should have checked," Shaw bellowed into North's face.

"Son of a fuck, I heard him!" North shouted back. "For the last fucking time, there is nothing wrong with my hearing."

Shaw settled back into his seat, beaming. "He's only saying that on account of toxic masculinity and machismo and the psychosexual dynamics of ageism because you know it's not just his hearing, but his eyes—ow, ow, ow, I'll stop!"

North sat back.

Shaw rubbed the nipple North had been twisting.

Auggie was trying to get his phone out.

At almost the exact same time, Theo and John-Henry sighed.

"As I was saying," Emery said. "The whole operation would have run smoothly if certain people—" He fixed first North, and then, of all people, Auggie, with dirty looks. "—had done what they were supposed to do when they were supposed to do it."

"And for the last time," Theo shot back, "I wasn't going to let Auggie take that kind of risk." A beat too late, he added, "Not by himself."

A shadow passed over Auggie's face, and then he smiled, leaned into Theo's shoulder and bonked his head lightly against Theo's. "But we did it, right? That's what's important."

"Two men were killed," Emery said. "Is that important? And what about the tiger?"

"They would have had to put her down anyway," Tean said. "She'd already attacked people before."

"Can't they find her a new home?" Shaw asked. "Somewhere safe?"

"Relocating animals is…well, it's a contested practice. She was raised in captivity, so she wouldn't know how to live in her natural habitat. Even if that weren't the case, you'd have to deal with the problem of dropping her into an unknown environment, where she'd likely be competing with established predators. And the reality is that animals that have killed humans often kill again in the new area. It seems like a good solution until you put it into practice."

"Can't they keep her in a cage or something?" North asked. "It seems shitty that humans did all this stuff to her, and now she's the one who's going to pay the price. I mean, it's not her fault."

Shaw made a small, adoring noise and touched North's arm. North jerked away and scowled at him.

Tean shook his head. "No, I don't think so. Wild cats are already dangerous to keep. One that has become accustomed to preying on humans—no, I think the best thing is to euthanize her."

"But what if they—" North began.

"Who's the fucking expert here?" Emery said. "Which one of us has the fucking doctorate?"

North shot him the bird.

"I had a question," Emery said, turning back to Tean, "about wildlife forensics—"

North started making a sound that was suspiciously familiar. Emery glared at him. North looked innocently skyward, while, at the same time, making an obscene bulge in the side of his mouth.

"—about wildlife forensics—" Emery tried again.

"Glug-glug-glug."

"Will you knock that off?"

"Knock what off?" North asked. "I couldn't even hear what you were saying. It sounded like somebody was—gosh, I don't know—sucking on a knob."

"I'm trying to have a conversation with an educated professional—"

"You're trying to swing on a giant knob," North said. "Tip: relax your throat; it'll go down easier."

"No, that's ok," Tean tried to say. "We don't have to talk about—"

But as Emery launched into a blistering response, Jem tugged on Tean's sleeve and whispered in his ear, "They're both enjoying it."

Tean gave him a look.

Jem grinned and nodded.

"And Emery is totally sucking up to you," he whispered, his grin widening, those crooked front teeth peeking out for an instant.

"All right, all right, all right," John-Henry said. Then he barked, "Enough!"

North and Emery settled back into their seats. They did, Tean thought after a moment, both look incredibly pleased and like they were trying not to show it.

"You were saying—" Emery shot a dark look at North. "—before you were rudely interrupted?"

"Good Lord," Theo muttered, and Auggie laughed into his beer.

"I was going to say I talked to Chief Cassidy about the likelihood of recovering evidence." Tean shrugged. "I'm not sure the odds are good."

"I'm surprised he talked to you at all," Shaw said. "He just yelled at us."

Tean couldn't imagine why. But he said, "He did some yelling too. He wasn't happy to have his theory about Missy proven wrong, much less that he was eventually going to have to let her go. But he did ask a lot of questions."

With a grunt, Emery sat back in his chair and looked out at the hotel corridor. "Jonas was always good at getting the information he wanted. Even if it wasn't the truth."

"He seemed...frustrated. A large part, perhaps the primary part, of wildlife forensics is determining which specific animal was behind the attack."

"Seriously?" Auggie asked. "Like, CSI but for bears?"

"The only bears you have to worry about wear leather harnesses," North told him.

Theo's expression darkened. Jem smirked and covered the expression by turning his head. Auggie burst out laughing.

"North has a leather harness," Shaw said.

"I do not have a leather harness. I have a tool belt. For tools."

"But he's definitely a bear."

"I am not a bear, dumbfuck."

"Your chest is all hairy; sometimes I have to comb it while you're asleep." Shaw brightened. "Maybe you're a cub."

"He is a cub," Auggie said through a fresh wave of laughter. "He's definitely a cub."

North spared him a long look and a middle finger. "Cubs are young, and—"

"Your eyes, I know," Shaw said. And then, bellowing again, "And your hearing. The ravages of age."

"Jerk water," North snapped, "yell in my face one more time—"

"Oh, I've got it! You're a sun bear!"

North's face was so red Tean was beginning to worry about the possibility of a stroke. "I am not—"

"He actually does kind of look like a sun bear," Jem said. "I can see it now. Right?"

The question was directed at Tean. "Uh."

"The snout, definitely. And—"

"The snout?" North asked with a note of horror.

Jem elbowed Tean, and because Jem was an inveterate bad influence, Tean said, "Stockily built. Small, rounded ears."

"The chest hair," John-Henry put in.

Theo rocked slightly, as though Auggie had bumped him under the table, and he grumbled, "You mean the underfur."

John-Henry flashed a smile. "Check: the underfur."

North's stare panned across the group. "Fuck all y'all squishy-dicked motherfuckers."

"Oh, oh, there's a pill for squishy dicks—" Shaw began, but North spun and clapped a hand over his mouth, and Shaw dissolved into laughter. The two of them began their own private wrestling match. Tean was surprised to find a smile on his own face.

"If we can continue our conversation," Emery said.

"You can," Jem said.

"Permission granted," Auggie said.

Emery made a strangled noise, John-Henry rubbed that spot on his forehead, and Auggie and Jem not-so-discreetly bumped fists behind Theo.

"Typically," Tean said, "we'd analyze the victim, look for the physical characteristics of wounds, gather evidence, etcetera. The problem, of course, is that Yesenia's body still hasn't been recovered."

"And probably won't be," Emery said.

"No, probably not. Rod wasn't a vet, but he'd been around animals his whole life, and he knew how to stall an investigation. I imagine he, uh, disposed of the body using the cats. The chance of collecting DNA evidence from Sita's claws, fur, and teeth is more complicated because she attacked Dusty and Rod. I told Chief Cassidy there's a possibility something identifying—hair, a scrap of fabric—might remain undigested inside Sita. They've asked me to stick around and do the necropsy, mostly because they don't have anyone else to do it."

"But there won't be a trial," John-Henry said. "Rod's dead. This is where it'll end."

"What about the Rangel brothers?" Jem asked. "Or the guy with the bad knee?"

John-Henry shrugged. "It's going to be hard to prove anything about the murder. Cassidy will probably go for assault charges, maybe false imprisonment. He might even go for attempted murder. I understand he's going to talk to your friend Kristin, but all she had were suspicions—I'm not sure she'll be able to prove anything, one way or another, about the wildlife trafficking. It depends on a lot of factors, but mostly what the county attorney thinks they can make stick. I don't think you have anything to worry about from them, if that's what you're asking."

"What about the people they work for?" Jem asked.

It took a moment before John-Henry answered, and the chatter of daytime television filtered into the chinks in the conversation. "I don't know. It might be better—safer—if you went home as soon as you finish whatever work the county has contracted you to do."

"They know you're not easy meat," Emery said, "but if Rod was telling the truth and they're looking for you, the best thing you can do is clear out of here."

"We can protect you," Shaw said from inside a headlock. His butt stuck up in the air as he tried to wiggle free. North scowled and squeezed him more tightly. "We're so good at protecting people!"

"Hello? Tean?" Missy stood in the opening to the bar. She was wearing the same clothes Tean had seen her in when she'd been arrested, but they seemed to hang on her now. She was thinner, although he tried to convince himself it was his imagination, and her hair was flat and lusterless in its low fade, her eyes ringed by shadows. She was the same Missy—the earbuds around her neck, the tattoos, the smile that was, today, understandably worn out. But she wasn't the same, Tean understood. Wouldn't be the same for a long time. Maybe not ever.

"Oh my gosh," Tean said and scrambled out of his seat. He made it over to her, and before he could second guess himself, pulled her into a hug. "You're ok. You're out."

He released her almost as quickly, and Missy stepped back, wrapping her arms around herself. Her smile trembled. "I'm out. I understand—I mean, the police weren't exactly thrilled, but I guess I'm here because of you."

"Not really," Tean said.

"Yes," Jem said loudly from the table. He'd even cupped his hands around his mouth. "He's amazing. My husband, everybody. Line starts here for autographs."

"North," Shaw said, "we have to get his autograph."

North doubled down on the headlock.

"Everybody helped," Tean said. "It was—I mean, I'm so glad you're ok."

Her smile tuned in and out. Her eyes looked empty, and she was looking at Tean, but also through him.

"Would you like to sit down?" Theo asked, getting up from his seat and favoring his stiff knee. Auggie was holding Theo's hand. Clutching it might be a better word.

"No, thanks." Missy went blank again. After a moment, she said, "The hotel has my stuff in storage, and now I have to convince them to rent me a room—any room—so I can shower, and then I have to get out of here." A laugh snaked its way out of her on the last few words. She seemed to fight it, and then, after a long moment, managed to bite off the sound.

"You can use our room," Jem said.

"No, I couldn't—"

"Yes, please," Tean said. "Let's get your bags, and we'll take them upstairs right now. Take a shower. Rest for a little while. If you decide you still want to leave today, we'll help you pack, and if you want to get your own room and have a night to recharge, well, they'll still have plenty of rooms later today."

Missy waffled.

"Come on," Jem said, bounding out of his chair. "Sorry, folks. Show's over."

"North," Shaw wailed, "we didn't get his autograph."

"Here," Emery said. "Let me show you the sleeper hold. How long do you think his brain can go without oxygen?"

Tean refused to look back.

They collected her bags from where the resort had stored them after the arrest, and then they took the elevator up to their floor. There didn't seem to be much to say. Missy stared out from the dark hollows of her eyes and seemed to be seeing somewhere else.

The resort's cleaning staff had straightened up the room: the bed was freshly made, the curtains drawn back, the water in the reservoir coppery in the afternoon light and shimmering like a struck gong.

"Take as long as you need," Tean said. "Do you want someone to stay? Is that weird?"

Missy shook her head. "You didn't have to—thank you."

"Do you need anything else?"

"Let's give her some privacy," Jem said, taking Tean's hand.

"If you need anything," Tean said, "text. Or call. Or—do you have Snapchat? Jem made me get it."

"We'll be downstairs," Jem said, and a smile fluttered on Missy's lips before it was gone again.

They rode the elevator down.

"I guess now that Rod's—" Jem stopped himself. "I guess we're never going to know why he went after Missy, are we?"

"I imagine it was because he hated her and, of course, because he thought he could get away with it. But no, we'll never know for certain." Tean stopped. "She looked—we shouldn't have left her alone."

"She had her whole world turned upside down," Jem said. "She never thought she'd be through something like that. She spent the last few days having her foundations washed out from underneath her, slowly starting to believe she was going to be convicted of a murder she didn't commit. That's a lot. It's going to take her some time to find her way back to the world she knew."

Tean touched his eyes.

"She'll be ok," Jem said, and he pulled Tean against him in a one-armed hug. "She's tough."

The elevator rocked slightly when it stopped at the lobby.

"The hot water," Tean said.

Jem grimaced. "Oh. Damn."

"Nobody told her about the hot water."

"She can call the front desk."

"She's too—" The word Tean wanted to use was dangerous, so he said, instead, "—tired. I'll just knock on the door and tell her how to get it running."

Jem didn't sigh. He didn't frown. He nodded, squeezed Tean's shoulders in that one-armed hug, and hit the button to send them up again.

When they got to their room, Tean knocked.

No one answered.

He tried again, and, after another moment, he used his keycard. When he opened the door an inch, the steady hiss of the shower filtered out to him. He caught a hint of the hotel soap.

"Sounds like she figured it out," Jem said. "Come on."

"Missy?" Tean called into the room. "It's Tean. Did you figure out the hot water?"

"I know you want to make sure she's ok," Jem said, "but she needs some time alone."

The air shifted, and the smell of the lake came in. Tean frowned and nudged the door open another inch. "Missy? Jem, the slider's open."

"So?"

"So maybe she—" He didn't want to finish that sentence either. He leaned into the door, ignoring the way Jem hooked a belt loop. "Missy? Hey, it's Tean. Can you hear me? Jem!"

Missy's suitcases lay on the floor, overturned. Clothes and personal items—a hair dryer, a lone Chuck high-top, a mesh bag, the kind you wash delicates in. On the other side of the room, the curtains drifted on currents of hot, swampy air seeping into the room.

"Maybe it felt good," Jem said, but he didn't sound convinced. "Maybe she wanted to throw things around. Maybe she wanted fresh air after all those days in a cell."

"Missy?"

Tean advanced into the room. His imagination went to work, delivering possible scenarios: Missy opening the door, totally naked, and Tean having to resign from his job and never work in any veterinary fields again, and possibly move to one of those islands where they used to send rebellious monks. But another scenario: Missy on the floor. A stroke. Or she slipped and fell.

"Hello," Tean called again. "Missy, we're worried about you. Can you please say something?"

Jem's hand tightened around Tean's arm, fingers biting into his flesh. He stopped Tean. Then he shouldered past him and gave Tean a push toward the hall.

"What—" Tean began.

But Jem already had the paracord in one hand, the dark metal of the hex nut swinging at the end of the loop. He reached the bathroom door. The only sound was the spray. Then, after some internal decision, he threw the door open.

The first thing Tean noticed was that the shower curtain needed to be replaced. There were holes in it. Then he noticed the shadow bunched up along the side of the tub. Then the arm and hand that protruded from under the curtain and lay on the tile.

Jem cleared the room, checking corners as he talked. "Get an ambulance, hotel security, the police—"

But Tean had already pushed past him. The curtain rattled back under his touch. Missy lay on her side in the tub, naked, the cold spray needling her face. She had been shot twice.

25

"You need to leave," Emery said. "We'll handle this."

It wasn't a war council; that sounded too much like The Chronicles of Narnia, which Jem was plodding through (between volumes of *Goosebumps*). Still, the air in Emery and John-Henry's hotel room had a charge—an energy that Jem couldn't dismiss. The others felt it too: Theo with an arm around Auggie, who pressed into him; the unfamiliar gravity drawing down the lines of Shaw's face, and the darker mirror in North's expression; John-Henry's guy-next-door smile was gone; Emery was a thundercloud. Tean, though, was a tempest of emotions that wouldn't settle, making it impossible for Jem to get a read. Every time he thought he had it—grief—those psychic winds would pick up again, and the turmoil in Tean's features erased Jem's certainty.

Jem checked the part in his hair; the gesture was automatic, reassuring. "They were trying to kill me."

"You've been through a lot," John-Henry said.

That was putting it mildly. Chief Cassidy had been...well, enraged came close. And that anger had found its outlet in Jem and Tean. Hours of waiting. Hours of questioning. And now this, here. The midnight hours, with this midnight council, in a borrowed room. The curtains over the sliding door were drawn back, and on the other side of the glass, the shape of the reservoir was the rumpled irregularity of the mouth of a sack being cinched. Stars filled up the water until it looked miles deep, and the distant red of the aircraft warning light was like a signal from another world. It all sounded dramatic, a detached part of Jem observed. But also, somehow, right.

"Those pieces of shit broke into our hotel room and tried to kill me. Us." Jem glanced over; for a moment, fury blazed in Tean's expression, and then storm winds carried it away. "They wanted to kill both of us. Somehow they knew we were going up to our room. Somehow those fuckers knew."

"Rod said they had people in the resort," Tean said. The words were neutral, with a drained-battery quality. "Rod said this—this group, whoever they are, he said they're paying people to watch us."

"All the more reason for you to leave," Theo said. If he realized he was tightening his arm around Auggie, it didn't show on his face. "I'm sorry for your loss, sorry for what you've been through. But you've got kids you need to take care of. You need to think about them. You need to watch out for yourselves."

"They shot her through the fucking shower curtain," Jem said. He could hear his voice, the cutting side turned outward toward these men, these strangers. These not-quite strangers who had come for him, to rescue him, in a hail of bullets. He tried to soften his voice. "They came in through the fucking balcony and shot her without even bothering to check they had the right person."

Tean was staring at Jem, but not seeing. His eyes looked lost.

"Why?" North asked.

Jem looked at him.

"Why are they trying to kill you?" Shaw clarified.

"Yeah," Auggie said. "It doesn't make any sense. You stumbled onto their operation, ok. They didn't like you poking around Yesenia's disappearance because they didn't want you to look too closely at Rod. All right, fine. They didn't want you looking at Rod because Rod might flip on them and start talking. But Rod's dead now. And you're just some out-of-towner. Why not lie low and wait for you to leave?"

Jem glanced at Tean. Tean didn't meet his eyes, but he nodded.

From between his feet, Jem grabbed the plastic Piggly Wiggly bag he'd rescued from a convenient trash can. He emptied it onto the small hotel desk. Prescription bottles spilled out, many with their labels partially removed. Plastic bags with powders and pills, with squares of dehydrated animal parts, with horns, with dried leaves. Passports, Social Security cards, driver's licenses. Rings, necklaces, earrings.

The room was a held breath.

"They want it back," Shaw said.

"We knew it wasn't only animal trafficking," John-Henry said as though speaking to himself. "We already knew that. So, what the hell is it?"

"This is what they were looking for," Theo said. "When they searched your room. When they searched it again after they killed Missy. What is all this stuff?"

"Possessions of their victims?" Emery said, but it sounded like a question.

North made a considering noise, leaning forward, elbows on knees. The look he directed at Jem verged on impressed. "Where was it?"

An echo of a smile found its way across Jem's face. "The next room. Adjoining door."

North considered this and gave a nod. "Dumbfucks."

"I think Theo's right," Auggie said. He looked so young, Jem thought. Not in a bad way. Just...young. "I think you should leave. Drop this stuff in a dumpster and go."

"No." Tean raised his head. His eyes focused. They were a little red, but they were clear and dry. His voice firmed as he repeated, "No."

"I understand," Theo began, "but—"

"They were trying to kill us, and now Missy is dead." Tean braced his hands on his thighs. "They murdered her. We're not leaving."

"If you're in danger—" Shaw began.

John-Henry cleared his throat. "The best thing to do might be—"

"You all heard him," Emery said. The silence that followed had its own dark tattoo. "They're not leaving. The only thing left to discuss is what we're going to do next."

North opened his mouth, but Theo moved first, reaching for something on the desk. At the last moment, he stopped himself. He pointed at a ring mixed into a tangle of thin gold chains.

Auggie broke the silence. "Is that what I think it is?"

John-Henry, when he spoke, had a compressed anger in his voice—the sound of someone mastering a tremendous emotion. "Yes."

"What?" Jem asked. "What is it?"

"It's a class ring," Theo said. "From the high school where I teach."

"That answers one question," Emery said. "We're going to Wahredua."

The Girl in the Wind

Keep reading for a sneak preview of *The Girl in the Wind*, book two of Iron on Iron.

1

"I'll have my phone on," Theo said. "We both will."

Auggie bit back a comment.

"In case there's an emergency."

"We don't actually expect an emergency, by the way." Auggie sent Theo a smile. "In case that needed to be said."

"That's why I said in case."

This time, Auggie bit back a sigh. He didn't think anyone noticed; the Hazard and Somerset home was a maelstrom (SAT word) of chaos.

"We're going to have a great time," John-Henry Somerset said. The chief of police—and Auggie and Theo's friend—cupped the back of Lana's head.

"We're going to play Fillies," Lana said. The words were flat, almost affectless, one of the lingering effects of the terrible car accident she'd been in as a child. The leg brace was another. She was ten years old now, which was hard for Auggie to believe, with long dark hair that came to her shoulders. She had none of Theo's features or coloring—in fact, at a casual glance, she might have looked more like Auggie's biological daughter.

Emery Hazard looked at Theo. John-Henry's husband was a former police officer turned private investigator, and it didn't matter how many barbeques and baseball games Auggie went to, the unsettling weight of those amber eyes never changed.

"Fillies," Theo clarified.

Evie, Emery and John-Henry's daughter, looped through the room, being pursued by a scruffy puppy. She was five, almost six, and she had John-Henry's features, although, like Lana, she was dark where John-Henry was blond. As she ran, she screamed, "Biscuit, Biscuit, Biscuit!" The dog didn't have any problem keeping up with her—in fact, most of the chase seemed to consist of the puppy jumping up to put her paws on Evie, at which point Evie squealed and pushed the dog down to run some more.

"Come here a minute, you maniac," John-Henry said, catching her with one arm. "Do you remember Lana?"

Lana smiled and ducked her head.

"Lana's came over to play."

"We're going to play Fillies," Lana mumbled.

"She said—" Theo began.

"Biscuit is chasing us," Evie said. "Come on!"

Then, latching on to Lana's hand, she pulled her into a stumbling run. The brace made Lana's gait uneven, but Evie was smaller and younger, and Lana didn't have any trouble keeping up. Biscuit charged after them, yapping, and jumped. Both paws connected with Lana's waist, and she went down with a crash.

Theo started forward.

Before he could reach their daughter, though, Lana was back on her feet, laughing and pushing Biscuit away, while Evie shouted, "Come on, come on, he's getting us!"

"Her brace—" Theo said and took another step.

Auggie caught his wrist, and when Theo looked at him, he gave him a lot of eye contact.

After a moment, the tension in Theo's arm eased, and a rueful smile parted his beard.

"Knock it off!" The shout came from Colt, Emery and John-Henry's son. The teenager was as tall as Emery now, and although he wasn't their biological child, he had Emery's startling straw-colored eyes. He also had a thundercloud of hair, which he was—Auggie had been informed—trying to grow out. And about which, on pain of death, Auggie had been told to make zero comments. "Pops," Colt complained from the living room, "she won't listen to me."

"Evie," Emery said, "listen to your brother."

The girls stampeded past them again, screaming with laughter.

Theo smiled, but his eyes had that familiar tightness at the corners.

"Come in for a minute," John-Henry said. "Do you have time?"

"Our reservations—" Auggie began.

"Yes," Theo said. He followed John-Henry deeper into the house. Auggie watched them; when John-Henry said something about Lana's bag, Theo passed it over. Slowly. Like he was cutting off his own arm.

Emery stayed with Auggie, and he was watching too.

From farther back in the house came the swell of more voices, and after a moment, Auggie said, "Full house."

Emery made a face.

"You're coming with me," Colt said. He appeared in the opening to the living room for a moment, Evie slung over one shoulder, where she was giggling uncontrollably. "We've got to make your lunch. First day of school tomorrow. Lana, you can be in charge of the snacks."

"First day of school?" Auggie asked.

"First of the school year," Emery clarified. "She's got one more year before kindergarten; late birthday."

"I love snacks," Lana said, and she took Colt's hand as he carried Evie toward the kitchen.

"He's really good with kids," Auggie said.

For a moment, the change in Emery's expression was like watching sunlight catch glass. Then it was gone, and he scowled at Auggie. "Don't you have a regular babysitter?"

"I heard that," John-Henry called from the living room.

"I'm not objecting to watching Lana," Emery shouted back. "I'm pointing out a logistical reality of parenthood. They should have an on-call babysitter who has been properly vetted."

"We do," Auggie said. "She got arrested. Cocaine. She sold all of Theo's beard balm on eBay."

For a moment, curiosity peaked in Emery's expression. Then it flattened out. "I am surrounded by aspiring comedians."

He turned and headed toward the living room.

"She was very good until she tried to harvest our organs," Auggie said as he went after him.

As they reached the living room, Biscuit—presumably bored now without the girls to chase—rushed up toward Emery and began to bark at him. The scruffy little puppy was barely the size of a football, and Auggie grinned in spite of himself as the little thing locked her legs and began to tell Emery off.

Emery, being Emery, crouched and said, "Keep it up, and I'll make you into a handbag."

Biscuit whimpered and shot off into the kitchen, where she circled Colt's ankles and darted dirty looks at Emery.

"She's mad because you won't let her sleep with me," Colt said. He stood in the kitchen, visible through the opening that connected the two rooms, supervising Lana and Evie as they crammed a lunchbox full of goldfish packs.

"She's a dog. She sleeps where dogs sleep, in her crate."

"Dogs can sleep with people. I asked Dr. Leon. Dr. Leon, can't dogs sleep with people?"

Until that point, Teancum Leon had escaped Auggie's notice, which Auggie guessed was probably the idea. The wildlife vet, with his bushy hair and wild eyebrows, was hunkered down in an armchair, a book held in front of his face, obviously trying to pretend he hadn't heard.

"When Dr. Leon is your father, he can decide which animals are allowed to piss and shit in your bed. How does that sound?"

"Actually, most animals wouldn't—" Tean poked his head up above the book, and for a moment, Auggie was reminded of a wild animal testing the air. Then Tean ducked back out of sight.

"Hi, Tean," Auggie said.

"Hello."

"Is Jem around?"

"In the kitchen."

"He's smart," Emery said in an aside to Auggie as he headed toward the kitchen, "but zero social skills."

"Hmm," Auggie said in what he hoped was his most noncommittal tone.

The kitchen, it turned out, was the center of the madness in the house. Lana and Evie gabbled over each other as they focused their attention to loading the lunchbox with fruit snacks—only minimally supervised now by Colt. The boy had turned his attention to the other men in the room. To one man, in particular.

North McKinney had a thatch of blond hair, and he was built big and muscular in a way that made Auggie, even as an adult, feel a twinge of envy. In a gray tee that said BARNEY'S FISH AND CHIPS, he slouched against the cabinets, a beer in hand. "—you could paint it yourself, but that's a lot of work. And you've got to decide if you're going to spend your money on that, or if you want to save it toward the next one."

"Definitely the next one," Colt said. Lana tugged on his hand, and Colt made a dismissing noise without pulling his gaze away from North. "So, like, I should change my own oil, right?"

"Not this again," Emery said.

"You don't change your own oil?"

A flush rode Colt's cheekbones. "Uh, I mean, Pops said—"

"Because he doesn't know how."

"I know how," Emery said. "But I'm not interested in spending half a day doing a job I can pay someone else to do for forty dollars, thank you very much."

"Half a day," North said. "If it takes you half a day, you don't know how to do it."

"Maybe, um, you could teach me?" Colt's blush intensified. "I mean, I know you're busy, so, like, not right now —"

"He can't teach you because he doesn't know how," Shaw said. North's partner was wearing a black leotard and, probably only because North had insisted, baby blue shorts that only minimally covered his junk. He had cornered Ashley, Colt's boyfriend, and he broke off from whatever he'd been saying to speak over his shoulder. "One time North said he was going to change the oil, and it was hours and hours, and I went out there, and he'd taken off his shirt and he was all hot and sweaty and there wasn't any oil anywhere. So, I said —"

Colt's eyes darted to Shaw and then back to North. To North's chest, actually, if Auggie weren't mistaken. Only for a heartbeat. Emery must have noticed too, though, because the muscles in his jaw stood out.

"I know how to do it, for fu —" North shot the girls a look. "I know how to do it. I can show you."

"Seriously? That would be dope. Ash, did you hear that?"

Ashley didn't appear to have heard, though, because he was currently trying to wriggle free from where Shaw had trapped him. Shaw was talking nonstop—the only part Auggie understood was "Would it help if I summoned my Patronus first?" —but when Ashley slid a few inches farther, Shaw's arm shot out to block the escape.

"Good fucking Lord," Emery said under his breath. "Excuse me while I go blow my brains out."

"Not that one." The voice belonged to Jem Berger. Tean's husband worked in real estate, although Theo had said on more than one occasion that he didn't believe that story. Auggie wasn't sure; Jem was a puzzle. Clearly savvy, keenly trendy—although he skewed more toward vintage stuff, not really Auggie's vibe. But every once in a while, Auggie caught a glimpse of something else, like laughter or amusement that didn't quite line up with what was going on, and he wondered what he was missing. Right then, he was bent over John-Henry's phone, shaking his head. "No, definitely not. You're already fighting a losing battle in the ass department. Those are going to make you look like you're lugging around a couple of sacks of flour."

"Gee," John-Henry said, "thanks."

Jem flashed a grin, a hint of his slightly crooked front teeth making an appearance, and swiped on John-Henry's phone a couple of times. "What about these?"

"Uh." John-Henry seemed at a loss for words. "They look…young."

Jem burst out laughing. "We'll get them in this khaki color, and we'll go a little longer because I don't think you want to wear them above the ankle. I'm telling you, this is the pair."

"What are you guys doing?" Auggie asked as he worked his way across the kitchen.

"Bankrupting me," Emery said.

John-Henry flashed his husband a smile before saying to Auggie, "A little wardrobe update. Jem is really good at this stuff."

"He's motivated by existential despair, he told us. He wanted Tean to tell us about Sartre."

"To be fair, I'm motivated by existential despair about everything," Jem said. "We all are. Right, Tean?"

Tean's voice floated back from the living room: "I'm not listening."

"Let me see what you're getting," Auggie said, taking his place next to the men. "Ok, hold on, I know you said khaki, but what if you went for this one, a little more neutral?"

John-Henry said, "I like it, but Jem said—"

"No, he's right." Jem nodded. "Closer to the natural color. It's even better."

"And let me guess," Emery said from where he was picking an abundance of fruit snacks out of the lunchbox. "They cost sixty dollars."

The beat lasted a moment too long.

"Yes," Jem said. "Sixty dollars."

Emery paused. "How much are they?"

"I'd better check on Tean."

Jem slipped out of the room before Emery could catch him.

"John?"

"I, uh, better help."

And then, somehow, Auggie was alone.

"How much?" Emery said with that tone like he was picking each word carefully because the sentence was going to end in a murder.

"You know," Auggie said, "I actually didn't see."

Emery's silence seemed to grow by the second until he finally said, "I am going to remember this."

Auggie offered a smile.

"Did I mention that we charge for babysitting?"

"No," John-Henry called from the other room, "we don't."

"Speaking of which," Auggie said, and he tried to check his watch, only he wasn't wearing one—because, well, he never did. Emery even snorted. "We'd better get going, Theo."

"Right." Theo scratched his beard. "Let me just check on Lana—"

"She's fine," North said, gesturing with his beer. "She and Evie ran that way."

Theo looked in that direction.

"They had a bunch of kitchen knives," North said. "And they were running with scissors. Oh, and I think they were dousing each other with gasoline."

Theo shot him a dark look, and North smirked.

"It's ok if you have a third nipple," Shaw was saying to Ashley, who had now gone wide eyed and looked, frankly, a little desperate. "But it's not ok to lie about it."

"Not ok to lie about it," North said. "Look who's talking. I find you tits up in the bathtub, so blitzed you keep asking if your legs are balloons—"

"Balloon animals," Shaw said. To Ashley, who was trying to slide away again, he added, "I thought they were those little sausage dogs."

"—and you tell me all you did was have tea with Master Hermes."

"It was tea! It had the little mushrooms in it!"

"Those are shrooms, dumbfuck!"

Ashley made a break for it, his bare feet slapping the boards as he escaped.

North squinted at Auggie. "What product do you use in your hair, Short Round?"

"Uh."

"It's his eyes," Shaw said. "They're starting to go."

"Do you want to try that again?" Theo asked. "Maybe call him Auggie instead of a nickname that's borderline racist?"

But North's smirk just got bigger. "Daddy wants to play."

"Ignore them," John-Henry called from the next room. "North's being an asshole because he's bored."

"Language," Emery shouted as he scooped goldfish out of the lunchbox. "Am I the only one in this fucking house who remembers there are fucking children here, for fuck's sake?"

"Come on," Auggie said, catching Theo's arm and leading him into the living room. Theo, of course, kept his gaze on North until they'd left the kitchen.

To judge by the volume, Colt and Ashley and the girls were upstairs. Colt roared, "Because I'm a monster and I'm going to eat you," and Ashley shouted, "Come on, come on, in here," and Evie and Lana squealed with delight. Jem perched on the arm of Tean's chair, combing fingers through his hair while Tean tried to read, and John-Henry was flipping channels on the TV.

"Thank you again," Auggie said.

"No problem," John-Henry said. "Pick her up whenever you want."

"Not whenever you want," Emery said from the kitchen. "It's a fucking school night, which I already had to fight with Colt about. Fucking back-to-school party. Fuck me. One more fucking excuse to get tanked in a fucking cornfield."

"Ten o'clock curfew, Peewee," North called to them. "Actually, make that nine."

Theo's expression flattened.

"Leave it," Auggie whispered.

"Oh, hey, before I forget." John-Henry dropped the remote on the sofa. "A girl named Shaniyah came to the station. She dropped your names, wanted to interview me about a boy who'd gone missing."

"Wait, really? Is it—do you think it's related?"

The question brought a stillness broken only by the buzz of the TV. A week ago, the eight of them had found themselves drawn into the hunt for a killer. In the process, they had discovered a criminal organization operating in the region. One branch of their operations seemed to include theft or robbery, and they had found, among the stolen jewelry and IDs, a class ring from Wahredua High School.

"I don't know," John-Henry said. "That's what I wanted to ask you."

Auggie glanced at Theo.

"She's one of my students," Theo said. "Shaniyah. She's going into her senior year, and she's been working with Auggie on a digital media project for her college applications."

"And she needs to interview the chief of police about a missing boy?" Tean asked, his book now forgotten in his lap.

"I don't know about that," Auggie said. "The project is a collection of videos, but they're about social media use among teens—you know, TikTok challenges, BookTok, lip synching, cringey fails, the whole range."

"What are cringey fails?" Emery asked.

At the same time, Theo began, "What are—"

"Pops," Colt groaned from upstairs before roaring again like a monster.

"She hasn't said anything to me about a missing boy," Auggie continued. "What boy?"

"I don't know," John-Henry said. "I was in a meeting, and by the time I got out, she was gone."

A question hung at the end of the sentence, and John-Henry was looking at Auggie in a way that reminded him that, even with the buddy-next-door smile, John-Henry was still a cop—and an extremely good one.

"I swear," Auggie said. "Shaniyah hasn't said anything to me about anything like that. Not even remotely. She was down the other day, you know, upset. But that was because she didn't get a big scholarship she'd applied for. She didn't tell me she was going to change her project, though."

"Because if she had," Emery said, "and you two were planning on playing Lone Ranger—"

"How could the two of them play Lone Ranger?" North asked. "Isn't there just one Lone Ranger?"

"One of them is clearly Tonto—"

"We're not doing anything of the sort," Theo said. "Neither of us knows what Shaniyah is asking about, and we certainly didn't have anything to do with it."

The second floor rumbled with heavy steps and mock growls.

"Have you—" Auggie restarted. "It's been a week."

"Nothing," John-Henry said.

"We have jobs, remember?" Emery said. "We've been working on it, but it's going to take time."

Theo looked at Jem and Tean.

"We're still trying to run something down," Jem said. "Anything, really, but we've been trying to work the wildlife trafficking side."

"We haven't made much progress," Tean said.

"We haven't made any progress. But we're not giving up. And we've still got some time. Tean's working remotely, and my job is flexible."

"Our isn't," North said. "Some of us actually have to go to work."

"I'm sure watching dentists get blown by their mistresses is an incredibly demanding calling," Emery said.

"Look who's talking," North said. "Same job, bozo."

"And it is hard, Emery," Shaw said. "Sometimes they pull the curtains. And sometimes the dentists cry a little bit. And one time, one of them was—" Shaw mouthed, *Getting a hummer*. "—and his wig fell off. Oh my God, and one time my wig fell off! That was right after I fell on one of the mistresses."

"How did you fall on a mistress?" John-Henry asked.

"Sure," North said. "Great. Let's all give him exactly what he wants."

"I was wearing these polar bear feet—imitation!" The last part was a rushed assurance to Tean, whose eyes were huge. "And they were in this English basement—"

"What the fuck is an English basement?" Emery asked.

"I'll pop popcorn," North said. "We'll be here all day."

"—and it looked like she was doing something, you know, interesting, like, um, her technique, so I thought I should probably see with my spiritual eye—"

"He forgot the telephoto lens and humped his way right over the rail," North said.

"While North was getting his banger mashed," Shaw said with what might have been a note of vicarious pride.

"I was not—"

"He said this guy had hands that could crush walnuts."

North's face was turning a startling shade of purple.

"He couldn't sit down for a week. Well, he couldn't sit down front ways. That was before we were dating."

"What does—" Emery began.

At the same time, North shouted, "What the fuck does 'sit down front ways' even mean? I could sit down just fine, and Rodrigo didn't mash anything, since my sex life is now public fucking record." He snapped a look around the room, seized Shaw's arm, and said, "We're leaving. We'll be back when we can."

"John-Henry, my Pepsi—" Shaw tried.

But North dragged him toward the front of the house. Shaw's giggles came back to them for a moment, and then the door shut them off.

Emery rubbed his face. "God fucking damn it."

Laughing, John-Henry rubbed his shoulder. "Don't worry; they'll be back when they can."

Emery dropped his hands to give him a betrayed look.

"We need to get going too," Auggie said. "Listen, I'll ask Shaniyah why she wanted to talk to you, but in the meanwhile, is there something we can do? I mean, the class ring?"

John-Henry shook his head, but Emery was the one who answered. "We're working on the Cottonmouth Club, trying to figure out who's operating out of there. Tean and Jem are taking the animal angle, and North and Shaw are going to see if they can get a line on anything moving through St. Louis. There's nothing you can do right now without getting in the way."

"We didn't get in the way last week—" Auggie began.

"That's fine," Theo said. "We'll let the professionals handle it."

When they were in the Audi, driving away from the house, Auggie had to wrestle with the argument he wanted to start. Finally, he managed to swallow it, and as they drove toward Moulin Vert, he managed to say, instead, "Lana's going to have so much fun."

Theo nodded. He was staring straight out the windshield.

"She's going to be fine, Theo. Evie adores her, and she's got a house full of people who are going to make sure nothing happens to her. Colt and Ashley might need a three-day weekend to recover after this, but everyone's going to be fine."

"I know." Then Theo's mouth softened, and he said again, "I know. I'm sorry; it's hard to turn it off sometimes."

Auggie nodded and rubbed Theo's knee.

"They're going to have fun," Theo said.

"She loves other kids," Auggie said. "And I don't know if I've ever seen her run like that."

"She has to be careful—" Theo stopped.

Auggie rubbed his knee while they drove.

He didn't mean anything by it, not really. It just came out. "It's cute, isn't it? The—I don't know, the dynamic, I guess. At Emery and John-Henry's house."

"Cute like an insane asylum."

Auggie slapped his knee lightly. "It's busy, sure. But it's...warm. It's—" Full, he wanted to say, although that sounded like he was pitching a '90s sitcom. But it was the right word, that sense of fullness, of a house brimming with life. "It's happy."

Theo made a noise that could have meant anything.

"Didn't you think it was cute, watching Evie and Lana together? Or, God, Colt with his little sister?"

It was the wrong thing to say; Auggie felt it as soon as it left him. Theo pushed his hair back with both hands and looked out the windshield. He didn't knock Auggie's hand off his knee. He didn't do anything dramatic. He didn't need to.

"That's not what I meant," Auggie said.

Theo nodded.

"I was just saying."

"I know what you were saying," Theo said. The sunset caught his eyes and turned them into hard little mirrors. "I thought we weren't having this conversation again."

Acknowledgments

My deepest thanks go out to the following people (in reverse alphabetical order):

Wendy Wickett, for helping me with clarity and emphasis (and those pesky italics!), for so much wonderful help with continuity (the BLACK Mustang!), and for helping me deal with a particularly problematic moment for Shaw.

Jo Wegstein, for all her help making the conference as realistic as possible (and anything that falls short is my own doing!), for catching my mistake with bluestem, and for improving the text in so many other ways.

Mark Wallace, for spotting extra letters and missing spaces (and even some missing words!), for helping me with my singular and collective nouns, and for the laugh-cry emoji at one really good blunder.

Tray Stephenson, for catching my repetitions, righting errant characters, and lending his usual editorial prowess.

Nichole Reeder, for spotting my advance appearance of the Jeep, for catching (among other things) my missing end marks, and for helping me with the final EPUB formatting!

Pepe, for helping me orient readers to Auburn much more quickly, for giving Emery that wonderful line about the gummies, and for all the wonderfully helpful questions, most of which I hope I've answered.

Cheryl Oakley, for spotting so many things that others didn't, for checking my continuity (Auggie's laugh), and for asking so many good questions (the vandalism in Yesenia's room).

Raj Mangat, for her help with so many character interactions, for her genius suggestion about Yesenia's true fate, and for asking "Why Missy?" — such an important question!

Steve Leonard, for fixing Wavey the Snow Goose, my social media blunders, and the sausage-and-biscuit sandwich—among so many other things.

Marie Lenglet, for helping me with my fake mustache, for suggesting more explanation about the title of the book, and for encouraging me to rethink Hazard as the *deux ex machina*.

Austin Gwin, for fixing my cars (which always need fixing), my Pantera tee (big cats on the mind), and LouElla!

Fritz, for helping me with my tenses and my grammatical moods (subjunctive!), for catching so many of my typos, and for helping make my Clarice joke land!

Christine Fredrickson, for spotting that stray corgi brigade and, even more importantly, for giving me Emerson and Shawn (with Bryoney's help!).

Savannah Cordle, for fixing characters names (Ron), and continuity (DeVoy sitting up), and for sharing her enthusiasm for this book with me!

Jolanta Benal, for helping me with the corgis (more corgi assistance!), for fixing my Aves classification, and catching so many errors that had slipped through the proofing process.

Keren Abbou, for taking time to send me the typos she found.

About the Author

For advanced access, exclusive content, limited-time promotions, and insider information, please sign up for my mailing list at **www.gregoryashe.com**.

www.ingramcontent.com/pod-product-compliance
Lightning Source LLC
Chambersburg PA
CBHW052041240626
47153CB00006B/2185